TAKEN OUT OF LOVE

Gene Grant

TOKY Publishing International LLC

Fairview, Oregon

www.tokybooks.com

A note from the publisher:

TOKY Publishing International LLC and Gene Grant wish to extend our sincere thanks the following:

Transcription	Proofing and Editing	
Beverly C.	Beverly C.	Lois M.
Dana G.	David G.	Lorri M.
Brandon K.	Janet G.	Blake S.
John H.	Jean H.	Grant S.
Grant S.	John H.	

Last names have been withheld for privacy.

Without your help this project would not have been possible.

Dr. Richard Colton became wealthy while still in medical school after inventing two surgical instruments for which he had applied and received patents. Also contributing to his substantial wealth was his successful medical practice. In addition, his wife, Nancy, won a lottery jackpot when she bought their first, and only, ticket while on vacation.

Dr. Colton first met Nancy Marshall when she rented an apartment in the same building as the young doctor. Following her graduation from college, Miss Marshall became a legal consultant for Rizzoli Enterprises. Six months after they met, Dr. Colton proposed–Nancy accepted. Eighteen months into their marriage, Mrs. Colton gave birth to a healthy baby boy, Richard, Jr.

Four-and-a-half years later, Nancy was walking her son across the street to his preschool, when a silver Aston Martin ran a red light. Richard, Jr. died instantly. His mother stubbornly clung to life until her husband arrived. The silver Aston Martin and driver had fled the scene. Nobody recognized either the car or driver–at least not until Dr. Colton leaned close to his wife and whispered, "I love you."

At that, Nancy faintly moaned, "It was Mario Rizzoli…he killed our baby." Moments later, Nancy Colton died.

Dr. Colton mourned the deaths of his wife, and son. He remained single for many years before meeting and marrying his second wife, his office nurse, Barbara Manners. Dr. Colton contributed many hours of his time and medical knowledge to serving the underprivileged and homeless. Much of his efforts were spent helping people in Chi-town, a Chicago subway shanty for the homeless.

Chapter 1

"Dr. Richard Daniel Colton, you are hereby charged with the abduction and murder of one Marco Rizzoli, twenty-five years ago when he was five-years-old. How do you plead?"

"My client pleads NOT GUILTY, Your Honor," Defense Attorney Wesley Dill stated emphatically.

"Very well," Judge Byron Vang said. "I'll set a bail reduction hearing for the day after tomorrow at nine o'clock in the morning."

"Your Honor, bail is set at one million dollars. Prosecution requests bail not be reduced from one million, but be rescinded. Defendant is a licensed pilot who owns a private jet and is a reasonable risk of flight," Prosecuting Attorney Anthony Pizzo argued. "Defendant has lived a nomadic life with his wife and twin sons for the last fifteen years. He has numerous friends–"

"Objection, Your Honor!" Mr. Dill interrupted. "Dr. Colton has already surrendered his passport and visas. He sold his private jet two years ago and he is *not* a flight risk."

"You're only saying that because you're being paid," Prosecutor Pizzo protested.

"Excuse me, Mr. Prosecutor. I could say that about you; however, I'm not receiving a single cent to represent Dr. Colton. My firm has taken this case at request."

"Prosecution still asks bail be rescinded, or at least remain at one million dollars." Prosecutor Pizzo continued, "I see the defendant–"

"I object, Judge Vang," Dr. Colton sang out. "Anybody who hears the word 'DEFENDANT' will automatically relate that to guilt. The court requires respect from all who come before it. It only seems right–"

"Mr. Dill, you'll keep your client quiet or else he'll be found in contempt of court. Am I clear on this matter?" Judge Vang said sternly.

Dr. Colton opened the briefcase in front of him. He removed three pieces of paper and handed them to his attorney, Mr. Dill. "Yes, Your Honor," Mr. Dill responded. "I'd like to submit this federal order to the court and label it defense exhibit 1." Attorney Wesley Dill handed a paper to both the court clerk and the prosecutor, Anthony Pizzo. "Your Honor, my client has been granted co-counsel status by a higher court so his voice may not be silenced. To insist on him not speaking during this trial is grounds for a mistrial and/or dismissal of all charges."

"Your Honor, surely this document isn't legal," Prosecutor Pizzo urged. "Do we really need to allow 'the defendant' to speak whenever he wishes?"

"I don't agree with this so-called federal order Mr. Pizzo, but I'll honor it until such time as I learn it's fake or has been forged. The defendant may speak for now."

"I ask the court to acknowledge I have a running objection to everything the defendant has to say," the prosecutor said sarcastically.

"Your objection can be noted," Dr. Colton interjected. "In regards to, quote, the defendant unquote, I consider those words objectionable, disrespectful, and

1

highly inflammatory. My name is either Dr. Colton or Mr. Colton, therefore, it is requested that all future references be addressed as such."

"You're the defendant in this case, sir," Judge Vang spat angrily. "You broke the law; accept it."

Dr. Colton remained calm in his response. "And I suppose allowing illegally obtained evidence in Mr. Mario Rizzoli's trial means you *didn't* break the law, right, Your Honor? And as for *accepting* it, I've only been *charged* with breaking the law. Mr. Rizzoli proved your court broke the law and therefore received a reduced sentence of life, without the death penalty."

Attorney Dill already knew Dr. Colton was going to insist on equal respect from Judge Vang and Prosecutor Pizzo. He also knew Dr. Colton had just struck an extremely sensitive nerve.

"Because this will undoubtedly be our only meeting, I'll address you as requested, Mr. Colton," Judge Vang agreed begrudgingly.

"Criminals are criminals," Prosecutor Pizzo rebuked. "When caught, they lose the right to respect. You're not a doctor; you're a defendant and should be addressed as such."

Quickly Dr. Colton spoke up. "Of course, I understand Judge Vang is our judge, Mr. Dill is the lead defense attorney, I'm the defendant, and you, Mr. Pizzo, you're the prosecutor–or should I say the court liar."

"How dare you!" Anthony Pizzo shot back, "I don't lie; you child killer."

"Order! Stop this nonsense!" Judge Vang demanded. "You, Mr. Colton, would be wise not to anger this court. Do I make myself clear?"

"Yes, sir, you're understood. But I cannot and will not allow Prosecutor Pizzo to ignore a higher court ruling of which you're both now in possession. I stated that Mr. Pizzo lied. Please permit me to explain–"

"No, no explanations," Judge Vang glowered angrily at Dr. Colton. "We'll not discuss this any further. You are hereby ordered held for trial and there'll be no reduction of bail."

"Pardon me, Judge Vang," Mr. Dill interrupted. "Due to Dr. Colton being refused a bail reduction, would you see fit to order him held at Methodist Hospital?"

"Denied," Judge Vang said authoritatively.

Dr. Colton opened his briefcase and again handed Mr. Dill three sheets of paper.

"Your Honor, my client has just presented me with paperwork naming you and Mr. Pizzo as direct defendants in a $10 million lawsuit for the refusal of medical attention."

"What kind of game is this?" Prosecutor Pizzo asked.

"My question is, what kind of medical attention?" Judge Vang queried. "I haven't denied you medical access."

Turning to the audience, Dr. Colton spoke one word: "Doctor."

"Well?" Judge Vang leaned forward impatiently.

"My name is Dr. Adam Boot. Your Honor, the man on trial, Dr. Richard Colton, has an aggressive form of cancer. If he can't be home at night then it's

2

best he should be housed at Methodist. I'm the oncologist responsible for Dr. Colton's cancer therapy."

"Dr. Boot is already fully equipped at my home, Judge Vang. My insurance required me to pay $300,000 upfront. Treatment so far has been in excess of $1.5 million. At home I can fight the cancer throughout the evening as Dr. Boot is living with us during this trial."

"Your Honor," Prosecutor Pizzo interrupted, "The defendant is looking for sympathy from the court. Where was his sympathy for five-year-old Marco Rizzoli? He had none and I ask the court to deny the defendant's request."

"Mr. Dill, the court is going to deny any motion for bail reduction and/or housing at Methodist Hospital. Do you have anything else to present at this time?"

"Yes, Your Honor, we do. I've counted at least three times Mr. Pizzo has addressed Dr. Colton as "the defendant". He's blatantly defied the court's order to refrain from addressing Dr. Colton in said manner."

"Your point, sir?" Judge Vang said impatiently.

"My point is this: If I exhibited the same behavior of ignoring your instructions, I'd properly be found in contempt of court and undoubtedly fined for each contempt. I ask the court to follow its own rulings."

"Add it to your frivolous lawsuit. Request denied," Judge Vang said with contempt.

Dr. Colton once more handed papers to Mr. Dill. This time, he spoke, "Your Honor, I instructed Attorney Dill to follow the path we have presented. I'll now present this court with these final documents." Dr. Colton held up a third set of papers. "You'll notice these documents have today's date on them and are signed by Federal Judge Samuel Holt."

"This is my courtroom," Judge Vang hissed. "Judge Holt *does not* make rulings in my court. My ruling stands! No bail reduction, no medical hospital quarters, and no to your lawsuit and contempt request." Judge Vang crumpled the papers he had been served, and then set them aside, facedown.

"By your action, I take it we're finished here?" Defense Attorney Dill asked. "I mean, when do we meet again?"

"You have two weeks to prepare any further motions you wish to present. But I won't be hearing them."

"Thank you, Your Honor," Dr. Colton said, getting to his feet.

As Dr. Colton turned to leave, Sheriff Kelly stood up to block the way. "Where do you think you're going?"

"Home, until our next court date," Mr. Dill stated. "Judge Vang failed to fully read the documents handed to the court. Prosecutor Pizzo failed also. Had they read them, it would have resulted in a different outcome. As it is now," Attorney Dill paused briefly, "Dr. Colton is held under federal authority." Then recognizing Sheriff Kelly's name, Attorney Dill motioned to two U.S. Marshals present in the courtroom. "This is Sheriff Frank Kelly. I believe you have something for him."

"You're Sheriff Frank Kelly?" Marshal Tucker asked.

3

"Yup, that's me. What can I do for you men?"

"Don't move. You are under arrest for heinous crimes against humanity. Don't say a word," Marshal Tucker responded. Sheriff Kelly was placed in handcuffs and his duty weapon secured. He was then read his rights and immediately escorted from the courtroom. Transfixed, Judge Vang stood up.

"Federal officers have successfully arrested over one hundred people for very specific charges. Judge Vang, you'll need to come with me. I don't think you're going to like what I have to say. However, I urge you to listen carefully," an unknown man said.

"Am I allowed to inquire what this is about?" Judge Vang asked.

"It's believed you're an unknowing accomplice in a number of illegal acts. However, believe it or not, your name came up to be an official observer in Dr. Colton's trial, so you'll be seeing him again. As an official observer, you'll be allowed to ask questions. Once Dr. Colton's trial ends, you're to be appointed as special prosecutor in regards to the information which will come out during that trial."

"But I thought Dr. Colton kidnapped Marco Rizzoli and killed him because Mario Rizzoli refused to pay ransom."

"I'm really not at liberty to discuss much more. It might surprise you to know that Dr. Colton suggested you as an observer and special prosecutor. It might also interest you to know it was you who signed my son's adoption papers. My wife and I couldn't have children of our own. We ended up adopting two children. I'm Federal Judge Samuel Holt."

"And you say I'm just an observer who can ask questions? How'd you manage to pull that off? I can't see Mr. Wesley Dill agreeing to an observer who can ask questions."

"Wesley Dill may only be twenty-eight years old; however, he's a well-respected federal attorney. An official observer and special prosecutor was Dr. Colton's idea, which was agreed to by Mr. Dill. As an official observer you'll be connected by computer to the Judge's computer, Prosecutor Pizzo's computer, and both defense computers. But they'll have access only to their own computers and not yours. One thing you're not to do is suggest questions or express your thoughts or opinions."

"So why is Dr. Colton not behind bars?" Judge Vang asked.

"May I suggest you talk with the doctor and ask him yourself. I think you'll see that he has a deep-seated respect for the law. I can only promise shock and disbelief. Dr. Colton will be very trying for any judge."

"Why do I get the feeling court today was useless? I mean, the doctor isn't in custody, he's going home and he has no bail."

"If you're around Dr. Colton very long, you'll soon realize he's an exceptional genius."

"Officer, arrest that man!" Prosecutor Pizzo demanded. "He can't just walk out of court. His bail was set at one million dollars."

"I know," a U.S. Marshal responded. "I was in court too, but unlike you, I answer to someone with much more authority. Dr. Colton will be in court on his

4

next scheduled hearing date. The hearing today was merely a formality. We needed access to Judge Vang and Sheriff Kelly. And, because Dr. Colton provided both without causing undue alarm, he was granted special considerations."

"What do you mean by special considerations?"

"Mr. Pizzo, I'm one of his special considerations. I'm FBI Special Agent Xander Ward. Dr. Colton is a person of interest to our government. His special considerations include things such as no bail and no jail. You really ought to have read all the paperwork Mr. Dill handed you. The doctor's special considerations are all covered in those papers, sir."

"Xander Ward," Prosecutor Pizzo almost whispered. "You're the guy who went to Mexico alone and brought Kevin Vale back to face murder and drug trafficking charges."

"It was no big deal, really," Xander said casually.

"Rizzoli Enterprises wanted both of you dead. Avoiding all their hired guns took a lot of work."

"Well, thanks to you, Kevin Vale is in prison, right beside his boss."

"Xander," Dr. Colton interrupted. "My curfew is six o'clock and we need to stop for dinner."

"Mr. Colton," Prosecutor Pizzo looked at the doctor. "You deserve a jail cell, not freedom. I intend to offer time and effort to whoever the prosecutor is in your Superior Court trial."

Smiling, Dr. Colton responded, "Why, Prosecutor Pizzo, haven't you heard? You won't be helping anybody."

"Is that a threat?"

"No, Mr. Prosecutor, I'm not threatening you. What I just said is a promise based on fact. You won't be helping anybody, but somebody might be needed to help you. You, Mr. Pizzo, are going to hate me when this trial is over."

"What's that supposed to mean? I already hate you. I despise anybody who would harm a child."

Dr. Colton turned his back on Mr. Pizzo. As he and Xander walked away he said, "You're prosecuting my case, Anthony."

"He's going to fight twice as hard now," Agent Ward commented softly.

"And he'll draw strength from his blind hatred. If he blinds himself to the obvious, it's better for me."

"I don't know why you were in Mexico illegally, but you saved my life by flying me and that drug lord home."

"A little birdie told me you could use a bit of help. Plus, it was pure dumb luck," Dr. Colton half teased. "I brought a Mexican girl to the United States for surgery to repair two holes in her heart. When you were in Mexico, I was returning the girl to her family. I helped because you were American and I heard the villagers saying men were on their way to kill you."

"Well, thank you again, Doctor. You definitely saved my life. Oh, my wife and children thank you too."

Chapter 2

"All rise, the Honorable Judge Noah King presiding."

"Be seated and come to order," Judge King instructed. "This is the case of the People vs. Richard Daniel Colton. Is the defendant present?"

"Yes, sir, Dr. Richard Colton is present." Anthony Dill responded.

"Very well, I understand we'll have an official observer during this trial. Please identify yourself."

"Judge Byron Vang, Your Honor. I'm here to take notes, ask questions and pay attention to Dr. Colton's trial."

"Okay, thank you. You may ask your questions through the court. Is that acceptable to you, Mr. Pizzo?"

"Yes, sir, that's quite acceptable," the prosecutor replied.

"Judge King, I must protest," Judge Vang said. "I'll be asking questions of both sides. Therefore, I'm going to need a way of indicating I have a question. Forcing me to go through the court to ask a question hinders me from being neutral."

"He can always raise his hand," Attorney Dill quipped.

"We can do without childish remarks or suggestions. If you can't be civil towards one another, I'll find a method that suits me and you'll have to live with it."

"I meant no disrespect, Your Honor," Mr. Dill stated.

"Your Honor," Dr. Colton spoke up. "May I suggest a small battery-operated light which can be turned on and off by switch."

"Dr. Colton, you're the defendant in this case. You will not speak unless you're on the stand or addressed by me. However, your idea is good, so I'll look into getting that done today."

Leaning to his right, Dr. Colton opened a box and lifted out an already-built light from inside. "Judge King, I have a light right here. It was constructed by the FBI at Special Agent Ward's request."

"While I appreciate your foresight, I find it necessary to advise you one last time that *you are* the defendant in this case. If you have something to say, write it out and give it to Mr. Dill. If you speak again without permission, I'll find you in contempt."

"Judge King, may I invite you to turn your attention to folder 'A', document number two, page one, line sixteen. It states, Dr. Richard Colton is hereby ordered to act as co-counsel in his trial. As co-counsel, he is granted the privilege of making objections, asking questions, and in general asserting himself appropriately throughout the trial," Observer Vang interjected.

"Thank you, Observer Vang. I had not yet taken the opportunity to peruse these documents in *toto*."

"That particular document also states my co-counsel shall be given due respect. Meaning he'll be referred to as Mr. Colton or Dr. Colton, not as the defendant as some may wish to refer to him." Mr. Dill asserted.

6

"There are certain protocols in courts," Judge King said, softly rubbing his eyes. "They're in place to ensure the justice process goes smoothly. I'm not going to change this process just to accommodate one man."

"Your Honor, Judge King," Prosecutor Pizzo chimed in. "I ask you to take this afternoon off and investigate whether or not we must follow this ridiculous order."

"Judge King, sir," Dr. Colton spoke politely, "I'm charged with a capital crime–specifically, murder in the first degree. As with any and all capital offenses, the defense is entitled to dual representation. Now, as I understand it, both defense attorneys may speak up at any time. However, only one of the two attorneys is considered lead counsel. Mr. Dill is our lead counsel so he'll usually present our, or in this case, my defense."

"Mr. Colton, it's my advice for you to step aside as co-counsel and allow two educated attorneys who have passed the bar exam to represent you."

Defense Attorney Dill stood up. "Your Honor, I'd like to introduce the newest member of Dill and Barnes, Attorneys at Law: Dr. Richard Colton. Dr. Colton took and passed his bar exam two months ago. He is well-versed in state and federal law. Dr. Colton passed his exam at number two."

"It might also be noted that Dr. Colton is a board-certified physician and surgeon," Judge Vang stated to everyone in the courtroom.

"You're here to observe and ask questions, not make comments," Prosecutor Pizzo argued. "Why hasn't he been disbarred? He's a criminal, a kidnapper of children, and a murderer," he goaded.

"A provision in the law allows Dr. Colton to retain his status and represent himself. If he should be found guilty he'll be immediately disbarred," Mr. Dill explained to everyone present.

Stepping up to assert himself, Dr. Colton said, "Objection, Your Honor. Please inform Mr. Pizzo that being charged with a crime does not equal automatic conviction. The prosecutor is disrespecting this court and the procedures for a just, fair, and unbiased trial."

"Overruled," Judge King retorted. "Prosecutor Pizzo is stating his opinion based on facts as he understands them."

"Objection!" Attorney Dill yelped. "If we're to be allowed to state opinions based on facts as we understand them then, this trial will be nothing but a travesty."

"Again, overruled! The prosecutor is entitled to his opinion, and for argument's sake, you also are entitled to your opinions."

"Based on facts as we understand them," Mr. Dill sarcastically voiced. "Very well, the Defense apologizes to the mendacious prosecutor who believes himself above the law."

"That, Mr. Dill, is contempt. Any more of your nonsense and you'll be fined," Judge King sternly warned from the bench.

"Your Honor," Dr. Colton calmly joined in, "I believe my co-counsel was merely stating facts as he understands them: facts that have been found to be true and verifiable by courts of higher authority."

"*Enough*!" Judge King commanded. "Any more of this and I'll fine the violator."

"Fair enough," Dr. Colton responded. "I only wish to have a running objection noted in regards to the double standard just named by the court."

"Overruled, you just bought yourself a $200.00 contempt of court fine. Next time it'll be $500.00. Do I make myself clear?"

Dr. Colton took out his wallet, removed $200.00, and dropped the money in front of Mr. Dill.

"You'll need to wait until we recess to pay your fine. At that time you'll be allowed to pay the bailiff, who will give it to the court clerk."

"Yes, Your Honor. Thank you," Dr. Colton responded.

"You need to put your money inside your wallet."

"Put your money away," Dr. Colton whispered as he nudged Mr. Dill.

"I was addressing you, Doctor," said the judge.

"Yes, sir, I know, but that is Mr. Dill's money. I lost a bet, so I paid the man his money."

Judge Vang smiled. He had just watched Mr. Dill file for an immediate appeal with the State Supreme Court. He also saw the appeal accepted, given a case number, and then sent to Judge King—all in a matter of minutes, thanks to the age of computers.

"Now isn't *this* a new twist?" Judge King reflected. "It appears Mr. Dill has filed an appeal with the higher courts regarding the defendant's contempt fine."

"This is a high-profile trial, everyone involved is under a magnifying glass," Dr. Colton remarked.

Judge King banged his gavel. "Mr. Dill, you'll instruct your client to address the bench as 'Your Honor' or 'Judge'."

"Judge King," Observer Vang interrupted, "as an official observer I would be remiss should I not speak up. There's an outstanding federal court order requiring Mr. Colton to be addressed as Mister or Doctor, and not as the defendant. To do so, because he is acting as co-counsel, is considered inflammatory, especially when in front of jurors."

"The man is charged with kidnap and not only a murder, but the murder of a child. He doesn't deserve any respect," Prosecutor Pizzo spewed aggressively.

"So says the man who presents false evidence as truth and lies as facts. You, sir, are an arrogant, dishonest attorney. You may want to check yourself before you wreck yourself," Mr. Dill retorted in disgust.

"Mr. Dill, that's enough!"

"Just stating the facts as I found to be true, Your Honor. No disrespect intended towards the court or bench, sir."

"Or the prosecutor, Mr. Dill?" Judge King asked.

"No, sir! I meant total disrespect for the prosecutor. He's showing disregard for the law, so he'd best expect it to come back on him," Mr. Dill replied.

"In this courtroom, you'll show respect for your opponent," Judge King ordered.

"Objection! Objection! Objection!" Dr. Colton snapped. "You order us to be respectful to Mr. Pizzo. But he's allowed to be disrespectful and contemptible towards Mr. Dill and myself, and especially towards me."

Judge Noah King was now clearly angry. Slamming down his gavel he barked, "We'll take a fifteen-minute recess. Mr. Colton may either pay his contempt fine at that time or go to jail when we dismiss for the day."

"No offense, Your Honor; however, I suggest you read your packet of federal procedure documents which have been handed down by the federal court. And, of course, I'll pay my fine. My attorney is buying the coffee."

Chapter 3

At noon, Dr. Adam Boot entered the courtroom. He sat patiently observing Dr. Colton as the proceedings progressed. Twice Dr. Colton faltered in his speech and motor skills. On the third time, Dr. Boot exited the courtroom. He quietly identified himself to an officer and requested assistance. Upon entering the courtroom again, Dr. Boot waited. He watched the officer approach Judge King. It was a mere sixty seconds later when he was addressed by Judge King.

"You may come into the courtroom, Dr. Boot. Do I understand correctly that you're a cancer specialist?"

"Yes, sir, I am, and Dr. Colton needs to take a break. He has to eat and get some rest."

"We'll be finished in about an hour," Mr. Pizzo said. "He can take his medicine and rest then."

"Now!" Dr. Boot insisted. "I'm charged with keeping Dr. Colton alive for this trial. You have no physical proof of any kind. All you do have is conjecture, theory, and circumstantial garbage. But, that's only my personal opinion, Your Honor."

"Dr. Boot, the defendant cannot leave until we're finished going over the jury questions," Mr. Pizzo smirked.

"Judge King, federal orders in your possession give me the authority to end today's proceedings if Dr. Colton's immediate health is in jeopardy. If you allow Dr. Colton to eat food and drink some fluids, he can stay until you're finished. If not, then he must leave. And, Mr. Prosecutor, don't speak to me unless you can be civil."

"I'll agree to let Mr. Dill continue jury questions, Your Honor. I trust his judgment with the questionnaire," Dr. Colton interjected.

"Prosecution will agree to allow the defendant to leave until tomorrow morning," Mr. Pizzo said.

"Granted, you may leave," Judge King conceded.

Dr. Colton spoke briefly with Mr. Dill. Turning to Judge King, he addressed the court. "I object to Mr. Pizzo's ongoing display of disrespect. I ask the court to admonish him for his negative attitude and behavior."

"Objection overruled unless you wish to remain present. Your request is definitely denied."

"Thank you, Your Honor," Dr. Colton responded calmly as he closed his briefcase and exited the courtroom.

Chapter 4

"Be seated and come to order," Judge King said the next morning. "I received an extremely unpleasant phone call yesterday afternoon before I left for home. I was informed that for each time I referred to Mr. Colton as 'the defendant' I am to pay a fine of two hundred dollars. I am now duty-bound to fine Mr. Pizzo a total of two thousand dollars for his blatant disregard of the same federal order."

"But he *is* the–," Mr. Pizzo began to protest.

Holding up his hand, Judge King interrupted. "He *is* either Doctor, or Mr. Colton. No arguments, Mr. Pizzo."

Judge King was not fooled. To him, Mr. Colton was nothing more than a common criminal. It took nearly twenty-five years to catch him for his kidnap and murder of Marco Rizzoli, but thanks to an anonymous tip, the police were now able to link a previously unidentified ambulance service as a heated rival to the Rizzoli Enterprises Ambulance. And, Rizzoli Enterprises' Ambulance was in fact based closer to the Nancy Colton Memorial Clinic. Additionally, evidence showed Marco Rizzoli had visited the Nancy Colton Memorial Clinic more than five times before his disappearance, which was cause for deeper investigation. The ash remains of a child on Gibson Road had to be those of Marco Rizzoli. Next to the ashes were Marco's shoes and an earring. Yes, sir, in Judge King's opinion, Mr. Colton was one guilty, egotistical son-of-a-bitch.

"I'll allow the defense to present their motions first, Your Honor," Mr. Pizzo said.

"Mr. Dill, do you wish to begin?"

"Yes, sir, in order to save the court's time, I'll simply refer to our motions as defense motion and a number such as, defense motion 1: motion to dismiss. Due to the lack of hard substantial evidence, we move to dismiss all charges with prejudice. The evidence is hearsay, a pair of shoes, an earring, and conflict-of-interest ambulances. The entire trial will be presented under reasonable doubt."

"Excuse me, please," Observer Vang interrupted while flipping his light switch. "Are you going to make your ruling on each motion as you proceed, or wait until after all motions are presented?"

"I can do either, as is best for both prosecution and defense. However, I think it would be better to hear all motions and make a ruling later. But in response to defense motion 1: motion to dismiss is denied."

"I believe the majority of my motions can be ruled on today," Mr. Pizzo volunteered. "I like the defense's idea of making this simple. Likewise, I'll refer to my motions as people's motion, with a number. Like people's motion 1: people wish to subpoena Dr. Colton's medical records."

"Is that personal or otherwise?" Dr. Colton asked.

"I'd say both," Prosecutor Pizzo replied.

"I'll allow only one or the other per motion," Judge King responded.

"Then I'll amend that to be a motion for his own personal medical records," Mr. Pizzo said.

"Objection! My personal medical records have no bearing on this case," Dr. Colton argued.

"Mr. Prosecutor, your rebuttal?"

"Your medical records have everything to do with this case. If you in fact don't have cancer, it'll show you to be deceitful and an outright liar. It'll prove you're delusional," Mr. Pizzo retorted.

"Mr. Pizzo, your argument lacks merit. Whatever I say is irrelevant unless I decide to take the stand and testify in my defense."

"Regardless of merit, I'm going to grant people's motion number one. Dr. Richard Colton's personal medical records will be turned over to the people."

"Very well, when defense receives a copy of the people's motion, signed by the court, my medical records shall be provided," Dr. Colton conceded.

"Your Honor, defense wishes to submit defense motion 2," Mr. Dill continued.

"Proceed, Mr. Dill."

"Defense motion 2: defense petitions the court to order a polygraph examination of Dr. Colton regarding Marco Rizzoli's alleged murder. Did Dr. Colton really kill a child–any child?"

"Objection! Polygraphs are not admissible evidence in any court of law."

"Sustained. The court denies defense motion number two. I don't recognize polygraphs as evidence. The defense is already aware polygraphs are easily manipulated and therefore not admissible in any court, let alone mine. Mr. Pizzo, do you have any more motions?"

"People's motion 2: Your Honor, the people petition all Nancy Colton Memorial Clinic medical records."

"That's a direct violation of all, and I do mean each and every single HIPAA law. Therefore I object."

"Dr. Colton, as much as I'd enjoy overruling your objection, the law is on your side regarding this subject. Objection sustained," Judge King said. "People's motion 2: denied."

"In that case, Your Honor, the people would modify people's motion 2 to read: 'All Nancy Colton Memorial Clinic medical records pertaining to Marco Rizzoli.' Submit this as people's motion 2."

"Your Honor, we again face HIPAA restrictions. Those records, the same as all medical records, are considered confidential for all time. And that includes the medical records of Dr. Colton which the court has violated by ordering his records surrendered," Mr. Dill argued.

"Your client professes to be ill from cancer," Judge King responded. "His medical records can only help his claim should he be telling the truth. His records will be surrendered. The medical records of Marco Rizzoli will be released to the court. It seems very unlikely HIPAA laws would apply to a deceased child. Marco Rizzoli's father, Mario, is in prison for life. He has no right to keep his son's files from *my* court. I'm granting people's motion number three, the release of Marco Rizzoli's medical records."

"Your Honor," Dr. Colton interrupted, "HIPAA privacy rules are excluded regarding a person who has been deceased for more than fifty years. Enforcement of the rule for a person who has died is the same as for the living. Only the person with authority may act on the behalf of the deceased."

"Your Honor, the records will assist the prosecution in proving the ashes found on Gibson Road are those of Marco Rizzoli," Mr. Pizzo claimed.

"Judge King, I must protest the release of Marco Rizzoli's medical records. Authorities have never found a body. So, on the premise that Marco Rizzoli is alive, I would assert he most definitely would not want his medical records divulged to anyone," Mr. Dill stated.

"Your Honor, Marco Rizzoli hasn't been seen since the day he left the Nancy Colton Memorial Clinic," Mr. Pizzo asserted.

"Should the court be wrong, and Marco Rizzoli files a lawsuit for violating his medical right to privacy, I fear the city and quite possibly the state could lose a multimillion-dollar lawsuit for the aforementioned violation," Mr. Dill countered.

"I'll risk the lawsuit, Mr. Dill. I've seen the boy's ashes so I'm not overly concerned about a lawsuit," Judge King shot back.

"Objection!" Dr. Colton said, rising to his feet. "Your Honor, I've been looking at photographs of the alleged ashes of Marco Rizzoli. However, there's absolutely nothing which solidly proves those ashes are the remains of Marco Rizzoli. As I understand it, there's no possible way to perform a DNA test to prove or disprove the theory that the ashes found on Gibson Road are the remains of Marco Rizzoli. I caution you to remember, if you're wrong, it could cost this county and court everything. As an advocate of HIPAA, I must report this violation."

"Marco Rizzoli is dead, Dr. Colton. You know this better than anyone else. I'll put my reputation and career on the line because I'm certain you killed Marco Rizzoli," Judge King said in anger.

"Your Honor, that causes me to request you disqualify yourself from hearing this case. You just stated in open court you're certain Dr. Colton killed Marco Rizzoli. With that conviction, you can't in all good conscience say you are unbiased," Attorney Dill stated.

"I beg to differ with you, Counselor. I'll be quite fair to your client and co-counsel Dr. Colton. To consider otherwise is singularly ridiculous. I'll not disqualify myself from this case."

"Begging your pardon," Dr. Colton interjected. "If you're certain I killed Marco Rizzoli, then you must have no doubt I kidnapped him as well."

"Is that an admission of guilt?" Prosecutor Pizzo quickly asked.

"No, *it is not*! I asked Judge King a question and you jumped in, preventing him from answering me."

Turning to Judge King, Dr. Colton asked, "Do you believe I kidnapped Marco Rizzoli, even though there is no solid factual evidence to support it?"

"Yes, I believe you kidnapped and killed Marco Rizzoli."

"Then I wish to file a motion to dismiss you as the judge for this trial. You can't be unbiased if you truly believe I'm guilty and aren't willing to give me the benefit of the doubt until all evidence is presented."

"Your Honor, by stating you believe my client is guilty you set grounds for a reversal or at least a finding of mistrial due to inability to be neutral," Mr. Dill said firmly.

"I'm willing to take that chance, Mr. Dill. I'll be remaining as judge for this trial," Judge King said, showing extreme agitation. "You may complain all you want. File your motion and do whatever you wish. This is *my* courtroom!"

Dr. Colton opened his briefcase and pretended to be ignoring the events happening around him. He held his defense motions in a blue packet. These he handed to Mr. Dill, then turned his attention back to his briefcase.

"Your Honor, are we boring Mr. Colton?" Mr. Pizzo inquired.

"When I get bored I'll let you know," Dr. Colton calmly replied without looking up. "No, sir, I'm not bored; I'm merely multitasking and looking for papers I've been ordered to surrender." Then, with a minor bit of flourish, Dr. Colton waved his left hand containing a medical file. "This is my medical file pertaining to my cancer."

"You were ordered to turn over your entire medical file," Mr. Pizzo jumped in.

"Objection!" Mr. Dill protested. "The court doubted or doubts Dr. Colton is battling cancer. You clearly stated his records can only help his claim, should he be telling the truth. The medical record proves Dr. Colton is indeed battling cancer."

"Counselor Dill, you're trying my patience. I want Dr. Colton's complete medical record. Not just the part pertaining to his cancer."

"Very well," Counselor Dill sighed in defeat. "We'll offer the following folder as evidence. Do you want me to name this as a defense exhibit?"

"Objection," Mr. Pizzo protested. "The prosecution motioned for those files. They should be people's evidence."

"I agree," Judge King said. "Objection sustained. Your attempt to manipulate this court *is not* appreciated. Mr. Pizzo will make copies of the file and return the originals to you."

"Thank you, but I really don't need them," Dr. Colton said. "I already know what cancer is doing to me. Mr. Pizzo, read it carefully. You'll discover I have cancer." Turning to Judge King, he continued. "Defense motion 4: we wish to call an expert witness to testify regarding the alleged remains of Marco Rizzoli." Dr. Colton knew full well that expert witness requests didn't fall under motions. He expertly diverted the court's attention after realizing he nearly revealed his mental health records were with his regular medical files.

"Motion denied. You can put your expert on the list of witnesses you expect to call."

Leaning towards his client, Mr. Dill whispered to Dr. Colton, "Put your mental health records away; we need those in front of the jury and not before. They contain your polygraph results."

"Your Honor, people's motion 4: people petition the court to seize all property and freeze all bank accounts belonging to Dr. Colton."

"Excuse me," Dr. Colton interrupted. "I'm broke, so seizing and freezing will serve absolutely no purpose other than proving that I'm flat broke."

"Petition granted. All of Dr. Colton's personal belongings are to be seized immediately. I'll order his bank accounts frozen. Dr. Colton, you have a retirement fund. That, sir, has also been seized."

"Along with all of your property, including your expensive motorcoach, your jet aircraft, and that fancy houseboat. They're going to be sold and the money used to pay for your trial," Mr. Pizzo gloated.

Dr. Colton sat at the defense table, half laughing and definitely smiling. Turning to his briefcase, he brought out a thin file.

"Do you find this amusing, Mr. Colton?" Judge King inquired. "Are you so self-absorbed that you think your possessions won't be gone by day's end?"

"He's just a smug criminal who got caught and now he's lost everything," the prosecutor interjected.

"Objection, Your Honor," Dr. Colton said immediately. "The prosecutor has no right to address me in this manner. I request you find Mr. Pizzo in contempt, and remind him of the conversation you told us about earlier. If required, I'm one hundred percent certain Federal Judge Samuel Holt would be willing to address Mr. Pizzo in person."

"Sustained," Judge King barked. "Mr. Prosecutor, you'll apologize for your rudeness and be warned. Any further disparaging remarks shall result in a stiff fine."

"Yes sir, Your Honor. I do apologize to Mr. Colton for my comments," Prosecutor Pizzo said, putting extra emphasis on the word *Mister*. "It's just that this case really bothers me. I put Mr. Rizzoli in prison for life. I fully intend to prosecute this self-righteous, arrogant doctor to the fullest extent of the law for the murder of Rizzoli's son."

"Your Honor, Mr. Pizzo, this file will show my house, motorcoach, jet, and boat were sold when I first learned I had cancer. The house went to a well-known family in the city. They offered cash. The jet is owned by a corporation which allowed me to use it before I was grounded. I've had a medical hold placed on me, and am no longer allowed to pilot aircraft. My two sons jointly own the motorcoach, boat, jet skis, quads, and the car I drive." Taking a deep breath, Dr. Colton continued. "My bank account—*not accounts*—was quickly depleted when I learned of the cancer. My wife, Barbara, has her own retirement fund. Should you attempt to go after my retirement fund, you'll discover it is federally protected. You can have what is left after I die. Until such time, I receive limited funds each month."

"You'll understand when I don't take your word regarding these things?" Judge King responded.

"Consider this file as defense exhibit—whatever number it is." Dr. Colton waved his hand as he handed the file to Mr. Dill who passed it to the court clerk.

"We'll take a thirty-minute recess," Judge King said as he rose to leave the courtroom.

"Your Honor, if Mr. Dill and his client are agreeable, we can turn this time into our lunch break. It's only another thirty minutes until lunch."

"Personally, I think that's an excellent idea," Judge King affirmed. "What I'm going to do is recess at this time until one o'clock. With that, the court is adjourned."

"Are we going to continue with motions when we return?" Mr. Dill inquired.

"Yes," Judge King answered, walking away.

Mr. Dill and Dr. Colton remained in the courtroom to secure their files.

"Excuse me, Mr. Pizzo," Dr. Colton said, addressing the prosecutor. "Do you think Judge King would mind if I set this little brown bear out to remind me of my wife? And would it bother you?"

"You'll have to ask Judge King if he is okay with your toy. Personally, I could care less."

"Just leave it, Richard. If Judge King objects, he can tell you to remove it," Mr. Dill interjected as he packed up his files. Turning to the bailiff, Mr. Dill asked, "Is there a secure place to leave our files? We're not allowed to take them into the lounge."

"I just locked the doors. This place will be secure enough," the bailiff replied

Dr. Colton left his briefcase on the table and his file box on the floor. "Do you really think Mr. Pizzo will look inside my files? Surely he knows the courtroom is video recorded."

"This case has no merit and no grounds. They have no evidence, Mr. Pizzo is under tremendous pressure to bolster their case against you, and Judge King isn't above doing cover-ups. I haven't been able to verify it, but there are rumors that the video recorder in this courtroom is disabled. Leaving your files behind is a rookie mistake."

"I heard the same rumor from Sam Holt, so let's get out of Mr. Pizzo's way and allow him to make an ass of himself. I also put a false file in my briefcase."

"Was it the property file we talked about?" Mr. Dill asked.

Smiling, Dr. Colton snickered. "Yup, as though I'd ever own property on Catalina Island off the California coast. Trust me, Mr. Pizzo will believe it. He'll also spend time and money trying to prove it's true. When he starts probing into the matter, we'll be alerted by friends who actually own property and you can discredit Mr. Pizzo in front of the jury," Dr. Colton stated.

During the recess, Dr. Colton and Mr. Dill began making phone calls. When they finished, Mr. Dill informed Dr. Colton that the well-known author, Blake West, had called from Catalina.

"Mr. West has agreed to be present to testify. An attorney by the name of Pizzo, claiming to represent Mr. Colton, called Mr. West asking if Mr. Colton owned property on Catalina Island. Mr. Pizzo won't be able to deny the phone call, because Mr. West recorded the conversation."

16

"When we return to court, I want to present a new motion for Mr. Pizzo's phone records," Dr. Colton told Mr. Dill. "And I expect Judge King to deny my motion."

Mr. Dill changed the subject. "Your son Royce called. You are now a grandpa to baby Nancy Marie Colton. Royce promised to bring pictures. They'll be flying in to be here during the trial. Royce asked me to thank you for sending the corporate jet. Baby and mother are doing fine."

"Thank you, Wesley. Has anyone heard from Mario Rizzoli? I would imagine he's put a contract out on me by now."

"No contract. The infamous Mario Rizzoli wants to see how this works out. He's issued an order of hands-off, because if you're convicted, he'll see you in prison."

"I want that sorry excuse to be here so he can hear for himself that my deceased wife, Nancy, named him as the hit-and-run driver who killed my baby boy before she died. I want him to feel what I have felt since he killed my wife and son. I want him to be reminded of the ashes and other items he found on Gibson Road."

"Doc, I'm really glad you've never been angry at me or my mom and dad. I'd hate to be in a fight against you," Mr. Dill said fervently.

"I think our recess is nearly over. I drank my lunch and still feel steady–so let's go piss off Mr. Pizzo and the judge!"

Chapter 5

Prosecutor Anthony Pizzo knew his evidence against Dr. Colton was weak. What he needed was proof the good doctor was guilty beyond any sort of doubt, let alone reasonable doubt.

Seeing Dr. Colton's briefcase, Prosecutor Pizzo noticed both clasps were open. He was alone in the courtroom. This was his playground and he knew the court video surveillance cameras had been temporarily disabled because of a digital recording issue their IT was trying to resolve. It would take no time at all to peek inside the doctor's briefcase. Then there was his file box. This could be a gold mine to be used against Mr. Dill and his client.

Anthony Pizzo believed in winning–not coming in second. Coming in second was losing. In court, you either both win and send all defendant scum to prison, or you lose. Losing means the defendant gets to commit more crimes.

"Dr. Colton, you're going down. I've got proof you've been lying to the court," Prosecutor Pizzo smirked, as he slipped three files inside his own briefcase. Looking inside Dr. Colton's file box provided him with witness names plus a paper with the words: "REMEMBER–You're supposed to have CANCER–act like it" Now Mr. Pizzo had evidence to prove Dr. Colton was faking his terminal cancer.

Back at his office, Mr. Pizzo went directly to the copy machine. He made only one copy of each document, being careful to put them back in the exact order prior to returning them to the courtroom. He put everything back in its proper place and went to his office.

Sitting at his desk, Mr. Pizzo dialed the prosecutor's investigator. "Mr. Hill, I need you to check on a couple of items for me. There's a file on my desk labeled *Defendant C–Lies*. Please research the contents and get your results to me ASAP, and *do not* share what you're doing with anyone. It's imperative that information about what you're doing isn't leaked out to the defense."

"I'll pick up your file before I leave for lunch," the investigator replied. "And nothing I do gets leaked unless I want it that way."

Setting his phone back in its cradle, Mr. Pizzo smiled. "Now for that witness list," he said to himself. A short time later he buzzed for his paralegal.

"Yes, sir," the paralegal, Ms. Gigi Green said upon entering Mr. Pizzo's office a couple of minutes later.

"Take these names and fill out subpoenas for them. I want Judge King to sign each of them this afternoon."

"Where'd you get these names?" Ms. Green inquired. "The heading says; *Defense Witnesses*."

"I also want you to check each of these people out. Get their backgrounds to me this afternoon." Then Mr. Pizzo fudged the truth: "The defense left the list lying on the table, open for anyone to see. What you have in your hands is my only copy. I want it back."

"I'll get on it right away," Ms. Green answered.

With two out of four files being worked on, it was time to check on the file titled; *Getaway*. Opening the file, Prosecutor Pizzo was drawn to the large letters spelling; FRANCE. In what he thought to be Dr. Colton's own handwriting Mr. Pizzo read:

I keep my passport in the corporate jet. I can still fly–I just don't have a license. I'm glad the corporation keeps a pilot and copilot on call twenty-four hours a day for me. To go anywhere all I have to do is call the pilot, tell him I want to get out of here and two hours later I'm flying to England. Refuel in England, then off to France. Everything I need is kept in the jet. One of the things I can see myself doing is living in Agde. It's only two hundred miles, as the crow flies, to Cannes. The cottage at Seventeen Bayonne Street is fantastic.

Louis Romily helps people lose themselves for the right price. He helped me find my cottage. Getting bored can be cured by going to work in a nearby Grandes Ecoles in Medicine. Oh yeah, Grandes Ecoles have great schools for military service and other fields. But what I really want to do is live in my cottage and enjoy the beach scene in Southern France.

To learn French as a child, as I did, is the best way to become proficient. The region of Agde grows some of the finest grapes, resulting in fabulous wine. France; Agde is where I feel most alive. I want to disappear in Agde and live my life in total beauty.

"Gotcha, you child killer," Mr. Pizzo said, feeling a deep sense of self-satisfaction. "Now I can get your sorry ass locked up in jail where you belong. This proves you are planning to play rabbit," he smiled to himself. "Judge King is going to love what I've found out about you, Dr. Colton. Maybe this bit of information will put you away for life, starting today after lunch."

Had the prosecutor paid attention to everything that was written, he would have seen *from the desk of Barbara Colton* printed in small letters above the word FRANCE.

Opening the fourth file, Prosecutor Pizzo gasped, "Oh my God, I know this place! I've been there with my parents. Oh Lord, that's Alaska! I grew up in Alaska! This place is between Fairbanks and Anchorage. I had a friend who lived in Ferry, Alaska. Dad used to take me to Anchorage on the train. His working as a mechanic for the railroad had its benefits, but what's Dr. Colton doing with pictures of this place?" Picking up his telephone, Mr. Pizzo dialed the paralegal.

"Gigi Green speaking."

"Ms. Green, could you check the lists I gave you to see if there's an address in Alaska?"

Moments later, Ms. Green spoke: "I see one address for Ferry, Alaska."

"What's the name and address, please?"

"Fred Block–it's a P.O. Box and there's a contact number."

"Thank you, Ms. Green." Mr. Pizzo hung up the phone. "What are you up to, Doctor? Are you going to bring up the hunting accident when I was twelve? Damn it, I didn't mean to shoot Kenny–he was my friend. It was an accident. You do know what an accident is, don't you?"

19

Anthony Pizzo began to cry softly. This document had brought hurtful memories. But how in the world did Dr. Colton find out about Ferry, Alaska? Why would he call Mr. Block as a witness? Another quick call and Mr. Pizzo had Fred Block's contact number. Fifteen minutes later, he was talking with Fred Block in Ferry, Alaska.

"You probably don't remember me, sir. I'm Anthony Pizzo; or if you do, the memory isn't a very nice one."

"Anthony, I remember you very well. You're the boy who shot Kenny while the two of you were hunting."

"Yes, sir, you remember me. Can I ask how Kenny is doing? The last time I saw him I was on my way to Fairbanks."

"Kenny works for your dad on the railroad. He got married two-and-a-half years ago. Their second child is due in three weeks. Your dad said you're an attorney."

"Yes, sir, I work in the prosecutor's office. That's why I'm calling you."

"What's on your mind, Anthony?"

"I'm beginning a child kidnap–slash–murder trial. I was wondering what you might know about Doctor Richard Colton. Do you have any idea why he'd list you as a possible witness in his trial?"

"What do I know about Dr. Colton? Well, let me tell you this: Dr. Colton was in Alaska on vacation with his wife. They were riding the Alaskan Railway as part of her bucket list of things to do. We flagged down the train, which stopped to pick up Kenny after the accident. Even though it was snowing hard, Dr. Colton wouldn't let the train move until he had Kenny's bleeding under control. Dr. Colton didn't get to see anything except Kenny all the way to Anchorage. The next day he hired a helicopter to bring you and your dad to see Kenny at the hospital. Anthony, you were so upset that all you did until you saw Kenny was mope. You sat around doing nothing because you didn't want to hurt anyone else. If the doctor has me listed as his witness, it's probably to testify that he'd never hurt a child. Dr. Colton would rather break the law than kill any child."

"Well, sir, your good doctor kidnapped a five-year-old boy. He demanded a ransom. When the ransom wasn't paid, he killed and burned the boy's body to ashes. I have pictures of the burned body, or in this case, the ashes."

"Anthony, if Dr. Colton calls me to testify, I'll be there to share what I know. I'm sorry you don't believe he's a good man. Our conversation is over, Anthony. I'll tell Kenny you called."

"Thank you, Mr. Block. You'll be receiving a subpoena from my office, so you'll be a witness for the Prosecution instead of the Defense."

"Do what you must, Anthony. Goodbye."

Prosecutor Anthony Pizzo sat back. "That went well. But I'm no closer to why the man would kidnap and kill Marco Rizzoli." Opening his office door, Mr. Pizzo nearly bumped into Ms. Green.

"Pardon me, Mr. Pizzo; here are the subpoenas you requested."

"Thank you, Ms. Green."

"Sir, are you okay? You seem a bit shaken, like you didn't get any lunch."

"I've been too busy. I'll get a big supper tonight. Right now I have to be in court.

Chapter 6

"All rise and come to order, the Honorable Judge King presiding."

"Be seated," Judge King quickly responded.

Speaking with anger in his voice, Judge King said; "I've just spent ninety minutes on the telephone trying to check on Dr. Colton's claim of no longer being in possession of his former properties. All I got with each phone call was four words. Those words were: *That is privileged information.* It's like nobody respects this court. When I contacted the Nancy Colton Memorial Clinic, they informed me that Marco Rizzoli's records were not available,"

"Begging your pardon, Your Honor, what does 'not available' mean?" Mr. Pizzo asked.

"According to the clinic, Mr. Pizzo, it means the Marco Rizzoli medical records have disappeared. They can't find them; *period.* I intend to send a deputy sheriff to the clinic with a search warrant to bring back all clinic records."

"You can't do that, Judge King," a spectator announced. "HIPAA laws protect those files. If you send a court-appointed physician to the clinic, he or she can go through the records."

"Exactly who are you?" Judge King shot back.

"I'm Samuel Holt, the federal magistrate assigned to this case. Pardon me one moment." The man then spoke softly; a tiny microphone could be seen in front of his mouth. Less than thirty seconds later, he turned his attention back to Judge King. "Did you check the hospital records where Marco Rizzoli was treated?"

"I've heard of a federal judge named Holt; is that you? Mr. Holt, nobody seems to know a five-year-old boy named Marco Rizzoli. The Methodist Hospital never treated the boy, so they have no records. I'll assign a doctor and two nurses to check records beginning tomorrow."

"Did you check for Mrs. Rizzoli's records?" Mr. Dill inquired. "We'd welcome those records as they'd prove my client's innocence." Continuing his diversion, Mr. Dill added, "The woman reported her husband was responsible for injuring their son. Maybe he's responsible for Marco's death."

"If I may make a suggestion," Dr. Colton interrupted.

"What?" Prosecutor Pizzo baited, "Drop the charges?"

Ignoring the prosecutor, Dr. Colton continued, "Check with the ambulance company I used to transport patients. They should have records." He then smiled at Mr. Dill.

"Stop helping them," Defense Attorney Dill ordered. "Other than yourself, I'm the only one fighting to keep you out of prison." Turning to Judge King he asked, "Your Honor, could we continue with our motions?"

"You may precede Mr. Dill."

Federal Judge Holt smiled to himself as he sat down to watch more of Dr. Colton's trial.

Mr. Dill continued, "Defense motion number five, motion for change of venue. Defense requests to move this trial two counties away, due to the notoriety of the Rizzoli name."

"Oh, nonsense, Your Honor," Mr. Pizzo objected. "What the defense requests is just plain ridiculous."

"Mr. Pizzo, you're out of order," Judge King replied. "I'll decide what is nonsense or ridiculous, unless I've missed something–because I'm certain this is *my* courtroom, not yours."

"My apology, sir," Mr. Pizzo answered respectfully.

"Change of venue motion denied. The Rizzoli name is well-known throughout not only this state, but neighboring states as well. Changing counties is out of the question. Next motion."

"Defense motion 6: move to sequester jurors for the duration of the trial."

"Denied!" Judge King snapped. "Unless I hear of a death threat towards a juror or potential juror, they'll be allowed to return home every day."

"Your Honor, defense motion 7: we request a closed hearing in fairness to my client. We ask that all media be banned from the courtroom."

"I'm inclined to grant this motion, unless the prosecution can think of any reason I should keep the hearing open to everyone."

"The prosecution would object to banning the media and closing Dr. Colton's trial to the public. Marco Rizzoli's death wasn't closed to the media. The defense wishes to keep Dr. Colton's dirty secrets from society. That's why they request closed doors," Mr. Pizzo argued.

"Your Honor, we make this motion in order for the court to provide due process."

"Mr. Dill, you amuse me," Judge King chuckled. "Even our clerk and recorder laughed at your ridiculousness. Motion denied."

"Your Honor, the prosecution has but two more motions, which I'm willing to combine in order to speed this process up. Also so we can hopefully proceed to jury selection in the morning."

Looking at Prosecutor Pizzo, the judge responded, "Would you like to share these motions with the court?"

"Oh, excuse me, my apologies," Mr. Pizzo said. "Defense motion 6: I think it is–"

"Objection Mr. Pizzo," Defense Attorney Dill said loudly.

"Over what?" Mr. Pizzo questioned. "I didn't even say what my motion was; you didn't let me."

"I think, Mr. Prosecutor," Judge King interrupted, "Mr. Dill is objecting to your choice of words. You present prosecution motions, not defense motions. Plus defense motion 6 has already been presented."

Both Dr. Colton and Mr. Dill chuckled. "I really appreciate people being human," Dr. Colton remarked. "I know it was accidental, but thank you for the chuckle."

"Dr. Colton's comments are ordered stricken from the record," Judge King commanded. "And off the record, I agree with the man. It *is* nice to be able to laugh occasionally."

"If we're back on the record, I'll wipe the egg off my face and try again," Mr. Pizzo said, smiling.

"On the record," Judge King smirked softly.

"Prosecution motion 5: the people wish to suppress pictures of Marco Rizzoli's ashes, and we request Dr. Colton be ordered to submit his DNA to the court."

"Objection to suppressing photographs of the alleged remains of Marco Rizzoli in the form of ashes," Dr. Colton responded. "Prosecutor Pizzo wants to try this case on nothing but hearsay– *his* hearsay. We have no objections to submitting my DNA. It can only prove I'm not responsible for the alleged death of Marco Rizzoli."

"Prosecution motion to suppress photographs is denied. Motion for Dr. Colton's DNA is granted," Judge King ordered. "And with that, if there are no further motions, we'll adjourn for the day."

"Defense submits motion 8: we wish to submit Dr. Colton's psych evaluation by Dr. Yvonne Hoch," Mr. Dill said.

"Objection!" Mr. Pizzo roared. "That evaluation was in order for Mr. Colton to resume his duties as a doctor, it has no bearing on this trial."

"Sustained!" Judge King quickly responded; "Motion denied!"

"Your Honor, the defense will submit, in writing, any final motions. Dr. Colton needs to leave. He neglected to eat lunch and is now feeling ill."

"Return tomorrow morning at nine o'clock. Adjourned."

Dr. Colton and Mr. Dill gathered their files and left. Dr. Colton removed his little bear.

The following morning, while sitting in Wesley Dill's office plotting their trial strategy they were informed that Judge King was delayed due to a family emergency.

"Shall we check Watchful Teddy the Bear?" Dr. Colton asked. "My files were definitely removed from their original resting spots."

"Hand me the micro SD chip and I'll put it in my computer. You know this recording isn't exactly legal," Mr. Dill said.

"It's not like I haven't broken a law or two in my life," Dr. Colton replied.

A short time later, the two men watched and listened to the contents from Watchful Teddy's chip. They expected to see the prosecutor going through Dr. Colton's papers. What they didn't expect was what they heard fifteen minutes before they were expected in court.

"Judge King, I'm glad you're early."

"You seem troubled, Mr. Prosecutor. Is there a problem I need to know about?"

"Well, yes, sir, I mean… I think… You see, Your Honor, on my way out of the courtroom I noticed the defendant and his attorney left some papers and files sitting out on the table. I, uh Your Honor, I…"

"You *what*, Mr. Pizzo?"

"I looked at the papers, sir."

"Did you see anything of importance?"

"The defendant lied to us. He owns six oil wells in Texas which produce an average of 100 to 150 barrels of crude per day. And that isn't all I found.

"Did you think to write any of this down? Did you see anything to help you convict the defendant?"

"I did something more than just write notes. I took the files and photocopied them. I'm going to ask you to replace me as prosecutor. What I did is grounds for disbarment for life."

"I want to read everything you copied. You're not to say a word about this to anyone. I'll accept all the help a defendant gives to convict himself. I want those copies before you go home today."

"Sir, I found the defendant's witness list as well. I had one of our paralegals fill out subpoenas for each of them."

Mr. Pizzo had just played a dangerous game with the judge and won. He now felt allied with Judge King in convicting Dr. Colton. The lack of evidence no longer seemed insurmountable.

"Excellent!" Judge King declared. "You've blocked their defense. I'll ask for witness lists this afternoon."

"Your Honor, the defendant has a file with newspaper articles on the kidnapping and death of Marco Rizzoli. One of the articles states they found blood around young Rizzoli's ashes. I'm having that particular evidence tested for DNA."

"I'm glad you petitioned for the defendant's DNA; now maybe you can conceivably find the golden bullet that convicts Mr. Colton."

"I was twenty-five when I led the prosecution of Mario Rizzoli. Granted, we lost our death penalty because my assistant, committed prosecutorial misconduct–or at least she was found guilty of it, anyway."

"We'll keep this quiet for now. This afternoon when we recess I'll remind everyone to secure all papers."

"Mr. Dill's client had the nerve to ask me if I thought you would object to his little stuffed bear."

"Let him enjoy his bear. It's no sweat off our brows. Give me those subpoenas and I'll sign them."

After viewing the SD card's video, Mr. Dill sighed, "Well, Doctor, it appears to me we can expect no fairness in this trial."

"I guess it's true: guilty until proven innocent," Dr. Colton replied. "I've been informed there is a bug on my phone line at home."

"Then I suggest we spoil Mr. Pizzo's little celebration. He's really going to hate you, Doc," Wesley Dill said. "Do you think maybe you could share just a little?"

"Wesley, I'm proud of you," Dr. Colton said, smiling at the young attorney. "No! I won't share, but only because you still have to work for a living."

"You know my dad told me you saved my life and helped him and mom adopt me."

"Austin always talks too much, but he loves you. That's what matters most."

"Not in my book. What matters most to me is, I would be nothing but dust if you hadn't taken me away from the torture I faced every day. I tried to commit suicide when I was seven by drinking a full bottle of my father's cooking sherry."

Dr. Colton chuckled, then stopped. "That was rude. I shouldn't have laughed. I apologize. I didn't know you tried to kill yourself."

"My father thought I needed to be disciplined. He made me drink spoiled buttermilk. I threw up for what seemed like hours. Then he used a razor strop to whip me. I had to learn my lesson. Even my mother beat me, only she used her stiff-bristle hair brush on my bare back. She always spanked me with a ping pong paddle. If it broke, she would get a new paddle and start over again because when she asked me how many swats she had given me; it was always the wrong answer. I learned to take my clothes off when I knew she was going to spank me. If any blood got on my clothing Mother would stop, clean up the blood, and then start over.

"When I told my teacher about my parents hitting me, she called the police, who took me out of the house. They put me in foster care, where I learned about sex. First it was two other boys in the house. Then one night the man walked in on us. I told him the other boys made me do what he caught us doing. I thought they'd get in trouble. I was wrong. He took off his belt and beat me. Then he did unspeakable things. I was locked in a room and only let out to be subjected to ungodly acts. He let the two teenagers beat me until one day, when he made me take a bath. Then, nobody touched me for almost an entire week."

Wesley Dill had been speaking softly, a tear on his cheek. "A social worker came by the foster house. She joined the foster mother in spanking me. They were evil, Dr. Colton. I finally pretended to like having the social worker French-kissing me. She lost her tongue that night and I escaped. The last I saw of the other two boys, they were drunk, dancing around the foster father and another man; both were dead. Someone started a fire which burned the house down. I was blamed for the fire until the foster mother testified that I was in a room with her confessing to biting the social worker. To keep out of prison, the foster mother swore it was the teenage boys who killed her husband and burned their house down."

"She evidently lied," Dr. Colton responded. "Am I presumptuous in thinking you know what really happened?"

"You're not stupid, Doctor. Yes, I know what really happened that night."

"I can understand if you'd rather not speak of it."

"I've spoken about this only twice in my life. I told my adoptive mom and dad when I was eleven years old because I kept having night terrors. Strangely, they ended shortly after I shared my story. What I told Mom and Dad is this; it was the foster mother who killed her husband and the second man. She then started the fire."

"You said *twice*. Who else did you tell?"

"Sam, the man who encouraged me to become an attorney. Recently he asked me to testify before a federal panel. I told him any testimony I give will be after I defend the one man to whom I owe my life."

Dr. Colton sighed. "Finding you under the pier nearly dead was pure luck–or divine intervention. I listened to my police scanner describing a runaway boy being sought for theft and assault. They described your clothing exactly. I thought a boy who had stolen money would have candy wrappers and other trash, like at least one pizza box lying around. Your feet were cut badly enough that after you were in the motorcoach, I chose to knock you out so those little feet could heal. You had deep cuts on your feet. They were bad enough I was surprised they weren't infected. You slept for three days, which gave me time to address your other physical injuries.

"I knew a couple in Florida were trying to adopt a child. I only hoped you'd be happy. You talked in your pain-filled sleep. There was no way I could return you to the abusive life you had escaped. What you didn't know is that the police found a garage with plastic tubs full of child porn. They managed to identify nearly all the adults and all the children. I was able to fool the police into thinking you died by dumping a gallon of cow's blood into the ocean in a riptide. All I had to do was drop my glass container full of blood against the barnacle-covered pilings. It was a long shot, but it fooled the police. Your blood-covered clothing was found in the water as well. The police decided not to send a diver looking for your body. I drove to Florida, being certain not to drive too fast. I was asked to pull over at one border. It turned out one of the guards had been bitten by an illegal spider monkey pet. I treated the woman while you slept in my motorcoach.

"Wesley, I didn't see the torture you went through, but I saw your injuries: the cuts, abrasions, and burns to your flesh. I also removed nearly a dozen tics from your body. I was very happy for you after I met Austin and Helen. I knew you'd be safe and not abused in any way."

Laughing to himself, Wesley shared his thoughts, "You're right. Growing up in a nudist resort where they do complete background checks on all new members is safe for everyone, especially when only families are accepted. Austin and Helen interview everybody, including kids. They encouraged me to tell them if anyone ever tried to get overly friendly. Mom even had a sister who moved to the resort with her two kids after Uncle Fritz died in a car accident.

"We had our own school and a market at the resort. I got to work in the market when I was eleven years old. I did deliveries using my wagon. My friend, Eric, worked at the market, too. We didn't get paid money. Eric's mom and dad managed the store; they gave us orange juice or flavored water when we finished our work. I learned how to swim at the resort and nobody ever hurt me again.

"Austin and Helen really did–and still do–love me. It was a perfect place for me to live and grow up. Thank you for not letting me die under that pier."

"You're welcome, my friend. I'm sure your mom and dad are proud of you, but know this; I am extremely proud of the man you've become. Now, let's find the wives and go to dinner."

"May I ask you a personal question?"

"Wesley, I've not hidden anything from you. Whatever you're curious about, ask and I'll answer your questions."

"How do you know Judge Holt?"

Smiling, Dr. Colton replied, "He's on the list of names I want you to ask me about when I testify. He and Sandra adopted Evan when the boy was five." Dr. Colton then explained his relationship with the federal judge, and how it became a friendship.

Chapter 7

Jury selection had gone smoothly for over an hour, when Dr. Colton tapped his attorney's arm. "I need a break; I haven't eaten since last night," he whispered.

"Your Honor, could we possibly take a fifteen-minute recess?" Mr. Dill asked, interrupting Mr. Pizzo. "Dr. Colton's vision is blurring."

"Can't this wait for thirty minutes?" Prosecutor Pizzo interjected in agitation.

"No, it *cannot* wait!" an angry Dr. Boot exclaimed.

"Quiet!" Judge King ordered. "This courtroom will not become a yelling match. We won't be taking a recess at this time."

"Your Honor–" Dr. Colton began.

"No!" Judge King spat. "I'm not granting you a recess."

"I was simply going to say that the defense will accept the current jurors, and we move to impanel them at this time."

Judge King's computer screen showed a message from Judge Vang, the official observer: *"You are violating a federal court order by denying Dr. Colton access to Dr. Boot."* Looking up, Judge King saw Samuel Holt glaring at him.

"If I'm not mistaken, we have Federal Judge Samuel Holt in our courtroom today. Judge Holt, may I have a few minutes of your time?"

Sensing Judge King's discomfort, Mr. Dill asked, "What about the motion before you?"

Turning his attention back to the court, Judge King responded. "Mr. Prosecutor, do you accept the presently seated jurors?"

"No, sir, the people would thank and dismiss Juror Number Ten."

"Oh, good," Dr. Colton quipped. "I didn't like her."

"Due to matters which I must discuss with Judge Holt, we'll recess for twenty minutes."

When all potential jurors had exited, Judge Holt left through another door. Dr. Boot stepped up to the defense table and instantly recognized Dr. Colton's problem. "From now on, you'll keep something to eat within reach. Eat a big lunch. Richard. I don't want my daughter, Ruth, angry with me because you failed to eat."

"Just close your eyes and she can't yell at you," Dr. Colton teased. "Besides, your daughter is adorable when she's mad."

"You think she can't yell? If I don't watch her hands fly, then she'll make sure I feel them! If you need anything, send a message to the court observer's computer."

Judge King remained in the courtroom instead of following Judge Holt. He listened to Dr. Boot talk with Dr. Colton. To his surprise he found himself liking Dr. Boot. Judge King called the court to order twenty minutes later. Two additional potential jurors were dismissed before the jury was finally impaneled. Four alternate jurors were added. Although it was only noon, Judge King was ready to quit for the day.

"Before we recess, let me remind our jurors not to discuss this case with anyone. Be back in court by two o'clock to begin trial. I require two hours. Court dismissed."

"Are you ready? It's time to take this fight to them?" Mr. Dill asked eagerly as people filed out of the courtroom.

"Mr. Pizzo is going to get angry," Dr. Colton replied.

"I'll buy that for a dollar." Both men laughed and secured their files.

Chapter 8

Once he was back in his office, Prosecutor Pizzo dialed Judge King's office phone.

"Judge King... Talk to me."

"Anthony Pizzo, sir. I have information which supports the defendant is planning to rabbit."

"Can you prove it in court, Mr. Pizzo?"

"Yes, sir, most definitely. In his own words, he wants to disappear in France."

"Bring it to court, you can present it to the court and I'll be able to legally revoke his free pass. Mr. Colton is going to jail this afternoon."

"Can I bring a camera to take a picture of his face when he learns his fate?"

"Gloating is for immature children. We're professionals. However, you may buy the celebratory drinks this evening."

"My next reason for calling is about those ten oil wells in Texas which Dr. Colton owns. All the money from them goes into a fund called C.A.R. I think the initials stand for Child Abduction Resource." Mr. Pizzo took a deep breath.

"Bring that information with you. I'm sure there's a way to let our jury learn about this abduction money."

"I'll bring other things my office has learned about the defendant so I can share the information with you," Mr. Pizzo said.

A knock on the prosecutor's door interrupted his telephone call. "Sorry to bother you, sir, but we just intercepted a telephone call from Dr. Colton's home phone. He just told somebody named Frank to take his files to the airport tomorrow morning."

"Thank you; bring me the information." Mr. Pizzo waited for his office door to close. "Did you hear my paralegal? She said the defendant is planning to get rid of potentially damaging files."

"I'll have the police intercept those files and bring them to the courtroom tomorrow morning. We'll give Counselor Dill a nice little surprise to see how he handles it."

Chapter 9

"Mr. Dill, you have a phone call from Blake West."

"Put him through, please," Mr. Dill requested.

"Yes, sir," Mr. Dill's secretary replied.

"Blake, Wesley Dill here. Did you get a phone call?"

"Yes, sir, I surely did. Should I tell you about it or send it to you by email?"

"If you email a recording of it, Dr. Colton and I can listen to what was said and take notes."

"Okay. I'm attaching an audio file now. I need your email address so I can get it sent."

Counselor Dill told Mr. West his email address and waited.

"When are we supposed to arrive for court?" Mr. West inquired. "Lucy can't wait to get out of here for a while."

"Blake, take Lucy to France. My wife owns a cottage in Agde. I'm certain she'd let you use it," Dr. Colton said.

"Email just arrived," Mr. Dill interrupted. "Mr. West, there's a shuttle plane on its way to pick your family up for a jet plane ride to our location. You have a reservation at the Victoria Inn beginning tomorrow morning." Mr. Dill paused briefly, then said, "I hate to be rude, but we need to listen to your file. Thank you."

A knock on the door startled both men as Attorney Dill hung up his telephone.

"Come," was Mr. Dill's response.

"Mrs. Colton is here with food and drink," his secretary replied.

"Let her enter."

Mrs. Colton sat and listened to the audio recording with both men. "I can transcribe the recording while you go back to court," she offered.

"Let's listen to it again first," Dr. Colton suggested.

The recording began: *"Hello, Blake West speaking."*

"Hello, Mr. West. My name is Anthony Pizzo. I'm calling to ask if you'd be willing to talk with me regarding Doctor Richard Colton. I'm an attorney working with him."

"I know Dr. Colton; he's a good man. What or how can I help you?"

"I have information that Mr. Colton owns property on Catalina Island. I was wondering if you would be able to confirm said information."

"Oh, yes. Mr. Colton does own a nice home on the island. He and his wife also own a boat they have anchored in the bay. Mr. Colton usually arrives on the island in his plane."

"Are you saying Mr. Colton is still a pilot?"

"Oh, yes, sir. He and his wife stopped here and spent two days not long ago."

"Would you know if Mr. Colton owns any other property?"

"I believe Richie is still listed as the owner of oil wells in Texas. And nobody has ever been named to replace him."

"Thank you, Mr. West. You've been extremely helpful. Is there anything else you can think of which might be useful to us?"

"Well, I still have the money Mr. Colton gave me to hold for him. The man doesn't trust banks. Did you know he can also fly helicopters?"

"Actually, yes, I do know that. I'll tell Mr. Colton you still have his money. Uh, how much are you holding, if you don't mind me asking?"

"Five hundred thousand. He called it his getaway money."

"Anything else I should tell Mr. Colton when I see him?"

"Yes! Please tell Mr. Colton his R-66 is ready for pickup. Repairs were made after he had his hard landing. There's a twenty-four thousand dollar repair bill he needs to pay. And Kent sold the property in Virginia for four hundred thousand dollars."

"You have no idea how much our conversation means to me. I'll be glad to pass on your information when I see Mr. Colton."

"Good day to you sir," Blake West said just before hanging up.

The recording ended seconds later.

"Well, we know what Mr. Pizzo is planning," Dr. Colton said.

"Richard, you are the one who keeps saying Mr. Pizzo is an extraordinary individual. But me, I think he stinks and I look forward to putting him in his place."

Turning to his wife, Dr. Colton smiled. "Time we went back to court. I've a judge and a prosecutor to piss off."

"I'll be praying for you," Barbara Colton told the men.

"We need a copy of this tape as soon as possible," Dr. Colton told his wife.

"I can bring it to you in an hour," Mrs. Colton responded. "Richard has meds to take at that time."

"Mr. Prosecutor turned in our bogus witness list. I noticed he had only two or three people to call at first." Wesley Dill smiled as he spoke.

"Let's stick to our plan," Dr. Colton urged.

Once they were back in court, Judge King called everyone to order and introduced himself, Prosecutor Pizzo, Defense Attorney Dill, and Dr. Colton to the members of the jury.

"Dr. Colton is acting as co-counsel in his trial. In addition to the four of us whom I just introduced, we have a special court observer, the Honorable Judge Vang."

"As a special observer I'll occasionally ask a question of both prosecution and defense," Judge Vang explained.

Judge King waited to a count of five before speaking.

"Dr. Colton is on trial for one count of kidnapping and one count of premeditated murder," Judge King stated.

"Your Honor, isn't the kidnap charge one with special aggravation due to ransom requests?" Prosecutor Pizzo asked; in an attempt to prejudice the jurors.

"Objection! Your Honor," Attorney Dill interrupted loudly. "The charge of kidnap is an illegal charge and must be dropped."

"Objection," Prosecutor Pizzo was on his feet immediately. "The defendant kidnapped Marco Rizzoli for ransom, and when–"

"Objection!" Dr. Colton bellowed; entering the conversation. "Objection!"

"Order!" Judge King calmly projected. "Mr. Dill, exactly, how do you support your theory for the charge of kidnap as being illegal?"

"Regardless of any special conditions, there is this thing called the statute of limitations, and it is long past. The prosecutor's office knows this, yet they chose to file the illegal charge, hoping we would not catch them."

"Your Honor, the charge of kidnap is not illegal," Prosecutor Pizzo argued. "It's an intrinsic part of the murder of Marco Rizzoli."

"To make that stick, you would have to say it was kidnap with intent to murder," Mr. Dill argued. "And to do that, you have to admit there was no ransom note. No, sir, Mr. Prosecutor. Your count of kidnap is not only illegal, but it must be dismissed with prejudice. You're not allowed to file false charges and not have them dismissed."

"I've quickly checked what Mr. Dill has stated, and he is correct," Judge King said. "While there is no statute for murder, there most definitely is for kidnap unless it is attached with intent to murder. So, I find that the charge of kidnap is hereby dismissed with prejudice. The jury will not consider kidnapping during the course of this trial. Is there anything else, Mr. Dill?"

"My co-counsel had an objection, Your Honor."

"Dr. Colton, your objection was regarding…?"

"The defendant is unhappy that I didn't refer to him as Doctor," Prosecutor Pizzo spat angrily.

"Mr. Prosecutor, you're defying a federal court order. In *my* court that is pure contempt. You will pay a five hundred dollar fine or spend five days in jail. From this point on you'll show respect. It's either Doctor or Mister, do you understand?" It wasn't really a question, but a distinct order. Judge King was clearly angry.

"Yes, sir," Prosecutor Pizzo replied.

"Your Honor, I'd like to request a quick conversation in your chambers," Mr. Dill interjected.

"Mr. Dill, you and Mr. Pizzo come up to the sidebar," Judge King instructed. "Dr. Colton, do you mind? There isn't a lot of space for sidebar conversations."

"I'm certain Mr. Dill will share what is said. I have no objections at this time."

Turning to Mr. Dill, Judge King asked, "Why are we here?"

"With the kidnap count dismissed, all evidence pertaining to that charge must be suppressed."

"Your Honor, those ransom notes show motive. You have to allow them into evidence," the prosecutor insisted.

"Ransom notes are related to kidnapping, and are therefore inadmissible in this trial," Mr. Dill argued softly.

Turning to his computer, Judge King typed, "Please join us in my chambers. Tell Mr. Colton to follow."

"We're wanted in the judge's chambers," Judge Vang said to Dr. Colton.

"The prosecution, defense, and Observer Vang are going with me to my chambers along with the court clerk to discuss admissibility of evidence," Judge King advised the jurors.

Once inside his chambers, Judge King spoke directly to the prosecutor: "Your ransom notes are inadmissible."

"Your Honor, they show motive," Mr. Pizzo argued.

"You're correct," Mr. Dill replied. "They show motive for kidnapping, not for the murder with which Dr. Colton is charged."

"Ultimately, it's not my decision, but Mr. Dill's argument is spot on," Judge King stated. "All evidence pertaining to ransom notes and kidnapping are inadmissible. If you have anything else to address, bring it out in open court."

Upon entering the courtroom, Judge King addressed his court: "We'll now begin this trial. Mr. Pizzo, are you prepared to proceed?"

"Yes, sir, however, I've a few things to address first."

"Proceed," Judge King said, knowing full well where Mr. Pizzo was heading.

"Your Honor, I have it on good authority Mr. Colton plans to abscond or leave the country and disappear. I've learned that Mr. Colton also has cash in excess of half-a-million dollars to aid him once he disappears. He owns a yacht, a helicopter, and property in other states."

"Is that all you wish to address?" Mr. Dill politely inquired.

"My sources tell me Mr. Colton has a C-A-R fund that I'm *sure* the court will be interested in; if he cares to explain it." Mr. Pizzo hesitated briefly for the defense to object. When nothing was said, he continued, "There's evidence of Mr. Colton owning oil wells in Texas. And beside my table, I have a box of confiscated files Mr. Colton was attempting to send out of the state."

"If that's all, I'll gladly respond to Prosecutor Pizzo's allegations," Dr. Colton said calmly. "The files Mr. Pizzo has in his possession were obtained through an illegal wiretap."

"Objection!" Mr. Pizzo blurted.

"Objection to what?" Defense Attorney Dill inquired. "Objection to the fact that you ordered an illegal wiretap placed on Dr. Colton's home phone? Or that the FBI found it and learned your office ordered the wiretap? Or could you be objecting to misrepresenting the truth to Judge King?"

"I object to your accusation that my office ordered a wiretap, *period*. I learned this information from a third party."

"Total hearsay evidence," Mr. Dill countered; "Federal Officer, Chris Archer, will testify in this court on how she discovered your wiretap and traced it back to your office." Defense Attorney Dill was shocked at how much he was enjoying putting the prosecution on trial instead of Dr. Colton.

"Your Honor, may we take a short five-minute break? I need to take my medicine and get a shot from Dr. Boot."

"Can this be done here in the courtroom or do you have to leave?" Judge King inquired.

"Shot goes in the left arm, and my wife has my medicine. I'll take the medicine with food which the court granted permission to keep beside me."

"I'll grant you a five-minute pause. Please proceed."

Dr. Colton received medicine from his wife in front of the entire courtroom. Dr. Boot administered the shot, passing on a verbal message as well. "Royce is outside. He wants to know if you need him or others in the courtroom yet."

"No, there's only two hours left today. Tell Royce to bring everyone into court tomorrow morning."

"Hold still. This is going to hurt," Dr. Boot spoke loud enough for the jurors to hear. Then in a whisper, "Take this memory chip. It is from Barbara. She said a copy of the audio file from Blake is on it along with your Teddy's video…whatever the hell that means."

"Thanks, that hurts," Dr. Colton told Dr. Boot.

Before returning to his seat, Dr. Colton saw a paralegal, from Mr. Dill's office, enter the courtroom carrying a large square briefcase. She spoke briefly with a court deputy before opening the case she carried. The deputy walked to Mr. Dill and informed him of the paralegal's presence, then returned to his station. Mr. Dill received the case and went back to his seat.

"Your Honor, I'm finished, and I thank the court for its patience," Dr. Colton politely addressed Judge King.

"All right, you're welcome. We're back on record and defense counsel may continue–"

"Pardon me," Prosecutor Pizzo interrupted. "Before the defense addresses anything else, I would like to ask the court to accept as evidence this file box of Mr. Colton's handwritten journals. I wish to submit them as People's Evidence Two, Three and Four. There are numerous other papers inside I'm willing to submit as People's Evidence Five."

"Objection," Mr. Dill said. "Those files and journals were obtained–"

Interrupting the defense attorney, Judge King spoke. "They were obtained through a seizure order I signed. If information came to me by acts which were questionable, feel free to appeal their seizure. Objection overruled. The files are accepted into evidence."

"Allow me to be absolutely clear regarding your decision," Dr. Colton stated. "Every item in that file box is ordered into evidence on the people's behalf."

"That is correct," Judge King responded.

"And there's nothing I can say or do to convince you to rescind your order."

"No, Mr. Colton, there is not. My order stands. If you're dissatisfied, file an appeal."

"I have a question, if I may, Your Honor," Court Observer Vang said, addressing the bench. "What relevance do these files have in the case against Mr. Colton?"

"The defense was ordered to turn over all personal files. They failed to comply, trying to send these files away," Mr. Pizzo said.

"From what you held up, I would suggest that what you're calling files are nothing more than journals," Observer Vang responded.

"I'll read them tonight and have a copy of every page to pass out to our jurors tomorrow morning," Mr. Pizzo said.

"That's all I had to say," Observer Vang replied.

"Shouldn't Judge King review my journals before you're allowed access to them, or given permission to photocopy them for juror perusal?" Dr. Colton asked Mr. Pizzo.

"I'll accept a copy once it is made," Judge King rebutted. "Until then, I see no reason to read your papers."

"Sir, we've just over two hours left in our day," Mr. Pizzo urged. "Can we address Mr. Colton's plans to disappear?"

"No," Mr. Dill snapped. "You claim sources reveal these things but you have no proof. There's no court on earth that's stupid enough to act on he-said/she-said hearsay. It's the same as if I said we have information that places you at the scene of an armed robbery. Please get real with your wild accusations and add at least one percent proof."

Not giving the prosecutor a chance to talk, Dr. Colton spoke calmly saying, "Judge King, Your Honor, because you have ruled to include my journals in this trial, and due to your having stated you'll read them once our jurors have a copy, I pray you'll accept these copies of those journals. However, I don't believe your ruling is proper."

Distracted from his point of interest, Prosecutor Pizzo freaked out upon hearing Dr. Colton's words. "What do you mean, copy of the journals?"

"What I mean is that Mr. Dill insisted we make copies of the journals because we knew you illegally placed a wiretap on my phone. Counselor Dill is a smart man and he planned ahead, knowing I have cancer." Dr. Colton handed Observer Vang a copy of the journals. He took copies to Judge King, the clerk, and then faced Judge King. "With permission I'll give each juror a copy, sir."

"Hand them to the bailiff. He can give our jurors a copy," Judge King instructed. "At the end of each day you will leave your copies of Mr. Colton's journals on your chairs, where they'll be waiting upon your return."

As the bailiff handed out the copies, each juror opened their copy and began reading.

"Your Honor, Mr. Colton is clearly planning to avoid prosecution. I'm more convinced of this than ever, due to his easy compliance regarding his journals," Mr. Pizzo pressed.

"Your Honor, we're willing to address this issue of Dr. Colton playing rabbit if Mr. Pizzo is so disposed. However, we'll present further evidence in the morning. Would the court call Royce Colton into the courtroom?" Mr. Dill requested.

Royce Colton entered the room. "Come forward," Judge King ordered. "Take a seat in the witness stand."

Royce stepped forward and into the witness stand. After the court clerk administered the oath Judge King said, "Please be seated."

"State your full name and age for the record," Dr. Colton said.

"Royce Adam Colton, I'm twenty almost twenty-one, sir."

"Royce, I want to ask you some questions regarding your dad's finances and property," Mr. Dill said.

"My dad doesn't own any property, and if he didn't get a small amount of money still coming from his medical inventions, he and mom would be nearly broke, even with mom's retirement fund of three thousand dollars a month."

"Does Dr. Colton own a helicopter or a yacht?" Mr. Dill asked.

"No, he does not," Royce responded.

"Does he own any property, anywhere?"

"No, sir, he does not."

"I'm good, Your Honor," Mr. Dill said, returning to his seat.

"Your witness, Mr. Pizzo," Judge King stated.

"Royce, are you trying to tell this court that your father, Mr. Richard Daniel Colton, *does not* have a friend holding a rather large sum of money for him?" Mr. Pizzo inquired.

"Your words are twisting–"

"Objection, Your Honor, please instruct the witness to answer the question."

"If you would shut up–"

"Pyramid!" Dr. Colton blurted out, interrupting his adopted son mid-sentence.

"Objection," Mr. Pizzo grasped. "*Pyramid?* What is that supposed to mean?"

"I apologize to the court and to you, Mr. Prosecutor. I've a problem with… well, Dad said *Pyramid*; which is a trigger word to get my attention. My words were mean and disrespectful. I must ask for your forgiveness."

"Mr. Colton, please answer Mr. Pizzo's question," Judge King instructed.

Looking at the prosecutor, Royce replied, "Please ask your question again."

"Are you trying to tell this court that Richard Daniel Colton *does not* have somebody holding a large sum of money for him?"

"No, I'm not trying to do that," Royce sighed. "The only one holding money is Mr. West; you should ask him."

"I asked you," Mr. Pizzo shot back.

"Mr. Blake West is holding nine hundred thousand dollars of *my money*, not my dad's. My dad has no money and he refuses to take money from my brother or me."

Mr. Pizzo phrased his next question carefully, hoping it would appear as a statement. "But your father owns property, *doesn't he?*"

"No, he *does not.*" Royce turned to Judge King. "Sir, how many times do I have to answer the same question? I mean, my answers won't change. I promised to tell the truth and I will. I'm being respectful, as I was taught by Mom and Dad, but I don't feel the prosecutor is showing any kind of respect, except *dis*respect."

"Personally, I don't care how you feel, young man," Mr. Pizzo retorted. "All I want from you is the truth."

"I told you the truth," Royce responded. "You want respect; you give the opposite. You want the truth; you tell lies," Royce voiced venomously, "You, sir; are a two-faced hypocrite."

"Royce Adam Colton, you will not libel, slander, or disparage other people simply because you think it warranted," Dr. Colton interjected.

"Yes, sir, my apologies to you, and Mr. Dill, Dad."

"What about Judge King and our jurors?" Dr. Colton asked.

"I apologize to you all for my behavior."

"Thank you," Judge King responded.

"I have nothing further," Prosecutor Pizzo muttered.

"Because he is outside waiting, I'd like to call author Blake West in this unusual hearing," Mr. Dill said as Royce left. "We have no questions on redirect."

"Mr. West can wait until tomorrow morning," Judge King replied. "I find Royce Colton's testimony to be hostile and guarded. I believe he's protecting Mr. Colton, and therefore I'm going to order Mr. Colton be remanded into the sheriff's custody."

"Begging your pardon, Judge," a man in the back interrupted, "I'm Special Agent Xander Ward. My orders are to be Dr. Colton's constant shadow and he will not be leaving my line of sight for any reason."

Dr. Colton waited for a moment of silence. He pushed the button on his computer and turned up the volume. *Judge King, I'm glad you're early.* Everybody recognized Prosecutor Pizzo's voice.

"Your Honor, I have the entire conversation between yourself and the prosecutor. Mr. Pizzo clearly states he looked at files, files that he claims were left out but were in fact inside my briefcase and file box."

"Your Honor, the defend...ants–" *Shit*, Pizzo muttered to himself.

"Objection," Mr. Dill immediately reacted. "How many times does Mr. Pizzo need to be reminded to call my co-counsel either *Doctor* or *Mister*?"

"Sustained, Mr. Pizzo; you are in contempt of court. You're fined one thousand dollars or one week in jail."

"Yes, Your Honor," Mr. Pizzo replied in resignation. "Sir, Mr. Colton was clearly spying on the court. It is quite evident he's attempting to blackmail the court and the prosecutor's office."

Skipping ahead in the recording, Dr. Colton again pushed the button. *Sir, I found the defense witness list as well,* the recording continued.

"Shut it off, Dr. Colton. I've heard enough. We'll recess for the day at this time. Jurors are reminded to leave their journal copies behind. You will not discuss this case. What is said and heard here, stays here. We'll resume at nine o'clock tomorrow morning."

All twelve jurors and the four alternates left in silence.

"All right, people, let's get this out of our systems," Judge King ordered.

"Mr. Dill and I are defending me," Dr. Colton flatly stated.

"Are we on or off the record?" Mr. Pizzo asked.

"Defense will speak *on* the record," Mr. Dill said.

"I think we can do this off the record like civilized gentlemen," Judge King suggested, trying to calm tempers.

"I consider only Mr. Dill and myself to be gentlemen," Dr. Colton countered. "We resorted to blindsiding only after Mr. Pizzo blindsided us."

"I never blindsided you," Prosecutor Pizzo flippantly rebuked.

"Your Honor, maybe you should know all the circumstances. I've re-queued this file and patched it into the courtroom television," Dr. Colton said.

"We think you'll find this informative," Mr. Dill added.

Judge King watched the video, seeing his prosecutor breaking numerous laws. "Mr. Prosecutor, you will issue a formal apology to Mr. Dill, Dr. Colton, and to me for your behavior. When you return to the prosecutor's office you will tender your resignation."

"Objection–one moment," Dr. Colton jumped in. "No resignation, no written apologies, and no removing himself from the case. I'll accept a verbal apology, as I believe Counselor Dill will as well."

"I'm open to a verbal apology," Wesley Dill agreed.

"Mr. Pizzo has made allegations against me in open court in front of the jurors. Tomorrow, we'll address each of his allegations in front of those same jurors," Dr. Colton asserted.

"Mr. Colton, may I ask you a personal question?"

"On or off the record, Mr. Pizzo?"

"Off the record, sir."

"Your Honor?" Dr. Colton queried.

"We'll adjourn for the day and pick up again in the morning."

"Okay, what's your question?" Dr. Colton asked.

"Does it hurt? I mean, does having cancer hurt?"

"Yeah, it does, but most days are tolerable. But I don't believe that was your true question."

"It wasn't. My question is this: Do you remember a boy about twelve years old named Kenny?"

"Do you have any more to go on?" Judge King inquired.

"It's not necessary," Dr. Colton responded. "Kenny was shot with a .243 caliber rifle. Kenny's father told me his son's blood type. Luckily, my wife Barbara was a match and she gave the boy blood. I had to perform surgery on Kenny on our way to Anchorage. We found one other person who had the same blood type. Kenny died twice that day. Of course you know he ultimately survived because you came to Anchorage via helicopter. The engineer stopped the train so I could stop Kenny's internal bleeding. I didn't close his wound. That was done after surgery in the operating room at Anchorage."

"I grew up in Alaska, and Kenny was the closest to being my best friend. I was afraid he was going to die."

"I'm going to go out on a limb and say you undoubtedly knew that when Kenny was in the hospital he told his father he was gay and he loved you," Dr. Colton said.

"That boy was more than just your best friend, wasn't he?" Observer Vang asked from behind them.

"What people don't know," Mr. Pizzo offered, "is that I leaned my rifle against a tree. I told Kenny I loved him. I was so afraid he would hate me if he knew I had a boyhood crush on him. When we hugged, I stumbled and we fell. Kenny knocked the rifle over and it went off."

"Kenny told the state trooper it was an accident. He pleaded with them not to arrest you. Even Kenny's father said you deserved no punishment. Me...well, I wasn't so forgiving." Dr. Colton smiled before continuing. "I thought you should be flogged, but nobody agreed with me."

"I remember afterwards, when my dad told me Kenny was alive, he led me into a room where they took my clothes. A male nurse checked me for injuries. The state troopers kept my clothes, so my dad bought me brand-new clothes."

Dr. Colton nodded. "My wife and I left once Kenny stabilized."

"Gentlemen, you've had an opportunity to talk, but tomorrow I expect Mr. Pizzo to do his job. Mr. Colton, don't think for a minute you've gained any favor with me or this court," Judge King advised.

"No, sir, you want a conviction. I don't believe you want the truth, only another conviction for your reelection campaign."

"I'm seeking a conviction," Mr. Pizzo told the judge. "I can't condone the kidnap, or, more disgustingly, the murder of a child."

"Let's go home," Observer Vang prompted. "I'm tired."

Chapter 10

"So what's really in those so-called journals? And why are they so dang-blasted important?" Mr. Dill inquired as he and Dr. Colton entered Mr. Dill's office.

"They really *are* my journals. I wrote about my daily interactions with patients, including Marco Rizzoli and his very distraught mother. There's an original audio chip in the box Mr. Pizzo has, and a typed copy in each file I gave our jurors."

"Audio files about what?"

"Marco, claiming his father hurt him in very descriptive ways. Marco talked about his mother spanking him all the time, and how his daddy broke his arm. The description is all in Marco's voice. The journals also contain test results proving there is cancer killing me. Not to mention my yearly psychiatric evaluations, and copies of Nancy's statement of Mario Rizzoli driving the car that hit her and Richard Jr. in the crosswalk. In my psych evaluations there are a series of questions, usually about twenty. The questions were a part of the polygraphs I was required to undergo. Plus there are the reports from the three polygraph tests given to me by the FBI polygraphers."

"All of that was disallowed by Judge King," Wesley Dill protested. "What were you thinking?"

"Correct me if I'm wrong. Seven out of ten of our motions presented for immediate decision were denied."

"True, we were dumped on by Judge King."

"And every single motion Anthony Pizzo requested was granted, even when they were or are illegal. Everything the prosecution asked for he received."

"Okay. Again you're correct. What's your point?"

"When I was found in contempt of court I was instructed to pay the fine at our next break. Mr. Pizzo has yet to pay his fines. So, if we want the jury to see positive evidence, it has to come from the prosecution. If Judge King complains or tries to blame us, all we have to do is remind him that we objected and he overruled us."

"Dr. Colton, you're one sneaky, conniving, manipulative genius. And once again, I'm glad you're my friend."

"Thank you, Wesley; I accept your compliment. In the journals are statements which prove I treated the boy and then left."

"Come on, cough up more," Mr. Dill coaxed.

"You heard Mr. Pizzo tell Judge King there were blood drops near the body's ashes. Well, that blood belongs to Mario Rizzoli. There's a DNA report in my journals stating this fact. And there are papers detailing that my medical invention monies have been deeded over to a well-known children's hospital. Other documents prove I have no property or money. Things Mr. Pizzo and our extremely unbiased judge will be upset over."

"It appears as though your journals were a home-run hit out of the ballpark. I saw nearly all of the jurors reading them."

"You know I applied for a concealed weapon permit in at least five different states."

"What's your point?"

"Three of those five states make you do a state polygraph, and all five of them require mental and physical health examinations. The examinations are given to a review board before you go for a face-to-face interview."

"I'm beginning to feel sorry for Mr. Pizzo."

"Wesley, I need to find a way to get Mario Rizzoli ordered back here from prison."

"I know why you want him here, but I think it would be harder for him if he stays where he is, separated from the society he considered beneath him."

"What do you mean harder for him?" Dr. Colton asked.

"If Mario Rizzoli was here he'd have first-hand information as it happens. In prison, all he gets is hearsay or whatever they say on television in the news; ergo, harder for him," Mr. Dill was smiling.

"Makes sense, plus some of his people might try to break their boss out of jail if he were here." Dr. Colton's next remarks seemed a bit distant to Wesley Dill. "It's better this way Nancy. That scum will learn you named him as the killer of you and our son. I'll see him dead or tried for double murder."

"Eh...Doc, are you okay?" Mr. Dill asked, nudging Dr. Colton.

"Yeah...sorry, just thinking of Nancy and Richard Jr."

"I heard," Wesley replied. "Doc, you need to get some rest for tomorrow. Mr. Pizzo will be finished with his witnesses before lunch, then it's our turn."

"Do you think our judge and prosecutor will have much to say when they read the newspaper articles in my journals about their various case reversals due to their...shall we say...misbehaviors?" Dr. Colton snickered. "So, what's the bet my journals will not be returned to our jurors?"

"I confess it intrigues me to think what Judge King will say to cover removing the journals from your trial."

Laughing, Dr. Colton got to his feet. "Barbara is holding dinner for me and my shadow."

During the fifteen-minute drive to Dr. Colton's rented house, Special Agent Xander Ward began reminiscing: "You know, I hated you when I woke up one day and found myself alone, with my two best friends gone. I lived in constant terror over having to face the Dragon Society again. I cried myself to sleep every night, wishing I was dead. I tried to believe you were good, but only one person came to see me twice a day with food. During the day I played a video game where I killed monsters. I saw you as each and every one of those monsters. The person who came to see me–"

"Wore a ski mask and sunglasses," Dr. Colton half-whispered, interrupting Agent Ward.

"How'd you know that?"

Dr. Colton didn't answer; his eyes were fixed straight ahead. His breathing was slow and shallow. "Hang in there, sir–I'll have you home in three minutes." Xander Ward leaned forward, switched on his flashing lights and turned on the vehicle's siren. He used his radio to call ahead for Dr. Boot to meet them at Dr. Colton's house.

"We were talking on our way home when the doctor went silent. His eyes were blank, as though he was looking but seeing nothing."

"Pressure on his brain," Dr. Boot replied. "Barbara, fill your spa tub with cold water; let's see if that will help him again. I'll increase his medicine. From now on, Richard must rest every three days."

"Dr. Colton has court every day," Xander said. "We'd best tell Judge Holt so he can break the news to Judge King and Prosecutor Pizzo. They won't like it."

"Take Richard to St. Mary's Hospital," Barbara Colton directed. "Dr. Boot and neurologist Peyton Payne can do as Richard has already said he wanted done."

"We can try the cold water first," Dr. Boot insisted.

Dr. Colton blinked his eyes five minutes after being placed in the tub of cold water. "How long was I out?"

"Between fifteen and twenty minutes," Barbara responded. "Royce arrived about ten minutes ago. His wife and baby girl are also here," she said.

"Kent?" Dr. Colton asked.

"He'll be here around midnight. If you go to bed after eating, I promise to wake you up to see him."

"I want to see my granddaughter and her mother tonight. I'll see Kent in the morning. I'm hungry. What's for dinner?"

"I made lasagna, cold beets with onions, Italian dressing, peas and toasted garlic bread."

"Do we have any beer? Or do I have to be refined and drink wine?"

"You can be refined if you want. Me, I'm drinking beer," Barbara replied.

"Mom, is Dad talking?" It was Royce.

"Yes, Dad is talking. Ask Dr. Boot if your dad can have a beer. He'll be out in a few minutes."

Dr. Colton held his granddaughter and wept. He looked at Royce, "Thank you, son. I'm very proud of you and your brother. Nancy Marie is a beautiful, beautiful baby."

"Well, we promised to name our first daughter Nancy Marie after Richard Jr.'s mother. You gave Kent and me good lives. I wish we could do more."

Chapter 11

"All rise–"

"Be seated and come to order," announced Judge King. "I see we have quite a number of visitors this morning. Could it be that you've angered such a large number of people, Dr. Colton?"

"Would it be possible to ask our visitors their names?" Mr. Dill asked, with full knowledge of who they were. "And do they expect to be here for the entire trial?"

"My only objection to these people being here is if they plan to testify," Mr. Pizzo commented.

"Because there are so many of you, I'm interested in who you are and why you're here." Judge King spoke with concern.

Two young men stood up immediately. "I'm Kent Colton; this is my brother, Royce. If we're called to testify, we will." Others in the gallery followed suit.

"Xander Ward; I don't expect to testify and you already know my interest."

"Wesha Canyon; my parents sent me."

"Evan Holt; I received a letter advising me to appear."

A woman stood and was accompanied by a young man in military camouflage fatigues. Her hands began moving. "The woman's name is Ruth," the man said. "Father wanted me to come."

"And who are you?" Judge King asked.

"Ethan Rau; I'm here because I want to be here."

"Your Honor," Dr. Colton spoke up. "I expect to call some, if not all, of our visitors during the course of this trial. After my original witness list disappeared from my briefcase, I named these people as my current witnesses."

"If you received a subpoena, you'll have to wait outside until you're called to testify, excluding Mr. Ward," Judge King ordered.

Prosecutor Pizzo let Dr. Colton's comment regarding his witness list go un-rebuffed.

As Dr. Colton's adopted sons were exiting, Kent turned. "Take your medicine, Dad," the young man said. "And eat some food. You look like hell, sir."

"Young man," Judge King shot out in a loud voice, "there will be no profanity in my courtroom."

Looking at the judge, Kent replied, "I didn't curse. *Hell* is in the dictionary and in the Bible, if you care to read it, Your Honor. But because it offends you, I won't say it again, sir."

"Thank you," Judge King responded calmly. When he glanced towards the jurors, he saw them reading their copies of Dr. Colton's journals. Lips were moving and heads nodding.

"I think our jurors are more interested in your journals than either the judge or Mr. Pizzo. I haven't seen either of them even look at your journals," Mr. Dill softly told Dr. Colton.

"Well, don't expect me to say anything."

"Okay, people, it's time for us to begin this trial," Judge King remarked, bringing focus back to why they were in court. "Yes, Observer Vang, you have a question?"

"Am I allowed to make an observation?"

"As I understand your purpose, it's to ask questions, not to make observations or comments," Prosecutor Pizzo interjected. "If it were up to me, you wouldn't be here at all."

"I'm of the same understanding," Judge King stated. "However, Mr. Pizzo is out of line with his last statement."

"I've no questions, thank you," Observer Vang replied. "*Nicely done! I tried to warn them,*" he typed into his computer and sent it to Mr. Dill.

"Mr. Prosecutor, you may call your first witness."

"Your Honor," Dr. Colton interrupted, "yesterday Mr. Pizzo accused me of intent to abscond. May we revisit his false accusations at this time?"

"I thought we handled that yesterday after I dismissed our jury for the day," Judge King responded in disgust.

"Judge King," Mr. Dill interjected, "Mr. Pizzo claimed Dr. Colton plans to disappear. He stated Dr. Colton is clearly planning to avoid prosecution because he complied with your court orders regarding his journals."

"Your Honor," Dr. Colton added, "Mr. Pizzo's allegations must be addressed. He mustn't be allowed to slander me. I believe the jury has the right to know how he comes to his conclusions."

"I'll say this one last time," Judge King said, his anger barely under control. "This was taken care of yesterday. We will not address this issue again. Mr. Pizzo, call your first witness."

"Defense requests a running objection," Mr. Dill said.

"Denied! Mr. Pizzo, call your first witness!"

"Prosecution will call Mr. Blake West to the stand."

"Objection, Your Honor. Mr. West is a witness for the defense," Mr. Dill protested.

"Your Honor, my office subpoenaed Mr. West two weeks ago. You signed the subpoena yourself," Mr. Pizzo retorted.

"That explains where my witness list went," Dr. Colton muttered.

"Overruled," Judge King said as he banged his gavel.

Reaching over, Dr. Colton touched his attorney's arm. "Let Blake come in. This'll be fun."

Blake West raised his right hand. "Yes, sir, I promise to tell the truth, even though that Mr. Pizzo feller tells folks lies."

"Mr. West, you will refrain from calling Mr. Pizzo a liar," Judge King admonished.

"My apologies. I thought I just promised to tell the truth."

"Mr. West, you'll answer questions and not give your opinion of people."

"Excuse me, Mr. Judge, sir. But if this here man," Blake West pointed a finger at Mr. Pizzo, "asks me if Dr. Colton is capable of hurtin' a person, then he is asking my opinion."

"Don't worry, I won't ask you that question," Mr. Pizzo countered. "Do you remember talking to someone from my office?"

"I remember talking–"

"It's a yes-or-no question Mr. West; just answer the question."

"Yep, sure do," Blake West replied.

"Does Mr. Colton own property on Catalina Island?"

"Yep, he sure does."

"Does Mr. Colton own a helicopter or a boat at Catalina?"

"Yep and nope."

"Which is it, Mr. West, yes or no?"

"It's both. You asked two questions. I answered them in the order you asked."

"Do you remember saying over the telephone that Mr. Colton owned a yacht?"

"Yep."

"Mr. West, how much money are you holding for Mr. Richard Colton?"

"Not one red cent."

"Did you not say that you are holding five hundred thousand dollars for Mr. Colton?"

"Yep."

"So what you've said is that if Mr. Colton told this court he had no property, yacht, money, or a helicopter, he would be lying?" Mr. Pizzo was pleased.

"I'm not allowed to give an opinion."

"Never mind, I have nothing further," Anthony Pizzo said.

"Your witness, Mr. Dill."

"Mr. West, you testified that Dr. Colton owns all these things and he has five hundred thousand dollars. Is that correct?"

"No, sir," Mr. West replied, now speaking in a far more formal manner.

"Explain please, sir."

"I said *Mister* Colton owns all those things, not *Doctor* Colton. And Mr. Colton doesn't own the yacht. Even though he has unlimited use of it, I believe his father-in-law actually holds the title."

"Forgive me, I'm a bit confused. If Dr. Colton isn't Mr. Colton, then who is?"

"I've always referred to the Colton boys, Royce and Kent, as Mr. Colton. I call their father 'Doc' or 'Doctor Colton'. He's more than earned the title. I address the boys individually by their first names."

"So Dr. Colton doesn't own any of those items?"

"No, sir, as I've explained, they're owned by his sons."

"Mr. West, with whom did you speak to on the telephone?"

"Anthony Pizzo; he asked if I'd talk with him about Dr. Richard Colton. He said, and I quote, 'I'm an attorney working with him.'"

"In that conversation, did you talk about Dr. Colton?"

"No, sir, I *did not*. Mr. Pizzo asked me questions about Mr. Colton. He never once asked about Dr. Colton. But I answered his questions anyway."

"Would your answers be the same if Mr. Pizzo asked you specifically about *Doctor Colton*?"

"No, sir," Mr. West replied. "Doc doesn't like Catalina Island. Furthermore, when he was diagnosed with cancer, he was medically grounded."

"Whose money are you holding? I mean, for which Mr. Colton?"

"Royce, sir."

"Thank you, Mr. West." Mr. Dill sat down in his chair. "Nothing further."

"One more thing," Dr. Colton interrupted. "Mr. West, I note you spoke with something of an accent while speaking with Prosecutor Pizzo here in court today. Is that your normal manner of speech?"

"No, sir. When people treat me like I'm ignorant and act like an idiot, I'll talk to them like an idiot."

"Nothing further," Dr. Colton said.

"Mr. Prosecutor," Judge King said, raising one eyebrow as he spoke. "More questions?"

After an uncomfortably long moment of silence, the prosecutor said, "Yes, sir. Do you remember saying, 'Richie owns oil wells in Texas and no one has replaced him'?"

"Yes, I remember saying it."

"So Dr. Richard Colton still owns those wells in Texas?"

"Dr. Colton never owned oil wells. I said Richie owns them."

"Richard...Richie...what's the difference?"

"Richie died when he was just a little boy. Maybe I should've said Richard, Jr."

"Wouldn't ownership go to Dr. Colton?"

"No, and don't ask who. I cannot tell you."

"Your Honor, please instruct Mr. West to answer my question."

"Objection, Your Honor," Dr. Colton said, getting to his feet. "Obviously, Mr. West knows but is not at liberty to disclose that information."

"Then who can authorize Mr. West to disclose the information?" Judge King inquired.

"Excuse me, Judge King."

"Yes, Mr. Ward. Do you have something useful to say?"

"If you want information about the Colton oil wells in Texas, you might ask Senator Lucas Connor. But I warn you, he isn't going to tell you anything."

"You call that useful, Mr. Ward?"

"No, Your Honor, I call it information."

"I've no more questions, Your Honor," Mr. Pizzo said.

"Just a few more," Dr. Colton interjected.

"Go ahead," Judge King consented.

"Mr. West, have you ever known me to lie, cheat, steal, or harm another person?"

"Objection, calls for an opinion," Mr. Pizzo challenged.

"Dr. Colton asked for my knowledge of him, not my opinion," Blake West corrected. "My answer is, *no*, to each of the things he asked."

"Objection!"

"I'll let the answer stand. Mr. West didn't give his opinion."

Dr. Colton now asked the question he had been patiently waiting to ask. "Mr. West, you were called by Mr. Pizzo to testify. Does that mean you received a subpoena from his office?"

"Yes, sir, I did. I brought it with me. You want to see it? I have Mr. Pizzo's subpoena in my briefcase next to the one I received from Wesley Dill's office over one month ago after agree–"

"Objection. Argumentative," Mr. Pizzo blurted out.

"I'm not arguing anything, Your Honor. I simply wish to know how the prosecution came to subpoena my witness, Mr. Blake West, who received my summons nearly two weeks prior to Mr. Pizzo's."

"Sustained," Judge King responded. "Your question is not pertinent to this trial."

"Mr. Judge, sir," Blake West interrupted, "can I file fraud charges against Mr. Anthony Pizzo for misrepresenting the truth?"

"I can't advise you on any legal matters."

"Defense has no further questions," Dr. Colton said.

"You may step down, Mr. West. Do not discuss your testimony or this trial with anyone, including Dr. Colton."

Blake West exited the courtroom, a smile on his face.

Chapter 12

"Mr. Pizzo, do you have any more witnesses?"

"Prosecution calls Mr. Joseph Hill."

Mr. Hill entered the court and was sworn in. "Mr. Hill, take the stand and state your name and occupation for the record."

"Joseph Hill, investigator for the prosecutor's office."

"Do you know Sheriff Frank Kelly?"

"Sure, I know the man. He's one of over one hundred people arrested for child crimes."

"What kind of crimes, Mr. Hill?"

Joseph Hill took a deep breath, sighing as he exhaled. "Porn, abuse, kidnap, murder...and that is just the beginning."

"How do you know–scratch that," Mr. Pizzo paused. "Was Mr. Kelly a good sheriff?"

"Objection," Mr. Dill protested. "Calls for an opinion, and opinions are not allowed."

"I'll rephrase the question. Do you know him to be a good sheriff?"

"Yes, Sheriff Kelly–"

"Objection; It's a yes or no question, no commentary," Mr. Dill said.

"I'll allow the witness to finish his answer."

"Kelly was a good sheriff. Our juvenile crimes receded while he was sheriff."

"Did Sheriff Kelly come into contact with Dr. Colton?"

"Objection; conjecture and irrelevant, Your Honor," Mr. Dill interjected.

"Sustained."

"Dr. Colton was interviewed–"

"Mr. Hill, I said sustained, that means you do not continue," Judge King cautioned.

"Your Honor, I'll ask a different question. Mr. Hill, during your investigation of Dr. Colton, did you come across Sheriff Kelly's name?"

"Yes, sir."

"What did you find?" Mr. Pizzo asked.

"Sheriff Kelly interviewed Dr. Colton regarding the kidnapping of–"

"Objection, Your Honor. Mr. Pizzo was warned of this by the court and yet he persists," Mr. Dill protested.

"Objection sustained. I'll see all the attorneys and the witness in my chambers immediately."

Once inside Judge King's chambers, he turned to face the four men, "Mr. Pizzo, if I hear one more thing about the kidnap or ransom of Marco Rizzoli from any of your witnesses, Mr. Dill won't have to object. You will be placed in handcuffs and escorted to a six-foot-by-twelve-foot jail cell. Do I make myself clear?"

"Yes, sir," Anthony Pizzo replied. "Your Honor, Sheriff Kelly and a detective questioned Mr. Colton regarding the missing child, Marco Rizzoli."

"Then I suggest you restrict your questions to *missing* and not *kidnapping*," Judge King instructed.

"Judge King, I suspect the files lifted from my briefcase led Mr. Hill to investigate Sheriff Kelly and myself. Should this witness continue, I'll be forced to disclose Mr. Hill's involvement in covering up Mr. Pizzo's prosecutorial misconduct in Mario Rizzoli's trial," Dr. Colton said, staring straight at Judge King.

"That, Dr. Colton is open blackmail," Judge King stated.

"No, sir, it is not. It's an open statement of what I'll do. And should I make that information public knowledge, Mario Rizzoli will have grounds for a mistrial."

"Mr. Pizzo has never had evidence to support his case," Mr. Dill said. "Even his present behavior is questionable. If Mr. Hill goes back on the stand, I'll question him as to where he obtained the forms and information regarding certain Rizzoli Enterprises scams."

"I'm under federal court order not to discuss that information with anyone," Mr. Hill informed those present.

"Not that I know anything," Dr. Colton countered, "but Mr. Xander Ward and Judge Holt just heard you put Mr. Kelly and myself together. I don't think the feds will be very happy with what they heard in open court."

"Mr. Pizzo, this witness is finished," Judge King snapped.

"Yes, sir, Your Honor."

Upon returning to the courtroom, Judge King announced, "We're back in front of the jury, Mr. Hill is on the witness stand and we'll continue on the record."

"I've no further questions, Your Honor," Mr. Pizzo muttered.

"I've one question," Mr. Dill said. "Mr. Hill, correct me if I'm wrong. All the information you might have to tell us is nothing but hearsay. Is that correct?"

"Yes, sir, that's correct."

"That's it for now. I've nothing else."

"You may step down, Mr. Hill," Judge King instructed. "Mr. Pizzo, call your next witness."

"The prosecution's next witness is Louis Romily; however, I don't believe he's here yet."

"That's odd," Dr. Colton remarked. "Louis Romily was the third name on my missing witness list. Your Honor, Mr. Romily lives in Agde, France. He'll not honor a summons from this court. Mr. Pizzo can go to his next witness. Louis isn't able to travel at this time."

"My next witness may not be outside yet," Mr. Pizzo stalled. "May I go check to see if he has arrived?"

"Go," Judge King waved his hand in a *go away* motion.

Mr. Pizzo quickly left the courtroom. He was relieved to see his witness sitting on a bench next to his childhood friend, Kenny Block, and his father. "Kenny! Oh my God! I never thought I'd see you here. Are you testifying for Mr. Colton?"

"Only if he calls me," Kenny replied. "He saved our lives, Anthony. Dr. Colton kept me from dying when I was shot. He saved your life too. You thought the accident was your fault. It was my fault as well. You've been my friend for a long time. We grew up together, and when you went to college I felt so lost."

"I grew up, Kenny. I went to college, found girls and learned that I like girls more than boys. I'm not gay."

"Who're you trying to convince?" Kenny asked. "Frankly, I don't care one way or the other. My wife knows all about our friendship."

"Excuse me, Mr. Pizzo, Judge King sent me to find you," the court bailiff interrupted.

"Yes, he just arrived," Mr. Pizzo lied. "Mr. Tooth, you're next. Whatever I ask you, *do not* bring up the Rizzoli kidnapping or ransom."

Mr. Toth nodded and followed Mr. Pizzo.

"My witness is here, Your Honor."

"Step forward and be sworn in, sir," Judge King said.

"State your name for the record," Mr. Pizzo instructed.

"I'm FBI Agent Francis Toth, that's F-R-A-N-C-I-S T-O-T-H."

"Mr. Tooth,"

"It's Toth, T-O-T-H," the witness corrected. "Not Tooth."

"My bad, I apologize for the mistake. Mr. Toth, do you know Dr. Richard Colton?"

"Yes, I do."

"Objection," Dr. Colton said, standing. "Mr. Toth does not know me. The man only knows who I am."

"Sustained. Mr. Pizzo will rephrase his question."

"Do you know who Dr. Colton is?" Mr. Pizzo asked.

"Yes, I do."

"Do you see Dr. Colton in this courtroom?"

"Yes, he is wearing a dark blue suit and sitting directly across from the jury box."

"Let the record show that Mr. Toth identified Dr. Colton," Judge King instructed. "You may continue."

"Did you question–never mind, scratch that. How do you know of Mr. Colton?"

"I was the lead investigator in the disappearance of Marco Rizzoli. I spoke with Dr. Colton over the phone regarding the boy's injuries, treatment, and disappearance."

"And what did Mr. Colton tell you?"

"He declined to discuss Marco Rizzoli at first. When I obtained a court order, Dr. Colton cited HIPAA law preventing him from discussing the situation. I threatened him with jail, to which he replied, 'You gotta do what you gotta do.' He did, however, tell us whatever he could without violating HIPAA laws."

"Did you think to get a court order for Marco Rizzoli's medical records?"

"Yes, we got them. But just like some court documents and most government documents, the medical file we received was heavily redacted."

"Did you suspect Mr. Colton in the Rizzoli boy's disappearance?"

"Dr. Colton was never suspected in Marco Rizzoli's vanishing act. Our primary suspect was Mr. Rizzoli, especially after Mrs. Rizzoli and her bodyguards were found dead."

"Why didn't you suspect Mr. Colton? He was one of the last people to see the boy."

"Dr. Colton left the hospital thirty minutes before the ambulance. His vehicle was seen five miles away. The ambulance transporting Rizzoli was found abandoned in a Rizzoli Enterprise parking garage. The ambulance driver was found dead days later. The FBI is convinced Mario Rizzoli abused his son. We have video recordings from around the time Marco disappeared. Four Rizzoli lackeys were seen roughly escorting Dr. Colton into Mario Rizzoli's office."

"Did you question the doctor regarding his meeting with Mr. Rizzoli?"

"Dr. Colton shared what the meeting was about and I informed him we suspected Mr. Rizzoli of killing his own son."

"When Marco's ashes were discovered, Mr. Colton became a suspect, did he not?"

"Yes, he did."

"Why?"

"He had a motive."

"Can you explain his motive?"

"Dr. Colton's motive was simple. He claimed his wife and young son were killed by Mario Rizzoli in a hit-and-run. He swore that before his wife died, she identified the driver as Mario Rizzoli."

"Did you return and question Mr. Colton once again?"

"No, we kept him under surveillance, but nothing came of it."

"So, Mr. Colton had a motive, a twisted reason, for exacting his own sense of revenge."

"Objection; again speculation, putting words in the witness's mouth and testifying himself," Mr. Dill protested.

"Overruled. I'll allow it."

Touching his attorney's arm, Dr. Colton whispered, "Let it go."

"Yes, he did," Mr. Toth professed.

"Nothing further, Your Honor."

"Defense," Judge King called.

"Thank you, Your Honor," Dr. Colton responded. "Mr. Toth, the one and only time we spoke, didn't I reveal my claim regarding my wife and young Richard's deaths?"

"Yes, you did."

"And at that time I was not a suspect in Marco Rizzoli's disappearance?"

"No you weren't."

"Who decided I should become a suspect, and when did this decision come about?"

"I did, after I interviewed Dr. Yvonne Hoch."

"Did you happen to receive and read Dr. Hoch's evaluation? It was a simple one-page report."

"I didn't read Dr. Hoch's report."

"Did you receive her report?"

"Yes, sir, I did."

"And yet you failed to read it?"

"Yes, sir, I followed my gut feeling."

"If I showed you a copy of that report, would you recognize it?"

"Not really. I never opened the envelope."

"I notice you have a copy of my journals in front of you. Did Mr. Pizzo give those to you?"

"Yes, I do, and yes, Mr. Pizzo sent me a copy via overnight mail."

"Those journals were submitted as prosecution evidence and accepted by the court, so let me direct you to page 126. It is titled *Psychological Evaluation of Dr. Richard–*"

"Objection!" shouted Mr. Pizzo. "Your Honor, defense's motion to present this document was denied."

"Your Honor. Mr. Pizzo is correct; we were denied submitting this document into evidence. But, if attention is paid to what Dr. Colton said, it will be clear, this isn't defense evidence. It's prosecution evidence which we argued over before you allowed Mr. Pizzo to enter it into his evidence against Dr. Colton."

"Your Honor, the defense didn't disclose the contents of Mr. Colton's journals when they dispersed their journal copies."

"It's not our responsibility to disclose Dr. Colton's journal contents. We argued they were inadmissible. You, Mr. Pizzo, insisted Judge King allow them into evidence. Dr. Colton and I merely accepted Judge King's decision. Now you complain, or object, over documents you submitted into evidence."

"I think this is a good time to take our morning break. We'll take a twenty-minute recess. The witness may step down. He is admonished to refrain from discussing this case or his testimony with anyone. Dismissed!"

Chapter 13

Prosecutor Anthony Pizzo exited the courtroom angry. He found himself wishing his father had come from Alaska with Kenny and Fred Block. It was Fred Block who intruded on his thoughts. "I have a letter from your dad," Mr. Block said, handing a letter to Anthony. "Jonathan told me to let you know he has a job for you in Alaska if you ever decide to leave this life."

"I'm not leaving, Pop-Pop," Mr. Pizzo said with a tone of affection and familiarity. To him Fred Block was like a second father. "I enjoy being the person who takes trash out of society and puts it in the dump. Look at Mario Rizzoli and all his ill-gotten gains. The only thing he came out on top of was the garbage heap of human waste."

"Maybe you can visit your dad when this is over. Your mother is doing really well. Please call home, Anthony."

"Yes, sir, Pop-Pop. I'll call today. Maybe I can get a week or two away to visit when this trial is over."

"Anthony, I want you to know Kenny calls his oldest boy 'TAB'. It's short for Tony Andrew Block. He named his son after his best friend."

Looking around, the prosecutor saw his childhood friend talking to Dr. Colton. "Well, I can't talk to Kenny now. He's probably a witness for the defense."

"You sure ain't very smart for being a top-notch attorney," Mr. Block said sarcastically. "Kenny came to see his friend. I'm the defense witness, but don't expect Doc Colton to protest. He knows I won't talk about anything important. Come with me." Fred Block didn't wait for a reply. He took a firm grasp on Mr. Pizzo's arm and walked to his son and Dr. Colton.

"You come with me," Mr. Block told Dr. Colton. "You talk to Mr. District Attorney," he said to Kenny.

"Fred, we can't talk. You're a defense witness," Dr. Colton warned.

"I just moved you so those two could talk," Mr. Block said. "Kenny has to leave tomorrow afternoon. His return trip home requires two airline changes with an eight hour layover in California."

"When does Kenny have to be back at work?"

"Monday morning."

"I'll make arrangements to have Kenny flown home nonstop, Sunday. He can spend Friday and Saturday here with his friend. But you and Kenny have to promise that you won't tell anybody I had anything to do in helping Kenny stay an extra day."

"I'll try to remember to not mention this when I testify," Fred Block said, winking at Dr. Colton.

"Fred, you can't testify. Mr. Pizzo will tell the court we spoke out here and that I coached you on what to say."

"That's preposterous," Fred Block objected.

"Fred, I'm sorry. There's more at stake here than I can tell you, but I will say it's Federal. The feds are monitoring this trial. My babysitter, Xander Ward, is more than merely an FBI agent. He's an intelligent man who became a federal agent."

"You aren't an evil man, Doc," Fred Block said.

"Thank you, Fred. I've always tried to help people. But sometimes my methods are rather extreme."

"So why's this Agent Ward mad at you?"

"He isn't mad at me. Several months ago he knocked on my front door. When I opened the door, he said: 'Hi, remember me?' 'Yeah, I remember you,' I told him. That's when he asked, 'Can we talk for a few minutes? I need your help.' Of course I agreed."

"What'd he want?" Mr. Block asked.

"That, I'm not at liberty to discuss, sir."

"Don't you go calling me sir, Doc. I never went above a Gunnery Sergeant, so if you have to call me anything it's Gunny."

"Okay, Gunny, I'm not at liberty to talk about a lot of this."

"How, pray tell, did you meet Mr. Ward?"

"Now, *that*, I can tell you..."

Chapter 14

"This is the story: My association with Mr. Ward all began one night while working late at the clinic. A side door had been left propped open. A shabbily-dressed woman walked in.

"I'm sorry to bother you, ma'am. My name is Mary. My daughter is very sick," the strange woman said.

"How'd you know we were here?" Nurse Barbara Manners asked.

"More importantly," I interrupted, "where's your daughter?"

"She's in Chi-town. Maurice is with her. I left to buy food and children's aspirin."

"I'll grab my bag," I said, opening my wallet.

"Take Nurse Manners and buy your daughter some hot food. You can also pick up a warm blanket." I handed Nurse Manners one hundred dollars in cash.

"Below the city streets, in Chi-town, I greeted people as we passed. There were three young boys who were definitely out of their element. I nodded to the boys, "Good evening, boys."

"There ain't nothin' good about it, mister," one boy replied.

"Yeah," a second added. "Nobody here even talks to us, but at least they aren't trying to touch us."

"If you follow me, I'll take you to Maurice. He'll get you some food and a place to sleep."

"We don't need no one's help," the first boy replied.

"Suit yourselves. I have to go see a girl who is sick. Her mother will be back soon. The woman's name is Mary. Find her if you want food or clothing," I said, eyeing the one boy who had closely shaved red hair, and wore only a cloth diaper.

"The three boys said nothing more as they followed me to Mary's small area. Mary's daughter, Sally, was sitting up coughing. It took me only minutes to diagnose the girl with pneumonia. Upon returning with Nurse Manners, Mary watched the nurse give her daughter an antibiotic. Nurse Manners then encouraged Mary to bring her daughter to the clinic for further treatment.

"Sally needs breathing treatments, antibiotics, and fresh air to get well," I advised.

"Part of the clinic is being remodeled," Nurse Manners said. "Is it possible to maybe–"

"Yes," I replied with a smile. "I see no reason why Mary can't bring Sally to the clinic. She can receive treatment and I'll have Mr. Nicholson, our janitor, put a bed out in the courtyard so Sally can get lots of fresh air."

Mary objected, "I've already cost you money just coming to see my baby. I have no money to pay for these things. That's why we live in Chi-town, the old abandoned subway."

"I wanted to argue with the woman and started to, but I knew Mary wouldn't accept the offer. It was the memory of the three boys I had just met which provided a reasonable answer.

57

"Did you see three nearly naked boys, new to Chi-town, on your way back here?"

"They're waiting for you to finish with Sally before coming inside for the night," Mary said.

Stepping outside the cubicle I saw all three boys a few feet away. "Hey guys, I need your help. My name is Dr. Colton; please come inside. I have a request."

"We ain't doing nothing weird, mister."

They entered the cubicle and stopped. "What?" one of the boys asked.

"Miss Sally, here," I motioned towards Mary's daughter, "has pneumonia and needs medicine. Sally's mother won't accept free medicine, so I need you to help her. If Miss Mary brings Sally to the clinic, I'll give her money to buy clothing at Goodwill for you."

"Do we have to go with her to Goodwill?" the red-haired, diaper-clad boy asked.

"No, you don't," Mary shot back. "Dr. Colton can measure you for me."

"Are you a weird doctor?" the boy with black hair wanted to know.

"No, he's not," Mary defended. "And you watch your mouth. You boys coming down here to Chi-town dressed like you are–what's your problem?"

"My name is Dyson, lady," Dyson Compton hesitantly offered. "The three of us ran away from the Dragon Society."

"Oh my God–oh my God! You poor boys–oh my God," Mary stammered. "What's the Dragon Society? Never mind. I don't want to know, not if that's the way you dress."

"Come to the clinic; nobody will harm you, I promise," I told them. "I can call the police and you can tell them what happened."

"Mister, you really are stupid," the black-haired boy said. "I'm David Kelly and my father is a deputy sheriff. I ran away because of what he does."

"And don't say tell a judge," Dyson interjected. "Judge Towzer sends people to prison for the kinda stuff he does."

"Okay, I get the picture," I half-sighed in resignation. "No police, and you can stay in Chi-town for a while."

"Does anybody have pants that'll fit me?" the diaper-clad boy asked. "This thing is ready to fall off. A real weirdo made me wear it."

"That weirdo is your father," Dyson said.

"What's your name?" Nurse Manners inquired.

"Brody Green, ma'am."

"If you come with us, we'll buy you some pants, underwear, and shirts tonight," Barbara offered.

"Can you bring them back here?" Dyson begged.

"No, I won't. I'm willing to go out of my way, but only to a certain extent. Either come with us or stay here with your diaper until tomorrow."

"Why won't you come back here?" Brody asked.

"I said, accept my offer, or stay here. Miss Sally is the only child in Chi-town. Maybe her mother will let you wear one of Sally's dresses. I'm taking Nurse Manners home, then I'm going home and going to bed, alone!"

"Let's go with them, Brody," David Kelly urged.

Looking at me, Barbara spoke softly. "Richard, let's take all three boys. You need to examine them to see if they need medical attention."

"If we take them, how do I get you back home?"

"I can take a taxi from your house, and tomorrow Mary can go shopping for clothes while Sally is at the clinic with you."

"Who's going to stay with the boys while I'm at work?"

"It's my day off. I'll come to your house and stay there. After Mary buys clothing she can take them to the clinic. Then you can bring them home to the boys."

"I know better than to argue with good logic. Boys, are you staying or going?"

"Will we still get pants tomorrow?" David asked.

"Yes, I promise you'll still get pants tomorrow," Barbara answered.

"I left with Nurse Manners and the three boys. I put my coat on the backseat of my car for Brody to sit on; then, thinking quickly, I popped the car's trunk lid and opened a travel case. Motioning for Brody to follow me, I took him between my car and another. I slipped one of my T-shirts over his head. "If you give me your diaper, I'll get rid of it for you." Brody unpinned the cloth diaper and handed it to me.

"Once we arrived and went inside the house, I asked the three boys if they were hungry. A 'yes' in unison was their answer. Knowing all boys like pizza, Barbara ordered a large pepperoni pizza to be delivered.

"I led the boys to a guest bedroom and bathroom. "You can sleep in here. It's a king-size bed. All three of you will fit. You decide who is first to take a shower. I'll return with towels for each of you. After your physical examination you can eat and watch TV or go to bed."

"What about clothes?" asked Dyson.

"Check it out," Brody quipped, lifting the T-shirt slightly. "It's almost like a pajama top."

"Remember to clean up all messes." I left the boys alone as I went for fresh clean towels. Twenty minutes later all three boys appeared in the dining room where Barbara and I were playing cards. One at a time each boy came to my office to be examined. After what they claimed happened to each of them, I wasn't surprised with my findings. I asked each one questions and was amazed at their frankness in response. Not a single one of them showed any modesty in covering themselves when Nurse Barbara entered to take a blood sample.

"They've been conditioned to keep their hands away from covering up," Barbara said. "Did you notice how they only put on T-shirts after you examined them?"

"They still expect us to abuse them. We're looking at a lack of trust due to years of abuse. No child should go through what these boys told me happened to them."

Barbara was sickened. Her heart ached, trying to think of some way to help the boys. "Can you tell me exactly which policeman or judge did this to you?" she asked the boys.

"Yeah, if we could remember every adult's name. But if you tell the police we'll only have to go back home and it'll be worse than ever," Dyson offered.

"Let's go to my home office. I'd like to check one or two more things. Barbara, you can use the Corvette to drive home and bring it back in the morning." I handed her my car keys. "Garage door opener is on the visor. Please make sure you close it before leaving. I really don't want the neighborhood watch committee waking me up or fining me for not securing my house after dark."

Barbara laughed, "Good night, Doctor."

"Gentlemen, boys, say goodnight to Nurse Barbara and come to my office." With that, I left the four to say goodbye. Then Dyson, Brody, and David entered the office. I instructed them to sit on the couch facing my bookcase.

"Okay, boys, you can't go back home. Each of you have been betrayed by your parents. In a few minutes you'll go to my basement. In my basement, I can video-record what you've already told me. You'll have to tell it all again, even naming the people you do know. If you do this, I'll help you escape the abuse and from those responsible. This offer comes with a price, however. It means you'll never be able to see each other again."

"Why can't we see each other anymore?" David asked. "Dyson and Brody are my friends. We all live on the same street."

"After you've given a sworn statement on video, I'll explain why you can't see each other any longer. Okay, who's first?"

"In the basement all three boys sat in comfortable chairs, eating pizza, a blank wall behind them. "My name is David Kelly. I swear that what I'm about to say is the truth. Nobody is paying me to say this and under my shirt I am naked because I ran away from home. I'm ten years old, almost eleven. My father is Deputy Sheriff Frank Kelly; my mother is Court Attorney Kay Kelly, prosecutor. My mother and father are members of a club called the DS, or Dragon Society. They make me go to Dragon Society meetings and outings with other Dragon Society members. I've got a small seagull tattoo. I also have a star around it. It tells other Dragon Society people what they can do to me. I'm not allowed to say 'no' to any Dragon Society member for any reason. If I say 'no', I get punished. Punishment is long and painful. The Dragon Society puts locators in all the kids' arms. My father, Deputy Sheriff Kelly, told me that they can always find me because of the locator in my arm. If I'm caught now, I'll be killed as a warning to other DS kids."

"Hi, I'm Brody Green. I'm nine years old. My daddy is John Green. He's a security guard at the mall where the Dragons meet on Saturday nights in the big conference room. They use the conference room because my daddy has the keys. The Dragon Society had a Dragon Santa at Christmas. Boys and girls were made to sit on his lap. It makes me sick. I have four lines part way around my seagull tattoo, but some kids have more. My father makes me wear diapers because my baby sister died. I wasn't allowed to go #1 or #2 without wearing a diaper. When my diaper was changed I had to go #1 or #2 right away in my new diaper or else I was punished. If I don't wear it, they punish me by spanking me with a strap ten times. I have a bad diaper rash. My sister died when she was two years old and my mother doesn't live with us. I ran away from home, I think my daddy hurt Sissy before she died." Brody hung his head and quit talking. He then mumbled, "They cut my hair really short when they marked me for death."

"What you're going to hear is nothing but the truth. My first name is Dyson, my last name is Compton. I had my first experience with the Dragon Society when I was four years old. My seagull tattoo is inside a star. That means Dragon Society members can order me to do any act that doesn't kill me. Adults shouldn't hurt any kid ever. Someone needs to tell my mother and father that I once loved them. They lost my love when they hurt me. Last year in school I had to take Health. My teacher was a Dragon Society member. We learned what it means to be a virgin. A lot of kids laughed and made jokes. I cried, because I felt dirty and ashamed. Some people call my mother 'Candy Kathy'. She's a stripper at the adult club called *The Bar Belle*, but she strips for the Dragon Society members at the meetings too. My father is a security guard at my school. The Dragon Society meets there for their form of entertainment in the gym, pool, and locker rooms. I ran away from home and I'll kill myself if I'm forced to go back. I want to live in Canada where nobody knows me. I'm ashamed to be seen by normal people. Today for the first time since I can remember I feel safe. In one whole night no one has tried to hurt me." Dyson continued. "Stephen Fellitch, a judge in the city, was the last person to make me do something ugly."

"I shut off the camera. "I promised to tell you boys why you'll never see each other again. David, I have a friend in California who isn't married. He was abused as a boy and he hates abusive people. He's the man who can help heal you, spirit and soul. Dyson, a man and woman in Texas want children; however, they can't have any. The man is a pilot who is away from home a lot. His wife is a real estate agent. They like taking trips to all areas of the world. And Brody, you're going to live on a ranch. The man is both a rancher and a hunting guide. Amy will be your mother. She used to be a teacher and is going to home-school you. Zach will teach you how to track animals. You won't have to be around people who look at you with abuse in their minds. I promise you, no more abuse. Instead, you'll all wear clothes. But most of all, you get to be normal boys."

"How do you know they'll want us to live with them?" Dyson asked.

"You may be angry, but I already contacted them. I've known all of these people for many years. They heard your sworn statements as you made them. My friends asked for you to live with them. You'll have a new name, new life, and somebody who really wants to love you."

"Do we still get new clothes?"

"Yes, Dyson, you still get new clothes," I replied.

"He's Brody," David corrected.

"Time for bed, boys. I have to start paperwork for your new lives. However, there is one thing you have to remember: *do not* say anything about what I'm doing to anyone–especially Nurse Barbara."

"Why not?" Dyson asked innocently.

"Because everybody must think you ran away and if the police ever question Nurse Barbara she can't slip and accidentally tell them."

"We won't say nothin, but what about these things?" David asked, showing Dr. Colton his tattoo.

"If a Dragon ever sees our seagulls, they'll know we're Dragon kids," Dyson said.

"I can remove the RFIDs so you can't be traced. Your tattoos will take a bit longer."

"What's an RFID?" Brody asked.

"RFID stands for Radio Frequency Identification. It's how the Dragon's track you," I explained.

"When you take these trackers out of us, are we gonna be asleep?" David inquired.

"Yeah," Brody added. "Dr. Flynn, a dentist, is one of the Dragons. He gases kids then takes their clothes. I saw it one day after he used gas on me to take out what he called a 'pacted tooth'."

"He means 'impacted'," David offered. "My sister took me and another kid. I had to watch what Dr. Flynn did after he gassed the kid."

"You'll be awake, and feel a needle-prick, but nothing else. You decide who's first. I'll remove them in the morning. You're safe here tonight."

"The following afternoon, Dyson Compton briefly felt the needle enter his arm. I separated him from his two friends at that time. The last thing he remembered of that day was eating a double cheeseburger, fries, and a large Coke. Dyson awoke in a room with a bed, radio, and videogame. He appeared to be awaiting the arrival of his father Ralph. He acted as though he expected to be beaten or worse.

"Dyson was secreted in a storage container which had been delivered months before, when the clinic first began remodeling. It was common knowledge that I used the container as a private office from time to time. I also used it to store sensitive case files.

"Dyson was the first to leave my protection. His two friends needed more time. Dyson occupied his days playing video games and watching television. I entered Dyson's room twice during his stay. Both times, panic showed in his eyes. From then on, I only put food and water bottles in the room and did not enter.

"One afternoon, I fed Dyson pizza for supper. He ate all three slices. I waited for Dyson to fall asleep before giving him the aforementioned shot. Removing Dyson from the container was easy. A clinic laundry cart filled with smocks and blankets supported the boy's drugged body as I moved him to a waiting liftgate box truck. Inside the truck I moved Dyson to the right front seat. Sixteen hours later, Dyson awoke in a strange bed wearing pajamas, with a strange woman sitting beside him. "Hello son, you're safe now."

"From Brody Green, I got, 'Traitor, I hate you!' he yelled, when I informed the three boys I'd called the police to come and get them. Brody nearly succeeded in getting his finger into his throat to vomit, but the drugs in his cheeseburger and soda had taken effect. I placed him in a room containing a single bed, toilet, sink, comic books, and a video game. This was done after I performed three minor

62

surgeries. At first Brody complained of pain but I knew it was a ruse. When food was put in his room, he refused to eat. On day two, I placed prepackaged food in the room and he ate. I offered only bottled water or unopened sodas. At first, he screamed and shouted, yelling for help, but soon realized nobody was going to help him. I monitored Brody constantly, and learned he thought the Dragons were going to take him to a meeting and fulfill their promise to kill him, should he or anyone else ever run away, or tell on them. He had done both.

"One morning, I moved Brody to a new location as he slept. When a tall man dressed entirely in camouflage clothing entered the room, Brody nearly cried. "Stand up and turn around," the man ordered. "What's your name, boy?"

"Brody, sir," he said in a trembling voice.

"Oh, I like being called sir; it shows respect. I guess this is the wrong room. I'm looking for Scott Lawson, my son."

Turning around, Brody cried, "I'm scared, sir; another man said he was my daddy. He let his friends do bad things to me. They hurt me, sir."

"I won't let anyone ever hurt you again, son. The boy you were before I arrived no longer exists. Shall we go home? Your mother is waiting for us."

"Yes, sir, I like the name Scott." Brody removed his pajamas, shedding both them and his old name. He dressed in camouflage clothing, including a hood which covered his head so he could not see his surroundings.

"We're flying on a charter jet with other people. We have to be quiet, so we don't upset a lady who is very ill. Our seats are in the back. If someone comes to use the bathroom, I have to put the hood over your head to cover your face."

Scott visibly relaxed. "Okay," he said. "Can I grow my hair again, sir? They shaved me when they put me in diapers and marked me for death."

"I think Mother is going to insist on it," Mr. Lawson replied.

Chapter 15

I opened the garage door to the kitchen, entering the house. David watched me walk into the kitchen. He saw me kiss Barbara before she used the telephone. A few minutes later she left the house in my car. I told the boys, "There's no Chinese food, and Nurse Manners didn't cook anything for dinner. I didn't want Chinese so I bought fast food. Double cheeseburgers, fries, and sodas for you boys; for me, single cheeseburger, no fries, and a beer."

"They make us drink beer at the meetings," David offered. "I hate beer."

"My beer is for me or another adult only," I told the boy.

"You promised us new clothes," one of the boys said.

"Miss Manners went to get them. Let's eat and get cleaned up before she returns."

"Is she your wife?" David asked between bites of food.

David wasn't really hungry; he ate small bites of food, drinking gulps of soda as he ate. He swallowed the last of his double cheeseburger as I answered him, "We aren't married." I waited, then said, "The police have been looking for you boys. They came to the clinic after being in Chi-town. I heard there's a reward placed on each of you. I get the reward; you're going home. I told the police to come get you."

David found himself lying on a mattress instead of a bed. He had blankets, handheld video games, and a bathroom. I heard him say he wasn't mad at me. The Dragon Society would've found him or anyone else, no matter where they hid. He would wait, do everything demanded of him, and one day he would kill all the Dragon Society members he could, even if it meant he died in the process.

The only food I offered David was inside freeze-dried packages. He drank only water, using a small microwave to heat water for his food. There were no mirrors, but he didn't need one. His head was shaved bald, and a bandage covered a small wound on his scalp where I found and removed an RFID. Another bandage covered his arm where I had removed his tattoos. After his fifth day, in the room David removed his bandages. Examining his arm, it looked worse than before. Country music played every day from speakers he couldn't see.

One day all music stopped and the light turned off, leaving David in total darkness. After an agonizing 120 seconds, an extremely bright light shone into his face. "Stand up, turn around, and don't move," a strange voice commanded. A dark cloth bag slipped over David's head. Strong hands grasped his shoulders, turning him around. He felt soft cloth at his feet. "Lift one foot at a time and stand still. Lift your arms boy." Warm sweatpants were pulled up to his waist and a fleece shirt covered his torso. "Your father hired me to make sure you get home safely. Do exactly what you're told and things will be good. Do you understand?"

"Yeah, I understand."

"That's no answer. *I want yes, sir or no, sir—got it?*"

"Yes, sir! I got it."

David was helped upstairs before hearing a door open. Three more steps up, then he was gently seated, and a seat belt strapped him into the seat. He was in total darkness, keeping his eyes closed. An engine started; they were moving slowly away. Within thirty seconds, more country music came from nearby speakers. No words were spoken by the man, and soon David's eyes closed in sleep. He had not meant to fall asleep, and he awoke nearly six hours later.

"Hi, sleepyhead," a man driving a motorcoach said. "Are you hungry? I have venison jerky."

"Who are you, sir?"

"Aiden, I'm your dad, Kyler Grant."

Tears began flowing down the boy's cheeks. "Yes, sir, I'm real hungry. Do you have any water, please?"

Pointing to a bottle, Kyler answered, "Drink your fill. We have more in the refrigerator. We'll stop at the next rest stop so you can see the motorcoach better."

"Please, sir, don't stop. Thank you for taking me home." With his bottle of water emptied, Aiden asked, "Is it okay to get more water, sir?"

"Yes, it is," Kyler replied. "Bring one back for me, if you please. There are chips in a cabinet if you want some."

The change to being Aiden Grant was easy. Aiden was treated with respect, David with contempt. Aiden ordered food for himself; David ate what he was given. David was constantly in fear of offending others. Aiden felt at ease, openly laughing at Kyler when he did something silly, stupid, or downright ridiculous. Aiden felt no fear when he found his sweat pants and shirt missing from the motorcoach bathroom. They were parked in a state park for the night, so he wrapped a towel around himself and walked to Kyler.

"Where's my clothes, sir?"

"Well, nudist boy," Kyler teased, "I know you call them clothes you had on 'freedom', but I called them 'stinky'. I had to make a decision: either burn 'em or wash 'em. I chose to wash 'em. There's new clothes in the drawer under your bunk."

"Thank you, Mr. Grant. Can we go to the store, sir?"

"What did you call me?"

"I'm sorry, sir. Dad, can we go?"

"Why? We have enough food and drink."

"I ain't got no shoes."

"Check under your bunk–left drawer. And it's, 'I don't have any shoes', Aiden." Kyler put his arm around Aiden's shoulder. "It'll be okay, son. I forgot to tell you where to find your clothes and shoes. Please forgive me."

Aiden hugged his new dad, a sense of comfort and love filling him for the first time in his life, tears trickling down his cheeks. Aiden cried openly as he and his new dad hugged each other.

Chapter 16

"I removed electronic trackers from the boys' arms. They'd been safe in my house, because Nancy insisted on a thin lead lining being put in place on the roof and beneath the siding all around. She wanted protection from solar flares and the radiation. She convinced me when she told me the ionizing radiation released during solar flares includes x-rays and gamma rays.

I learned of the trackers originally while examining a toddler, Axle Banner. I also learned there were a total of ten bars associated with the Dragon Kid tattoos. Each was part of a star that enclosed the seagull. Eleven bars like David's meant death. As the years passed, I would come to see many kids branded with a seagull tattoo, and not all of them were located on an arm.

Each tracker removed from the three boys was dropped into a small lead box. They were either destroyed or used later. If destroyed, I left tiny bits behind. I hadn't lied to the boys. I did call the Sheriff's office, notifying them that David, Brody, and Dyson had approached me in Chi-town for help. As a doctor, I was naturally obligated to assist the boys medically. I admitted going a step further by taking the boys home where I gave each five dollars, a T-shirt, and a double cheeseburger. I said the boys slipped out of my house.

When the deputies came by the house, they were allowed to search everywhere. I answered all questions, meeting Deputy Sheriff Frank Kelly himself. "I trusted those boys, and all they did was steal from me. One of them stole an autographed Cubs baseball. I'm also missing a .243 caliber rifle with scope, and a box of ammo."

"Damn it! If David has a rifle, we've got a problem!" Deputy Sheriff Frank swore to himself.

"Is anything else missing, Doctor?"

"Yes, sir, but it's no longer missing. My golf cart was found by the lake. Its batteries were drained. Now, I have to replace them at a thousand dollars apiece."

"How did you find it?" Deputy Sheriff Kelly asked.

"Actually, your office notified me of its whereabouts about ten minutes before you arrived. I was warned that I have an hour to remove it or it'll be impounded."

"I can arrange to give you a few more hours, Doctor. We thank you for your cooperation," Deputy Kelly responded. "Now, did you say the boys left wearing the shirts you gave them?"

"No, sir, they wore whatever they already had on plus the T-shirts I gave them. I'm sorry I couldn't keep them here for you, but first the red-haired one went to use the bathroom and his blond friend tagged along. I went to check on them about ten minutes later. I never thought to check on my golf cart. It's usually parked in my garage next to my motorcoach."

"We'll have to search your motorcoach, Doctor," a deputy said.

"Go ahead; it's in the first extended bay. Next to it was my golf cart which I'll probably sell to make room for the houseboat I bought as a tax write-off, and for fishing on Lake Michigan."

"Where's your houseboat, sir?"

"Still in the factory being fitted the way I ordered. It won't be here for another month."

"You know I have to ask, sir," the deputy covered.

"If you didn't ask, I would be offended." I noticed the single dot between the thumb and forefinger of the deputy, a mark which the boys explained while staying with me.

Deputy Sheriff Kelly left my house disappointed. He drove directly to where my golf cart was found behind a warehouse building. Four sets of fingerprints were discovered on the golf cart. Those of David Kelly covered the steering wheel. Brody sat beside David with Dyson behind David. It was totally clear the boys took my golf cart. Their blood was all over the back of the cart. I left behind a bloodied knife and the smashed remains of an RFID tracker.

I honestly hated separating the boys and leaving them alone in different rooms. They had to believe I was betraying them until the last moment when they met their new parents.

When Nancy and I bought our house, years before she died, she insisted on bunkers being added to the garage add-on we had built. Nancy was forever concerned about a nuclear attack and insisted on a so-called safe haven. Entrance to the bunker was hidden, ergo, the sheriff deputies couldn't find it. It had been difficult to put fingerprints on my golf cart, but it was worth all the effort. I returned home after parking the golf cart where it had been found by deputies. I used my bicycle to return home.

"That's how you met Agent Ward?"

"My word of honor, Fred," Dr. Colton promised.

"Which of those three boys became Agent Ward?"

"Now that, my friend, is something you can ask Xander for yourself. You're invited to dinner at my house."

"I'll be there, Doc. Text me your address."

"Will do; dinner is at 6:30 sharp."

"Dr. Colton, two minutes left," Mr. Dill said as he headed to the courtroom.

"Here's my address; see you at dinner."

"Is Kenny invited?" Mr. Block asked.

"He is, but I think Kenny will be spending time with his long-time friend." Dr. Colton nodded towards Kenny and Prosecutor Pizzo.

Chapter 17

Judge King entered the courtroom, a stern look on his face. "I'm not a happy man," he said to everyone in court. "Mr. Pizzo, if I didn't know that you seek a conviction in this case, I'd almost swear you conspired with the defense to get these journals into evidence. I took into consideration Mr. Dill arguing to keep Dr. Colton's journals out of evidence as well. Then I asked myself a simple question: 'Why was Dr. Colton sending these files away?' I had no answer to the question. I've wrestled over what I'm going to do with Dr. Colton's journals. I confess you managed to get items into evidence which I disqualified in earlier hearings."

Dr. Colton held out his hand to Mr. Dill. Taking out his wallet, Mr. Dill removed a single dollar bill and placed it in Dr. Colton's hand.

"What are you doing?" Judge King inquired, with agitation in his voice.

"Excuse me," Dr. Colton asked in feigned confusion. "Was this bad timing? I told Wesley you'd blame us for this situation. I won our gentlemen's bet."

Slamming his right hand soundly down on the bench, Judge King loudly retorted, "This is not a game or a joke, Mr. Dill. You and Dr. Colton had best start taking this trial seriously."

"Your Honor—"

"Not a word, sir, *not a single solitary word*, or I shall find you in contempt and fine you one thousand dollars. Do you understand?"

Dr. Colton remained silent. Making exaggerated gestures, he put the single dollar bill inside his wallet.

"I said, do you understand me, Mr. Colton?" Judge King was now shouting.

"Yeah," Dr. Colton snapped sarcastically, "I understand. You've been working with Mr. Pizzo to convict me. I take this trial more seriously than you think. Counselor Dill and I both tried our best to keep those journals out of evidence, citing they were illegally obtained. Mr. Pizzo screamed to have them admitted and you readily accepted my journals into evidence. Neither of you even read them, but the jurors have been reading every page."

"That's enough, Dr. Colton. You just earned yourself a contempt of court fine. Your little antics with betting in court will add to that fine. You'll pay my clerk twelve hundred dollars before we leave today."

"Your Honor, I'll be glad to pay your outlandish fine, once Mr. Pizzo pays his fines of over $3,000."

"Don't tell me what to do, Mister!" Judge King spat.

"Judge King," Mr. Dill interrupted. "I can understand how you might think we manipulated you. For argument's sake, let's say we did. You can't deny that if Dr. Colton got one over on you, it took a lot of planning and guts."

"Why else would Mr. Colton send his journals out?" Mr. Pizzo asked.

After twenty seconds of silence, Judge King spoke. "Well, Mr. Colton, why were you sending your journals away in an aircraft?"

"Ask me in open court on the record."

"I warn you, sir. Your answer had better not be disrespectful on the record."

"I promise you, I'll only say why the journals were being sent away."

"Judge King," Mr. Dill interrupted. "I've researched the many contempt of court fines issued to Mr. Pizzo over time. His fines now total over $3,300 which have never been paid."

"My fines are none of your business, Mr. Dill."

"Mr. Pizzo, your disregard towards paying the fines levied against you is unprofessional. I cannot hold the defense to higher standards than the prosecution. I can't expect Mr. Dill or his client to pay their fines when you've seen fit to ignore paying yours." Turning to face the defense table, Judge King addressed Dr. Colton. "Your $1,200 contempt fine is hereby rescinded. Mr. Colton, I ask you to tread lightly, please, no more betting in my courtroom. If you do place bets, I request you settle after court."

"Thank you, sir. I promise to honor your request." Dr. Colton tapped his attorney's leg. When he looked down, Mr. Dill saw Dr. Colton motioning to indicate he was owed money.

"Your Honor," Mr. Dill said. "I'm not a fan of Mr. Pizzo, however, I recognize he's only been following his normal protocol, so now I find myself asking you to dismiss all fines imposed in this court by you."

"I'll have to consider your request; mainly because I wonder why you make such a request."

"Believe me, I'm not being altruistic. My motives are selfish."

"Explain," Judge King instructed.

"I want Mr. Pizzo to acknowledge he obtained information regarding Dr. Colton's journals through an illegal wiretap," Mr. Dill responded.

"Fat chance," Prosecutor Pizzo snapped.

"Okay, make the twerp pay his fines."

"Enough, gentlemen. Let's remain pleasant. Shall we proceed on the record? We have a trial to continue." Taking a couple of deep breaths, Judge King kept going, "We'll now go back on the record. I have reached a decision regarding Dr. Colton's journals. But first, I have a question to ask Dr. Colton."

Lifting his head to look at the judge, Dr. Colton said, "Yes, sir?"

"Why were you sending your journals away?"

"Frankly, Your Honor, I was sending them to a hangar where the C.A.R. Foundation houses its jet. My wife, Barbara, will use that jet to leave the United States and disappear into France. Barbara plans on writing a book about our life together. The journals were meant to assist her in her writings. Barbara wants to take my journals with her. She's in the process of finalizing papers for her new home in France. Your Honor, I honestly do have cancer."

"The journals were presented as evidence by you, Mr. Pizzo. What are your thoughts regarding Dr. Colton's journals?"

Mr. Pizzo took a moment to consider his reply. "Mr. Colton's journals contain items deemed inadmissible by the court. I believe he manipulated the court into admitting certain documents into evidence."

"Excuse me, please," Mr. Dill said, "How could Dr. Colton know you would find out about his journals?"

"Regardless of that," Mr. Pizzo retorted, "I still stand on having his journals submitted as evidence."

"Thank you, Mr. Prosecutor," Judge King responded. "I said before that I'd made my decision. I believe your information source is faulty, Mr. Pizzo. However, Dr. Colton's journals shall remain in evidence. I'm ordering the originals to be turned over to Mrs. Colton."

"Your Honor, on behalf of Doctor and Barbara Colton, we thank you," Mr. Dill quickly responded.

"Mr. Pizzo, do you have any more witnesses?"

"Objection, Your Honor," Dr. Colton stood to speak. "We, as yet, have unfinished business and a witness to finish questioning. I am, of course, referring to Agent Toth, who was testifying before we adjourned."

"Dr. Colton is correct, Your Honor. With a ruling of the journals as evidence, we are entitled access to them." Mr. Dill refrained from smiling, then, to himself, "I completely forgot about Agent Toth."

"Very well," Judge King said. "Bring Agent Toth back."

Francis Toth walked back to the witness stand. "Okay, people, I'm still under oath, so let's continue," he rudely said before anyone else could speak.

"Defense, the witness is yours," Judge King said.

"Thank you, sir," Dr. Colton addressed Judge King. "Agent Toth, you stated earlier that you suspected me only after the alleged ashes of Marco Rizzoli were found. Why'd you decide to make me a suspect?"

"We discovered a scorched rag that was soaked with ether. It only made sense, especially after we found blood splatter close to the ashes."

"Did you do a DNA test on the blood splatter?"

"I didn't see the need. It was apparent the blood came from the body which had been cremated."

"Well, sir, would it surprise you to know that it was Mario Rizzoli's blood near the ashes?"

"Objection, Your Honor. Pure speculation. Guessing and projecting his own hopes. Mr. Colton has no real idea of whose blood was splattered next to the ashes," Mr. Pizzo argued.

"Quite the contrary. We, the defense, paid to find out whose blood had been found."

"Are you going to share that information, Mr. Colton?" Judge King queried.

"Page 364 in my journal, Your Honor," Dr. Colton replied. "The drops of blood belong to Mario Rizzoli."

"Which lab performed the DNA test, if I may be so bold as to ask?" Mr. Pizzo inquired politely.

"The same one used by your office for my DNA comparison to those drops," Dr. Colton replied.

"Thank you, sir," Judge King said to Dr. Colton.

"Mr. Toth, you're still in possession of a copy of my journals. Did you read Dr. Hoch's evaluation?"

"No, I didn't."

"Then I'll read it for you. Listen carefully."

"Your Honor, do I have to listen to this man read his psych evaluation?" Agent Toth inquired.

"Not if you want to read it yourself," Judge King responded.

"Fine, I'll read it." Agent Toth turned to page 126 and read:

This evaluation of Dr. Richard Colton has been ordered by Administrator Beltran. It is quite obvious that Dr. Colton mourns the deaths of his wife, Nancy, and toddler son, Richard, Jr. Dr. Colton stated he is angry at our justice system. He reported his wife's dying identification of the hit-and-run driver as Mr. Mario Rizzoli. Dr. Colton is frustrated at nothing having been done to resolve this issue. He has further stated it is not in him to take a life, regardless of the situation. He went to medical school and became a doctor to save lives, not to take them. Dr. Colton admittedly expresses strong loathing toward Mr. Rizzoli. However, there is no way he could harm Mario Rizzoli's family in order to get back at the man. Dr. Colton misses his family, and while he detests Mario Rizzoli, it pains the doctor to see the results of the abuse Marco suffers at home. It is this writer's opinion that Dr. Richard Colton is fit to practice medicine. Dr. Colton is not harboring evil malice towards the man he claims killed his family. He honestly believes justice will prevail. It should be noted that Dr. Colton has just received a patent for yet another surgical implement.

"Okay, I've read the report," Agent Toth stated.

"If you'd read that report when you received it, would it–scratch that–*could it* have changed your suspicions?"

"Yes, I admit, it could, and most likely would have, had I taken the time to read it."

"Why was nobody ever arrested?"

"Insufficient evidence. We lacked evidence that would hold up in court."

"I've no further questions, Your Honor." Dr. Colton sat down and cradled his head in both hands.

"Are you all right?" Mr. Dill softly asked his co-counsel.

"Yeah, just gotta drink some water and eat a snack."

"If there are no more questions, Agent Toth, you may leave," Judge King said.

"Nothing further, Your Honor," Mr. Pizzo volunteered.

Chapter 18

"Prosecution now calls Quincy Nichol."

"Sir, do you promise the testimony you are about to give will be the truth, the whole truth, and nothing but the truth?"

"I don't abide by lies, lying, or liars. I'll tell it true."

"Take a seat on the witness stand," Judge King instructed.

"Please state your name and spell it for the record," Mr. Pizzo said.

"Name's Quincy Nichol and I spell 'it', I-T. What a crazy thing to have me spell."

"Mr. Nichol, I wanted you to spell your name, sir."

"Then you should have said that, young fella. Quincy, Q-U-I-N-C-Y, Nichol, N-I-C-H-O-L, okay-okay. Next question."

"Mr. Nichol, do you know a man–"

"Can't you just ask if I know Dr. Richard Colton? Yes! I know him. Knew his daddy too–"

"How do you know Mr. Colton, sir?"

"We were both jarheads in Vietnam, in '68. I was a sergeant; he was a top notch scout. I believe he was recon."

"Mr. Quincy," Mr. Pizzo addressed his witness in exasperation, "I'm asking about *this* Mr. Colton."

"Then why didn't you ask me about Doctor Colton? Why'd you ask me about his daddy? I'm–"

"Objection, Your Honor. Will you please instruct the witness to answer my question?"

"Mr. Nichol, you will answer Prosecutor Pizzo's questions and stop playing games."

Quincy Nichol sat without responding.

"Mr. Nichol, how do you know Mr. Richard Colton?"

"They've made Quincy angry," Dr. Colton whispered, leaning over so only Mr. Dill could hear him.

"Answer the question, Mr. Nichol," Judge King ordered.

"No! You didn't say please. That moron is being an arrogant fool."

"Mr. Nichol, if you continue to refuse to answer the prosecutor's question, I'll have you arrested and put in jail."

"Mr. Judge, I'll answer his questions, but I want to say something first. I've been–"

"Silence!" Judge King slammed his gavel down. "Bailiff, arrest this witness."

"Your Honor," Dr. Colton interrupted, "Quincy Nichol is my godfather. He's also the man who saved Senator Lucas Connor's life in Vietnam. Quincy Nichol needs only make one phone call and you'll no longer be a judge."

"Are you threatening me, Mr. Colton?" Judge King snapped.

"No, sir, I am not," Dr. Colton shot back. "Senator Connor owes his life to Mr. Nichol. If you put that man in your jail, the Senator will step up and order his immediate release through Homeland."

"Why should I believe you?"

"Because Dr. Colton's mother is directly related to Senator Connor," Wesley Dill answered.

"Mr. Pizzo, did you do any kind of background checks on the people you're calling to testify?"

"Your Honor, I…" the prosecutor stammered.

"No, no…don't answer. It's becoming quite clear you're not properly prepared to try this case."

"Your Honor, may I offer a suggestion? " Court Observer Vang inquired. "My idea might be helpful."

"Put your suggestion in the form of a question, otherwise you're out of order."

"Would it be possible to start Mr. Nichol's testimony over and ask specific questions using 'Doctor' instead of 'Mister'?"

Taking a deep breath, Judge King saw the sense of Observer Vang's question. "If Mr. Nichol is willing to start over, the court is open to the idea."

"I'll agree," Quincy Nichol stated.

"All right," Mr. Pizzo joined in. "Mr. Nichol, is it true that Dr. Colton is your godson?"

"Yes."

"When was the last–no, scratch that. How often do you communicate with Mister–excuse me, Doctor Colton?"

"Define 'communicate'."

A note passed from Dr. Colton. *He's still mad!* was written on the paper.

"I'll reword my question. Do you call each other on the telephone?" Mr. Pizzo kept his question basic.

"Yes."

"How often do you call Dr. Colton?"

"Two, maybe three times a quarter; that's three months."

"So you don't call very often?" Mr. Pizzo declared.

"More often than you call your parents," Mr. Nichol retorted.

"Your Honor," Mr. Dill interrupted. "Mr. Nichol stated he's in contact monthly with his godson. Mr. Pizzo's remarks were unwarranted."

"Agreed," Judge King replied. "Mr. Pizzo, stop baiting the witness."

Without acknowledging the judge, Mr. Pizzo continued, "Do you write letters to Dr. Colton?"

"No, he's a doctor. They write funny, but we email each other."

Judge King and a number of jurors chuckled.

"Do you think Dr. Colton is capable of killing a child?"

"Yes."

Prosecutor Anthony Pizzo couldn't believe his ears. This was ideal. "Have you ever seen Dr. Colton get angry?"

"Yes, I have."

"Can you think of a reason why Dr. Colton might kill a child?"

"Objection. Prosecution is asking the witness to guess or offer an opinion," Mr. Dill stated.

"Additionally, it is speculation and an inappropriate question," Dr. Colton offered.

"Overruled. I'll allow the question."

"Yes," Mr. Nichol responded.

"What would that reason be, sir?" Mr. Pizzo was elated.

"Same reason I faced in 'Nam: to protect his people from being killed in combat."

"What about a five-year-old child here in the United States?"

"No! He wouldn't kill that Rizzoli boy, no matter what the boy's father did to Richard's family."

"But you stated earlier that Dr. Colton was capable of killing a child. Now you say he wouldn't kill the Rizzoli boy. Let me ask you this: Is Dr. Colton capable of killing Marco Rizzoli, if he wasn't already dead?"

"Yes, yes, he is. But so are you. Did you kill him? Everyone alive is capable of killing another human being, including any member of the jury panel."

"Do not be flippant in my courtroom Mr. Nichol," Judge King admonished.

"Mr. Judge, I'm not being frivolously disrespectful, shallow or lacking in seriousness. The seriousness of Mr. Prosecutor's question requires a pointed answer."

"Really, Your Honor? Do we have to sit here and listen to Mr. Nichol's superfluousness?"

Snapping his head towards Mr. Pizzo, Defense Attorney Dill interjected, "I'm impressed, Anthony. However, I believe Mr. Nichol's answers are not excessive. We, the defense, think his answers are sufficient and very much required."

"Enough, gentlemen," Judge King interrupted. "Objections were not voiced, so I let you speak. Now, if you have no further questions, the defense may begin cross."

"Nothing else," Mr. Pizzo waved his hand in dismissal.

"Defense witness–"

"Hi, Pops," Dr. Colton said, addressing Mr. Nichol. "I'm going to let Mr. Wesley Dill ask our questions. However, did you receive a subpoena to testify at this trial?"

"Objection," Mr. Pizzo said. "He's a witness, so evidently he received a subpoena."

"Then it shouldn't matter if Mr. Nichol answers the question." Mr. Dill countered.

"Objection sustained. Go to your next question."

"I'll continue, if that is acceptable," Mr. Dill stated. "Mr. Nichol, you're Dr. Colton's godfather, correct?"

"Yes, sir, I am."

"You met Mr. Colton, your godson's father, in the military?"

"Yes, sir, I met a lot of good men in the Marines."

"Objection. Questions are becoming irrelevant to this trial."

"Your Honor, allow me just two or three more questions and the relevance will become evident."

"Overruled. Be quick about it, Mr. Dill."

"You met Lucas Connor in the Marines; how?"

"We were in an elite recon squad. Lucas was our point man. Mr. Colton, our scout, surprised a small group of NVA. He was battling–"

"Objection. Irrelevant."

"Overruled. Be silent, Mr. Pizzo," Judge King warned.

"Colton was fighting for his life. Lucas Connor jumped in without hesitating. I killed one NVA about to shoot Connor and then a second who lunged at Connor with a U.S. Army bayonet."

"Is that why the three of you became friends?"

"Just one of many–"

"We all know Dr. Colton is capable, but do you believe he would kill another person, regardless of age?"

"Objection. Calls for an opinion," Mr. Pizzo protested.

"Your Honor, I asked for Mr. Nichol's belief."

"Sustained; beliefs are opinions," Judge King responded.

"Mr. Nichol, how are you related to Senator Connor?"

"Lucas married my sister."

"Your Honor, my point is that Mr. Nichol, the Coltons, and Senator Connor are all related. That is how Dr. Colton knows what Senator Lucas Connor's actions or reactions would be if Quincy were arrested."

"Your Honor, Mr. Dill's questions and conclusions are out of line. I object, and ask that the defense be told *enough*," Mr. Pizzo urged.

"Judge King, my reasoning is this–"

"Save your explanations for the jury in closing arguments. I'm going to sustain the objection. Do you have any more questions for this witness?"

"Just one," Mr. Dill replied. "Quincy, have you ever eaten lunch at O'Toole's? I'm buying–oh sorry, that's not a question pertinent to the case. I'm done, thank you."

"Mr. Pizzo, any further questions?"

"He's done, Mr. Judge. He's scared of me," Quincy Nichol chuckled.

"Get him out of here, Your Honor," Mr. Pizzo snorted.

"We'll dismiss for lunch," Judge King said as Mr. Nichol left the courtroom.

Outside the courtroom, Fred Block grasped the hand of Xander Ward. "It's an honor to meet you, Mr. Ward."

"I understand you've been talking to Dr. Colton about his intervention. Did he tell you everything?"

"Only the 'before'. You and your friends were very brave."

"We were afraid, Mr. Block. We were filled with hatred. We trusted Dr. Colton. He gave me a family who wanted me. My mom and dad were the best a kid could ever have. I expected to wake up and find a fat hairy man beating on me for running away. Simon Ward was an airline pilot; he still flies commercially. Lori sold real estate, so my family had a nice place to live.

"When I arrived in Texas, I stayed indoors. Lori home-schooled me for over a year before I was willing to attend public school. I was so afraid some adult would continue what had already been done, so one night I took my bath and went into the living room nearly naked. I looked at Simon and Lori and then in my bravest voice said I was ready for them to do whatever they wanted. Simon walked over to me, removed his shirt, and put it over me." Xander stopped talking for a moment. "I still didn't trust adults."

"I'm sorry, Mr. Ward," Fred Block comforted. "I didn't mean to bring up these memories."

"These are good memories, sir. And please, call me Xander."

"I can do that. Would you like a drink?"

"The only thing I drink is water. On occasion, I will drink tea or a soda." Then, smiling, Xander added, "Thank you for asking, but I'm going to pass for now. Did Dr. Colton tell you what he had to do after he rescued me?"

"No, he didn't. Doc said you were taken out of love. He told me any more information had to come from you."

"When Dr. Colton examined me following his removing an RFID tracker from my arm, he told me I'll never have children unless I adopt. I suffered too many kicks to my groin. The 'Doc', as you call him, performed surgery to remove ruptured masses and repair a hernia. Are you picking up what I'm laying down, Mr. Block?"

"Loud and clear, Xander. Would you mind if I ask you something personal?"

"If your questions are too personal, I'll let you know."

"Call me Fred. My question is: Why isn't your voice high-pitched, if you suffered such injuries?"

"I've had shots since I was twelve. My parents arranged for implants after my voice deepened at age thirteen. Those implants made me feel whole again. I'm now happily married and have adopted three wonderful children. Does that answer your question?"

"Yes, but after you went through so much as a boy, how did you manage to become the man you are today?"

"Simon and Lori; without them to guide and support me, the hate in my heart would have grown. I'm afraid I would have hunted down Dragon Society members and killed as many as I could. Simon found my plans to kill Ralph and Kathy in their home by using homemade explosives I learned about in chemistry class. At eighteen, I became a Marine. At nineteen, I volunteered for Recon. I channeled all my hatred into what I considered 'training' to one day destroy those who nearly destroyed me; only I planned to do it legally. I left the Marines and became FBI Special Agent Xander Ward."

"You mentioned Simon and Lori. Tell me about them."

"Simon is an airline pilot. He encouraged me to learn how to fly planes and then helicopters. He bought me a motorcycle, even though mom was against me riding one. I was afraid of everything. It was my mom and dad who challenged me to face my fears. Mother's favorite saying was; *FEAR: False Evidence Appearing Real; challenge your fear and it will disappear.*

"Mom is a real estate agent. She taught me what to look for when buying a house. Together, Simon and Lori taught me how to be human. They showed me how to care about others the way Dr. Colton does, through their love for me. Mr. Block, my parents gave me so much, but they also took a lot away from me. They took my pain, my scathing hatred, and my dirty little secrets. They removed nearly ten years of mistrust, chewed it up, filtered out all the ugly, and then returned the good through love.

"I remember right after I went to live with Simon and Lori, there was a two-week period where I wouldn't take a bath. Dad finally decided enough was enough. He picked me up and took me outside. I thought he was going to throw me in the swimming pool. Wrong! Dad took me to an outside shower. He turned on the water and told me to wash. He stood there and waited. I remember him telling me I was safe. Nobody would ever hurt me again. That shower lasted for over an hour. When it ended I was clean and Dad looked like a drowned rat. Afterwards, he wrapped me in a big brown, soft towel; I was carried to the house. I went to my bedroom alone. Later when mom came to get me for supper, she found me crying. Mom held me until I fell asleep. When I woke up the next morning, I was wearing pajamas.

"To me, my new parents were the best. They never hit me, spanked me, or disciplined me in anger. Oh, they still disciplined me and expected me to do chores. I owe my parents more than anyone can imagine, but I would be dead if Dr. Colton didn't care about a frightened little boy. Truth be told, I envy Kent and Royce; they were blessed by God when Dr. Colton and Nurse Barbara adopted them."

"Dr. Colton told me he helped three boys once. It hurt him to separate the three friends, but they were safer living far from each other. At first I was curious about your true identity. Now I know Xander Ward is your true identity."

"My name was Dyson. When I became an FBI agent, I disclosed all of my past. I asked to work this case. If my friends are alive, I want to find them. I don't know the names they were given. However, Dr. Colton promised to reveal everyone's names."

"How many boys and girls did Dr. Colton help?"

"I only know of five: Royce, Kent, my two friends, and me. The FBI is sure he kidnapped others and killed them when ransom money wasn't paid."

"Do you really think Doc killed little kids?"

"I'm here only because the FBI believes it's true. Otherwise, I'd be investigating a case in California."

"You're waiting for Dr. Colton to slip and admit he killed one of those kids so you can arrest him. What if he never confesses?" Fred Block found himself admiring Xander Ward.

"If Dr. Colton admits killing a child, even accidentally, his wife loses her immunity from prosecution."

Chapter 19

"People call Mr. Fred Block to the stand," Mr. Pizzo called.

"Do you promise to tell the truth, the whole truth, and nothing but the truth?" Mr. Block was asked.

"No, I do not."

"Mr. Block, you've been called to testify in open court. You must take an oath to tell the truth," Judge King instructed.

"The way I see it, Mr. Judge, sir, is, if I swear to tell the truth and then lie, you'll put me in jail."

"Mr. Block, do you know Dr. Colton?" Mr. Pizzo interjected, trying to entrap the man.

"Nope, never heard of Dr. Colton."

"Were you not at Dr. Colton's house last evening for supper and drinks afterwards?"

"Didn't I see you at O'Brien's trying to kiss a man who isn't gay?"

"Mr. Block, you'll either take an oath to–"

"Objection!" Dr. Colton stood and spoke clearly. "Mr. Block is listed as a witness for the defense. Since when is the prosecution allowed to call defense witnesses? Furthermore, Mr. Block clearly stated he will lie if forced to testify."

Judge King watched the jury's reaction as Dr. Colton verbalized his objection. "Mr. Block, will you promise to tell the truth, sir?" Judge King asked.

"No!" Fred Block spoke in a clear voice.

"You may leave, sir," Judge King said. "Mr. Pizzo, do you have any prosecution witnesses?"

"Maurice Kelso," Prosecutor Pizzo replied.

Mr. Kelso entered the courtroom. He was dressed in an ill-fitting suit and ratty second-hand thrift store shoes. He was sworn in and took a seat. Spelling his name made Mr. Kelso feel as if he was the most important witness ever.

"Mr. Kelso, do you know the defendant?" Mr. Pizzo asked.

"Objection! Intentional disregard of court instruction," Dr. Colton protested.

"Sustained," Judge King responded. "Mr. Pizzo, you are found in contempt of court. You're fined one thousand dollars. Should you violate my order one more time, I'll immediately declare a mistrial."

"Yes, it's..." Maurice Kelso began to answer. He wanted to prove he was a good witness.

"Silence," Judge King barked. "When you hear 'objection', you shut your mouth. If I say 'overruled', then you answer. Am I clear?"

"Yes," Maurice replied meekly.

"Ask your next question, Mr. Pizzo. Your witness knows Dr. Colton. You can pay your fine at lunch break."

Ignoring the judge's last words, Mr. Pizzo proceeded: "Mr. Kelso, how do you know Dr. Colton?"

"He was a big shot down in Chi-town. Only doctor who came down there acting high and mighty."

"Do any children live in Chi-town?"

"Only one lived in Chi-town, a girl named Sally."

"Has Dr. Colton ever brought any children to Chi-town?"

"Sure did. I seen him with strange kids all the time."

"Did you see a young boy around five years old with Dr. Colton in Chi-town?"

"Sure did. So did Mary, she said that boy—"

"Objection. Hearsay, Your Honor. Mr. Kelso is testifying for Ms. Mary, who will testify for herself," Dr. Colton said.

"Sustained; let others testify for themselves."

"Who was the boy with Dr. Colton?"

"The only name I know was Marco Rizzoli."

Court Observer Vang flipped his light switch.

Judge King interrupted the questioning. "Mr. Vang, you have a question?"

"I have more than one question," Mr. Vang replied.

"Go ahead," Judge King consented.

"Mr. Kelso, do you understand sign language?" Observer Vang asked, verbally and through sign.

"Yes, I do, sir," Mr. Kelso nearly bragged.

Observer Vang faced Judge King. "Now I would ask Prosecutor Pizzo a question."

"Granted, you may continue," Judge King agreed.

"Why are you signing answers to the witness?"

"Mr. Dill, do you have any questions for Mr. Kelso? Prosecutor Pizzo is now finished with this witness," Judge King said in disgust.

"Yes," Mr. Dill responded. "Nice clothes. How much did Mr. Pizzo pay for you to testify here today?"

"One hundred dollars and my new suit."

"Mr. Kelso, how long have you lived in Chi-town?"

"I quit counting the years," Mr. Kelso squirmed.

"Now, in all honesty, Mr. Kelso, you have seen Dr. Colton only once in Chi-town and that was when you broke a leg. Dr. Colton treated you in Chi-town and no other doctor has been to Chi-town, isn't that correct?" Mr. Dill waited a few seconds. "Your Honor, the witness has lied under oath. I retract my last question with nothing further."

Judge King addressed the witness. "Mr. Kelso, you are finished testifying. You're fined seventy-five dollars. If you can't pay the fine, you can spend a day in jail."

Dr. Colton remained quiet. He knew Maurice would be run out of Chi-town once it was known the man testified in court—for any reason.

"Mr. Pizzo, I expect a written explanation for this debacle on my desk tomorrow morning. You're lucky I'm not asking for your resignation or commencing disbarment proceedings against you."

"Yes, sir," Prosecutor Anthony Pizzo replied. "Mr. Kelso was my last witness available to testify this morning. I have one witness scheduled for after lunch."

"If Mr. Dill and Dr. Colton have no objections, our jurors can retire to the jury room to read Dr. Colton's journals," Judge King offered.

"We have no objections, Your Honor," Counselor Dill responded in agreement.

Observer Vang's light lit up.

"Yes," Judge King acknowledged.

"Open question, Judge King. It's an unusual move and seldom encouraged, however, if Dr. Colton is willing, they could utilize this time to present evidence until the noon recess."

Following a few minutes of private conversation, Mr. Dill addressed the court: "That, Observer Vang, is a suggestion, not a question. However, Dr. Colton is willing to give some testimony at this time. If he…," Mr. Dill hesitated, looking for the right words. "If Dr. Colton says 'Next', we request you ask another question. But keep the skipped questions for later."

"Your Honor, you can't allow that! The def…, you can't allow Dr. Colton to set conditions for testimony," Mr. Pizzo objected.

"I'm not obligated to testify, Mr. Prosecutor."

"The man is right," Judge King agreed. "He's not obligated to answer any question you may have, and you know it. I thought his offer was more than acceptable."

"Fine, I'll go along with Dr. Colton's offer."

Mr. Dill leaned over to Dr. Colton. They whispered a few words before Dr. Colton spoke, "I have a new offer. If you reject it we will understand." Turning to the prosecutor he continued, "Mr. Pizzo removed a few items from my briefcase. We all know it's true, he's chomping at the bit to learn more about what he found and what it means. For example, I had *Arrest Frank Kelly* written on a sheet of paper. Judge Vang and Mr. Pizzo were present when Mr. Kelly was arrested. Frank Kelly is better known as the Black Dragon. His only son ran away and I helped him."

"Are you saying that you kidnapped Frank Kelly's boy?" Mr. Pizzo asked.

"I *did not* say that," Dr. Colton replied. "Those are your words, Mr. Pizzo, not mine. I said 'helped'. I helped the boy run away."

"Let's bring the jury back in and let Dr. Colton explain a few things," Judge King suggested.

"What you're about to hear is true," Dr. Colton told the jury once they'd been re-seated. "Caleb was six years old when I came across him. I was on vacation in Germany. Caleb lived in a hamlet village with his mother, father, and four older siblings. I spent two weeks secretly observing Caleb's family. What I saw sickened me. If you look at our monitor, I'll narrate what you see. My first picture is of Caleb drinking water from a dirty bowl like a dog. You see him on his hands and knees. Next we can clearly see Caleb wearing a dog collar; shock collar, to be precise. Picture number three shows the boy being shocked. Look closely at Caleb's neck in this next picture. Those marks on Caleb's neck are from being shocked until he wet himself."

"Dr. Colton, your pictures are very graphic–maybe too graphic," Judge King interrupted.

"I can tell you about Caleb," Dr. Colton offered. "You can look at the pictures yourself later."

"That sounds reasonable," Judge King said.

"Caleb's father whipped him with a leather leash as the boy whimpered like a dog. Caleb had to lick the hands of his family members whenever they were around him. He ate food scraps which his siblings would dump on the ground and not in the bowl."

"I really do find this hard to believe," Mr. Pizzo said. "It honestly sounds like a tall tale."

Tapping the keys of his computer, Dr. Colton opened a file. "Come up here for a moment, Mr. Pizzo; you'll see I'm telling the truth."

"I must agree with our prosecutor, Dr. Colton," Judge King interjected. "What you say sounds unbelievable."

Moments later, a short video began playing on the courtroom monitor. Everyone present saw everything exactly as described. A boy was seen barking, licking hands, and being abused. The boy's father slapped him; then, using a small tree branch, the man struck his son repeatedly. When the boy begged for mercy, he was kicked.

"Two days after Caleb was slapped and beaten by his father, I slipped the boy some warm food containing a sleeping pill. Once Caleb was asleep, I cut the shock collar off his neck, removed his chain, wrapped him in a blanket and carried him to my rental car. I thought about keeping Caleb in my vacation cabin, but I was the stranger in town. When people found him missing, I knew they would be knocking on my door. My relief came when I went to a flea market-type sale. I bought a nice large trunk and Caleb easily fit inside."

"You put a child inside a trunk? That's barbaric," Mr. Pizzo said in disgust.

"Look at the photographs, Mr. Prosecutor. What happened before I rescued him was barbaric. What I did was humane. Had I not rescued him that day, he would have died." Dr. Colton looked around, meeting each juror's eyes without flinching. "You wonder how I know Caleb would have died? I'm a doctor. I know the specific effects of certain poisons. Caleb was being murdered by his family. I had to get him out of Germany, which was no easy task. We finally ended up in France, where my jet was waiting. I flew home with Caleb wide-awake, healthy, and very happy. Caleb spent his days, before we flew home, running on the beaches of southern France. In these final two photographs, you can see Caleb buried in the sand and in an open-air market before we left France."

"Mr. Colton, how do we know this story of yours is true?" Mr. Pizzo queried.

"I guess that's a fair question," Dr. Colton responded. "If you want confirmation, Mr. Pizzo, I think maybe I should return to my seat."

"Excuse me, Mr. Colton. How can that prove you're telling the truth?" Judge King asked.

"Maybe you would believe Dr. Colton if I took the witness stand," a young man in the audience interjected. "My name is Caleb. I'm the Dog Boy Dr. Colton rescued. He saved my life. What Dr. Colton left out is that I'm now a US citizen, again."

"Will you come forward, please?" Judge King requested.

"Please state and spell your full name for the record."

"Sir, my name is Caleb, C-A-L-E-B. I don't use my real name, nor will I divulge my last name. The people from whom I was rescued are still looking for me. Germany's justice system is not like the United States'. If you want proof that I'm the boy in those photographs, I invite any three people in this room to accompany Dr. Colton and me into the judge's chambers, where I will show you scars that cannot be erased. Dr. Colton provided the Prosecutor in Germany with a full set of photographs, videos, and medical reports so the Dragon Society can be prosecuted. My stepfather kidnapped me and fled to Germany. I refused to do what I was told by my stepfather, a Dragon Master. What Dr. Colton witnessed was my punishment. Dr. Colton said he already–"

Caleb," Dr. Colton interrupted. "This is not the place to disclose that information." Then turning to Judge King he added, "Caleb is one of the witnesses against Frank Kelly for internationally distributing porn and other illicit photographs. Frank Kelly was extradited yesterday and has already been flown to Germany. Caleb flies to Germany tomorrow to testify against Mr. Kelly."

"Mr.–sorry, Caleb, we are…," Judge King stammered as he spoke to Caleb. "What happened…" Judge King paused. "How old are you?"

Caleb smiled. "Truthfully, I'm eighteen years old. And thank you for caring."

"When you turn twenty-one I'll buy you a drink," Judge King said.

"You can buy me a drink today," Caleb countered. "I like double lattes from the coffee shop."

"May I ask a question?" Prosecutor Pizzo asked.

"You just did," joked Caleb. "Sure, ask another."

"Where have you lived all these years?"

Caleb looked at Dr. Colton who nodded. "I lived in France. A friend of Dr. Colton's helped me disappear. I almost screwed the pooch–you know, messed up royally. While I lived in France, I was supposed to be in cancer recovery. But I played soccer and Dr. Colton found out."

"And Dr. Colton wrote, 'You're supposed to have cancer, act like it'," Prosecutor Pizzo offered.

"Yes, sir. He reminded me I was still being hunted. In two weeks I'll testify in front of a French magistrate following my testimony before a German tribunal. Then I go to college. I want to be a doctor."

"Hopefully not like the one on trial here," Mr. Pizzo chimed in.

"You're wrong!" Caleb shot back. "I want to be exactly like Dr. Colton. He rescued me, he saved my life. Dr. Colton would never hurt anybody." Caleb was becoming agitated.

"Breathe, Caleb, breathe," Dr. Colton said firmly. "Calm your breathing, you're losing control," Dr. Colton walked to the witness stand, calmly talking to the eighteen-year-old.

"Your Honor, Caleb isn't a witness in this trial. I move to strike his testimony," Mr. Pizzo said.

"Denied. Mr. Pizzo, you asked questions, offered comments, and were just as curious as I've been in what this young man had to say," Judge King reprimanded the prosecutor. "Caleb's testimony will stand, even though he isn't listed as a defense witness." Turning to his right, Judge King addressed Caleb. "I think Dr. Colton will agree with me when I say, become a doctor but don't be like him or anyone else. Just be yourself."

"Dr. Colton already told me that, sir." Caleb began to cry softly. "It's not fair. I love Dr. Colton. He's the father I never had, and now he is dying of cancer."

"Caleb, you may leave now," Judge King said. "Thank you for sharing your story."

Caleb left the witness stand. He paid no attention to the jurors watching him as he walked away.

"We'll adjourn for lunch. Be back at one-thirty. Mr. Pizzo, I expect you to have a *prosecution* witness ready. Court adjourned." Judge King waited until all jurors were gone. "Mr. Ward, come forward. We have heard testimony of a crime having been committed in Germany. I suggest you make an arrest and get this garbage out of my courtroom. If I never see him again, it'll be too soon."

"I agree," Mr. Pizzo said gleefully. "The people will gladly drop all charges once you make the arrest."

"I guess you got me," Dr. Colton responded, walking over to Judge Vang. "Thank you for staying on as court observer," he said, extending his hand.

As Judge Byron Vang grasped Dr. Colton's hand, he found himself twisted and slammed face-down onto the table. "Byron Vang, you are under arrest. You have no rights, so shut up and don't say a word." Dr. Colton spat.

Agent Xander Ward quickly placed handcuffs on another Dragon Society member in hiding. He read him his Miranda rights. "Anthony, you just dismissed the charges against Dr. Colton," Xander smiled as he escorted Byron Vang out of the courtroom.

"Your Honor, I distinctly said–"

"Relax, Mr. Pizzo," Dr. Colton said unperturbed. "He was jerking your chain."

"Go to lunch, people," Judge King ordered. "We know he's curious, so tell Mr. Pizzo why the young man was here."

"Caleb made a positive identification of Mr. Vang, or should I say, Leo Pardes. His mother was Asian, his father German. Byron, who grew up in Nevada, went to Germany avoiding prosecution for his actions. After I took Caleb from Germany, Byron Vang was disciplined. The Dragon Society cut off Mr. Vang's two ring fingers."

Upon leaving the courtroom, Dr. Colton found Caleb talking to Barbara and joined them. "You did good, youngster. You know where Barbara is going to be living. You'll have a place to live while attending an excellent college or great school."

"There'll always be plenty of food, and all expenses for school will be paid by Richard's medical patent monies," Barbara told Caleb.

"Is anybody in this little party hungry?" Wesley Dill asked. "I've a table reserved at Dumar's."

"I'll let you eat in peace," Caleb offered.

"Kid, you are family," Mr. Dill said. "Dr. Colton saved my life, too. That makes us family. You eat with us."

"You can argue while you eat," Dr. Colton interjected.

As they entered the restaurant, Dr. Colton immediately recognized Dr. Adam Boot; his wife, Janet; and daughter, Ruth. Adam greeted Dr. Colton with a big hug and a whisper in his ear; "We told Ruth she was adopted years ago. I promised her the true story, if you're up to it."

Greetings were made and food ordered. "Ruth is another one of my special people," Dr. Colton told Caleb after the small group had begun eating.

Ruth's hands began flying in speech, "Tell me what happened. Daddy said you helped them adopt me."

"I first met Blanche, your birthmother, two years after you were born. Blanche had a broken arm; you were still in diapers. When Blanche left the clinic, she slapped your head really hard with her good hand. Over the next two years I treated you for a concussion, burns, a broken leg, cuts, and a slice to your right arm. When Blanche brought you into the hospital with a severed tongue, I had you admitted into the hospital and notified the court of your injury. I had a top surgeon in reattaching limbs flown in to do your surgery. He finally said it was better to completely remove your tongue after, and only after, your heart stopped twice during surgery. It broke my heart to see you injured that way. While you were still under medication, I promised that you wouldn't be harmed again."

"Richard, eat some food," Barbara warned. "I don't want you wiped out tonight."

Between bites of food, Dr. Colton continued, "I didn't make much of a plan. Blanche was charged with abuse and you remained hospitalized for two weeks. I knew when you were cleared for discharge, so it was easy to plan your demise. When the ambulance came to take you away, they accidentally took the wrong patient. Nobody realized what happened for over an hour, and by then you were at my house in a safe room. Taking care of you was easy; I enjoyed being around you. Blanche confessed to kicking your chin when you stuck out your tongue. It was my testimony regarding your injuries that sent Blanche to prison. She got pregnant in prison and gave birth two months after being released. The infant was found dead from malnutrition, which sent Blanche back to prison. When you were healthy enough to travel, I took you to a friend I met in med school. Adam and Janet practically begged to adopt you."

"We would have paid good money for you, too. Mother and I wanted you to be our daughter. When Richard said he'd send the adoption papers, we couldn't stop smiling."

Ruth's hands moved with grace, "Mother taught me sign language right away. Father taught me little things about medicine. I learned how to read and was

84

home-schooled with other children who used sign language. Reading was fun, especially reading about herbs. I escaped to other worlds through reading. I'm now a world-renowned herbalist, and I'm only twenty-eight years old."

"That's all good now," Janet interjected. "You learned to swim and we couldn't get you to wear clothes for years unless we were going somewhere."

"I did too wear clothes," Ruth protested.

"You wore swimsuits," Adam Boot retorted.

"I still love to swim. My children are like fish and my husband spends his weekends in our pool."

"You're married?" Barbara blurted out, surprised.

"Yes, I am. Three children and a fabulous husband whom I met in college. Justin invested money in the stock market. He's now a sports agent who has over twenty top professional athletes to represent. When I gave birth to my oldest son, it was quick. I used herbs to help me with the pain and dilation. I did the same thing with my next two babies."

"And she spoils them, to boot," Adam teased.

"You're the one who spoils our grandchildren," Janet corrected.

"It's my job to spoil them."

"So, Dr. Colton saved other kids from being beaten?" Caleb asked. "I thought it was just me and his sons."

"Excuse me, sir," a dark-haired man interrupted the group, "I need Caleb to come with me. The jet is ready for departure."

"Agent Dalton Tucker, meet Dr. Richard Colton and his wife, Barbara," Xander addressed his friend. "I'm guessing Russell Flynn has been arrested."

"Dr. Flynn's body was found an hour ago. According to my information he was executed yakuza-style. They want Caleb and our prisoner gone right away." Caleb rose without saying a word. He stopped next to Dr. Colton. They hugged briefly, and then Caleb walked away.

"He'll be fine, sir," Xander said to Dr. Colton. "Vang has been deemed a terrorist and will be moved out of the country on the same flight. He'll be in a secure holding pod where he'll neither see nor hear anything."

"I'm not worried about Caleb. What he just whispered in my ear bothers me. I need to talk with Sam."

"Tonight soon enough?" Xander asked.

Dr. Colton wrote a quick note to Agent Ward before he began eating again. Xander read the message, then put it in his coat pocket.

While Dr. Colton conversed with Xander Ward, Mr. Dill cut in. "Did you hear about the new law they just passed? Now it's illegal to hang a man with a wooden leg."

"What? Why?" Barbara responded.

"Well, the law now says you have to use a rope." Mr. Dill's humor helped to lighten the mood.

Chapter 20

"Come," Judge King called in response to the knock on his office door.

"A sheriff deputy sent word that Dr. Colton will be a bit late returning from lunch," the bailiff announced.

"Did anybody say *why* he will be late?"

"Something about an accident of some kind."

"Please tell me he was practicing medicine without a license. Go tell my clerk to call the prosecutor's office and tell Mr. Pizzo we'll be delayed an extra thirty minutes for lunch."

Dialing a number, Judge King waited for an answer. "This is Judge King. I need to find out what kind of accident Dr. Richard Colton was involved in, and if he administered first aid."

"Dr. Colton was involved in a traffic accident. He was seen getting into an ambulance with his wife. Both appeared to have suffered injuries. We have reports of multiple fatalities associated with the accident."

"And with whom am I speaking?" Judge King queried.

"I'm Detective Aubrey." Unbeknownst to Judge King, Detective Aubrey was in reality Marshal Marshall.

"Let me know when you hear more. Did Dr. Colton administer medical assistance to people involved in the accident?"

"Not that we're aware of, Your Honor. Is that important?"

Yes, it is. His medical license has been suspended. If he is practicing medicine, then he'll be in jail before he knows what hit him."

Thirty minutes later, Judge King's telephone rang.

"Noah King–talk to me."

"Detective Aubrey said to tell you the answer to your question is no."

"Thank you," Judge King responded.

* * * * *

On Friday afternoon, Judge King entered the courtroom. "Be seated and come to order. Let the record show everyone is present. We're resuming court forty-eight hours after our lunch dismissal on Wednesday. I note Dr. Colton's right arm is in a sling. Does the defense have an explanation for Wednesday's events which caused this delay?"

"Your Honor, we sent word that there was a three-car accident. Dr. Colton's shoulder was dislocated. Mrs. Colton suffered numerous cuts from glass to her upper back and legs. I'm unable to lift my left arm without a lot of pain," Mr. Dill replied curtly.

"Not to mention, but I will anyway," Dr. Colton added. "We weren't allowed to return to court until today due to an ongoing investigation. The young man, Caleb, was killed along with a female driver of another car, who slammed our vehicle after she was broadsided in the intersection while Mr. Dill was turning left. Do you need to hear more, sir?" Dr. Colton didn't attempt to hide his anger.

86

"Mister, your attitude is out of line," Judge King reprimanded.

"My anger is justified, Judge, sir. You treat us as though this delay were our fault, even after you were informed immediately following the accident. We had no say about how long court would be delayed. Plus, if you think I'm out of line, I'm certain I can find a crappier attitude."

"Mr. Colton–" Judge King began.

"Dr. Colton, Your Honor, is still a doctor," Mr. Dill interrupted. "I've personally contacted the American Medical Association. They've stated the man will remain a doctor until he is convicted, *if* he is convicted."

"Mr. Dill, you're out of line. Do not presume to tell me how to address people in my courtroom."

Dr. Colton stood up. "My apologies, Your Honor. Wednesday we were in an accident with fatalities. Now I ask, can we continue this trial? I really need to distract myself so I don't become depressed."

"You're not running this court, sir, apology or no," Judge King admonished. "We will start when I'm ready and satisfied with the reason for Wednesday's delay."

Mr. Dill remained silent, signing against his leg for Dr. Colton to follow his lead.

"So, you've nothing to say, Counselor Dill?"

Dr. Colton typed on his computer keyboard, ignoring Judge King's agitation.

"Your lack of communication with the court leads me to believe you lack respect for my courtroom. For your total disregard for this court, you'll both pay a $1,000 fine."

As Judge King was speaking, the court clerk's telephone light began flashing. "Judge King's courtroom…, Yes, sir, one moment, please." The clerk made a quick hand gesture notifying Judge King he had an important phone call.

"I have to accept a call. When I return, *you* will have an improved attitude. We're now off the record."

"What a tyrannical jerk," one of the jurors murmured as the judge exited and could not hear.

"Who said that?" the bailiff queried. "If I find out who slandered the judge, *you will* be detained."

Unable or unwilling to restrain himself, Xander Ward replied, "Detained for what? Telling the truth? I'll tell your judge he is both a tyrant and a jerk. Look at Mr. Dill and Dr. Colton. They're both injured. What kind of person doesn't recognize that fact?"

"Mr. Ward, you may be a federal agent, but you will show respect in this courtroom," the bailiff ordered.

"Gentlemen, is all of this necessary?" Mr. Pizzo asked.

Within just a few minutes, Judge King returned. "We are back in open court, and we're now on record."

The bailiff stepped over to the court observer's table and typed a message. Judge King, having read it, turned to the courtroom and spoke, "Disparaging remarks in this courtroom are unacceptable. I must ask that all comments or opinions be kept to oneself."

Judge King continued, "Okay, it appears that these proceedings are being monitored. On the phone I was told exactly what someone in here said. In the interest of justice, I'm going to overlook this ugliness and continue Dr. Colton's trial. Mr. Dill and Mr. Pizzo, approach the bench, please." At the bench, Judge King addressed only Mr. Pizzo. "You will address Dr. Colton as 'Doctor' from this point forward. *Do not protest.* I've been informed that you'll do this or face jail time for your past indiscretions. Do you understand?"

"Yes, sir. I don't like it, but I'll do as you say."

"Return to your seats, gentlemen."

When everyone was ready, Judge King addressed the prosecutor, "is your expert witness here?"

"No, sir, she is a no-show."

Bailiff, put out a warrant for Ms. Fangle."

"Your Honor," Mr. Dill stood as he spoke. "By any chance would Ms. Fangle's first name be Sasha?"

"Yes, it is," Mr. Pizzo replied. "Why?"

"Sasha Fangle was killed in the accident we were involved in after lunch Wednesday. She died in my arms," Dr. Colton explained.

"Mr. Pizzo, do you have any other witnesses to question?" Judge King inquired.

"No, sir. Ms. Fangle was my final witness. Prosecution will have to rest, sir."

"Do you mean there are no more expert witnesses who are qualified to testify regarding this case?"

"No, sir. Not on this short notice. Ms. Fangle came from California."

"Very well, Mr. Dill, you may begin presenting your defense."

"We aren't exactly prepared to present our case, Your Honor. Our witnesses aren't scheduled until Monday."

"I suggest you call somebody and get them here within the next ten minutes."

"Judge King, you were willing to allow Mr. Pizzo more time to obtain another witness. Can we have a bit longer, say, maybe until Monday morning?" Dr. Colton inquired.

"You heard me. You now have seven minutes remaining. You'd best stop wasting time–you're running out of it."

"Defense will call Cindy Plante," Dr. Colton responded. "She is outside, and she definitely wants to tell you that you are being a horse's patootie."

"A horse's what?" Judge King snapped.

"Dr. Colton was being polite," responded a young woman, entering the courtroom. "I said you are being a horse's ass. I'm Cindy Plante. You can save your threats and fines. I don't scare easily, and I *will not* donate any of my money to this kangaroo court." Ms. Plante walked to the witness stand. "You can swear me in now."

"Ms. Plante, you'll refrain from using profanity in my courtroom. And I *do not* appreciate your reference. If I fine you, it'll be paid or you *will* go to jail. Do you understand?"

"Sure, I understand. I just don't care. You're an arrogant, self-important, power-hungry man who likes to intimidate people whom you consider to be inferior."

"I beg your pardon, young lady. You'll show proper respect in this courtroom."

"May I swear to tell the truth so we can get past all this petty banter? I have an appointment with my therapist at four this afternoon."

"Why are you in therapy?" Judge King asked harshly.

"Your Honor, I–" Mr. Dill started to protest.

"Let it go, Wesley," Dr. Colton whispered, "She's a big girl."

"Yes, Mr. Dill?" Judge King said.

"Nothing, Your Honor. I was going to suggest Ms. Plante be sworn in, to keep it real."

"Excellent idea. Swear in the witness and let's proceed. Place your hand on the Bible."

"I don't believe in it. I promise to tell the truth. I won't lie no matter what. I hate liars. If the truth hurts, then you have a guilty conscience. Yes! I'll tell the truth, so help me."

"State your name for the record," Judge King instructed.

"Cindy Plante, C-I-N-D-Y P-L-A-N-T-E; please call me Cindy."

"Cindy, why are you in therapy?" Dr. Colton asked. "And, please, start at the beginning."

"I'm dealing with PTSD due to the abuse I suffered as a little girl."

"Can you share this with the court?" Dr. Colton encouraged.

"I was number six in a family of eight. The next youngest is five years older than me. When I was two or three, the physical abuse began. I received whippings, not spankings. I got slapped every day for one reason or another. They called it 'discipline'–I call it 'sport'. Even my siblings slapped me. Everyone else in my family took hot showers; I had to bathe in cold water. My bathwater was always dirty. It had to be, because my brother always bragged about peeing in my bathwater. I can't remember ever having new clothes or even warm ones. I had to wear hand-me-down rags. The only time my rags were cleaned was when I took a bath. I had long filthy hair and I was sick a lot. My first immunization shot was given to me at age seven, after I no longer lived in that home."

"Ms. Plante, do you really expect us to believe this drivel?" Mr. Pizzo questioned.

"Objection, Your Honor. The prosecutor is out of line," Dr. Colton protested. "My witness clearly requested to be addressed as Cindy. Since when is Mr. Pizzo allowed to be disrespectful towards a witness?"

"Your Honor, I address all witnesses by their last name," Prosecutor Pizzo defended.

"Not true, Mr. Pizzo. You asked a question of my son. You said, and I quote: 'Royce, I want to ask you–' And a second time: 'Royce, are you trying to tell this court'."

"I never addressed your son by his first name."

"Dr. Colton not only has a photographic memory, but he remembers things with the same exactness of what he hears. Busted, Mr. Pizzo," Counselor Dill stated.

"One more thing, Your Honor," Dr. Colton interjected. "Cindy Plante is a defense witness. He can question her after the defense is finished, not before."

"Your Honor–"

"Quiet, Mr. Pizzo; objection sustained. Mr. Prosecutor, be more respectful in the future."

"Yes, Your Honor. I retract my question."

"Oh, no you don't." Cindy corrected. "You dare to question my integrity when yours is so soiled you can't see through the crap because you're ten feet below it. I've no reason to make this up. No child would want this to happen to them. And right now, you can believe what you want. I don't care what you think."

"Cindy, I have a copy of your medical records. Will you give me permission to place them into evidence?" Dr. Colton asked politely.

"Go ahead; all it'll do is prove I'm telling the truth."

"Submit medical records of Cindy Plante as Defense Exhibit Number...whatever number it is," Mr. Dill said.

Dr. Colton addressed his witness. "Cindy, how'd you get away from your family?"

"I broke my arm. Actually, one of my brothers broke it. I was six, and he hit me with a baseball bat."

"Why'd he hit you?"

"I told our mother that Roger and his friend were boyfriends. I caught them in Roger's bed."

"How'd breaking your arm help you escape?" Dr. Colton queried.

"It was two nights later when you found me asleep on the floor at the clinic and then you took me away."

"Excuse me," Judge King interrupted. "Did you just say that Dr. Colton kidnapped you?"

"I said 'took'. 'Kidnap' and 'took' mean two different things. Kidnap means to take by force or fraud, to use as a hostage or to exact a ransom. 'Took' is the past tense of 'take', and if you take something you get possession by voluntary action. Dr. Colton took me away from all the pain and abuse. There's no kidnapping involved. I went willingly, and I could've gone back anytime I wanted, but I was free from all the hatred."

Dr. Colton sat down. "Cindy, did Dr. Colton ever hurt you?" Mr. Dill asked.

"Him? No, he's got a heart of gold. Dr. Colton wouldn't hurt anybody. Especially a–"

"Objection; speculation and an opinion," Mr. Pizzo said.

"That's fine; I have no further questions."

90

"Mr. Pizzo, your witness," Judge King said.

"I've no questions, Your Honor," Mr. Pizzo declined sullenly.

"Call your next witness, Mr. Dill," Judge King ordered.

"Defense calls brothers Kent and Royce Colton to the stand."

"Objection, Your Honor," Mr. Pizzo chimed in. "There's no precedent for allowing two witnesses to testify at the same time."

"Judge King," Dr. Colton addressed the bench, "Royce and Kent are identical twins. They'll mostly testify to the same thing with only minor differences. Please allow them to enter so you can see for yourself. They're wearing different sport coats, but identical shirts and ties."

"Objection. What Mr. Colton is arguing is irrelevant. There's no precedent for what he is asking," Mr. Pizzo argued.

"Then let's make one," Mr. Dill suggested.

"I'm going to object, Your Honor," Dr. Colton said softly. "Mr. Pizzo continues to defy this court's order to be respectful."

"Sustained! Mr. Pizzo, you are fined $500 for contempt of court. Dr. Colton will be shown respect in my courtroom. I'm going to allow Dr. Colton's sons to enter. I reserve judgment as to whether they testify together or individually," Judge King stated.

The court bailiff summoned Kent and Royce. Once they were inside and standing in front of the court, Judge King addressed the twins: "Please remove your coats, gentlemen. We'll ask Dr. Boot to hold them for you briefly."

Both young men complied and waited.

"Step forward and state your names for the record."

Taking a few short steps, the twins stopped in front of Dr. Colton and Mr. Dill. Facing the jury, they introduced themselves.

"I'm Royce Adam Colton. I turned twenty-one years of age last month."

"Kent Franklin Colton, a.k.a. KFC. I, too, am twenty-one."

Slight chuckles could be heard from the courtroom upon hearing Kent's initials.

"Okay, Kent is on our jurors' left and Royce is to their right. Dr. Colton, you'll write each of your sons' names on a 3 x 5 card. When you're finished, you'll turn your back so we have the opportunity to rearrange Kent's and Royce's positions."

"Your Honor, it won't matter. We were never able to fool Mom or Dad growing up, sir."

"That's okay, Kent; I'm just testing him."

"It's Royce, sir; I'm Royce."

"Whenever you're ready, Your Honor," Dr. Colton offered, turning his back to Judge King, his sons, and the jury.

Judge King repositioned Kent and Royce to new locations, then addressed the jurors. "So there's no confusion, Royce Colton, raise your right hand."

Royce held up his right hand as instructed.

"All right, now we know who is who," Judge King continued. "Dr. Colton, please turn around and place a name tag upside-down in each twin's hands."

"Your Honor," Mr. Pizzo interrupted. "Can't the man just tell us which of these young men is one or the other?"

"Fine, Doctor, walk over to Royce," Judge King said.

Walking over to Royce, Dr. Colton smiled. "I told you this would happen. This is Royce Adam Colton. And even though I can tell them apart, I know our jurors could easily think someone was playing games if one left the courtroom with his twin walking in afterward."

"Point well presented," Judge King stated. "They may take the stand together. Bailiff, please bring their coats forward. Gentlemen, put your coats on and be seated. Clerk, swear them in, please."

With his adopted twins before him, Dr. Colton spoke. "You've already stated your names for the record, but please give your first names once again for all who don't know you. Then Mr. Dill will ask you questions."

"Kent–I'm wearing a dark blue blazer, sir."

"Royce–This is my favorite black sport coat, sir."

"Please tell us where each of you work, are you married, and are you paid to be here?" Mr. Dill stood in front of the defense table as he spoke. "Please start with Kent."

"Sir, I'm a master chef. I graduated from culinary school at age eighteen. I became a top master chef at nineteen and opened my first restaurant six months ago. I'm single, but am engaged to a very sweet and caring woman who has a son. I'm not being paid to be here, sir." Kent nudged his brother.

"Royce Colton; I'm not at liberty to discuss my job. I work for our government. Married with a child–not paid to be here, sir."

"May we address you by your first names?" Counselor Dill inquired. "I mean, you're both Mr. Colton."

"Yes, sir, first name is acceptable," Royce answered.

"What about your brother?"

"Kent is fine, Mr. Dill, sir," Kent said in affirmation.

"I notice you say 'yes, sir', 'no, sir', and address people as 'sir' when you talk to them. Why is that?"

"Oh, please, Your Honor," Mr. Pizzo interrupted. "Evidently they feared Dr. Colton growing up. Probably still do."

"No, sir, we don't fear our mom or dad," they both said in unison.

"Objection," Mr. Dill said quickly. "Mr. Pizzo is speculating. I don't use 'sir' with strangers, yet these two young men do. The only thing evident is we're witness to respect."

"Excuse me, Judge, sir," Kent replied. "There's only one whom I fear. And it's not my dad. Our parents taught us to show respect by saying 'sir' or 'ma'am' by example".

"It amazes me, Your Honor, ladies and gentlemen of the jury," Royce sighed. "Had I said 'sir' after addressing the court or jury, it would have been a form of insult for whoever was not addressed as 'sir' or 'ma'am'. However, you, sir," Royce nodded toward Mr. Pizzo, "display a sense of insecurity, low self-confidence, and yet you're an extremely arrogant man."

"I beg your pardon," Mr. Pizzo sputtered incredulously.

"Be very careful, Mr. Prosecutor," Judge King cautioned. "I believe we just caught a glimpse of what the young man does for a living."

"No, sir; I'm not a profiler," Royce countered. "And Mr. Pizzo appears to use his position as prosecutor to make disparaging comments."

"Gentlemen, leave Mr. Pizzo alone." Mr. Dill held up his hand to get Royce's attention. "Tell me, did Dr. Colton ever spank or hit you at any time?"

"Hold that thought," Dr. Colton interrupted, motioning to Mr. Dill; the two men spoke quietly.

Turning to face the Colton twins, Mr. Dill continued, "I asked a two-part question. First answer: Did he spank you?"

"No, sir," Kent replied. "Mom and Dad never spanked us."

"They punished us in a different way," Royce answered.

"Did they ever hit you?" Mr. Dill asked.

Both Royce and Kent laughed. "Dad taught us self-defense and how to fight," Royce offered.

"We thought he hit like a girl until we saw him disarm a man who was pointing a gun at our mom one time. Dad never hit us out of anger or for discipline," Kent said.

"Thank you," Mr. Dill acknowledged. "How were you punished?"

"We were grounded. We had to take our bath, put on underwear, and sit on our bed," Royce answered. "Dad told us we had to think about why we were grounded. We didn't get to play, watch TV, listen to the radio, or go outside at night."

"Sir, may I add?" Kent said, seeking permission to speak.

"Proceed," Mr. Dill encouraged.

"We lived in a motorcoach. If I was grounded, I was restricted to my bed. I didn't get to see stuff my family saw. When we stopped for fuel, I had to stay on my bed inside the coach. If they did a black or gray water dump, I couldn't help. That kind of thing made me want to behave. I didn't want my parents to be disappointed in me. That, sir, is how I was punished."

"If you lived in a motorcoach, how did you go to school?"

"Mom and Dad home-schooled us. My brother and I are fluent in French, Latin, German, and Russian. Plus, I'm fluent in Dutch," Royce added.

"Before I get deeper into Kent's and Royce's testimony, I'll ask Mr. Pizzo if he has any questions, while Dr. Colton takes his medicine," Mr. Dill said.

"This is unprecedented; however, I'll allow it," Judge King responded.

"Thank you, Mr. Dill," acknowledged the prosecutor. "Royce, did you learn your 'acid tongue' from your father, Mr. Colton?"

"Objection," Mr. Dill said, jumping to his feet. "Mr. Pizzo is again ignoring court direction when addressing or referencing Dr. Colton. And, Mr. Pizzo has overstepped the line of questioning."

"Sustained on your first point," Judge King responded. "Mr. Pizzo, you have earned yourself a contempt of court fine of one $1,000. Secondly, the witness will answer the question."

"Sir, my dad taught me to tell the truth. I can understand how some people would consider the truth as being caustic because it hurts them so deeply."

"So you were never spanked or whipped by your father?"

"Ted and Myra Binns beat us and whipped us for no real reason. So, the answer to your question is yes. They spanked and whipped us daily."

"Excuse me," Judge King interjected. "I believe Prosecutor Pizzo is referring to Dr. Colton."

"My brother and I have clearly stated that Mom and Dad didn't spank, whip, or hit us in any disciplinary fashion, sir."

"What about birthday spankings?" Mr. Pizzo queried.

"Barbaric," Kent and Royce answered together. "If you love someone, why would you ever hit them?" Kent asked.

"Just answer the question," Judge King admonished.

"Nothing more at this time," Mr. Pizzo conceded.

"Anything more from the defense?" Judge King asked.

"Yes, sir." Turning to the twins, Mr. Dill inquired, "You're adopted, true?"

"Yes, sir."

"Am I correct in assuming you changed your last name when you were adopted?"

"Let me interrupt," Judge King said. "For the sake of my court reporter, please state your name before responding."

"Royce: No, sir; that is incorrect, and yes, sir; we'll say our name before answering. We changed our whole name, not just our last names."

"You said, 'we'. Whom exactly do you mean by 'we'?" Mr. Dill resumed.

"Royce: We, my brother Kent, and me, sir."

"Do you remember your previous names?"

"Kent: Yes, sir; my name was Heath Peter Binns."

"Royce: Sir, my name was Garrett Randall Binns."

"Why'd you change your names?" Mr. Dill asked.

"Your Honor," Mr. Pizzo interrupted, "is this really necessary? These young men were kidnapped by Mr. Colton and his wife. They must've been brainwashed by the Coltons into believing they were adopted."

"Your Honor, may I submit to you these documents as proof of the twins' adoption into our family?" Dr. Colton said calmly.

"Bring them forward," Judge King instructed. "Mr. Pizzo, any further disregard for court instruction shall result in jail time."

"Did Dr. Colton kidnap you boys? I mean as children?" Mr. Dill asked as Dr. Colton handed the adoption papers over to Judge King's clerk.

"Kent: My brother and I were abandoned in the desert and left to die. Mom and Dad saved us."

"Royce: May I get my briefcase, Your Honor? It contains items which can only prove what we say is true."

"Bailiff, please bring Mr. Colton's briefcase forward," Judge King requested. "Or should I say Mr. Royce Colton's briefcase?"

"Thank you, Your Honor." Royce respectfully turned to face Judge King. Opening his briefcase, Royce removed a tablet computer. "Your Honor, on my tablet I have pictures of my brother and myself the day Mom and Dad found us in the desert. May I show them to you, sir?"

"Objection; if Royce or Garrett or whoever this young man may be wants to present evidence, he needs to do it properly," Mr. Pizzo protested.

"Overruled! I'm going to allow Mr. Royce to proceed."

"Question for Kent: Whose idea was it to change your names and why'd you choose Kent Franklin?" Mr. Dill asked as Royce started his tablet.

"Kent: Once we were safe, I started crying. I begged Dr. Colton and his wife not to make me go back to our mother, Myra, and father, Ted Binns. They left us to die in the desert, to die naked, sir." Kent struggled to keep his composure intact. "Dad said we wouldn't return to our parents and he asked us if we liked the names Royce and Kent."

"Royce: I'm ready to show you these pictures, sir."

"Proceed, young man," Judge King instructed.

Royce clicked a button on his tablet and almost instantly an image appeared on a large-screen TV facing the jury.

"Your Honor, would it be okay if Dad narrates these pictures?"

"How do we know these pictures are really you and your brother, and not some other boy or boys?" Mr. Pizzo queried.

"Show the video first, Royce," Dr. Colton suggested.

"Yes, sir. Mr. Prosecutor, you'll see us as five-year-old boys and you'll hear us say each other's name. I warn everyone, we're naked and very sunburnt. Mom took a video of us as we walked up to the motorcoach. You'll hear them talk briefly."

"I'll allow Dr. Colton to narrate the pictures if we get to them." Judge King looked directly at Mr. Pizzo, silencing any objections in advance.

The video was brief, less than three minutes. It showed the twins walking towards Dr. Colton's motorcoach in absolute agony, evidenced by their facial expressions and gait.

"Kent: Every time I was touched, it hurt. The only thing that didn't cause pain was cool water on my skin. I still have two scars on my back from that sunburn. Also, I had nightmares until Ted and Myra Binns were arrested and sent to prison."

"We'll take a fifteen-minute recess. Nobody, Defense or Prosecution, is to speak with our witnesses at this time. I, on the other hand, wish to see Kent and Royce in my chambers. Bailiff, please escort Dr. Boot to my chambers with Mr. Ward and yourself."

Chapter 21

"All rise."

"Be seated and come to order," Judge King commanded. "Before we bring Kent and Royce back, I wish to inform our jurors that I asked the twins if they might allow Dr. Boot to examine them. They agreed, and while they're healthy young men at this time, Dr. Boot assured me the twins suffered abuse as young boys. I showed Royce's video to him, and he was visibly shocked. At my request, he'll be sitting at the court observer table during this testimony. Kent Colton was not lying about having scars on his back from being sunburned."

"Your Honor, I don't doubt the horrible ordeal suffered by the two witnesses, but how can we be certain the abuse wasn't caused by Mr. Colton after he kidnapped those children?" Mr. Pizzo asked.

"I'm going to object, Your Honor," Dr. Colton said. "Mr. Pizzo is casting aspersions upon me. By his remark, he has claimed Royce and Kent have been lying on the witness stand, and he continues to focus on uncharged alleged crimes. Mr. Pizzo is also ignoring specific court instructions in reference to me."

"My apologies to Dr. Colton, Your Honor," Mr. Pizzo snapped.

"Your Honor, Mr. Pizzo offers a superficial apology in appeasement," Mr. Dill interjected.

"Sustained. Mr. Prosecutor, you will kindly show restraint from such remarks in the future. Now, if the bailiff will call Royce and Kent Colton, we shall continue."

Dr. Colton's sons resumed their seats. Each raised his hand and identified himself.

"We are back in court; our witnesses, Kent, and his twin brother, Royce, are reminded they're still under oath to tell the truth," Judge King said. "We watched a short video before our brief recess. Royce asked Dr. Colton to narrate pictures he is presenting. Are you ready to continue with the pictures?"

"Royce: I have another video to present, sir. It shows Dr. Colton treating my brother and me after Ted and Myra didn't return."

"Run the video," Mr. Dill instructed, facing the large television.

"Objection!" Mr. Pizzo exploded loudly.

"Overruled," Judge King responded. "Run your video."

Sounds of empathy for the two little boys being shown could be heard throughout the courtroom. When it ended, one female juror wept openly.

"Royce: Your Honor, is it okay to show the pictures now?"

"Proceed," Judge King said.

Dr. Colton began his narration: "This photo was taken at a park in Grant's Village. Barbara and I were on vacation when we first met Ted and Myra Binns. As promised, my beautiful wife, Barbara, and I took time for ourselves. My wonderful, supportive wife had never been west of Ohio, so we loaded up our motorcoach and headed west. We held no agenda, just wishing to see certain sites.

"Barbara showed me her bucket list of places to see. It surprised me that nothing was in order, so I had the honor of showing my wife her various desires of places to visit. We left Chicago, using the interstates. We took Interstate 93 through South Dakota. I loved Sturgis, all the lovely motorcycles, but our goal was Mount Rushmore. We marveled at the famous sculptures that receive thousands of visitors each year.

"Our next stop was Yellowstone National Park. Barbara and I stayed three days at a nice little place called Grant's Village. We wondered if President Grant visited this place, as it is rumored that our great president passed kidney stones at Grants Pass, Oregon, ergo, its famous name.

"Grant's Village was where we met five-year-old twin boys, Heath and Garrett, and their very difficult parents, Ted and Myra Binns. We met them because they parked their beat-up, garish trailer next to our motorcoach. It turned out that Mr. Binns and his family were traveling as he photographed various sites requested by a magazine that had hired him. Mrs. Binns wrote articles for the same magazine. Our first night in the campground, we were interrupted while eating supper. Mr. Binns was administering a whipping to one of his sons. The man screamed, 'You made me do this! Who made you be so stupid?'

"'Mommy did it, Daddy. She called me a fish,' the boy wailed as his father's belt struck him.

"The noise ended when Mr. Binns took his son away in their vehicle. Our peace and quiet came to an abrupt halt a half an hour later. 'What kind of hook did you put in this boy's ear?' Mr. Binns shouted.

'It was an accident, Ted. I was trying to practice my fly-fishing, but you know I don't have real fly-fishing equipment. I used one of the hooks we bought for steelhead fishing.'

"'And now it's in his ear until we can get it removed,' Mr. Binns chided his wife.

"Having heard enough yelling for one day, I exited the motorcoach and visited our neighbors. 'I may be able to help,' I said, approaching Mr. Binns. 'I'm a doctor. We see this kind of thing quite often.'

"'Do tell,' Mr. Binns replied sarcastically. 'How you going to take that thing out of my son's ear?' The man was definitely ill-educated.

"'I'll pull it out the way it went in, and I won't destroy your hook.'

"'And just how much money do you expect me to pay? We ain't exactly rich,' Ted Binns said.

"'Five dollars for the tetanus shot, unless he's had one recently,' I replied calmly.

"'Go ahead,' Mr. Binns retorted. 'I gotta see this.'

Removing the hook was easily accomplished. Ted paid me five dollars, and his wife went with their son to our motorcoach. Inside our coach, with Mrs. Binns standing outside, I gave Garrett a shot. 'Pull your pants down and bend over. This will sting for a second,' I warned him. 'Pull your shirt up a little.' I noted some angry welts on his buttocks, but those on his back were worse. 'I guess your daddy spanked you, didn't he?'

"Nodding 'yes', Garrett offered, 'With his belt.'

"After Garrett pulled up his elastic banded pants, I sent him out to his mother. 'If you would like, I'll give your other boy a tetanus shot and there is no fee; they both need up-to-date tetanus shots just to be safe.'

"Myra brought Heath to our motorcoach. Heath's backside showed nearly identical marks. My heart went out for those boys. 'Children ought never to be treated like whipping posts. I would sure like to use that belt on Ted Binns' backside,' I told Barbara as we finished our meal. We left Grant's Village looking forward to visiting Yellowstone and Old Faithful. Our time in Yellowstone was pleasant until we once again crossed paths with the Binns family.

"Ted Binns complained to his wife, yelled at his children and acted like a total buffoon. Other visitors intervened on the children's behalf. Back at the motorcoach, we ate lunch and watched as Ted Binns carried one of his sons to their vehicle. It became evident the boy had a twisted ankle. What I found most disturbing was a cut on the child's back. My language stank for a few seconds. 'I thought Chicago had all the pricks that treat kids like shit.'

"'Take a deep breath Richard, the world is full of pricks. We can offer to help,' Barbara proposed.

"'Look, a park ranger is approaching the Binns' car. Let him deal with that family,' I shot back at Barbara.

"As we passed, I heard Ted Binns boldly pronounce, '–glass on the walkway. My son tripped and fell on the glass. He yanked his ankle at the same time.'

"Barbara and I relaxed noticeably once we were away from Ted and Myra Binns."

"Is that when you plotted to kidnap the twins?" Prosecutor Pizzo asked loudly.

"Sustained," Judge King quickly interjected. "Mr. Dill, you don't need to object. Mr. Pizzo, you will apologize for your childish outbreak or face jail time this evening."

"Yes, sir. Dr. Colton, I apologize."

"Dr. Colton," Judge King said, "please continue your narration."

"Yes, Your Honor. We drove to Bozeman, Montana and spent an entire day in blissful relaxation. We stayed on Interstate 90 into Idaho, then into Washington. I wish to point out that Barbara and I enjoyed Spokane, Washington. Spokane to Seattle was a comfortable ride. I enjoyed letting Barbara drive. It gave me an excellent chance to fix my favorite lunch of peanut butter, banana, and strawberry jam for my beautiful wife.

"I previously made reservations for dinner in Seattle at the Space Needle. I didn't tell Barbara of our reservations; it was a surprise. To my horror, I made a huge mistake. I made those reservations for an afternoon the evil Binns parents showed up with their children. The nerve of Ted Binns, bringing his children to lunch. Why do I say that? Both boys had black eyes and if memory serves, Ted Binns showed a swollen split lip. I wished only to sit where they were out of sight.

"'Excuse me,' I said to the waitress. May we sit at a table with a bit more privacy?'

"'Please follow me. I'd much rather assist you people than that gentleman,' our waitress answered.

"'Did you just say gentleman?' Barbara asked.

"'I could get fired if I said what kind of person he really is,' the woman replied. 'My boss told all of the staff here that we're going to have an arrogant jerk and his family here for lunch. I'm just grateful they sat in Valerie's section and not mine.'

"'That man isn't just arrogant, he's...well, maybe we'd best forget them,' Barbara said.

"Our food was absolutely the finest. Our view, which constantly changed due to the rotation, was second to none. I had only one remaining request of our waitress. One I was willing to tip her an additional thirty dollars for fulfilling. 'Please help us leave without having to share the elevator with the Binns family,' I requested. We exited with another couple, a couple who weren't as lucky as my wife and me. They sat two tables away from Ted Binns and family.

"I drove south on Interstate 5 from Seattle in the rain. I chose a rest stop at random. We carefully looked for Ted Binns' trailer. Grateful when they were not in sight, my mood pleasantly improved. We finally managed to avoid Mr. Binns.

"Our fourth meeting with the Binns' family was in Oregon at Crater Lake, the deepest lake in the United States. At 1932 feet at its deepest, Crater Lake is in the crater of Mount Mazama; now an inactive volcano. Rainbow trout and Kokanee salmon are found in Crater Lake. Fishing licenses aren't needed, as it's a national park. The Binns family appeared at the boat rides. The twins were standing beside Mr. Binns, who was looking at the icy-cold lake water, when suddenly both boys were pushed from the boulder into the clear water twenty feet below.

"We shared a boat ride to Wizard Island. Only ten people stayed on the island. My heart ached when Ted Binns forced both boys to swim in the lake again after he failed to catch a fish within a half an hour of trying. Ted Binns spanked–or more accurately whipped–both boys when one of them tore a worm in half and used both halves to feed a large trout. Mr. Binns took the T-shirt off one of his sons before pushing him into the lake. He then forced the other son to jump into the icy-cold water as well."

Dr. Colton had to stop and take a deep breath. "Barbara took these photographs. It hurt both of us to see what these boys were going through." Dr. Colton drank some water, then continued.

"We witnessed Ted Binns make his sons stay neck-deep in the icy cold water. When they were allowed to come back on shore, their parents continued to abuse them. Ted's final act was to make his wife wring the boys' clothing out while they shivered. Barbara and I remained out of sight, sickened at what we observed. How can parents be so cruel to their children?"

"And that's when you decided–"

"Mr. Pizzo, silence," Judge King interrupted. "I don't want to hear your remarks at this time. Look at the expressions on our witnesses' faces. Mr. Pizzo, respect the pain these young men have gone through."

Not allowing the prosecutor to reply, Dr. Colton continued, "I stepped out into the open view of Ted and Myra. They quickly dressed the boys, and then kept to themselves. Back at the boat dock, I spoke with a worker who agreed to take Barbara and me back up the trail, using their small tractor. Yes, it pays to be a doctor at times.

"We informed the authorities in Oregon of the incident at Crater Lake. We left Oregon, taking Interstate 5 south towards Sacramento. Lake Shasta, in northern California, was on Barbara's bucket list. From there we continued south to Sacramento and took Interstate 80 to Reno, Nevada.

"Now I'm shocked: Barbara can gamble! She lost $1,000 in just one hour. I was tempted to insist she stop gambling, but decided she was finally relaxing. Losing money, yet she looked at ease. I was nursing my third beer when an alarm sounded. I paid no attention to the commotion. Instead, I sat at my blackjack table and won an easy $100. I was ahead by $400.

"'Shall we go get something to eat?' Barbara asked.

"'Sure,' I replied. 'I'm ahead by $400. I'll buy lunch.'

"'I started with $2,100 and lost $1,800,' Barbara smirked. 'But I outdid your four hundred. My jackpot just now was $10,000. I put two silver dollars in a slot, and it paid off for me.'

"Me–I smiled from ear to ear. 'You won how much?'

'You mean total, or just on two dollars?' Barbara teased. 'I lost $1,800 in the beginning, but then I came out ahead by $1,300–so in total with what I just won my profit comes out to $11,300.'

"My wife got lucky, and I loved it. I lost our personal bet, which meant I had the privilege of driving south on Highway 395 out of Reno. Our path took us to Lone Pine, California. We were headed to Death Valley; the lowest, hottest, driest place in the United States. We refueled in Lone Pine and decided to remain at a nice, smelly spot called Dirty Socks; an actual place and name. A sulfur spring bubbled out of the ground. It was caught in a large pool and offered visitors hours of hot spring relaxation. When we pulled into Dirty Socks, there were no vehicles visible, but more importantly, no people. I parked our motorcoach, changed clothes, and walked to the hot pool with Barbara.

"An hour after we arrived, Barbara started supper. It was fry-eggs-on-the-sidewalk hot, so I started our motorcoach air-conditioner. I was showering around five o'clock in the afternoon when Barbara screamed, 'OH MY GOD, NO!'

'Two small twin boys came out from the burning desert. They were completely naked and dirty from sweat and dust. Barbara grabbed her camera and began video-recording.

"I had to help both boys step up into our motorcoach. Barbara recorded everything. I watched as Barbara directed the boys to a seat. Being a nurse kicked in for Barbara and she handed each boy a cold bottle of water. I cut off pieces of my steak and left it on my plate.

"'Give them some food, but not too much,' I said. 'I'll go outside and get the coach ready for travel.'

"'Is it safe to bathe them?'

"'Use very little water and your hands, no soap,' I told her. 'A wash cloth will only rub against burned skin.'

"It took me less than twenty minutes to get us ready for the road. I put a cool sheet on the floor after closing the slides, then went to speak with Barbara. 'There's a sheet on the floor for them to sit on for now. For the next eight hours we'll use four cool, wet sheet wraps. Let the boys air dry, and wash the sheets. I'm going to take off, so be careful.'

"Only after we were on Highway 395, headed south, did I begin to relax a bit. There was plenty of traffic, but no sight of Ted and Myra. And this was one time that I *wanted* to see their ugly trailer. Barbara, along with two sunburned, black-haired, blue-eyed boys joined me up front about an hour after leaving Dirty Socks.

"'They may not like the taste, but I want each of them to drink about four ounces of wine. It will relax them and make their sunburns more bearable. Plus, they'll sleep easier. We'll buy them clothing later. Keep watch for that ugly trailer, too. We can stop in one of the towns ahead of us.'

"I turned off Highway 395 when we saw a sign indicating the town of Ridgecrest was five miles away. The land around this area was barren. I was surprised to see a thriving community off to our left. You can only imagine my sense of relief when we found a super-store. I spent nearly forty-five minutes finding clothes and other items we would need."

Dr. Colton paused. "I can stop this information if you wish," he told Judge King.

"No, please continue. I find your narration very interesting." Judge King responded.

Dr. Colton continued, "I bought plastic sheeting for use on the motorcoach sofa bed where the boys would sleep. When I returned to the motorcoach, a city police officer was standing outside talking to Barbara.

"'Is there something wrong?' I asked innocently.

"'The officer noticed a water drip under the motorcoach,' Barbara informed me.

"'That's just condensation from the air conditioner. It's the same as your cruiser, Officer,' I offered. 'Only our motorcoach is larger so we drip more than your vehicle.'

"'What are you?' the officer retorted. 'Some sort of know-it-all mechanic?'

"'No, sir,' I replied politely. 'We're on vacation. I didn't know it was illegal for my air conditioner to wet the ground.'

"'You know, I was willing to give you a warning and have you get it fixed before leaving town. Now you're getting a ticket for pollution. Any more sass and I'll arrest you for soil pollution as well.'

"When it happened, I didn't think about being licensed in California; I just reacted. A woman, exiting the store with a cart full of food, didn't look before stepping out into the path of a car whose driver was distracted by others inside the vehicle.

"'Excuse me,' I said quickly. 'Call for an ambulance. Then call your hospital; they'll need x-rays. She has a broken leg, and I see abrasions on the side of her face.'

"'Wait a second,' the officer ordered. His command fell on deaf ears. 'Who the hell do you think you are?'

"'My name is Dr. Richard Colton. We all just witnessed that woman being hit by a car. She's seriously injured. Stop behaving like a child and do your job. I don't mean to be disrespectful, but that woman needs immediate medical attention and I intend to help her.'

"I didn't wait to see what the officer would do next. I put my purchases in our motorcoach, saw the twins were sleeping, and then went for my medical bag. Barbara was already attending the woman when I arrived. The woman's leg bled profusely and her breathing was labored as shock set in. When the ambulance arrived, I identified myself and advised them to start an IV. I gave the attendants all of the information they needed to know.

"When everyone had left, I found the officer. 'I'll have one of your local mechanics check the motorcoach air conditioner drain so we don't have any more pollution.'

"'Don't sweat it,' he responded. 'I checked with my sergeant, who said air conditioner runoff is acceptable. It's the radiator overflow that pollutes. I want to thank you for your help. Not many people are willing to risk themselves that way.'

"Realizing I was very tired, I inquired, 'Would it be alright to get some sleep here in the parking lot before we leave?'

"'You folks don't appear to be vagrants, so I think it'll be alright for a few hours.'

"The officer left, and Barbara went shopping to relax. I put plastic under two moving blanket pads covering the sofa bed cushions.

"'Who're you?' I asked, teasing the boys when they awoke in pain. It was then that I knew: they could never return to Ted and Myra. I decided we had to give them new names. I changed their names to Kent and Royce.

"'Kent and Royce,' I said to the twins. 'Those are the names I'd give you if I were your daddy.' I gently rubbed aloe mixed with coconut cream and rubbing alcohol on the boys' sunburns. Barbara returned while I was attending to the twins. By the time I'd finished medical treatment, my thoughtful wife had made macaroni and cheese and had dinner ready and on the table for all of us.

"'I heard you gave those two little guys new names,' Barbara mentioned as she ate.

"Defending myself, I responded, 'I told the boys I would name them Kent and Royce if I were their daddy. They liked it and chose which name they wanted. Kent wants Franklin for his middle name, and Royce likes Adam for a middle name.'

"'That means we call them by new names,' Barbara stated with conviction. This led to a chant of Kent and Royce for over thirty minutes.

102

"We left Ridgecrest after midnight. I checked our road maps for an Arizona town and headed out. Barbara and I discussed changes to make with Kent and Royce. We needed to alter their appearances, not to hide them, but to boost their small self-esteems. Barbara gave them crew cuts. I removed a mole or two, did minor surgery on both boys, and had a clinic in Victorville give them immunization shots. The twins adapted to their new names, Kent and Royce, with ease. We let them wear next to nothing all day as we traveled. This was easier on their little sunburned bodies, which by now had blistered.

"In Arizona, I traded in my $489,000 motorcoach and special-ordered a new one, which we'd take possession of in Indiana. I rented a small, class-C coach for the trip to Indiana, which took another six weeks. Our new coach was painted identical to the old one. I ordered it this way to keep nosey neighbors from asking a lot of questions. The new coach had bunks for the boys, a half-bath for them, and a larger dinette to seat all four of us. In addition it included a washer/dryer so laundry could be done inside the motorcoach. Barbara was pleased with a larger refrigerator, a full-size oven, and a dishwasher. The new motorcoach cost $830,000, including our old one, but it was by far a better arrangement.

"I reached out to a federal attorney and disclosed how the twins came to live with us. My main concern then became reaching home safely and adopting the twins. Kent and Royce were legally adopted four months later in federal court," Dr. Colton said, ending his narration.

"Are there any questions for the twins or myself?" Dr. Colton inquired.

"Kent, you said there is only one you fear; who do you fear?" Mr. Pizzo asked.

"It is *whom*, sir. And the one I fear is God."

"Royce, you stated that you're not a profiler. Exactly what is your job?"

"I'm an analyst. That's all I can disclose, sir."

"Kent, who taught you to speak so many different languages?"

"My mom and dad, sir."

Mr. Pizzo peered at his notes. "Royce, when did you first learn you were adopted?"

"When Dad brought my adoption papers home, sir."

"Royce, do you remember Ted or Myra Binns?"

"Yes, sir, and I'm glad they're not a part of my life. They'll never meet my wife or children. Ted and Myra are evil."

"Kent, how do you feel about your real parents?" Mr. Pizzo asked, looking down.

"Sir, my real parents are Richard and Barbara Colton. They raised me, protected me, and most importantly, they loved me. Ted Binns merely put his seed inside Myra. Neither of them gave half a squat about us."

"Dr. Colton, how many interactions did you have with Ted and Myra Binns before you kidnapped–excuse me, scratch 'kidnapped'–before you adopted their children?"

"Kent: "Mr. Pizzo, sir, my brother and I told you Ted and Myra left us for dead."

Dr. Colton chimed in: "My interactions with the Binns took place in the locations I previously disclosed. When we left Oregon, I was glad Ted and Myra were far away. In California the twins came out of the desert nearly dead. Had either Ted or Myra appeared, I would've lied and told them we had not seen the twins."

"Dr. Colton, what changes did you perform on Kent and his brother Royce?"

"They each had a mole on their right shoulder, which I removed." Dr. Colton stopped, turned to Kent and whispered, "They don't have to know, son."

"We don't have to know what, Doctor?" Judge King asked.

"It's okay, Dad. You can tell them," Kent responded.

"I performed a double orchiectomy on Kent. Myra kicked him repeatedly before leaving him to die in the desert. I also removed warts from their hands."

"What kind of therapy have the twins received?" Mr. Pizzo queried. "With that severity of abuse, surely you saw fit to have them see a psychologist?"

"That, sir, is privileged information. I refuse to violate their rights under HIPAA laws."

"Kent, what's the worst thing you can say about your dad?"

"He wouldn't give me the motorcoach. No! Scratch that, sir. He made Royce and me pay for our flying lessons. And he refused to cosign a loan for my car."

Every person in the courtroom chuckled.

"Which one of you had the fish hook in his ear?"

"Objection! Irrelevant," Mr. Dill interjected.

"Your Honor, both boys had their ears pierced around age ten," Dr. Colton volunteered.

"Sustained." Judge King responded.

"Dr. Colton never yelled at you when you were young?" Mr. Pizzo asked.

"Royce: Sir, I promise Dad got mad. Even Mom got mad, but neither of them yelled at Kent or me. Our parents taught us to never let our anger control us."

"Why are you testifying today?"

"Royce: Sir, I received a summons from Mr. Dill and I'd do anything for my parents."

"Does that include lying in court and perjuring yourself?"

"Royce: Sir, you might lie in court—"

"Objection, Your Honor. Please instruct the witness to answer the question."

"No! I won't lie in court, sir," Royce responded clearly angered, yet maintaining control of his voice. "You lie, sir; I don't."

"Your Honor," Dr. Colton interrupted. "Mr. Pizzo has consistently disregarded orders by the court regarding witnesses on my behalf. I object to his behavior and his allegations."

"Sustained. Mr. Pizzo, I will not tolerate this any further. You may expect—no you *shall* make plans to spend this evening in jail."

"Your Honor, I merely asked a question," Mr. Pizzo defended.

"Do you have any further questions, Mr. Pizzo?" Judge King asked, ignoring the prosecutor's justification.

"Nothing further," Mr. Pizzo stated.

104

"You may step down. Mr. Dill you will have another witness ready for tomorrow morning. We'll reconvene at nine o'clock sharp." Judge King leaned back as he spoke.

"Yes, sir, Your Honor. Our next witness is ready."

"I give everybody my usual admonitions not to talk about this case. Court adjourned until Monday morning at 9 o'clock. Mr. Pizzo, you'll report to the jail immediately for your overnight stay. My clerk will accept payment of all court-assessed fines or you will spend more time in jail."

"Your Honor," Dr. Colton interrupted. "May I offer a possible alternative to Mr. Pizzo spending the night in jail? Tonight there is a meal for the homeless in Chi-town. Granted, community service isn't jail, but for some people, community service is worse than jail."

"Mr. Pizzo, your fines will remain as given. Your jail time is commuted to five days of community service; begin tonight at the Chi-town soup kitchen," Judge King ordered without hesitation. "Don't be late!"

Chapter 22

As they exited the courtroom, Dr. Colton observed a young adult male watching him. "Sam– Judge Holt, do you have a moment?" Dr. Colton asked.

"For you, yes," Judge Holt replied.

"Barbara wants me to invite you, meaning the Holt family to dinner tonight. She fixed lasagna. Dessert is a flaky French pastry."

"That would be fine. I'll call Sandra and ask if tonight is okay with her."

"Drinks are whenever you arrive, with dinner at six. Wesley and his wife will be there."

"Don't forget me," Xander Ward quipped.

"Let me make a phone call," Mr. Holt said. "Be right back."

"Dr. Colton, I heard what you said in court. Royce and Kent are lucky guys," the newcomer said.

"Barbara and I definitely love the boys. They went through hell before we adopted them."

"I'm glad my dad brought me to court today," Evan Holt said, identifying himself.

"Richard," Sam Holt interrupted. "Sandra is waiting for Evan and me at home. We'll see you at five-thirty, if not a bit sooner. We told Evan you helped us adopt him. He's known since he was ten years old. Maybe you can answer a few of his questions."

"We can talk when you come to the house. You deserve answers. I'll tell Mrs. Colton you are coming with your mom and dad."

At six-thirty that evening, Evan Holt sat on a chair across from Dr. Colton.

"Is it true you helped me get adopted?"

"Yes, it's true, Evan. I called your dad and asked if they were interested in adopting a five-year-old boy."

"What happened to my biological parents?"

"Your birth parents had problems. Do you want to hear how you came to be adopted?"

"Yes, please," Evan replied.

"We, too, would finally like to hear Evan's entire story," Sam Holt confessed.

"Your story begins with Nurse Barbara becoming my wife. I returned home from vacation in Europe and went back to work in the clinic. Barbara helped me treat three boys who were being abused by their parents and other adults."

Xander Ward held up a hand. "I was one of those boys."

"Barbara and I dated for over four months before we became serious. One year after our first date, I invited Barbara out to dinner. I proposed, she said 'yes' and we were married fourteen months later. We'd been married six months when Barbara entered my study as I worked filling out reports. Walking around behind me, she wrapped her arms around my neck.

"'My love, what has made you so upset? Please do not say everything is fine. I haven't seen you this agitated since you asked me to watch those three boys who disappeared.'

"I told her, 'What I'm worried about has nothing to do with those three boys.'

"'Who is Axel Banner?' she asked, seeing the name on my computer monitor.

"'He's a four-year-old boy who keeps coming into the clinic. His parents claim he's accident-prone, but their explanations are ludicrous at best.'

"'What happened to him?' Barbara asked.

"'Two months ago, his mother brought him to the clinic. His groin was swollen. Mrs. Banner said her son ran into a chain-link fence post. What I believe is that someone kicked or hit him repeatedly. When I first met the boy, he had a blue line on his arm. Today he had a faded DKT henna tattoo on his right arm.'

"'Why was he brought in today?' Barbara asked, walking around to the front of my desk.

"'I treated him for a dog bite on his side,' I answered.

"'That doesn't sound abusive to me,' Barbara said.

I explained: 'Tony Banner, the father, said Axel was running away from the dog, but the bite marks didn't match Mr. Banner's description of how his son was bitten. Unless the dog was upside down when it bit the boy, Mr. Banner's description just doesn't make sense. That's what has me stalled. I can't complete my report because this simply couldn't happen the way he claims. Professionally, I'd look like a buffoon if I filed this prevarication.'

"'Richard, do you know what DKT means?' she asked, hesitantly.

"'No, I'm sorry; I don't,' I lied.

"'I once spent an entire day with three very talkative boys,' Barbara informed me. 'They all started as a DKT; Dragon Kid Trainee. They told me what happened to them as Dragon Kids and why they ran away. My God, Richard, those boys were ten years old. This boy is only four. He's facing a lifetime of hell. I don't know if you helped those boys escape the Dragon Society, but I really hope you did.'

"'What could I do? Those boys were runaways.'

"'You fed them, you gave them clothes, regardless of what you say, that, by itself, is a lot more than what other people would've done,' Barbara argued.

"'I'm just amazed that a well-known and highly-respected professor could turn his back to the abuse his son has been through, let alone be a part of that abuse,' I stated.

"'Richard, the Banners used to take their son to Loyola General, but they stopped entirely last year. If you tell them you can no longer treat their son, they'll have to take him to Methodist,' Barbara reasoned.

"'I fail to see how sending them to Methodist will solve anything. Next time that child gets hurt, he could die.'

"She went on to explain: 'Methodist is small, and they'll contact past treatment providers for a history, which they are obligated to report to state police. But, best of all, no cameras because of their budget.'

"'Exactly what are you suggesting?' I asked, letting it be her idea.

"'If he isn't in their home, he can't be abused.'

'Did those boys who talked a lot say anything about how the sheriff knew they'd been in Chi-town?'

"'The dark-haired boy said they had RFID locator chips under their skin,' she recalled. 'He said the sheriff would find them using those chips.'

"Looking into my devoted wife's eyes. 'I love you, Barbara, but I haven't been exactly honest with you about my past.'

"I spent the next two hours telling my wife about the children I had already rescued. I explained how Mario Rizzoli had killed my first wife and son. I also told her how I planted evidence against Mario Rizzoli for the disappearance of Benjamin Beam, whom I rescued before Barbara became my wife. When I finished baring my soul, I added, 'I'll understand if you turn me in to the police. I'm not ashamed of what I've done. At least I know six children are safe from harm.'

"'Then let's make it seven. I want to help,' Barbara offered compassionately, without hesitation.

"'We do this my way,' I said firmly. 'No arguments and no surprises. We discuss everything. If anything goes wrong I take all the blame. Agreed?'

"'Agreed,' Barbara replied. 'What do we do first?'

"'I file my report stating I believe the Banner boy is being physically abused,' I strategized aloud. 'The next time they bring their son in for medical attention, I confront them, decline to be involved in a cover-up, and suggest they take the boy to Methodist.'

"'What can I do to help?'

"'Learn to drive the motorcoach. I think we need to take a few days and visit Geneva…You know, Geneva, Ohio. I know a judge whose little boy was killed. I called Sam from the lobby of Rizzoli Enterprises this afternoon, before I came home. Sam hates anybody who abuses their child. He wants me to call if the boy is put up for adoption. I went on to explain how I'm able to provide adoption papers which are foolproof. And it's Rizzoli Enterprises who provide the paperwork.'

Continuing his story, Dr. Colton said, "It had been quite some time since the last child had been rescued, so I explained that the Banner boy's parents are abusive. They have money, and they need to pay for everything they've done to Axel.

"I told Barbara, 'I'll have to work at the hospital for a few nights, so I can restock a couple of items we'll need to find and remove Axel's tracker. Also, you need to build extra hours in exchange for time off.'

"'I have access to all of the hospital, so if you give me a list of what you need, I can get it without signing for it,' Barbara explained.

"'No!', I shot back. 'I *want* to sign for the items—for an alibi in case something goes wrong. When the boy goes missing, he's going to need a few toys, a stuffed animal, and an open potty chair he can use by himself.'

"'Who's going to wipe his bottom?' Barbara asked out of concern.

"'Nobody; you can't go to him every five minutes. He's going to cry, but we have to be strong. We live in a gated community, so if anyone comes here we'll have a short warning, hopefully. And the boy *cannot* see my face, because he could recognize me.'

"'He doesn't know me,' Barbara responded. 'I can check on him.'

"'We'll take turns. He's going to be with us for two to three weeks. We *do not* change our daily routine for any reason. It'll be hard for him during the day, but he'll live.'"

Chapter 23

"I didn't wait for the Banners to bring their son into the clinic again. I went to a used truck rental sales lot and paid cash for a brownish yellow van. Using an old abandoned warehouse, I attached old lead-lined x-ray covers to the van's inside. I knew Axel would have a tracking device somewhere on his body, and the small newly-equipped van was the only safe place to hide the boy.

"I did my due diligence, found the Banner home, then made my preparations. Twenty-three miles outside the city, at a campground, I parked our motorcoach. Barbara arrived forty-five minutes later in her BMW. I reminded her to be careful and we returned to the motorcoach daily.

"Axel Banner was at the park with his babysitter, twenty-year-old Debra Jones, an active member of the Dragon Society. The boy played in the park water fountain under Debra's watchful eye. As she had done every day for the past week, Debra took Axel into the park's female restroom. I prepared a syringe to use on Debra. Once she was asleep, I could make it appear as though she had assisted in Axel's disappearance.

"When I entered the restroom ahead of Barbara, Axel's hands were over his head, waiting for his shirt to be removed. Debra Jones turned in time to see Richard Nixon push a needle into her side. She tried to remove Nixon's face, only to have her arms pinned behind her by Frankenstein. I was grateful for our latex masks. They kept my face from being scratched and scarred by Debra's long fingernails.

"Axel was given a sedative and placed in Debra's car. She and Axel were driven out to where Marco Rizzoli's body was alleged to have been incinerated on Gibson Road. A short section of chain link fence was attached to the van's back bumper. This was to help eliminate any tire tracks. Any footprints found were nothing more than two sets of size-thirteen Converse shoes, valued at twenty-four dollars a pair. My foot size is ten.

"Axel slept until nearly midnight. The tracking device was easily found in his left leg. Once it was out of his body, I dropped it inside Debra's car door. Drops of Axel's blood were smeared in places which would indicate he had tried to escape his captor. Blood was on Debra's passenger door, front right fender, and bumper.

"Barbara drove the van with Axel sleeping behind her. I took charge of Debra's car, taking it and her to yet another location. We moved Axel to a safe place. When all of my misdirection was finished, I took the van to a scrap yard where a former resident of Chi-town put the van through a shredder. In less than twenty minutes, the van no longer existed.

"Axel Banner slept in a warm bed, fifteen feet below ground. His clothing drifted toward the city sewage reclamation plant. His hair had been cut short in my guest-bathroom tub. All evidence of Axel's presence washed down the drain with the dirt and grime. All of our neighbors were now used to seeing Barbara driving the motorcoach. She was able to put fuel in it once Axel was safely hidden.

110

"I called Sam from a payphone downtown. 'You can take custody of your son, Evan, in two weeks. If you're not at Colorado and Fifth in Convention City on the fifteenth at noon the adoption will be canceled. Look for a short, red-haired boy dressed in green. Remember, Mr. Holt, you have two weeks.' The message took less than twenty seconds.

"The day Axel disappeared, Professor Banner received a note among papers he was to critique for his students. Mr. Banner didn't review the papers until he was at home waiting for his wife and son to arrive.

The note read: *Your son's safety will cost five hundred thousand dollars. You will put the money in an army duffle bag, then fly out over Lake Michigan following the coordinates provided. You'll depart Chicago Midway Airport at exactly 4:00 p.m. You are to fly and maintain 110 knots following the coastline south toward Indiana Dunes National Lake Shore, remaining outside O'Hare's Class B airspace. Once south of the 30 mile mode C/ADS-B radius you will turn your transponder off and descend to 1600 ft MSL. At precisely 4:40 p.m. you will toss out the duffle while parallel to the Indiana Dunes National Lake Shore. Once you have done this you will turn due north, increase speed by ten knots and return home. If you fail to follow these instructions your son will go swimming in chains and you will lose your standing with your twisted Dragon Society friends. Trust me, Debra was very helpful in this endeavor. I'm watching.*

"A previously hidden transmitter inside the Banner home revealed the professor wasted no time in seeking the help of fellow Dragon Society members. 'I believe someone is playing games. My son's tracker has been located in the same place as hers. They are presently at the bowling alley.'

"Thirty-two minutes later, Mr. Tony Banner received news that his son was missing, and that Debra Jones kept professing her ignorance of how she came to be at her present location. She could not explain the money found beneath her driver's seat. When a train ticket was discovered, she denied it being hers.

"It was later disclosed by a rescuee that; Patricia Banner felt nothing for Axel except contempt. She held him responsible for his own disappearance. Once he was back in her care, she would sell him for a snuff video. His last use on earth would be to die for money, and she would be a Dragon Society heroine.

"Tony Banner followed all instructions given to him, including those given by the newly-elected Sheriff, Frank Kelly, who shoved the army duffle bag out of the plane.

"'We'll get these bastards,' Sheriff Frank promised. 'I put a tracker inside your duffle bag. We'll find them, Tony. This has to be the same scum who stole our other Dragon Kids.'

"When the men made their drop, Barbara, a twelve-year PADI-certified master diver, was less than thirty yards away from where the duffle bag splashed down. She quickly attached a five-pound weight to the bag, adjusting her buoyancy control vest as she and the money sank. At fifteen feet below the surface, she began putting money into another bag. Having received instructions to be cautious, Barbara felt the hidden tracker amongst a bundle of money. Ten minutes later, she finished her task with only half her air tanks exhausted.

111

"As planned, Barbara allowed the original bag, with the tracking device inside, to sink, leaving the five-pound lead weight attached. She swam to a depth of ten feet in a southwesterly direction. I sat on the deck of my new enclosed party boat. Since anchoring I'd caught seven fish. Other fishermen trolled by and a couple of boats dropped anchor well away from me to catch fish for themselves.

"Barbara, being a veteran scuba diver, conserved her air. My flashing light beneath the houseboat easily caught her attention. I landed fish number eight, when I heard scraping below the houseboat. Going inside, I lifted a three-foot square trapdoor, which I had ordered installed for winter fishing. I passed a rope with a clip to Barbara. 'Hand me the money and hang your gear. Then I'll help you up and you can get changed,' I told her.

"Barbara made her presence aboard our party-houseboat known when she reeled in a nice-sized fish, shrieking and acting as though she had caught her very first fish ever. I moved the money one more time to my large, elaborate tackle box. Three cinder blocks, along with numerous slices which Barbara had made using her dive knife, allowed the second bag to sink quickly into the murky depths.

"'Shall we barbecue hot dogs and offer to share with some of our fellow fishermen?' Barbara asked.

"'Hot dogs, soda, and beer!' I responded.

"'Anybody want a beer?' Barbara shouted to the other boaters.

"Three of the outlying boats came close enough to receive food and drink from us. Barbara cooked more hot dogs than needed. She prepared a large fish, removing even the smallest of bones.

"As a group, our small huddle of boats left the area. I hauled Barbara's scuba gear on board. Our new friends helped us trailer the boat, thanking Barbara for sharing our food. We stopped at a flushing station to rinse lake water from the boat engine. Barbara used the station pressure-washer to clean the deck, pontoons and trailer. She passed out more beer to men who were nearby.

"'You folks have any luck today?' a game warden asked.

"'We caught nine,' I offered.

'Only took all day, too,' a gentleman, who accepted food and drink from us said.

"'I got a top-of-the-line fish finder on board,' I explained. 'Without that thingy, all I catch is water.'

"Everyone laughed at my joke. We were cleared to leave once our boat had been cleaned, flushed out, sewage emptied, and secured to the trailer. At home, I watched Axel Banner eat hot dogs and fish. I removed all the fish bones before giving him anything to eat.

"'Can I stay here?' Axel asked. 'Mommy will be mad. I no want a spanking.'

"'Drink your milk, then you can play,' I told him. 'I'll come back when it is time for bed.'

'Yes, sir,' Axel said, looking at President Nixon.

"The next morning, I performed minor surgery on Axel to remove a birthmark on his lower left back. I removed a small webbing between thumb and forefinger

112

on the boy's right hand, and a mole on his chest. This was the day he went from being Axel Banner to becoming Evan Holt. All identifying marks were gone from his body. It was amazing to watch Evan eat, play, and become a happy boy for a change. He especially liked chicken, burgers, fries, and of all things–peas.

"Barbara, in disguise, made a bubble bath for Evan one night and let him blow bubbles from a bottle of bubble soap she brought home from work. On another night, she gave him a spray tan from a can, hoping to alter his appearance just a bit more.

"One afternoon, I helped Evan dress in underwear, pants, shirt and shoes. When we finished, he ate a snack. I carried him into our motorcoach and put him in a soft bed of blankets beneath our king-sized bed. Barbara left the house, driving the coach. I drove to the hospital shortly after Barbara departed. Both of us made our presence known when we drove away from the hospital in the motorcoach. It was four in the morning, while Barbara was driving when we heard Evan crying.

"'I'll bring him up here with us,' I said. 'We're nearly alone this time of night.'

"'He needs to be fed,' Barbara replied. 'If I pull off the road we can trade places.'

"'Okay, pull over. Remember, wear your mask and put a seat belt on him at the table. I made peanut butter-and-honey sandwiches for him before we left home.' Evan sat quietly as he ate.

"Anticipating the Holt's eagerness to meet their new son, we stationed Axel on the street corner fifteen-minutes ahead of schedule. Barbara and I entered a cafe across the street, and took a table in front of a window where we could watch the boy unobserved. Sam and his wife, Sandra, arrived at the location indicated ten minutes early. They were surprised when they saw the boy waiting patiently. Sam took an envelope from the boy; inside was a note, birth certificate and adoption papers.

"The note was short and read: *Hi, I am your son, Evan Holt. If you do not want me, leave so I am not hurt by people who do not love me. I am five years old. Please do not hurt me.*

"Sandra then took Evan's hand. 'What's your name, honey?' she asked as she held him close, tears beginning to glisten in her eyes.

"'Note says it's Evan,' Sam said. 'Evan is our adopted son. It appears as though some benevolent people decided to let Evan have a new life and new name.'

"That's how Evan was taken out of love," Dr. Colton confessed. "If you decide to be angry, then direct your anger at me. The fewer people who knew, the safer Evan was, not to mention I was safer as well."

"Dr. Colton, how can I be mad at you?" Sandra Holt interjected. "You healed my broken heart by bringing a fantastic boy to our home. I was clinically depressed until Evan came to live with us."

Evan lifted his arm, a needlepoint-thin line barely showed. He remembered the star on his leg. "I think the only thing I'm angry about is that you wore masks.

But at least now I understand." A tear formed in Evan's eye. "Maybe it's a blessing that I don't remember anything but those stupid masks. What I do remember is that my childhood was better than anyone can imagine," Evan said.

"My confession:" Sam Holt began. "I've kept Evan's origin a secret all these years. If I had told anyone it would've only endangered Evan. I love Evan; he's our son. Until recently we didn't know who, but thanks to a woman who had an operation a couple of years after Evan came to us, we learned the Dragons were looking for him. Dr. Colton was the surgeon who performed her operation. It turned out the woman talked while under anesthesia. She also answered questions revealing a plot to find the person or persons responsible for Dragon Society children gone missing. All the children were being sought. When found, they would be sacrificed in Dragon Society snuff films."

"Who was looking for Evan?" Barbara inquired.

"Judge Vang and many others," Dr. Colton replied. "I heard the Dragon Society seekers' names, and when Caleb testified, Judge Vang sent messages to other Dragon members. So far, we've arrested Vang and one other."

"How many Dragon people are out there?" Evan asked.

"One is too many," his father answered.

"Caleb recognized one of the people who abused him in Germany," Dr. Colton informed the group.

"Who? Who did he recognize?" Judge Holt requested.

"Juror Number Eleven, Macy Turnock. I suggested we leave her on the jury to smoke out other Dragon Society seekers and members."

"Well, they managed to kill Caleb," Judge Holt lamented.

"He wasn't in the car when we were hit. And we suffered only minor injuries," Dr. Colton responded.

"Okay, Doc," Mr. Dill laughed. "Now you're telling fairy tales. But you outright lied in court."

"Fine, they think Caleb is dead and we were injured, but the truth is, nobody is dead or injured. Mr. Pizzo's expert witness was recognized by Caleb. The FBI took her into custody during lunch."

"Who bashed into your car?" Evan asked.

"That thing was a junk runner. Xander arranged to borrow it for realism. Our injuries were faked by Barbara," Dr. Colton admitted.

"Do you need me to stay here?" Evan inquired. "I mean, at the trial. Kent invited me to go fishing tomorrow."

"Go," Dr. Colton responded. "I promised your father I'd tell you everything."

"Did you?" Evan asked.

"Catch!" Dr. Colton tossed a bank book to Evan. "Not all of it. I demanded a ransom for you. They paid it, and for the past sixteen years, that five hundred thousand dollars has been collecting interest. I paid taxes on the money every year. From now on, it's your responsibility."

Opening the bank book, Evan softly uttered a single word: "Wow!"

"May I see that?" Sam Holt asked his son. Evan handed his father the bank book. "Whoa!" Sam gasped. "Richard, did you put any of your own money into this account?"

"Not a cent. Everything over five hundred thousand is entirely interest."

"There are scars behind Evan's ears," Sandra interjected. "Did you make them?"

"I reattached Evan's ears. Somebody pulled his ears so hard they caused damage. I did my best to keep the scars small."

"At least I don't have elephant ears," Evan joked.

"That's not the only elephant thing you don't have," Mrs. Holt teased. "Unlike you, elephants supposedly never forget, or so the saying goes. You can't remember to put gas in my car after you use it, or clean your room."

Everyone laughed and enjoyed their evening.

Chapter 24

"All rise, the Honorable Judge Noah King presiding."

"Be seated and come to order. Counselor Dill, do you have a witness available at this time?"

"Yes, sir, defense calls Hunter Lyon to the stand."

Hunter Lyon walked to the witness stand. "Do you promise to tell the truth, the whole truth, and nothing but the truth as you testify in this court today?"

"Yes, sir."

"Mr. Lyon, do you know Dr. Colton?"

"Yes, sir, Dr. Colton diagnosed me as having alopecia areata."

"Please describe your condition, and what alopecia is," Mr. Dill probed.

"Look at my head," Hunter replied. "I have a disease that prevents me from growing hair."

"You mean no hair anywhere?" Mr. Dill asked.

"No hair here, there, or anywhere, including eyebrows. Even hormone therapy doesn't help. I know because we tried it when I was younger."

"Has your disease caused you problems in life?"

"Alopecia has always been a challenge. I remember getting punched by my first father because I wasn't perfect."

"What do you mean, 'your first father'?"

"Lucas Lyon is my adopted father. He and Juanita adopted me when I was eight years old. Even though I think of Lucas and Juanita as my real parents, they are my second mother and father. Does that make sense?"

"Yes, it does," Mr. Dill replied. "Why weren't you perfect?"

"No hair. Dennis and Cynthia Stewart always made it clear. I was defective, worthless junk and they wished I was dead."

"How'd you meet Dr. Colton?"

"A baseball hit me in the face at school. The boy who threw it laughed at my broken nose. I walked over to the jerk and hit him one time with a right hook to his face. When I got home, Dennis beat me with his belt. He told Cynthia to take me to a clinic when they couldn't get my bleeding to stop."

"Why wouldn't the bleeding stop?"

"I'm a bleeder. A hemophiliac," Hunter said calmly.

"So you met Dr. Colton at the clinic," Mr. Dill stated for the record.

"Yes, sir, Dr. Colton gave me something to stop the bleeding. He talked to me and I told him what happened at school and at home. Dr. Colton reset my nose and gave me my first physical. As we were leaving, the other boy came in with his mother. They told Cynthia I started the fight and hit him for no reason."

"Did you see Dr. Colton again?"

"Yes, sir, Dennis pushed me down. I fell backwards and broke my wrist. The next time, three months later, I saw Dr. Colton for two broken toes after Cynthia dropped her clothes iron on my right foot when I wasn't wearing shoes. I learned to ride a bicycle and Dennis put a shovel handle in the front wheel spokes. I had a broken rib and bruised two others."

"Did you ever tell a teacher about these things?" Mr. Dill queried.

"Yeah, and then I got beat by Dennis and Cynthia. I didn't get any food all weekend. When I was almost eight, I tried to kill myself. I ended up in the hospital with Dr. Colton looking down at me."

"Did Dr. Colton say anything to you?"

"Dr. Colton kinda scolded me and said, 'Don't you *ever* do that again. *If you want help–ask.*' Then I said, 'Please help me. They don't want me. I'm trash.'"

"Do you remember what Dr. Colton told you?"

"He said, 'Be in Chi-town in three days. If you're there, they'll never hurt you again.'"

"Did you go to Chi-town?"

"Black eye, split lip, torn shirt and no shoes. Yes, sir, I went to Chi-town and Dr. Colton was there waiting for me."

"Tell the court what happened after you went to Chi-town."

"Objection; irrelevant narrative," Mr. Pizzo protested.

"This is Mr. Lyon's life. He is telling of his first-hand life experience," Mr. Dill rebutted.

"Overruled. I'm going to allow Mr. Lyon to continue."

"I rode a small electric cart with Dr. Colton. We went to a nice house with a hidden area where I got my own place. Dr. Colton took my clothes and then took blood from my arm. He let me take a bath in all the hot water I wanted. He gave me brand-new clothes, new shoes, and all the food I could eat. He never said anything mean. Dr. Colton made me feel good about myself. I was allowed to watch TV and I didn't see anything about my disappearance. There wasn't even what they now call an 'Amber Alert' for me.

"I lived with Dr. Colton for three weeks before he told me about my mom and dad, Juanita and Lucas Lyon. He gave me a shot to make me sleep. I woke up in a bed wearing new pajamas. Lucas and Juanita sat on another bed staring at me. They took me home and never treated me like some freak."

"Is Hunter your first name, even before Dr. Colton helped you?"

"My name is Hunter Lyon. I'll always be Hunter Lyon. I'll never acknowledge that other name."

"Did Dr. Colton ever hurt you?" Mr. Dill asked.

"Only once," Hunter replied. "He stuck a needle in my spine for some medical test."

"Nothing further, Your Honor," Mr. Dill said.

"Excuse me," Hunter said, raising his hand. "May I use the bathroom?"

"My questions will only take a few minutes," Mr. Pizzo offered.

Dr. Colton stood, "Your Honor, due to bladder scarring prior to Hunter's seventh birthday, he only feels a need to relieve himself when he absolutely must."

"Bailiff, escort Mr. Lyon to the restroom. We'll wait here for our witness to return."

Xander Ward rose to his feet. "Judge King, may I speak with you briefly?"

"Come forward to my side, Agent Ward."

"Sir, reliable sources have informed the FBI of a possible attempt to harm your jurors. The agency requested you contact them at this number," Xander spoke loud enough for all to hear him.

"Everyone will remain seated. Will the court clerk please place a call to the number Agent Ward has provided.

"Yes, sir, one minute please."

Judge King lifted his phone once the call had been placed. "This is Noah King. Agent Ward advised me of your request to talk... Yes sir, he mentioned that possibility. How real is that threat? Are you positive...? I agree, it is my only option–Very well, I'll take care of it immediately. Thank you, sir, goodbye," Judge King said as he hung up the phone. After getting the clerk's attention Judge King handed her a note.

Hunter Lyon and the bailiff returned to a subdued courtroom. "Thank you, sir," Hunter told the judge.

"You're welcome. Ladies and gentlemen, we're as of this moment a closed-court proceeding. I'm dismissing the jury to our deliberation room. I must ask everybody to remain seated as the jury exits." One by one, the jurors left.

"As of this afternoon, all visitors must pass through a metal detector. We've received information, which has now been verified, regarding threats on the jurors' lives. I've been instructed to sequester the jury. My clerk will make arrangements for housing the jurors until this passes. Mr. Dill, I request that you and Dr. Colton inform the court clerk of where your witnesses are staying."

"Your Honor, if you'll allow me to call my son, Royce, I'll have him get our witnesses moved. We're living in a gated community. We were offered the use of our old house for a small fee."

"Defense witnesses have been staying at one of the court's approved hotels," the clerk informed Judge King.

"Dr. Colton reserved eight rooms in the hotel for our witnesses," Mr. Dill said.

"It's not required, but if you choose to relinquish those rooms, you'll be reimbursed for the money you have spent." Judge King advised.

"Sounds good," Mr. Dill responded.

"May I ask a question?" Agent Ward queried.

"Ask," Judge King replied.

"If there's a threat against the jury, how do you go to and from court without exposing them to possible harm?"

"We'll use the tunnels," Judge King answered.

"Are jurors allowed to move their vehicles?" Mr. Dill asked.

"No, sir. We'll relocate the jurors' vehicles to a secured parking garage. They'll remain there until this trial is over."

"What about phone calls?" Mr. Pizzo asked. "Is the court allowed to prohibit phone calls? They'll probably want to notify their families."

"The court clerks are notifying the families, without specifics at this time. None of our jurors are single parents, so we have more in our favor than usual."

"Out of curiosity, with no disrespect intended, is a defendant ever sequestered?" Mr. Pizzo queried.

118

"That would be protective custody jail," Mr. Dill answered curtly. "Do you think we need protecting?"

"No, it was only curiosity."

"Officer!" Judge King called out. "Are you one of the four deputies I requested for this trial?"

"No, sir, you're getting four U.S. Marshals. There's an internal investigation happening, thanks to Frank Kelly. I only came into your courtroom to inform you of the metal detector outside your door."

"Let's bring our jurors back and deliver the news," Judge King told both prosecution and defense. Once all jurors were seated, Judge King made a hand gesture to a U.S. Marshal. "Ladies and gentlemen, as of right now, you are a sequestered jury. There have been threats against your lives for reasons unknown at this time. We have secured rooms for you at a nearby hotel. I ask for your cooperation and patience." Judge King looked at each juror as he spoke.

"Ow!" a marshal yelped.

"Do you have a problem, Mr...?"

"Marshal, Bob Marshall, just a bit of feedback in my earwig."

Judge King held up his hand. "Let me get this straight: you're a United States Marshal, your name is Bob Marshall, and therefore you are Marshal Bob Marshall?"

"That's me, sir," the marshal replied.

"Take care of your earwax problem, Marshal Marshall," Judge King laughed lightly to himself.

"Where are we going to be, Your Honor?" Juror Number Three asked. "I need clean clothing and some personal items."

"Your families have been notified, and they're bringing necessary items to the court building. You'll be allowed five minutes with your family. A marshal will observe your visit. I warn you, DO NOT PASS OR ACCEPT ANYTHING DURING THIS VISIT."

"Are we allowed to hug and kiss our spouses?" a juror asked.

"Yes, you may. I apologize for this inconvenience, but your safety is the responsibility of the court. I'll need vehicle keys from Jurors One, Four, Six and Alternate Number Two. Family members will take the others."

One by one, each juror went into a private room with a marshal for their visit. As they re-entered the courtroom, they received the items brought by their families. One juror was missing when all visits had ended.

"Remain seated and come to order," Judge King commanded. "By now, everyone can see we are missing a juror. Because we were forced to sequester our jury, we discovered a hidden microphone and camera on the missing juror. The FBI has begun an investigation into the situation." Judge King paused for a moment. "Due to a fortunate event, each of our jurors will have his or her own hotel room. You'll have a continental breakfast available every morning. Lunch will be provided by one of three places. You'll eat in the deliberation room. Evening meals can be ordered from a menu at the hotel. We'll be dismissed for today and return tomorrow morning at nine o'clock. Jurors are now instructed to follow the bailiff to their hotel. Court adjourned."

"Hot damn!" Dr. Colton exclaimed. "I wonder if my first wife Nancy, and Bob Marshall were related?" he quipped to Mr. Dill and Agent Ward.

"Should I run his background?" Agent Ward asked.

"Yeah, let's do it." Mr. Dill replied.

As they were preparing to leave, Dr. Colton interrupted, "No, let it go. At this point it really doesn't matter."

Chapter 25

"We are back in court this morning." Judge King looked as though he had been awake all night. "The court clerk will now tell us who is replacing Juror Number Three."

"Alternate Number Four, please take juror seat number three."

"Mr. Dill, you may recall your witness to the stand," Judge King instructed.

"Please call Hunter Lyon," Mr. Dill requested.

"You're still under oath, Mr. Lyon," Judge King reminded the witness. "Mr. Prosecutor, cross."

"Mr. Lyon, what's the name you refuse to acknowledge?"

"Objection, Your Honor," Dr. Colton said. "Mr. Lyon said he won't acknowledge that name. Mr. Pizzo is inciting Mr. Lyon into a contempt of court by asking that question."

"I'm merely attempting to ascertain what his name was."

"Your Honor, again: Mr. Lyon clearly stated, his name is, and always will be, Hunter Lyon."

"Overruled," Judge King retorted. "Answer Prosecutor Pizzo's question."

Hunter Lyon sat on the witness stand saying nothing. After fifteen to twenty seconds, he turned to face Mr. Pizzo. "I can't tell you that name, sir. It's not that I don't want to–well yes it is in a way. I can't tell you because I was hypnotized to forget it."

"Your Honor, are we supposed to believe–"

"Oh, can it, Pizzo," Dr. Colton snapped." Your Honor, may I offer an explanation?"

"Pray, tell, Dr. Colton; what's your explanation?"

"Although Hunter knows his former last name, he suffers from PTSD, due to what he experienced as a boy. Hunter's former name was Clint Stewart."

Hunter Lyon froze in place on the stand.

"Are you okay, Mr. Stewart?" Prosecutor Pizzo asked.

"Object–" was all Dr. Colton was able to say before Hunter Lyon spoke.

"My name is Hunter Lyon. You will address me as Mr. Lyon, sir. You, Mister Prosecutor, are nothing but a self-important, arrogant bully.

"Mr. Lyon, you'd best adjust the tone of your voice. I'll find you in contempt if you don't lose the attitude."

"Judge, you had best tell your bailiff to shoot me if your Prosecutor comes near me. My attitude is justified and my assessment of Mr. Pizzo stands. My name is Mr. Lyon."

"Your Honor, I merely asked Mr. Stewart–"

"Objection!" Mr. Dill shouted loudly. "*Mr. Pisso* is baiting the witness. I introduced the witness as Hunter Lyon. I ask you to instruct him in proper courtroom etiquette regarding witnesses. Thank you, Your Honor."

"Objection sustained." Judge King faced the prosecutor. "Counselor Dill has made a good point. So has Mr. Lyon. You've been baiting Mr. Lyon as only a court bully would do to a witness. I, sir, am the one and only bully allowed in my court. You'll address this witness as Mr. Lyon, sir. Failure in following my instructions shall result in a forty-eight-hour period in jail for each infraction."

"Yes, Your Honor. I, uh-sir, I have no questions for the witness," Mr. Pizzo said in defeat. "And I object, Dr. Colton has no right to call me *Mr. Pisso*. He needs to apologize for his behavior."

"Overruled! Mr. Pizzo, if my memory is correct, it was Mr. Dill who addressed you incorrectly. I'm holding you in contempt of court." Judge King turned to Dr. Colton. "Does the defense have another witness to call?"

"Mr. Pizzo, you do have an apology, don't you?" Mr. Dill queried.

"I've done nothing to apologize for," the arrogant prosecutor protested.

"Your Honor," Hunter Lyon broke in. "Even if the man apologized, I wouldn't accept it, but that's because even I know his apology would lack sincerity. May I leave?"

"You're excused, Mr. Lyon."

Mr. Dill stood up as Hunter Lyon started walking out of the courtroom. "Your Honor, the defense wishes to thank Mr. Lyon for his testimony, and we now call Kimberly Annie Wolf."

Kimberly entered the room. "Your Honor," Kimberly spoke loudly. "My name is no longer Kimberly Wolf. I'm now married, so it's Kim Ann Bishop."

"So noted," Judge King replied. Kim Bishop was sworn in and seated.

"May I call you Kim?" Mr. Dill asked.

"Yes, sir."

"Kim, do you know Dr. Richard Colton?"

"My oldest son, Richard Allen, is named after Dr. Colton. Yes, I know him."

"How long have you known Dr. Colton?"

"Twenty-four years. He first treated me when I was three years old."

"How do you remember it was at age three that you met Dr. Colton? Most people don't remember things from that age."

"You never forget the first time a thrown knife hits you, no matter where you get hit."

"Who threw the knife at you?"

"My papa. He did a knife-throwing act for the circus with my mama."

"Your Honor," Mr. Pizzo interrupted. "What is the significance of Ms. Bishop–"

"*Mrs*. Bishop," the witness corrected.

"Whatever. Why're you testifying?"

"I received a subpoena. And I was asked a question."

"Mrs. Bishop, would you tell this court the events following your first visit to Dr. Colton's clinic?" Mr. Dill requested.

"Papa was fired from the circus. He threw two knives at the circus lion tamer after the lion tamer killed the only lion. My papa's and mama's names were Jerry and Irene Wallace. The first time Papa hit me with a knife was in my left butt cheek. The next time, I got hit in my right arm. After that, he threw a knife which sliced off my right pinkie finger tip. Papa began throwing blunted knives at me when he was drinking. Dr. Colton sent me to Methodist Hospital when my injuries were really bad."

"What do you mean, 'really bad'?" Mr. Dill asked.

"A knife in my leg. One hit my appendix. I lost the tip of my right ear. By the time I was eight years old, I hadn't gone to school for two years, and my teacher said I was way far behind the other students."

"Did the knife injuries stop?"

"Yes, sir; Papa didn't like the police. They threatened to arrest him next time I was cut, even if I did it myself. After that, Papa made a leather spanking paddle with lead sewn inside it. I went from having knives thrown at me to being hit with Papa's paddle. Papa hit me mostly on my head and the bottom of my feet. He used a ruler to spank my hands. When I was nine years old, I was taken to Methodist Hospital for food poisoning. Dr. Colton did tests on me, or my blood. He found high levels of digitalis from a flower. Firefox…Foxfire…or something like that, I think."

"Your Honor, I'd like to call Dr. Colton to present further information regarding Mrs. Bishop's testimony," Mr. Dill said.

"Objection," Mr. Pizzo argued. "Dr. Colton can answer questions when he's called to the stand."

"Sustained; there's no reason for Dr. Colton to testify."

"Your Honor, maybe the prosecutor can tell the court what this flower is called," Dr. Colton said, flicking a button to activate the large courtroom monitor.

"I'm not a florist," Mr. Pizzo countered.

"Neither am I," Judge King responded. "But I know that flower is called foxglove."

"It's the flower used to poison Mrs. Bishop as a child. A flower Irene Wallace cultivated in four different plots around their home. Irene Wallace professed to be an amateur botanist. She poisoned her daughter."

"Objection; speculation," Mr. Pizzo charged.

Holding up a sheet of paper, Dr. Colton reacted calmly. "This, Mr. Pizzo, is a deathbed confession from Irene Wallace given last year. In it she admits to killing her husband, Jerry Wallace, after finding him with another woman."

"That doesn't sound like speculation, Your Honor," Defense Attorney Dill retorted.

"Overruled. What else does this confession have to say?"

"Irene Wallace admitted to placing her daughter in harm's way, and when the girl begged her mother to keep Jerry Wallace from touching her, Mrs. Wallace used her hair iron to burn the girl. Should anybody find it appropriate to check records, you'll discover I addressed these issues before Kim Bishop was removed from the Wallace's house of abuse."

"Kim, when were you removed from the Wallace home?" Mr. Dill knew the answer, but he wasn't allowed to testify.

"I was nine years old. I cried when Papa threw a knife and cut my arm. I was running away from him. He was drunk again, calling me his special girl. They made me stand in poison oak, and I had to pull leaves off, then rub them on my arms, legs and face."

"How long did you stand in the poison oak?"

"I don't know, Mr. Dill. I can only say that I opened my eyes to see Dr. Colton looking down at me."

Dr. Colton looked toward Judge King. "May I fill in the blanks?"

"Make it quick before Mr. Pizzo objects."

"Irene Wallace called for an ambulance. She claimed her daughter was found in a cluster of eastern poison oak. I volunteered to make the trip. What we found made me sick. We transported Jerry and Irene Wallace's nine year old daughter to the hospital. The only areas not blistered by the poison oak were her head, neck and buttocks. To prevent any infections, I suspended her in distilled water and saline mix. The Wallace girl was in a coma for three days. Four days after awakening she left the hospital."

"Where did you go?" Mr. Dill asked.

"I don't know." Kim shrugged her shoulders. "The room I stayed in didn't have any windows. Dr. Colton gave me medicine every day until the poison oak was gone. One day he gave me a shot, and I woke up on an airplane with my newly adopted Dad, Rocky Wolf, sitting beside me. I left the plane with Rocky, and my mom, Nancy. I lived with them from that day on until I joined the U.S. Navy."

"How'd you get the name Kimberly?"

"Dr. Colton said I didn't have to go back home. I could change my name and live with people who wouldn't throw knives at me, hit me, or make me do things that would hurt me. He asked me if I liked the name Kimberly–Kim, for short. I chose my name: Kimberly Annie. I've always used Kim or Annie since that day."

"So Dr. Colton never hurt you. He's always done his best to keep you from being hurt?"

"Yes, that's right.

"Nothing further at this time, Your Honor," Mr. Dill said.

"Mr. Pizzo, your witness."

"Thank you, sir," Mr. Pizzo replied as he stood and adjusted his tie. "Mrs. Bishop, where are you currently employed, or do you work?"

"Yes, I'm employed. I work for the Bureau of Land Management. I'm stationed in Bishop, California."

"May I ask where you met your husband?"

"Objection; irrelevant," Mr. Dill barked. "Not pertinent to this trial or my direct questioning."

"Your Honor, I'll ask a different question," Mr. Pizzo offered. "Have you told Mr. Bishop the story you've told us in court today?"

"Objection; implies the witness is lying."

"Does your husband know what you have told us today?"

"Yes, and Dale has never implied I've lied to him. Your Honor, I'm very perturbed, I swore on a Bible." Mrs. Bishop wasn't yelling, but her words were blunt. *"The truth, nothing but the truth."* I've answered all questions *honestly*, without deception."

"Your Honor, may I dispute the witness's claim? She stated and spelled her name; which is not her true name. In fact, the witness's last name is legally Wallace. Her marriage is also a deception." Prosecutor Pizzo expected Mr. Dill or his client to object, but they were both silent. His confidence was bolstered thinking he could discredit the witness. Mr. Pizzo continued: "What's your true name with its correct spelling?"

"Kimberly Ann Bishop. I've already spelled it. For the record, my name was Kimberly Annie Wolf. I legally changed the spelling to Kimberly 'A-N-N' before I joined the Navy because I hated hearing 'Annie, Get Your Gun'. Something I heard growing up from nearly everyone. I didn't want to disgrace my parents, Rocky and Nancy, so I went to court, paid their fees, and, I repeat, *legally* changed the spelling of my name. Are there any more character assassinations you wish to pronounce?"

"Objection; argumentative," Mr. Pizzo protested.

"Justified; overruled. I'm also overruling the objection for lack of relevance."

"We would've withdrawn that objection, Your Honor," Mr. Dill stated.

"You asked where I met my husband: The U.S. Navy base in California called China Lake. My husband's name is Dale. Before the end of my enlistment, I was a Navy certified F-18 fighter jet and Apache helicopter mechanic. I could fly both as well."

"Nothing further at this time," Mr. Pizzo said in defeat.

"You may step down, Mrs. Bishop."

"Thank you, sir," Kim said as she stood.

"When Mrs. Bishop has left the courtroom, I have a letter from Dr. Joseph Callendar regarding hospital records he and two nurses were sent to research. I'm going to ask my clerk to read this letter out loud." Judge King passed a letter to his clerk, who read the following:

To the Honorable Judge King;

Per your instructions I went to Methodist Hospital in search of medical records for Marco Rizzoli. At no time did I, or either nurse, disclose the purpose of our audit. We researched all records looking for any mention of the name Rizzoli. There are numerous reports regarding Rizzoli Enterprises as the employer of many disgruntled workers. We did find one mention of Marco Rizzoli in the hospital archives: Born to Mario and Maria Rizzoli. While there is an infant footprint on the enclosed birth certificate photocopy, it regretfully does not contain fingerprints. I am not including a physical description of the boy, as everyone already knows, Marco Rizzoli is deceased.

In one reference to Rizzoli Enterprises, we discovered the name of Richard Colton. Nancy Colton gave birth to a son, Richard, Jr.. Nancy Colton was employed by Rizzoli Enterprises and very vocal concerning what she perceived as their shortcomings. I must report that other than what I have described above, there were no other files regarding the Rizzoli or Colton families. Furthermore, we discovered no file pertaining to Marco Rizzoli in the Nancy Colton Memorial Clinic records.

As you suspected, there is one entry in the now-defunct ambulance company records you requested we investigate. What I found revealed nothing new. Marco Rizzoli was listed as a transferee from the Nancy Colton Memorial Clinic to Mercy General. However, we learned new information, revealing Marco Rizzoli disappeared two blocks from Mercy General. This contradicts reports of Marco Rizzoli having been abducted while still at the Nancy Colton Memorial Clinic. This information places Dr. Richard Colton further from the abduction site. We have searched all areas requested and found no record of any of the individuals you requested.

Judge King's clerk passed the letter back to the judge and resumed her seat.

"I find it simply amazing. I asked Dr. Callendar to check on no less than six files. It makes me wonder whatever happened to these individuals. Marco Rizzoli isn't the only child to disappear completely." Judge King set aside Joseph Callendar's letter.

"Mr. Dill, you may call your next witness."

"Your Honor, in compliance with the court's order to turn over all of Dr. Colton's journals, we submit nine pages regarding three boys: Dyson Compton, Brody Green, and David Kelly."

"Objection, Your Honor. Before being allowed to submit anything, Mr. Dill needs to be instructed to allow their documents to be read by you first," Mr. Pizzo shot out.

"Need I *remind* the prosecutor, it was he who chose to submit my journals, unread, into evidence? Mr. Dill and I strongly protested, but it was *you* who was adamant of their significance. Now we asked to be allowed to comply with Judge King's order, and you complain. Fine! The defense retracts our request. Instead, we seek a brief recess." Dr. Colton returned the papers to his briefcase.

"Very well, you may submit your documents and I shall rule on their significance," Judge King said.

"Mr. Dill and I will discuss submitting documents during our brief recess. Mr. Pizzo objected to their submission so I withdrew them, they are now moot."

"We'll have a brief recess. Mr. Dill, may I see you in my chambers? Jurors will retire to our deliberation room. I encourage you to choose a jury foreman. You have ten minutes, people. Dismissed."

"I'm going to snack and take my meds," Dr. Colton said. "I've been feeling lousy all morning."

Wesley Dill entered Judge King's chambers and closed the door. "What can I do for you sir?"

"I have filed with the federal government to charge your client with multiple counts of child abduction for the purpose of ransom. Should my request be approved your client will immediately lose his status as co-counsel. You might want to consider finding a new co-counsel to represent Mr. Colton."

"Your Honor, I respectfully ask you to retract your request with the federal government. If you don't withdraw the charges Dr. Colton will be exonerated with prejudice. Regardless of how you choose to act, I thank you for the courtesy of a heads-up."

"How do you figure Mr. Colton would be exonerated?"

"Previous Federal Disclosures/Assistance Contract."

"I've never heard of such a thing, Mr. Dill. I do believe you are jerking me around."

"No sir; a statement of fact. Aside from all of this other nonsense, have you finally received your scuba certification?"

"Yes, I have. Are we still diving in Cancún when this trial is over?"

"I'm ready anytime. I thought I'd go collect golf balls this weekend. I get paid ten cents a ball and usually come up with over fifty dollars every time. It's a good way to log dive time, even in shallow waters."

"Isn't the water muddy?" Judge King asked.

"Not really. I usually hit the ponds around eight in the morning before all the bad golfers show up. Water is shallow, cool, and I've never had to use my tank when I clean the stream. You're welcome to join me, get a few extra dollars, plus usually pick up a couple of free beers afterwards. Those I take home to drink later."

"How many more witnesses do you have?"

"More than a few. One of my witnesses is a dad-blamed millionaire. He isn't a patient man, but at the same time he never raises his voice."

"Thank you for the notice regarding your witness. You may submit the files offered in open court when we return."

"Begging your pardon, but if I know Dr. Colton, and I do very well, the good doctor has undoubtedly shredded those documents.

* * * * *

Dr. Colton smiled as the court was called to order. "Your next witness, Mr. Dill," Judge King said.

"Scott Lawson, Your Honor."

The bailiff asked, "Do you promise to tell the truth, the whole truth, and nothing but the truth?"

"I see no profit in telling tall tales. Yes, sir, I'll be telling the truth."

"Be seated and state your name for the record," Judge King instructed.

"My name is Scott Lawson. It changed when I was nine years old." Scott spelled his name."

"Mr. Lawson, do you remember your name before it was changed?" Mr. Dill asked.

"I sure do," Scott replied, "but I don't acknowledge that name anymore. Now I only respond to 'Scott Lawson'. My dad and Dr. Colton both have warped senses of humor. They liked calling me 'Scooter'. I hated it, and that's why I only answer to Scott. No more 'Scooter'!"

"Does the name 'Brody Green' upset you?"

"No, sir, it ain't my name. Brody Green died at the age of nine. Two of his best friends died then as well."

Xander Ward now recognized his childhood friend. They had suffered hell on earth together. He wanted to reassure his friend that everything would be all right.

"Do you know why you received a subpoena?" Mr. Dill asked.

"Yes, sir, my father, Zach Lawson, said it was because the doctor who saved my life was on trial for murder."

"What would you say if asked what happened to Brody Green before he died?"

"Torture, rape, beatings, intimidation, humiliation, to start. Then I'd tell you to use your imagination because one of Brody's best friends went through far worse."

"Does the name 'Fellitch' mean anything to you?"

"Yes, sir, one day when I was eight, he ordered Deputy Kelly to shoot me in the leg, using a .22 caliber pistol."

"Do you remember why or what you had done?"

"Yes, sir, I refused to go swimming at Mr. Mario Rizzoli's estate."

"Why would you refuse to go swimming?"

"Only boys went swimming at Mr. Rizzoli's home. I remember when even Marco Rizzoli didn't like swimming or playing in the water when his father's men were around," Scott answered.

"You knew Marco Rizzoli when you were eight or nine years old?"

"No, sir, I knew Marco when I was seven and he was five. I refused to go swimming because when the boys arrived at Mr. Rizzoli's, we were stripped and searched. Everyone knew his home security guards looked for boys they could take to Judge Fellitch according to Mr. Rizzoli's orders."

"Your Honor," Dr. Colton interrupted. "Defense seeks to release this witness and place him into the custody of the U.S. Marshals."

"May I approach the bench?" Xander Ward requested.

"Come," Judge King commanded.

After a brief conversation with the judge, Xander approached the witness. "Scott Lawson, stand up, turn around with your hands behind your back. You are under arrest for the murder of Judge Taylor Fellitch. Do not speak anymore."

"I didn't kill anybody. What is this crap?"

"Put him in cell three," Judge King instructed. Marshal Marshall accompanied Xander and Scott out of the courtroom.

"We've lost our witness," Judge King said. "Mr. Lawson will not be returning for further testimony. Would you care to call your next witness?"

"Our next witness is Aiden Grant."

Chapter 26

Outside the courtroom, Xander Ward stopped. "I've been searching for you, Mr. Lawson–or should I say *Red Man.*"

Scott Lawson stopped in his tracks. "Only two people know that name. Who are you, pig?"

"PIG? This from someone who used to call me 'smarty-pants'. Marshal, remove those handcuffs, please"

Scott looked at his old friend. "Oh, thank God! I thought you're dead." Arms embraced Xander. Tears of joy filled both men's eyes.

"I've believed that I alone survived," Xander continued. "Oh, my name is Xander Ward now. I've been working with Dr. Colton for quite some time."

"Why'd you arrest me? We all wanted Fellitch dead."

"Red–sorry I mean Scott, he isn't dead. Fellitch is alive in a new unopened private prison in California. There are now over two hundred Dragon Society members and supporters in jail. Frank Kelly was arrested last month, John Green two days before, and yesterday, Kay Kelly was arrested."

"What do you mean, 'working with Dr. Colton'? Are you guys helping other kids escape?"

"Working with him means I'm a federal agent assigned to Dr. Colton during the course of this trial. He's on trial for first degree-murder. He swears that he's innocent, but just because he helped us and others escape an abusive life doesn't mean he didn't kill Marco Rizzoli. We believe it was revenge for his wife and son's deaths, which he blames on Mario Rizzoli–something he cannot prove."

"Are you really a cop?" Scott asked.

"Total FBI Special Agent. The people I went to live with treated me like I was some kind of royalty. Simon, my dad, taught me to fly airplanes. He did cabinetry as a hobby and fishing was the first thing we did together. We had a super-great house with our own pool and I had my own bedroom with a bathroom. Simon and my mom, Lori included me in planning family vacations to different countries every year. I learned to snow ski in Sweden. I can yodel and I got my first motorcycle when I was twelve. After every vacation we'd begin planning our next destination so I could start learning the language. I speak five different languages. Dad and Mom taught me so much all year long. I spent six years in the Marines then another two years in Japan. Mom's a real estate broker, so when I moved out she helped me find my own house. I learned how to cook from Mom."

"My parents are Zach and Amy. They're survivalists," Scott confessed. "Zach operates a 10,000-acre ranch and hunting reserve. Amy home-schooled me, which let me graduate early. I went fishing in the ranch's big water ponds and 500-acre lake. I was allowed to go swimming in the stream whenever I wanted. Mom and Dad let me hunt rabbits and deer. I shot a deer in our orchard every year. I made 300 yard shots from the barn loft, even on windy days. I killed an elk from over five hundred yards after my dad's hunter missed three times. I only shot because the hunter said to take the shot. That happened when I was thirteen.

I began guiding with my dad after my fourteenth birthday. One hunter thought I was too young, so he sent his son with me and he went with Dad. My hunter got his deer, but dad's hunter came back empty. Dad helped my hunter clean his kill."

"But the best thing was, nobody ever treated me like I was their property," Xander interjected.

"The only one I'm intimate with is my wife," Scott said.

"Yeah, but I worried about it for a long time. My dad and mom let me talk about what happened. They always gave me support. What helped me the most was my girlfriend. She knew about my past but she didn't let it bother her. She's the love of my life. We didn't have sex until after we were married. Now we have twin girls, and a son," Xander told his old friend.

"Did I tell you that I hated Dr. Colton for over a year? One day, my dad told me Dr. Colton removed my tattoos and trackers. He said Dr. Colton protected me. I remember being in a room with no windows. I had a television and games but didn't get clothes right away. I was afraid our DS parents were coming for me every day." Scott admitted.

"The Dragon Society was watching Dr. Colton after we ran away," Xander said. "Deputy Sheriff Kelly searched Dr. Colton's property twice, but they never found anything. My tracker was found in Mario Rizzoli's office with my blood on his desk. I still don't know exactly where I stayed until I went to live with Simon and Lori. My room had a bed, a bathroom, warm blankets, a chair, and video games. What I didn't have was threats of violence or sex."

"Am I going to testify anymore?" Scott asked.

"Not until we know which juror is a Dragon. We picked up transmissions coming from the courtroom. Judge Vang, or should I say Byron Chow, and a juror were arrested but there is still a signal coming from the courtroom."

"Get me out of here," Scott replied. "I know a guy who can find that signal within a matter of hours. My friend is freaky smart."

"You're leaving in ten minutes. Marshal Mack will be taking you to a safe phone. Call your friend, ask him to come see me or call this number," Xander said, handing a card to Scott.

"When will we see each other again?"

"Tonight, we're having dinner with the Coltons. Hope you don't mind. Time for me to get back."

130

Chapter 27

"Mr. Grant, you may take the stand."

"Would you spell your name for the clerk, please?" Mr. Dill requested.

"A-I-D-E-N G-R-A-N-T, did you want me to spell my middle name, too? It's Noel, N-O-E-L, like *The First Noel*, my favorite Christmas song."

"Mr. Grant, do you know Dr. Colton?" Mr. Dill asked.

"I met Dr. Colton one time. May I make a request? Please call me Aiden. Mr. Grant is my father."

"I think we can call you Aiden. However, first I'd like to ask you about another name. If I ask you about David Kelly, what would you say?"

"David Kelly was a boy who ran away from home. His heart was full of hate. Do I have to talk about this?"

"I can only imagine the feelings of pain this brings," Mr. Dill replied. "Maybe Dr. Colton would do better."

"Ladies and gentlemen of the jury–Your Honor," Dr. Colton said, taking over for his co-counsel; "this witness will be sharing explicit information. If his testimony makes you squeamish, then I ask you to consider how he and others have felt through the years." Turning to Aiden, he continued, "I'm Dr. Colton and no, you don't have to talk about it. I know what you went through and these people need to know about it, too. However, the final decision is yours. You're a strong young man whom I admire."

"I promised my dad I would do this; so I'll answer your questions, sir."

"Before you were called Aiden, was your name David?" Dr. Colton asked.

"Yes, sir, my name was David Lee Kelly."

"Do you know Frank Kelly?"

"Yes, sir, Sheriff Frank Kelly was my father."

"Was Sheriff Kelly a good father?" Dr. Colton queried.

"Objection; conjecture, calls for an opinion."

"No, he was mean!"

"I said objection," Mr. Pizzo corrected. "Now you wait for Judge King to make a ruling. When you hear 'objection,' you remain quiet until the objection is ruled on."

"Excuse me," Aiden responded. "I said no, he was mean. All I meant to him was money or prestige–"

"Objection, Your Honor. Please instruct the witness to be silent."

"With his Dragon Society friends," Aiden said, completing his answer, ignoring Mr. Pizzo.

"Your objection is moot at this point, so overruled," Judge King informed the prosecutor. "Mr. Grant, in the future please wait for my ruling."

Dr. Colton continued, "Why do you say he was mean? Don't most parents discipline their children?"

"Most parents don't beat their children, sir. I know that *I* don't, and neither does my wife."

"What did Sheriff Kelly do when he disciplined you?" Dr. Colton asked, using the title 'Sheriff' for impact.

"Usually he used his wide leather belt to whip me, and I wore only my underwear. One day we were at a Dragon Society meeting; where an older boy tripped me causing me to spill beer on Dragon Master Kelly. The man took my clothes, then whipped me with his belt. He also let other Dragon Society members beat me. That's the night they put a star around the tattoo on my right arm."

"Why a star?" Dr. Colton asked.

"The star meant I had to do anything a Dragon member ordered. If I refused, they could kill me and nobody would care."

"What were you told to do?"

"I was told to hit a girl until I split her lip. They made me kick another boy and hit him with a belt. One man told me to sit on some tacks. If I had refused they would have killed me."

"Objection; total fabrication," Mr. Pizzo asserted.

"Fabrication! How dare you accuse me of lying!" Aiden retorted angrily. "Were you there? Did you suffer humiliation daily? What about licking the bottom of someone's feet when they had athlete's foot? I'm not fabricating anything." Aiden was visibly upset.

"Objection is overruled." Judge King looked at Aiden, "Do you need a break, or should we continue?"

"I can keep going, sir. But that man objects too much. Nobody objected when this stuff happened to me."

"Aiden, you and two of your friends ran away from the Dragons, is that correct?"

"Objection. Leading question."

"Never mind, I can rephrase my question," Dr. Colton volunteered. "Why were you in Chi-town the night I met you?"

Aiden looked over at Prosecutor Pizzo. "What, not objecting? I ran away from the Dragon Society. That night I was hung upside-down and whipped with green hickory branches. They made me do something really gross and I threw up. Mr. Compton, a Dragon Highlord, rubbed my face in my vomit."

"Aiden, describe your tattoo to the jury."

"I don't have any tattoos, sir."

"I can respect that," Dr. Colton responded. "Please describe the tattoo you had when I first met you."

"My first tattoo was a DKT in henna. DKT stood for Dragon Kid Trainee. All the Dragon members make their children DKTs. The first permanent tattoo I got was a small seagull. A star was put around the seagull when I spilled the beer."

Did anyone else get a seagull tattoo?"

Before Aiden could answer, Marshal Marshall stepped forward. "I want to see everybody's hands above their heads except for Judge King."

"Bailiff, please open the deliberation room for our jurors," Agent Xander Ward requested. "Juror One please exit; all alternate jurors may also leave." Xander waited for the first four to leave. "Juror Number Eleven, you may leave."

Juror Eleven picked up her purse and stepped out of the jury box. When she had taken half a dozen steps, Xander Ward spoke, "Juror Eleven, stop where you are and do not move. Release your purse; let it drop to the floor. Put your hands on top of your head. All remaining jurors exit the jury box. Leave your possessions where they are; we've no intention of bothering your property."

Marshal Marshall stepped forward. "Annabel Rigsby, you're under arrest. You've been broadcasting these proceedings to your fellow Dragon Society members. You may be interested to know that the people you've been broadcasting to have received silver bracelets as well."

"You have the right to remain silent, and I insist upon it. You have the right to counsel, even if you cannot afford one. Accept the free counsel; we froze all of your assets. Anything you say will be used to convict you." Annabel Rigsby received her actual Miranda rights from Agent Xander Ward. All jurors were brought back into court and informed of the circumstances surrounding Annabel. An alternate juror was assigned to Juror Seat Eleven.

"Everything you've heard from our witness has been his honest testimony. Annabel Rigsby was an active Dragon Society member for over thirty years," Mr. Dill announced. "Now we believe Judge King may have an announcement."

"Thank you Mr. Dill. We're going to be dismissed earlier than usual today. I'm lifting the sequester order of our jury. Annabel Rigsby was our threat. Jurors may return to the hotel for their belongings."

"Excuse me, sir, Judge," Aiden interrupted. "May I say something? I mean, it's important."

"What is it, Mr. Grant?" Judge King asked. Unexpectedly, Aiden began speaking in Japanese. Instantly Xander Ward was on his feet. Using sign language, he spoke to a fellow FBI agent. Dr. Colton also understood Aiden's words, whispering a clipped translation to Mr. Dill.

"It appears that we have another possible Dragon Society member sitting outside."

"Objection; speak English," Mr. Pizzo complained.

"I apologize," Aiden responded. "I was hoping somebody understands Japanese."

"Your Honor, may I approach," Dr. Colton requested.

"Defense and prosecution may approach."

Dr. Colton spoke Japanese, knowing only he, Xander and his witness would understand. "Bring Kyler Grant into court before you arrest anyone." Arriving at the sidebar, Dr. Colton translated what he and Aiden had said in proper order.

"My God, is there no end to these people?" Mr. Pizzo asked in astonishment.

"If you only knew," Dr. Colton replied.

"Please return to your seats," Judge King instructed.

Five minutes later, Xander Ward entered. "Done and done," he said.

"Let's get back to this trial," Judge King responded.

Dr. Colton rose to his feet. "I'll ask again. Did anyone else get a small seagull tattoo?"

"Yes, sir, at age five, boys and girls who are Dragon Kid Trainees get a seagull tattoo on their arms. Boys on the right arm, girls on their left arm."

"Do adults have seagull tattoos?"

"Yes, but their small seagull is covered by a big dragon tattoo. All eighteen-year-olds get new tattoos from the Dragon tattoo artist."

"Part of your tattoo was a star. There are ten lines in a star. Did each of those lines mean anything?"

"Yes, sir, but thank God I no longer remember what they meant. What I do remember is that anybody could discipline me and I remember that if one of the Royal Dragons put a henna "X" on your seagull, you were their next snuff film star."

"Objection, Your Honor. This is preposterous. Snuff films? *Please*, are we really supposed to believe all this nonsense?"

"Is he allowed to malign me?" Aiden asked.

"It's his way of feeling important," Dr. Colton responded. "I'm sure Mr. Pizzo is a leading authority in snuff films. But before you make a ruling, allow me to direct everyone's attention to the court screen. I must warn everybody present, this is extremely graphic and gruesome."

Judge King watched the entire courtroom as a young child suffered severe abuse and stood in a steel-walled room in a corner. It ended when another boy, eight years old, fired two shots from a silenced .22 caliber pistol. Then he turned and walked away, directly towards the camera.

"I remember him," Aiden stated. "That's Buddy Jones."

Dr. Colton held his hand up, palm forward, telling Aiden to wait. "'Nonsense', Mr. Prosecutor? We just observed a snuff film from over twenty years ago."

"Overruled, and Mr. Pizzo will not jump to conclusions in the future." Judge King began to raise his gavel. "You know the boy in that film?" he asked, his gavel still at its apex.

"Buddy Jones, sir, and the boy killed was his cousin who kicked one of the Royal Dragons. Buddy died about a month later when I got the star tattoo on my arm. Buddy's death was my warning."

"What do you mean, your warning?" Prosecutor Pizzo turned to face Dr. Colton. "I apologize, he isn't my witness."

"Good question," Dr. Colton responded.

"My two best friends' fathers held me, forcing me to watch while my father hit Buddy with brass knuckles. A deputy sheriff used his hunting knife to emasculate Buddy just before stabbing him in the heart," Aidan said, visibly shaken.

"Judge King, may I approach the witness?" Dr. Colton requested, as he poured water into a glass.

"Yes, he's your witness. Do you need a short break?" Judge King inquired with concern.

"Here, Aiden," Dr. Colton interjected. "Drink some water, take a few deep breaths. Judge King has offered a short break if you want."

"No...I'm okay. I kept this inside me all my life. My dad was right."

"Your dad?" Dr. Colton queried.

"Kyler Grant, the man you promised me would never let anyone hurt me again. He said to tell the whole truth when I came here. He said telling the truth is healing, even when we don't think it will be."

"Sounds like an intelligent man," Counselor Dill extolled.

"Aiden, we know it isn't easy, but what else did you see?"

"That night, Sheriff Kelly became a Master Dragon because he proved his willingness to murder a child and put me, his son, up to be killed if I offended any Dragon member or if someone paid him $5000. I ran away two weeks later."

"Did you run away alone?" Dr. Colton asked again.

"No, sir, two friends ran away also. And before you ask, we went to the abandoned subway station called Chi-town."

"Aiden, I may have additional questions, but right now I'm finished. Mr. Pizzo, on the other hand, most definitely has a question or two."

"Ask away—I ain't hiding."

"Your witness, Mr. Pizzo," Judge King said.

"Thank you. Mr. Grant, can you explain what a DKT does before he or she receives a seagull tattoo?"

"At meetings, a DKT learns what Dragon Kids do by watching."

"What kinds of things, Mr. Grant?" Mr. Pizzo pressed.

"Have you heard of Caligula? Well, he's a saint when compared to the Dragon Society."

"Read journal number two, page 265 for a complete answer," Dr. Colton interjected. "Aiden gave an in-depth statement when he was rescued. His sworn statement is in journal two, page 250 through 350."

"Thank you," Mr. Pizzo responded. "Mr. Grant, when you were a Dragon Kid, did you do things to other DKTs?"

"No, DKTs were trained by Dragon members."

"What kinds of things do DKTs do Mr. Grant?" Mr. Pizzo pushed. "What kinds of things? Are you afraid to tell us, or are you afraid you'll remember the details—details that *are not* true, Mr. Grant."

"My turn; objection, Your Honor. Badgering the witness," Dr. Colton said, coming to Aden's defense.

"No, it's okay, sir," Aiden quickly responded. "What I remember isn't a lie. It's a violation of innocent trust. I remember everything, Your Ostentatiousness," Aiden said in a demeaning tone.

"What did you just say?" Mr. Pizzo spat incredulously.

"He said you are an arrogant jerk," Mr. Dill quipped. "I must say that Aiden hit the nail on the head, or in your case, the jerk."

"Because the witness replied, I will overrule the objection. I must admonish Mr. Grant for the acerbity in his responses." Judge King folded his hands on his desk as he spoke.

"Your Honor, in my defense, there was no sourness or bitterness in my response. What I said is, in my professional opinion, an accurate description of your prosecuting attorney."

"What is your profession, Mr. Grant?" Judge King inquired. "I find it convenient that Dr. Colton failed to ask what you do for a living."

"What I do sir, is—"

"Aiden—stop please," Dr. Colton again spoke in Japanese.

"English, Doctor, English in my court," Judge King voiced. "The witness will answer my question."

"I'm a government tactician, sir," Aiden responded.

"I'm going to check on your profession, Mr. Grant. If I find out you're lying, I'll have you arrested."

"I can have the witness's occupation verified by Senator Connor," Dr. Colton offered. "After all, it was Lucas— excuse me, *Senator* Connor who recommended Aiden for the position. If we can take a recess, I'll call Senator Connor and we can have him straighten this out immediately; or I could ask him to call you."

"Mr. Grant, do your best to refrain from further sarcastic remarks directed towards Mr. Pizzo."

"Objection, Your Honor. Objection, objection, objection!" Mr. Dill repeated in a rising crescendo. "Surely you can't mean it's acceptable for Mr. Pizzo to impugn Mr. Grant's integrity without consequences. Mr. Grant has simply stated a truth, and we all know it."

"Mr. Dill, you'll hold your tongue and abide by my rulings. Am I understood?"

"Yes, sir; I hear that double standards are the norm in your court."

"Silence, Mr. Dill. You're in contempt. You will pay a $500 fine or spend this coming weekend in jail."

Dr. Colton removed his wallet from his coat pocket.

"If I see you pass any money, Mister, the two of you shall spend the weekend in jail," Judge King threatened Dr. Colton.

"*Puh-lease*," Dr. Colton protested. "Your conversation with Mr. Dill had nothing to do with my actions. However, your having jumped to conclusions leads you to believe I'm disrespecting your earlier request that I neither make nor pay off bets in your court. I'm pointedly hurt by your assumption. My action with my wallet, sir, was to extract my medication," Dr. Colton said as he held up his packet of medicine. "Yet, with all things considered, may I be direct, Your Honor?"

"How do I respond to being reminded of my own directions within this courtroom? You may be direct, Doctor."

136

"Mr. Pizzo has continually ignored your directives. Don't get me wrong, sir; I'm not asking you to censure the man. What I am requesting is that if the prosecutor deems it necessary to act like a buffoon, please do not tolerate that type of behavior from any of the defense; meaning myself, Mr. Dill, or witnesses we call. And, finally, my last bit of directness would be to tell Mr. Anthony Pizzo to cease being an *enfant gâté*, which is French for 'spoiled child'."

"I think we need to get back to Mr. Grant's testimony," Judge King directed. "Mr. Pizzo, you may continue your cross-examination. I caution you to monitor your comments."

"Thank you, Your Honor," Mr. Pizzo replied. "Mr. Grant, please tell the court what was done to you by the DKTs that you remember."

"Excuse me, Mr. Pizzo," Aiden responded. "DKTs didn't do anything to anybody.

"Let me rephrase the question. As a DKT, what were you required to do?"

"Whatever we were told to do by Dragon Elders. I hated all of it. It made me sick. I gave a statement when Dr. Colton rescued me."

"What did you do as a Dragon Kid Trainee?" Mr. Pizzo asked. "Do you remember?"

"I can never forget the abuse I went through. I was a kid, forced to do things against my will," Aiden stated.

Aiden's emotions began eating at him. All the pain he suffered as a boy weighed on him, along with the knowledge others weren't as fortunate as he'd been. "Whether you like it or not, I tolerated what was done to me. I chose to survive, to live."

"Thank you for being honest with the court." Judge King offered. "Any more questions, Mr. Pizzo?"

"Yes, sir, I do," Mr. Pizzo answered. "Mr. Grant, how many snuff films did you witness?"

"Objection; irrelevant," Dr. Colton defended. "Not to mention, Aiden requested that we address him using his first name."

"I'll allow it." Judge King turned to Mr. Pizzo. "I won't tolerate your disrespect any longer. You will spend the weekend in jail for your contempt." Pausing, he continued, "You may answer, sir."

"Three," Aidan replied through tightened lips.

"What happened to your seagull and star tattoos? You said they were on your right arm."

"Uh–Objection–I think Your Honor," Dr. Colton interrupted. "I don't believe Aiden knows the answer to Prosecutor Pizzo's question."

"Why would he not have an answer?" Judge King asked.

"His tattoos were removed surgically by me." Dr. Colton looked at Mr. Pizzo.

"Prosecution accepts the possibility that the witness may not have known how his tattoos disappeared, if they actually existed."

"Objection, Your Honor; defense requests permission to prove said tattoos did in fact exist."

"Sustained. I'll allow you to present evidence of Aiden's tattoos' existence."

"Thank you, Your Honor," Dr. Colton responded. "On our monitor, you'll observe a full photograph of Aiden Grant as a child. Notice, you can see that his right arm very clearly shows both the seagull and a five-point star surrounding it." Dr. Colton looked at the jury. "Aiden had numerous piercings in or on his body. Note how his eyes are closed; he is under anesthesia which enabled me to perform minor surgery without causing undue stress or pain. These pictures are also located on the SD card in my journals along with a video I put on the SD card."

"What was your name as a Dragon Kid?" Mr. Pizzo inquired, resuming his interrogation.

"Excuse me," Dr. Colton said. "Tattoos existed. You may want to acknowledge that fact."

"It's clear that there were tattoos on a child's arm," Mr. Pizzo agreed.

"My name was David Kelly. My name *is* Aiden Grant. That's me in Dr. Colton's photograph."

"Nothing more for now, Your Honor," Mr. Pizzo said.

"Dr. Colton, any more questions?"

"No, sir. I wish to thank Mr. Aiden Grant for his openness and forthright honesty."

"Thank my dad, Kyler Grant," Aiden replied.

"Out of curiosity, where did you live with Mr. Kyler Grant?" Mr. Pizzo queried.

"DO NOT ANSWER THAT!" Mr. Dill quickly rebuffed. "Mr. Pizzo, you said nothing more."

"Am I dismissed?" Aiden inquired as he began to leave the witness stand.

"Dismissed," Judge King responded.

Chapter 28

"So, Kyler-how was Aiden as a boy? Did he give you headaches?" Wesley Dill asked during dinner at Dr. Colton's.

"Very spooky, leery and a lot of paranoia. His second week with me was probably his worst. But by the end of week three, he became much more relaxed."

"How'd you manage that?" Wesley inquired.

"One night, when he fell asleep from sheer exhaustion, I picked him up out of his bed and carried him to my recliner. All that night I held Aiden, calming him when his nightmares hit. I stayed with him all night. Next day we sat watching television together in my chair. He slept off and on throughout the day, as did I. When he had to use the bathroom, he went alone. I only told him to return when he was finished. After two days, I carried him to the bathroom. He had to learn that he could trust me.

"I filled the tub with water and told him it was time for him to take a bath. I left him alone to bathe, asking him to put his dirty clothes outside the door before taking his bath. When he did, I washed and dried his clothes. I knocked on the bathroom door to let him know it was okay to use more water. Only when I heard Aiden crying did I enter the bathroom. I asked him, 'What's the matter, son?' He cried and said he was too dirty. No matter how many baths he took, nobody would ever love him.

"I lifted Aiden out of the tub, wrapped him in a big towel, carried him to my recliner, and just held him. I cried with him, held him wet in my arms, and laid the blanket I kept at my recliner over him. When his clothes were dry I took him into his bedroom. He dressed by himself while I emptied the tub. We bought clothes he wanted. We ate pizza he ordered. At home, Aiden played with his video games while I watched. He sat beside me on the couch. We watched television together. When he fell asleep I held him, comforting him whenever his tortured mind frightened him.

"Three weeks after coming to live with me, Aiden wore pajamas for the first time. At one month, he began wearing shorts and going without his T-shirt. Two months after Aiden arrived, we moved into our new house."

"Wait a minute," Barbara interrupted. "Didn't I hear that you built a gated town? I mean a whole town. That was you, right?"

"Yes, ma'am, I bought land really cheap about five miles outside the town where I lived. It was in the desert and I paid $150 an acre. My house sold for $325,000 and all of that money was invested in land. I owned a construction company with thirty people working for me. Our town has grown far beyond my wildest dreams."

"How does one build a gated town?" Wesley asked.

"I started by allowing Cal-Trans of California to dump the freeway overpass and building debris on my property following a horrendous earthquake. Aiden was driving most of my heavy equipment by the time he turned twelve. All that concrete debris filled with rebar makes a great barrier on the town's eastside. We planted trees on both sides of the debris barrier and soon there was no eyesore visible. The front barrier consists of used ten-inch well casings, fourteen feet long, standing vertical and driven eight feet into the ground. The well casings are placed six feet apart. We have various sizes of juniper trees in front of those well casings so the general public is totally unaware of the barriers keeping them out. We have our own township police department as well."

"How do you protect–no–I mean, most gated communities restrict certain people from living in their area. How do you manage to keep certain people out, or do you?" Dr. Colton asked.

"If you want to live in our community, you have to pay a $1000 background check fee. Only after you pass an FBI investigation are you invited to lease one of the existing homes for $20,000 a year, plus a $10,000 security deposit. Before you can lease a house, you must sign a contract agreeing not to sublet it to anyone, including family. When you move out, if there is damage done to the house, you forfeit your security deposit. Although you lease the house, it still belongs to the township. If you prove to be undesirable, as a citizen, you are given forty-eight hours to move out. The housing authority assigns people to search your belongings and put them into a town-owned moving truck. Two people have been found undesirable, with one now in prison because of what was found while packing their possessions."

"How many empty houses are currently available?" Royce asked.

"We have over 150 houses; all are occupied. We broke ground on twenty-five more homes, ten of which are already leased. Our town has a filling station, a market, an Olympic-size indoor pool, and we even have a bank. The people who work at these places must live within the community. We've got a lot of room for expansion, including our school, which has over 300 students in attendance. There were seventeen high school graduates this year."

"How long has the town been around?" Barbara asked

"It became a town about fifteen years ago, but we've been building it since I was eleven," Aiden responded. "My most favorite place on weekends is our party barge, fishing. Dad still likes to do his cross-country run every Saturday morning."

"You know I'm going to ask you more questions in court," Dr. Colton said.

"I thought the judge dismissed me."

"He did, but you're still subject to recall."

"Why'd you have Dad brought into court?" Aiden asked.

"Aiden, I know things about Kyler that would surprise even you. He isn't into martial arts, but he is one deadly person with a throwing star. The shocker is, your dad has four ceramic stars on his person at all times. I brought him into court as a backup for your safety."

"Excuse me," Kyler Grant interjected. "How'd you know about my throwing stars?"

"Three years before Aiden went to live with you there was an incident in a bank in Garlock. Three armed men attempted to rob that bank. They didn't take into consideration a contractor trying to get a small business loan. I was in that bank withdrawing money."

140

Aiden interrupted, changing the subject, "What's Prosecutor Pizzo's problem? He's such a jerk."

"He has aspirations of being elected as head prosecutor in a couple of years. He gets convictions at any cost. Mr. Pizzo is very motivated and the more people he puts in prison, the better his chances of winning the office in two years." Dr. Colton ate as he spoke. "Wesley and I are going to break his heart and I suspect he's going to literally hate me when I am found NOT GUILTY."

"Why would he hate you? I don't understand."

"A *not guilty* verdict in a high profile case will destroy his election chances. So far we've embarrassed Mr. Pizzo in front of the jury, not to mention at least two news reporters," Wesley explained, smiling.

"And being ethical, as we are," Dr. Colton smirked, "we don't read newspapers or watch the news on television." Everyone laughed.

"Can a guy have another slice of meat?" Kyler asked. "I hope you like that eight-point mule deer. Aiden made an impressive uphill shot to bag that big guy."

"Speaking of Aiden," Dr. Colton said as he finished his meal, "would you like to see where you were hidden during your first day in this house? You might find it revealing."

"Sure, I remember that room as being small, but it was safe. Nobody treated me mean."

"Meaning, I wasn't mean to you. I couldn't get close to you or the other two because there were Dragon Society members watching me all the time. I'm sorry I didn't keep my promise."

"You kept me alive. I think being alive and naked was, and always will be, better than being dead and resting clothed inside a casket."

A short time later, Dr. Colton led Aiden to a door in the large garage next door. "This used to be my house. Go through that door, walk halfway down and pull the light cord to turn off the light. Pull it once and wait. After that, follow your instincts."

"What's in there?"

"Freedom, your life, maybe even a bit of redemption. Go, it's my last gift to you." Dr. Colton laughed when he saw Aiden open the door."

Aiden walked slowly to the light cord and pulled. Temptation to yank a second time came to him twenty seconds later. Resistance seemed futile until as his hand touched the cord again, then he heard an audible click. A panel on his left opened. Less than a minute later, Aiden turned another doorknob. Opening the door with a push, he froze, tears coming to his eyes.

"Don't just stand there; get your butt over here," a voice said from within.

"Is that really you? I thought both of you were dead," Aiden said through tear-filled eyes.

"We're all alive," Brody said smiling. "Dr. Colton changed my name to Scott."

"My new name is Xander. I saw you in court today."

"We lived," Aiden said with deep emotion. "We all lived. This is awesome! I'm sorry, guys. All my life I thought you were dead."

"Dr. Colton said your name was changed to Aiden," Scott informed his friends. "I think Dr. Colton saved our lives by letting us think the others were dead. I know that if I thought you were alive I would've looked for you."

"Me, too," Xander added. "But luckily I figured that if I had a different name, then so would you. Tonight, though, is the best night since the night we all ran away and met Dr. Colton in Chi-town."

"Dr. Colton said that this is the room where I stayed until I left," Aiden told his old friends. "It's bigger than I remember."

"Barbara told me they had three of these storage rooms. I stayed under their motorcoach in a secret room, and Xander was in the clinic office container," Scott said.

"Did you meet Kent or Royce?" Xander asked.

"I did," Aiden answered. "Do we have to stay here? This place is starting to feel weird. Where'd you guys grow up? I live in California in a gated town. It's called Harmony, border-line desert hot."

"I live in New Mexico," Scott offered next. "Zach and Amy Lawson are my parents. He manages the largest ranch I've ever seen."

"I'm married and have a family. I live wherever the FBI sends me. But I grew up in Texas. I'm super glad we ran away from the Dragons. I can't testify in court, but I think it's good the two of you can tell our story. Just remember, if you say anything about me, use Dyson."

"I might testify again tomorrow," Aiden said. "Mr. Dill told me they have evidence to send all Dragons to prison for life. I hope he's right."

"Don't stay down there all night," a voice called out. "We got cake and ice cream for dessert. Extreme dessert includes alcohol," Wesley Dill said as he entered the bunker. "Humph, wonder how many kids were lucky enough to stay in this room? Did you guys know Dr. Colton is a genius? Doesn't act like it, but it's true. Let's get back to the house."

"Back inside the house Dr. Colton stood waiting. As Xander and the others entered they saw Dr. Colton with arms outstretched, tears in his eyes. "I'm sorry– sorry for letting each of you think his friends were dead. All I can do at this time is ask for your forgiveness."

"Don't you dare ask us to forgive you," Scott said.

"Yeah, you have no right to ask for forgiveness," Aiden added.

"If you ask us for anything," Xander expressed, "it had better not be for us to forgive you." Aiden and Scott nodded, patting Xander on the shoulder. "It would be better to ask for our thanks. We owe you more than you'll ever know." All three teared up as they embraced Dr. Colton.

"Thank you for my dad," Aiden stammered.

"Thanks for getting us away from the Dragons," Xander said, "and for telling us how you killed Marco Rizzoli."

"Xander, I have a secret just for you. Let me whisper in your ear." Xander leaned close to Dr. Colton's lips. "I didn't kill anybody," Dr. Colton said in a normal voice. "But I still love all of you."

Chapter 29

"Mr. Dill, please call your witness," Judge King instructed.

"We'd like to recall Aiden Grant to the stand."

"Mr. Grant, please remember you're still under oath. Take the stand, please."

"Aiden, do you know of any surgery that you received as a boy?" Mr. Dill asked.

"Yes sir, Mr. Dill, I do. My dad–"

"Objection, Your Honor, please. You undoubtedly had surgery as a child. So what?"

"Overruled. I want to hear what Mr. Grant has to say."

"My dad took me to have surgery when I was twelve."

"What was the surgery for?"

"A tonsillectomy, sir."

"Have you ever taken a trip to Sweden?"

"Objection, irrelevant," Mr. Pizzo protested. "Do we really need to hear about a trip to another country?"

"Your Honor," Dr. Colton responded as he tapped a key on his computer, sending a signal to the courtroom television. "I showed this photograph to the court earlier. It clearly shows the witness as a boy prepared for surgery. I was the surgeon's assistant. I flew Aiden and his dad to Sweden."

"Overruled, please continue." Judge King leaned forward.

"Your Honor," Mr. Pizzo interrupted. "Didn't we just hear Dr. Colton admit to practicing medicine in another country? Isn't that illegal?"

"No, Mr. Pizzo," Dr. Colton responded. I *assisted* the surgeon. You know, handing her the instruments which I invented. I assisted the surgeon in performing her job, much the same way you assist in the prosecution of this trial. May I *please* continue questioning my witness, Your Honor?"

"Yes, you may. Mr. Pizzo, if you believe Dr. Colton acted illegally, then I suggest you do your due diligence."

Dr. Colton continued, "Aiden, do you know why you were in Sweden? I know it was for surgery, but do you know what kind?"

"My father said it was microsurgery to repair damage done to my body when I was little."

"How old were you?"

"I was twelve."

"Let me direct the court's attention to the numerous piercings Aiden suffered in his young life. To describe these mutilations can only be considered grotesque. These pictures were taken prior to his surgery, and at age twelve he was finally healed."

Mr. Pizzo stood up, "I know it's not my turn to ask questions," he said, "but who did this to you?"

"Prosecutor Kay Kelly did all the piercing using a big hypodermic syringe needle she took from Dr. Trask, an animal doctor. Prosecutor Kelly did this to me at a Dragon Society meeting on my ninth birthday."

"Aiden, why didn't you tell the police, a teacher, or even a judge?" Mr. Dill asked.

"Who would I tell? Sheriff Kelly? He is a Dragon. Oh, I know: tell Judge Felitich–nope, he's another Dragon. Judge Tauzer–Dragon! You see, Mr. Dill, Dragons are judges, attorneys, teachers, doctors, youth directors, and everybody else. I'm not saying every person is a Dragon Society member, but kids just don't know who they can trust."

"Why'd you trust Dr. Colton?"

"We ran away from the Dragons. We had to trust someone. While Dr. Colton was with the lady whose daughter was sick, the people in Chi-town said we could trust him."

"Thank you, Aiden. Your Honor, we've no further questions," Mr. Dill said. "Mr. Pizzo's turn now."

"Does the prosecution have any questions?" Judge King asked.

"Only one," Mr. Pizzo responded. "First, what you suffered was pure evil. My question is only this: how have you kept from being filled with hate?"

"My adopted father gave me nothing but love and accepted me. He let me talk without any kind of judgment and when I described all the ugliness, he loved me still. Kyler Grant never doubted my honesty; he supported me, giving me a life without abuse."

"My mistake–one more question," Mr. Pizzo admitted. "Did the surgery in which Dr. Colton assisted help to heal your injuries?"

"Yes, sir, the surgery healed my physical injuries. It was my dad who helped me keep from going insane."

"No more, Your Honor." Mr. Pizzo sat down and looked at Dr. Colton.

"Mr. Dill, do you have another witness? Mr. Grant, you may leave," Judge King directed.

"Yes, sir; the defense calls Cedric Sullivan."

A distinguished looking gentleman entered the courtroom.

"Do you swear to tell the truth, the whole truth and nothing but the truth, so help you..."

"Don't! I'm not an atheist, however, I do not believe in your oath to tell the truth. I promise to be totally honest. My name is Cedric Sullivan–that is C-E-D-R-I-C S-U-L-L-I-V-A-N. Your questions, please." Mr. Sullivan sat down in the witness chair.

"Mr. Sullivan, do you know Dr. Richard Colton?" Mr. Dill inquired.

"Only professionally. I'm a barrister for Sullivan and Williams. It's a small law firm in southwest London."

"Forgive me, sir, but why would a law firm in London be interested in Dr. Colton?"

"Inheritance funds, sir."

"Please explain," Mr. Dill encouraged.

"A woman–Amanda Bentley by name–lived in a small, unassuming bungalow. She wasn't related to the Coltons, but she did attend Richard and Nancy's wedding. While Nancy Marshall was vacationing in Europe, she came to the aid of Amanda Bentley, who had been in an automobile accident. This accident took the life of Amanda's son, Ford Bentley, and left Amanda Bentley paralyzed from the waist down. Nancy Marshall spent her entire vacation with Amanda, encouraging her to do physical therapy. When Mrs. Bentley began therapy, Nancy Marshall took a year off from school to help the woman."

"Are you saying Nancy Colton inherited money? Why?"

"Yes, as you Yanks would say, 'in a roundabout way'. Only not really cash." Mr. Sullivan went on to explain, "When I contacted Dr. Colton, he asked how much the inheritance would cost him, and did the fact his wife, Nancy, was deceased nullify the inheritance. I assured him the inheritance was still quite valid."

A puzzled look from Mr. Dill caused Mr. Sullivan to elaborate.

"I take it you Yanks haven't heard of Amanda Bentley. Therefore you would not know she sailed around the world alone. She made a fortune telling her story. Amanda Bentley was a world-class racing sailor. She won two championships before her accident. Her ship, the *Crystal Wind*, was still in dry dock. Dr. Colton said to me, 'Why not sell or donate it to a museum?' He isn't a sailor. I told him the last offer for the *Crystal Wind* was 3.5 million. I promised to arrange a sale in twenty-four hours. Word got out, and the *Crystal Wind* sold for over 5.8 million U.S. dollars. A week later, Dr. Colton flew home in his own private jet which Sullivan and Williams helped him purchase. Amanda Bentley had no living relatives except for her ex-husband, Roger. She owned 25% of the Bentley family business. This 25% translated to an additional 8.8 million."

"Let me get this straight," Mr. Dill said. "Dr. Colton received this inheritance from Amanda Bentley because his deceased wife Nancy was a Good Samaritan?"

"Yes, sir, that is what I just said."

"Your witness, Mr. Pizzo. I'm done."

"Mr. Sullivan, how much money did your firm charge Dr. Colton for handling the inheritance?"

"Amanda Bentley's estate paid us. And before you ask, we didn't charge for helping in the aircraft's purchase because our commission in selling the *Crystal Wind* was quite substantial."

"How substantial?" Mr. Pizzo inquired.

"Objection; irrelevant. Sullivan and Williams aren't on trial. Mr. Sullivan told the court how much Dr. Colton received in his dead wife's inheritance. Mr. Pizzo is reaching beyond my direct line of questioning."

"I agree, sustained. We aren't interested in Mr. Sullivan's funds. Dr. Colton disclosed the information on his own."

"How did Dr. Colton receive his money, sir?"

"I believe he left his funds in the Greater Bank of London. I assisted Dr. Colton in placing $500,000 in a separate account for use in refueling his jet and paying the crew."

"Have you been paid for your court appearance here today or your testimony?"

"Of course I'm being paid. I would be a fool not to pay myself vacation fees when I'm on vacation."

"You're done," Mr. Pizzo sighed.

"You may step down, Mr. Sullivan. Thank you for your testimony," Judge King said in dismissing the witness. "Mr. Dill, you may call your next witness."

"Defense calls Declan Hinkle."

Mr. Hinkle was sworn in and spelled his name for the record.

"Mr. Hinkle, do you know Dr. Richard Colton?"

"Yes–yes sir, I know him."

"And how do you know Dr. Colton?"

"He's a better pilot than he is a–sorry Doc, but the truth," Mr. Hinkle said.

"Than what, sir?"

"Oh, yeah–sorry. He's a better pilot than he is a piano player."

"You surely have to know what I'm going to ask."

Mr. Hinkle laughed lightly. "I was his piano teacher. Dr. Colton is a smart and really talented doctor–"

"Objection," Mr. Pizzo interrupted. "The witness is giving his opinion of Dr. Colton."

"Your Honor, Mr. Hinkle is stating the facts as he knows them," Mr. Dill rebutted.

"Your Honor, forgive me, but if I'd said Dr. Colton would starve if he tried to play music for a living, that would be an opinion. But if I testified that he's a really bad musician, I'd be stating facts based on my years of instructing others," Mr. Hinkle addressed the judge, finishing his testimony.

"I'm going to overrule the objection. You may finish what you were about to say."

"That's all right, Your Honor," Mr. Dill yielded. "I'll ask another question. Mr. Hinkle, have you ever worked for Dr. Colton as a pilot for his jet?"

"Two years, then he piloted his jet for himself. After that I only flew transatlantic flights with him."

"I thought all jets required two pilots. Or a pilot and a copilot," Mr. Dill said.

"A common misconception by lots of people, including other pilots," Mr. Hinkle replied. "Dr. Colton's jet could be flown not only legally, but quite easily by one pilot. Dr. Colton's jet was a cutting-edge jet aircraft.

"Were there any other times you flew Dr. Colton's jet?"

"At least twice a year I flew mercy missions, sponsored by Dr. Colton."

"What's a mercy mission?"

"Dr. Colton sent me from São Paulo, Brazil to UCLA in California with a little girl for an open heart surgery."

"Your Honor," Mr. Pizzo interrupted. "What's the purpose of Mr. Hinkle's testimony? This is wasting the court's time. Can we take a twenty-minute recess?"

"Excuse me, young fella, but you didn't say 'objection'. Therefore you're out of line. So please remain quiet," Mr. Hinkle politely directed his comment to Mr. Pizzo.

146

"Objection," Mr. Pizzo began.

"Overruled, no recess at this time," Judge King retorted.

"Mr. Judge, Your Honor," Mr. Hinkle spoke directly to Judge King. "Isn't that young man the one who accused Dr. Colton of not caring about people?" Mr. Hinkle asked.

"No, I believe the charge is murder," Judge King replied.

"Well, sir, if you kill someone then you sure don't care about them," Mr. Hinkle continued. "I'm here to testify that Dr. Colton is a caring man. And that isn't my opinion; *that is a fact*."

"Mr. Hinkle, you make a great point," Judge King turned to the prosecution. "Mr. Pizzo, let the man testify. You don't have to object so often. Proceed, Mr. Dill."

"Do you have any children, Mr. Hinkle?"

"Me! No, sir, once I retire it'll be time to marry a nice God-fearing woman. Right now I'm enjoying my life flying private jets for people who need my services."

"Are you contracted out to anyone at this time?" Mr. Dill inquired, looking at Mr. Pizzo.

"Yes, sir, as a matter of fact. Barbara Colton has me on standby to fly her to France. She has everything she wants to take with her in a hangar at the airport. Her passport is aboard the jet," Mr. Hinkle responded.

"What about Dr. Colton's passport? Is that on the jet too?"

"No, sir, Dr. Colton doesn't have a passport."

"Objection! Speculation, Your Honor," Mr. Pizzo immediately interrupted. "Mr. Hinkle has no real way of knowing where Dr. Colton's passport is located."

"Your Honor," Mr. Hinkle defended, "may I rebut the objection?"

"Your Honor, if I may," Mr. Dill pleaded. "Grant me one question before you rule on Mr. Pizzo's objection."

"One question, Mr. Dill, and I warn you, I'm leaning toward sustaining Mr. Pizzo's objection."

"Thank you, sir. Mr. Hinkle, how do you know Dr. Colton has no passport?"

"I personally handed all of Dr. Colton's visas and passport to Federal Judge Sam Holt. That's not speculation, it's fact."

"Okay, I'm going to overrule the objection. You may proceed, Mr. Dill."

Ignoring Mr. Pizzo's antics of throwing his hands up, Mr. Dill continued. "Have you ever heard Dr. Colton say that he wanted to disappear in France?"

"No, sir, Barbara Colton is the only person I ever heard say those words. Dr. Colton's cancer has made her want to disappear and those are her words to me."

"Now, Mr. Hinkle, you're more than just a pilot and part-time piano teacher. What's your profession, sir?" Mr. Dill stood with his hands behind his back.

"Which profession do you want? Psychiatrist, psychologist, behavioralist, or maybe profiler. I've been called upon to perform all of these, and yes, I'm considered to be an expert in each of the fields mentioned." Mr. Hinkle opened a folder and removed four pieces of paper. "These are copies of my certifications."

"Is it safe to say you've talked with Dr. Colton on a professional level?"

"We've spoken over fifty times in the last six months," Mr. Hinkle answered. "Dr. Colton has confided his actions to me. Other than Dr. Colton, I believe that I'm the only person who knows what happened to Marco Rizzoli."

"What did happen to Marco Rizzoli?" Mr. Dill queried.

"That, sir, is confidential information," Mr. Hinkle began.

"Objection," Mr. Pizzo said, leaping to his feet. "The prosecution asks that the court order this witness to answer the question."

Mr. Hinkle chuckled lightly. "You really are a horse's patoot. My refusal falls under doctor-patient privilege. As a psychiatrist for Dr. Colton I cannot be compelled to disclose the information you desire."

"Now is a good time to take a twenty-minute recess. The witness will not speak with anybody during this recess, including defense counsel. Dismissed." Judge King then rose from his chair and exited.

Exactly twenty minutes later, Judge King reentered the courtroom, a look of pure contempt on his face. "Come to order, we're back in session. Mr. Dill, do you have any further questions for this witness?"

"Sir, I believe we're finished for now."

"Mr. Pizzo, your witness. Keep it short."

"Mr. Hinkle, have you ever flown Dr. Colton's jet when he was accompanied by an underage male or female?"

"Ask a different question, Mr. Pizzo. Our witness is not at liberty to answer, due to doctor-patient privilege," Judge King instructed.

"When was the last time you piloted Dr. Colton's jet?"

"The day before he sold it."

"Have you flown Dr. Colton anywhere after he sold his jet?"

"Dr. Colton is grounded. Flying anywhere could kill him without warning."

"You testified that Dr. Colton is a caring person. What caring person takes a child from his or her family?"

"I'm sorry, sir. I can't answer that question as it calls for an opinion."

Dr. Colton nudged Mr. Dill under the table. "I think Declan is frustrating our prosecutor."

"I say Mr. Hinkle will finish soon," Mr. Dill signed back.

"We left him nothing," Dr. Colton responded.

Mr. Pizzo tilted his head back. "Is there anything you can tell us about your conversations with Dr. Colton?"

"He likes beer, loves his wife, his two sons, and he worships God. He misses his first wife, Nancy, and his son, Richard Jr.. His family comes first."

"Did you know that Dr. Colton basically kidnapped his twin boys?" Mr. Pizzo probed.

"Actually, you have your information twisted. Upon reaching home after rescuing Kent and Royce, Dr. Colton and his wife contacted the proper authorities to foster the twins. Ted and Myra were later arrested for crimes against an infant daughter, born six months before the Colton's filed for legal adoption of the twins."

"Were Ted and Myra charged with child abandonment?" Mr. Pizzo inquired.

"Yes, and their jury saw two very shocked faces when they saw the twins in court. Myra Binns confessed everything for a lighter sentence."

"What was her sentence?"

"Objection, Your Honor," Mr. Dill interrupted. "Mr. Pizzo's questions are irrelevant and they go beyond the scope of direct examination. Plus, Myra Binns died in prison."

"Sustained. Mr. Pizzo, do you have any relevant questions for this witness?"

"Nothing further, Your Honor." Mr. Pizzo shook his head as he sat down in defeat.

"Mr. Dill, call your next witness."

"Your Honor, defense calls Robin West."

Robin West took her seat in the witness stand, and after taking the oath, spelled her name.

"Hello, Robin, how're you feeling?" Dr. Colton began.

"I'm blessed by the best, sir. Thank you."

"Are you the daughter of the author, Blake West?"

"Yes, sir," Robin West replied.

"Would you tell the court how we met, please? How old were you?"

"I was eleven years old. I walked into a hospital with a knife sticking out of my chest. Both of my legs were blistered. The hospital people saved my life. The emergency room doctor asked me what happened and I told him."

"Can you tell this court why there was a knife in your chest?" Dr. Colton asked.

"My daddy stabbed me. It hurt and I couldn't pull it out. The doctor stayed with me even during my x-rays. He promised to take the knife out when I went to sleep. A nurse asked me my name. I said Victoria Payne and then I heard fire engine sirens blaring. Someone asked if my mother was at home or at work. My answer was that my mommy and my brother are dead. That he shot them with his gun."

"Your Honor, the witness's mother and brother were found inside their burned-down house, a bullet to the head of each. Mr. Payne could not be found," Mr. Dill informed the court.

"And you know this how?" Mr. Pizzo asked contemptuously.

"Police reports, newspapers, and television," Mr. Dill replied.

"Your Honor," Dr. Colton stood up. "Police Detective Child threatened to jail the doctor when he–Detective Child–was denied access to Victoria. The doctor informed the detective that the hospital also removed a bullet from just below the girl's left kidney. The moment Detective Child left, my assistance was requested. I advised the emergency room doctor to call First-Rate Ambulance Service, then send the patient to Methodist Hospital and notify Judy Franklin, wife of Judge Franklin, of the situation."

"Is the witness going to testify?" Mr. Pizzo inquired querulously.

"Relax, Mr. Pizzo," Judge King directed.

"Do you remember what you told the police?" Dr. Colton asked his witness.

"I saw Daddy kill Mommy and my brother. Daddy stabbed me when I left my bedroom to use the bathroom. Daddy had grounded me earlier for breaking a glass plate. I disobeyed him and he stabbed me. Daddy shot me when I went back to my bedroom. I played dead until Daddy went outside. The house was on fire when I walked to the hospital. Nobody offered to help me. I told Detective Child, my daddy, Arnold Payne, owned a boat. His brother, Uncle Danny, lived in Canada."

"Your Honor, Mr. Payne's body was found five years ago in an old building being demolished." Mr. Dill paused. "The building was owned by Rizzoli Enterprises."

"Due to her injuries, Victoria Payne was placed into protective services. The whereabouts of her uncle is as yet unknown," Dr. Colton explained.

"Dr. Colton," Robin interrupted, "on the day the metal staples were removed from my chest, as I walked out of the doctor's exam room, I fainted. I was rushed back to my doctor–"

"Objection! No question has been asked," Mr. Pizzo snapped.

"I'll ask a question," Dr. Colton countered.

"Sustained; the jury will ignore the witness's statement from Dr. Colton up to Mr. Pizzo's objection."

Dr. Colton calmly waited for Judge King to finish his ruling. Then he asked, "Robin, what happened to you after your surgery staples were removed?"

"I fainted and was rushed to my doctor–"

"Objection; more spewing of useless information," Mr. Pizzo petulantly protested.

"Your Honor, I asked a question. Mr. Pizzo is objecting to my witness testifying."

"Overruled! Continue."

"The doctor was baffled; everything appeared normal. By my choice, I didn't respond to any of the medical staff. My doctor thought something was seriously wrong, so he admitted me into the hospital to undergo testing. Staff finally left me alone in the room. When they returned, I was gone and so were my clothes."

"What? Dr. Colton *abducted* you, too?" Mr. Pizzo accused, seizing the opportunity to get the crime of kidnapping on the record.

"Objection; casting aspersions. Prosecutor Pizzo is once again ignoring the court's instruction."

"Sustained. Mr. Pizzo, you'll remain silent. You've been warned too many times. Two days in jail, plus four hundred dollars."

"Your Honor, in rebuttal to Mr. Pizzo's outburst: I found Victoria in Chi-town playing chess with one of the residents. She remained hidden for three months before she went to live with a new family. We talked often and she asked everyone to call her Robin," recalled Dr. Colton, looking directly at Judge King.

"Mr. Dill, please continue with your witness," Judge King said, ignoring Dr. Colton's statement.

"Robin, where'd you end up living?" Mr. Dill inquired with a warm smile.

"Catalina Island, off the California coast. I was openly welcomed by everyone on the island."

"Can you tell me, or us, how you got to Catalina Island?" Mr. Dill continued.

"Dr. Colton flew me to LAX in his jet. From there we flew in a helicopter to Catalina Island. I grew up on the island. Now I live there with my husband and our four children."

"Why did you go to Chi-town?" Mr. Dill asked.

"I heard someone say Chi-town is where to go if you want to disappear."

"You know I'm going to ask." Mr. Dill gently coaxed.

"Dr. Colton said it when I faked being asleep."

"Did Dr. Colton kidnap you?"

"Objection!" Mr. Pizzo erupted venomously. "Why can I not ask such a question but the defense is free to do so? Your Honor, I ask the court to admonish the defense regarding the word 'kidnap'."

Mr. Dill quickly responded, "I'm making certain the jurors know this witness was *rescued*, not kidnapped."

"Overruled," Judge King snapped back.

"No, he didn't," Robin stated emphatically.

"Robin, why'd you run away? You had an uncle in Canada where you could live?" Mr. Dill hinted.

"No offense, but who in their right mind wants to live in temperatures that drop to thirty or forty below zero? Not me! Uncle Danny killed a man on the road when he got angry. He just drove up beside the man and shot him. Nothing but road rage. I'm glad Dr. Colton helped me be adopted by good people. He's my hero."

"We have nothing further, Your Honor." Mr. Dill ended his questioning, a smile on his face.

"Mr. Pizzo, do you have any questions?"

"Yes, sir," Mr. Pizzo said. "When did you legally change your name from Virginia Payne to Robin West?"

"If I'm not mistaken, it was the day before we…, I mean, Dr. Colton and I flew to California. It was a federal judge who signed my name change."

"I have no further questions," Mr. Pizzo said dejectedly.

"You may step down. No, no you can't," Judge King corrected. "What did you say your name is?"

"Robin West; is there a problem with my name?"

"You said you're married?" Judge King questioned.

"Yes, I am," Robin replied

"What's your husband's name?"

"Your Honor, my husband is not part of this trial; therefore his name is irrelevant—and with all due respect—none of this court's business." Before Judge King could respond, Robin held up her hand. "Please don't threaten me with contempt. I'm stating a simple fact. I kept my maiden name. So I've told the truth under oath."

"You may leave, thank you." Judge King felt chastised, and he didn't like the feeling. "Call your next witness, Mr. Dill."

"Rebecca Preston, Your Honor."

Rebecca walked in, stopped next to the witness stand and spoke. "Rebecca Preston," she spelled her name. "I promise to answer all appropriate questions truthfully and ignore all mundane frivolous ones."

"Oh heck–I'll allow that as being sworn in," Judge King said in exasperation.

"Ms. Preston, may I ask your age?" Dr. Colton inquired.

"I'm twenty-eight, sir."

"What's your occupation?"

"Nurse, registered nurse to be exact."

"You like helping people?"

"Yes, I do. My mother is a nurse practitioner. That's my goal as well."

"What about your father?"

"He's a corporate attorney, but you know that already."

"Yes I do–but the court doesn't. What do you remember?"

"Objection," Mr. Pizzo interrupted. "Remember about what?"

"Your Honor, Ms. Preston knows what I'm talking about. But allow me to rephrase." Dr. Colton faced Rebecca. "Is Rebecca Preston your birth name?"

"No, sir, my parents explained everything. Tom Preston, my father helped me–"

"Objection," Mr. Pizzo interrupted again. "She answered, 'No sir.' Nothing else is required."

"Sustained," Judge King responded automatically.

"Rebecca, what did your father help you do?" Dr. Colton asked in order to allow his witness to answer without interruption from Mr. Pizzo.

"Change my name legally. I was Michelle Gates. Judge Samuel Holt changed my name when he signed my adoption papers."

"Thank you, Rebecca," Dr. Colton responded. "You were adopted by whom, and why?"

"Tom and Emily Preston; they paid for plastic surgery–"

"Objection! Irrelevant," Mr. Pizzo barked.

"Your Honor, just let the witness continue," Dr. Colton urged. "Otherwise, I'll have to continuously rephrase questions around Mr. Pizzo's absurd protests."

"Overruled! Mr. Pizzo, let the witness testify without undue remonstrations."

"Please continue, Rebecca," Dr. Colton prompted.

"I had plastic surgery, reconstructive surgery, and they paid all of my regular medical bills. They were accused of physical abuse when I broke a rib after crashing on my motorbike. The hospital told my parents that somebody abused me."

"Your Honor, journal number one, page 223," Dr. Colton offered. "Shall we take a recess to allow our jurors the opportunity to carefully read the entry?"

"It would be far more expedient if you share this information," Judge King advised. "Only remember Mr. Pizzo will be afforded the right to ask you questions regarding your narrations once your witnesses are finished."

152

"Yes, sir, I'll honor our agreement at that time."

"Please proceed," Judge King said.

Remaining where he stood, Dr. Colton began: *"Michelle Gates, three years old. She's been in the clinic six times in four months. She's suffered six life-threatening afflictions."* Dr. Colton paused. "Your Honor, if it pleases the court, I won't name her injuries as they are listed with detail in my journal entry. However, if you wish, I will list them."

"Um–no, I think what you have listed in your journal regarding her injuries will be sufficient for now. You may continue with your narration."

Dr. Colton took a moment for a swallow of water. He began: "*Journal number one, page 223. Ralph and Martha Gates have subjected their daughter to untold abuse. I thought my first rescue would be the only one. Now, I see this little girl will be dead in less than a year if I don't intervene. I notified the proper authorities twice before and they have done nothing. It will be risky! I have to– NO, I MUST rescue her. I leave for a convention in Texas two days from now. She'll have to go with me. I couldn't rescue the girl that night. Her parents signed her out of the hospital promising to watch her carefully. Watching their daughter meant she was in the same bedroom as her mother who entertained two men sexually."*

"Objection," Mr. Pizzo started.

"Either read the journal or listen, Mr. Pizzo," Judge King directed. "Overruled!"

"When I returned home from my secretive observation of the Gates, I prepared plans to remove Michelle from the house. To my surprise, it was easier than I had expected.

I called the Gates' home, pretending to work for a bogus pizza place. 'You won a free pizza,' I told Mrs. Gates. She told me what they liked. Martha Gates acted like a giddy school girl. Ralph liked sausage and mushrooms, she liked pepperoni. 'Do we get a free drink with that, Mr. Pizza Man?' she asked me. Martha Gates said her daughter is only three years old and she would give the girl part of a sleeping pill so she wouldn't need to eat. Mrs. Gates asked for two cans of beer.

Thirty minutes later I delivered the pizza. I crushed two tranquilizers on each half of the pizza right after I picked it up. Ralph Gates opened the door. 'Free pizza and beer. Must be my lucky night!' He exclaimed. I opened the pizza box so he could see the pizza. Greed is wonderful at times. Mr. Gates snatched a slice of pizza and took a big bite flaunting his good fortune.

Ralph tossed his pizza back into the box, grabbed pizza and beer from me and then spat out, 'Thank you. Now get the hell outta here.' He shut the door in my face, forgetting to lock it afterwards.

I waited a short time before knocking on the Gates' front door. Getting no response I opened it and stepped inside. I carefully retrieved every bit of uneaten pizza; the two beer cans were emptied in the toilet and flushed away. All evidence of my presence was removed, put inside a white Honda Accord and then I returned for Michelle. When the Gates woke up, their daughter would be gone forever."

"I notice your next entry on this subject, page 224, is months later," Judge King interjected. "Is that correct?"

"You are correct, Your Honor."

"You kidnapped that child," Mr. Pizzo stated.

"I was not kidnapped," Rebecca countered. "Dr. Colton saved my life. He rescued me."

Dr. Colton looked at the jurors. Some were reading, others watching him. "My journal reads: *Ironically, Michelle's disappearance wasn't discovered until Martha Gates' trial for murder. Reports indicate Mr. Gates became angry after finding his wife home at eight o'clock in the morning. Mr. Gates answered a phone call, only to learn that his wife had been fired for missing work again. His anger fueled, Mr. Gates began beating his wife. She fought back, reaching a knife on the kitchen counter. The moment Ralph Gates turned his back, Martha shoved the knife into her husband's lower back. Then she cut his neck before stabbing him repeatedly in the stomach. Ralph died in their living room. He had been stabbed seventeen times. Martha Gates fled the house, knowing she would be arrested for murder. Police were not summoned for two days. Ralph Gates' body was discovered by one of Martha Gates' regular clients. The man called 911 from the home.*"

"Excuse me," Judge King interrupted. "Are you saying Martha Gates was a 'lady of the night'?"

"Secretary by day, prostitute by night, sir," Dr. Colton answered.

"Let's continue," Judge King said.

"I was safely in Lubbock, Texas, meeting with the Prestons who were recommended as adoptive parents. I had no doubt the girl would be safe with these people. I left Michelle, now named Rebecca, and returned to my cheap motel room. I promised myself: no more, even if I did it out of love–it's extremely dangerous and illegal. When I returned home, I resumed my normal routine."

Mr. Dill stood up as Dr. Colton returned to his seat. "Do you by any chance remember any of what Dr. Colton has described?" Mr. Dill asked Rebecca.

"Some of it, but what I remember most was seeing Dr. Colton every time I had surgery. My father said–"

"Objection; hearsay," Mr. Pizzo groused.

"Sustained; you're not allowed to state what another person says," Judge King responded.

"How many times did you see Dr. Colton?"

"Lots; my dad would say–"

"Objection; again, hearsay," Mr. Pizzo said, pleased that the witness ignored the judge's earlier instruction. "Evidently Mr. Dill's witness didn't pay attention a moment ago."

"I listened," Rebecca shot back.

"Sustained," Judge King quickly responded.

"Mr. Judge, can I object?" Rebecca asked.

"No, you may not."

Dr. Colton stood up, motioning to Mr. Dill. "Rebecca, how would you know I was coming to see your family?"

"My daddy would," Rebecca glared at Mr. Pizzo. "Don't you dare say '*objection*'. Daddy would say, 'Doc is coming to see you, girly-girl. And that is firsthand information, not hearsay.'"

"Is that what you were trying to say earlier, before Mr. Pizzo objected?" Dr. Colton waited for Rebecca's answer.

"Yes, sir, it is."

"Your Honor, once again Mr. Pizzo is jumping to conclusions. So, evidently Mr. Pizzo is the one who didn't pay attention to your instructions to abstain from that specific behavior." Dr. Colton looked directly at Mr. Pizzo as he spoke. "My witnesses aren't here to be badgered, Your Honor." Dr. Colton resumed his position at the defense table.

"Excuse me, Rebecca," Mr. Dill interrupted. "Why be a nurse?"

"I was lucky. I know what happened to me because of the surgeries I've had in my life. I don't remember everything. I want to help others the way I was helped. I became a nurse because of Dr. Colton."

"I'm finished for now," Mr. Dill said, sitting down. "Mr. Pizzo may have some questions."

"Cross?" Judge King queried.

"He doesn't want to talk to me. He knows it's useless," Rebecca spoke calmly in a low authoritative voice.

"Ironically, Ms. Preston is right. She's been through enough, having been brainwashed into believing she was rescued, not kidnapped, by Dr. Colton," Mr. Pizzo said in a clearly angered tone.

"Objection!" Mr. Dill shouted, instantly on his feet. "Mr. Pizzo goes too far. Miss Preston has indeed been abused in her past. She's done nothing to warrant Mr. Pizzo's acidic tone."

"Sustained. The jury will ignore Mr. Pizzo's outbreak of disrespect toward this witness." Turning to the prosecutor, Judge King added, "Mr. Pizzo, I wish we could strike your comment from the record. You've just given Mr. Dill grounds for a mistrial." Then he addressed Rebecca Preston: "You may leave. Thank you for coming today."

Once she had exited, Judge King adjourned for lunch until one-thirty in the afternoon.

Chapter 30

"Dr. Colton, there's a young boy and girl here wanting to thank you for some reason," Agent Ward said as they prepared to leave the courtroom for lunch.

"I've no idea why any young kids would want to thank me. Let them have their say," Dr. Colton responded.

Two children, clearly brother and sister, approached Dr. Colton after Agent Ward motioned to them. "You don't know us, sir, but you knew our mother," the boy said. "Our mother's name was Ruby. She died six months after we were born."

"Your mother loved the two of you from the second I told her she was going to have twins," Dr. Colton responded. Seeing Mr. Pizzo hanging back, eavesdropping, Dr. Colton called to him: "You may want to hear this, Mr. Prosecutor, and realize I didn't kidnap their mother."

"Oh, *heck* no!" the boy exclaimed.

"Excuse me," Mr. Pizzo interrupted. "Who are you children?"

"My name is Lisa, and my brother's name is Wayne."

"Their grandfather is Baxter Axelrod, the multimillionaire," Dr. Colton said.

"Baxter Axelrod is wanted for the kidnapping of a twelve-year-old girl," Mr. Pizzo accused.

"Our granddad didn't kidnap our mother," Wayne countered.

"Easy, kids," Dr. Colton cautioned. "Their mother's name was Georgie Edwards. She was forced into being a call girl at the age of twelve by Rizzoli Enterprises, who called her 'Ruby'. She changed her name to Brandy Axelrod after being adopted by Baxter Axelrod when she went to live in Canada. Later, they moved to Alaska."

"Why would the woman move and change her name if she wasn't forced?" Mr. Pizzo asked.

"Our mother wasn't a woman," Lisa corrected him. She died four months, one week, and five days after she turned thirteen. We were six months old. Granddad moved to Alaska after Mother died."

"Ruby was merely twelve when she came to see me at the clinic. She was escorted by Mario Rizzoli's number-two man, Otto Primo. Otto never left her side during my physical examination of the girl. When he heard that Ruby's illness was morning sickness, the poor man nearly cried."

"Otto Primo testified against Mario Rizzoli in court. It was his testimony that ultimately convicted his boss," Prosecutor Pizzo revealed. "I bet he knew who got their mother pregnant."

"DNA tests have proved that our birth father is Mario Rizzoli," Wayne said. "When he went to prison, we celebrated."

"Ruby was returned to Mario Rizzoli–or more exactly, Rizzoli Enterprises–where she was savagely beaten. She stole a bicycle and came back to the clinic. I hid her," Dr. Colton admitted. "Otto stopped by the clinic looking for Ruby. He wanted to help her. Otto told me, the girl's father was either Mr. Rizzoli's chauffeur–or Rizzoli himself."

156

"Rizzoli's limo was blown up," Mr. Pizzo reflected. "Law enforcement thought Mario Rizzoli had ordered his chauffeur killed, but Mario Rizzoli paid $500,000 in ransom for his chauffeur's kid, so it didn't make sense for him to kill the girl's father."

"This will make you mad," Dr. Colton said. "Otto Primo killed the chauffeur and you granted him immunity from charges for crimes he committed while employed by Mario Rizzoli."

"Why should this interest me?" Mr. Pizzo asked. "Otto died of a heart attack last year."

"Uncle Otto gave Granddad a lot of money. He wasn't our real uncle, but we called him 'Uncle' because he helped our mother. It was Uncle Otto who demanded a ransom. He told us how he made Mr. Rizzoli pay for what he'd done to our mother," Lisa confided.

"Why'd you want to see Dr. Colton?" Mr. Dill finally asked the question that had been bothering him."

"Granddad heard that Dr. Colton has cancer. He told us how much Dr. Colton helped our mother," Wayne informed Mr. Dill. Wayne looked to his sister.

"We are Axelrods," Lisa said. "We owe our lives to Dr. Colton."

"Who brought you to court?" Mr. Pizzo harshly inquired.

"I did," the man behind Mr. Pizzo answered. "My adopted grandchildren have decided they don't want Mario Rizzoli's blood money. I'm Baxter Axelrod, and I didn't kidnap anyone. Granted, I changed Ruby's name to Brandy Axelrod when I adopted her. I adopted her infant children as well, which she requested. Otto gave me information on how to use Mario Rizzoli's adoption agency against him. I did, and it worked perfectly."

"What proof do you have that supports your claim of Otto Primo being the one who kidnapped Ruby and blew up the limo, killing the chauffeur?"

"Give him the paper, Wayne," Lisa urged.

Wayne handed Mr. Pizzo an envelope. Inside was a handwritten confession by Otto Primo of the kidnapping and ransom of twelve-year-old Ruby. He also admitted to killing the chauffeur, believing Mr. Rizzoli was inside the limo.

"We know we're what you call illegitimate, but Mario Rizzoli is our biological father. We want to file papers stating that we wish no claim against anything he still owns."

"Should you file those papers, it will alert Mario Rizzoli of your existence. I urge you to *not* file your paperwork, but leave it all until after he dies." Mr. Pizzo cautioned.

"We're going to lunch," Mr. Dill interrupted. "Your granddad can go with Mr. Pizzo so they can work out some kind of legal arrangement. Lisa and Wayne can eat with us."

"This doesn't change my opinion of you, Mr. Colton. We're not friends," Mr. Pizzo said defiantly.

"Thank you, Anthony," Dr. Colton responded. He knew that using Mr. Pizzo's first name would irritate the man.

"Dr. Colton likes you, young man," Mr. Axelrod said, as he and Mr. Pizzo walked away.

"I bet he'll hate me once I get him sent to prison for life," Mr. Pizzo responded.

"Right now, I'd rather focus on clearing my own name. I really do dislike that cursed cold climate in Alaska where we've lived since them kids' mama died," Mr. Axelrod asserted.

"With these documents, it should be easy enough to clear your name. I'll give Mr. Colton credit for knowing my interest in resolving Ruby's kidnapping."

"Mario Rizzoli got Ruby pregnant, then tried to kill the girl. Thanks to Dr. Colton, she came to us. In my opinion, Mr. Mario Rizzoli is lucky to be in prison. If I could get to him, I'd beat him bloody," Mr. Axelrod candidly admitted.

"So have you been raising Ruby's children–or I should say Brandy's children?" Mr. Pizzo asked bluntly.

"The wife and I are raising Brandy's children. They're our grandchildren."

"Letting your grandchildren go with Mr. Colton could be a mistake. He's on trial for killing a five-year-old boy."

"Mr. Prosecutor, Dr. Colton has been the children's doctor since before they were born. They're quite safe with him."

"You may be right, but your good doctor murdered Marco Rizzoli just to get even for what he claims Mario Rizzoli did to his first wife and child."

"But you never called Dr. Colton to testify against Mr. Rizzoli during the Rizzoli trial."

"We had sufficient evidence to convict," Mr. Pizzo replied. "Tell those children to keep the money–their loss is worth more than what they gained. Mario Rizzoli will never need it."

Chapter 31

"All rise, the Honorable Judge King presiding," The court bailiff announced.

"Be seated and come to order. I spent my lunch break deciding whether or not to declare a mistrial. Mr. Pizzo, the choice will be yours. You can issue a written apology to Mr. Dill's last witness, Rebecca Preston, by tomorrow morning or I *will* declare a mistrial. What's your decision?"

Mr. Pizzo looked at the defense table. "Your Honor, I'll apologize to Ms. Preston personally if she is here in the morning. Should she not be present, I'll hand Mr. Dill my written apology after you've read it."

"Very well. Mr. Dill, you may call your next witness."

"Defense calls Mr. Wesha Canyon to the stand," Dr. Colton called out.

A young adult with black hair, blue eyes, six feet-four, and wearing a deerskin shirt and pants with buckskin boots, walked into the courtroom.

"Look, it's Daniel Boone," Mr. Pizzo joked.

Wesha stopped walking. "You, sir, are *not* funny!"

"Mr. Canyon, do you promise the testimony you're about to give is the truth, the whole truth and nothing but the truth?"

"Yes, ma'am. And so no one needs to ask, my full name is pronounced Key-la Way-sha." He then spelled his name and continued," I'm nineteen, and I am *not* Daniel Boone."

"Mr. Canyon, do you know Dr. Colton?"

Wesha turned to Mr. Pizzo. "Okay, princess, pay attention. Yes, I know him. Dr. Colton saved my life."

"Objection. Your Honor, please instruct the witness to show a bit of respect," Mr. Pizzo complained.

"Sustained; do not refer to the prosecutor as 'princess'."

"Mr. Prosecutor calls me 'Daniel Boone' and you say nothing. I refer to him as 'princess' and you chastise me. And people say our courts are just."

"Mr. Canyon, you'll hold your tongue while in my court," Judge King reprimanded in anger. "Do you understand?"

"Yes, sir," Wesha replied. "I ask only that you chastise the prosecutor for his rude comment as I entered your court."

"That won't happen, Mr. Canyon. You may consider yourself lucky that I haven't found you in contempt of court."

"Mr. Judge, sir, I'm not worried about a contempt fine. I earn in one day what you earn in one year."

"Excuse me," Mr. Dill interrupted. "Could we get to the witness's testimony? Mr. Wesha has done nothing deserving of Mr. Pizzo's sarcasm."

"If your witness dressed–"

"Objection!" Dr. Colton shouted as he jumped to his feet, "Mr. Pizzo–" Suddenly, and without warning he slumped to the floor, lifeless.

"Bailiff, call 911 and get Dr. Boot," Mr. Dill ordered. Agent Xander Ward immediately

After his collapse, Dr. Colton was rushed to the hospital, where he spent two days under Dr. Boot's care. He required treatment for sleep deprivation, dehydration, and stress. His first day was spent flat on his back in the hospital. IV tubes fed nutrients into his veins, along with drugs he had been negligent in taking during the day. An additional day at home was required before Dr. Boot relaxed his vigil.

Dr. Colton had been spending hours after court every day, preparing for the next witness. He took time to write about each day's events in his current journal. Additionally, he wrote letters to all of those whom he had aided in escaping their torturous lives. Judge King stopped by the hospital to check on his condition each morning and afternoon. Although he professed concern, his true motivation was to prove Dr. Colton had feigned his illness.

During the time Dr. Colton could not appear in court, Mr. Pizzo brokered two convictions through plea agreements. He also received a letter from Mario Rizzoli. This he gave to Judge King. The letter read:

Mr. Prosecutor;

You should know that if you manage to convict that scum doctor of killing my son I'll forgive you for the underhanded way you convicted me. Find my one million and seven hundred thousand dollars. Understand me–you're both scum but I want my son's killer in prison with me. You are maggot scum, Mr. Prosecutor. I got no care for you. All I want is my son's killer, and thanks to your incompetence I'll see you when I'm once again a free man.

Mr. Pizzo counted it a blessing when Dr. Colton was hospitalized. He received news that the blood found next to the ashes of Marco Rizzoli belonged to Mario Rizzoli. The Rizzoli Enterprises building was closed down due to nonpayment on back taxes. With this news, it was easy to obtain a search warrant for the building. Mr. Pizzo became ecstatic upon finding evidence of Mario Rizzoli's involvement in illegal porn. This was a spectacular find which, he decided, must be turned over to the FBI.

The biggest news at the time was the discovery of two items, which had disappeared over twenty-five years ago. One, a necklace–reported missing from Maria Rizzoli's possessions when she was killed in Italy. By itself, it was no big find, however, the note beneath it provided additional proof that Mario Rizzoli ordered the death of his wife. The note read:

I sent Marco away with Thomas. I then ordered Rubio to kill Maria as you instructed. After Rubio fired six bullets into your wife's head and chest I shot him twice from behind in the head. We left the evidence you ordered, implicating our rivals.

The note was signed by an enforcer of the Rizzoli clan.

The second discovery was made by Royce Colton, a young man who enjoyed old cars. Royce invited Evan Holt to attend a storage auction. Inside the last of ten storage rooms was what looked like a pile of junk and old clothes. What people saw inside while inspecting the unit was an old flat tire with a rusted rim, two mattresses covered in dust, plus box after box overflowing with old clothing. A child's rusty tricycle sat upside-down on old plywood. Shelves holding old rusty cans lined both sides of the storage room. Old televisions, VHS players and three old computers sat in front. Several bidders complained of the older items not being worth the time or money. When bidding opened Evan started at $50. Two other bidders raised the bid to $200 before backing out. Evan finally offered $210 for the room and won.

Royce paid his half of the money, then called his brother. Kent arrived forty minutes later with a large rental box truck. He was surprised to see more trash than useful items. Only when he saw the antique silver Aston Martin did his eyes brighten.

Evan explained that computers had gold inside them, enough to bring over $2,000. They would make money, but how much exactly, no one could tell. Royce suggested they pull the Aston Martin out of the storage room to inspect it.

Xander Ward knocked on Dr. Colton's bedroom door. "Doc, I have good news and bad. Kent, Royce, and Evan Holt found a silver Aston Martin which has been sent to the FBI headquarters for processing. The right front of the car is heavily damaged, and its windshield is damaged from the outside."

"Okay, what's the bad news?" Dr. Colton was now sitting upright. "Please don't tell me one of the boys got hurt."

"Nobody's hurt, but my bad news is that Judge King is petitioning the federal court to be allowed to file habitual criminal charges against you and revoke your bail status. He claims you staged the incident in court to garner jury sympathy. Judge Holt is being pressured to grant Judge King's request. A nurse named Gina Kelso gave a sworn statement to Judge King that you're faking the seriousness of your cancer. She said you weren't at the hospital."

"It's time we went back to court. Contact Wesley and tell him we return tomorrow. We'll talk with Sam and ask him to bring guests."

"Will Dr. Boot clear you for court?" Xander asked.

"Adam cleared me to return this morning. Did anyone think to take pictures of that Aston Martin?"

"Royce is printing them out from his computer as we speak," Xander replied.

"Maybe I'll file for that mistrial to shake up our prosecutor and judge."

Chapter 32

"All rise, the Honorable Judge Noah King presiding."

"Be seated and come to order."

"Your Honor, may I approach the bench?" Dr. Colton requested.

"Come," Judge King replied.

Dr. Colton picked up two file folders and stepped to the judge's bench. One folder he dropped in front of Mr. Pizzo, and the other he handed to Judge King himself.

"Inside those folders is my complete medical history. You ordered them turned over; you now have them. I have additionally submitted an incidental copy of these reports to the federal judge, Samuel Holt and his associates, whom you've petitioned to have additional charges attached to this case."

"Silence, Doctor! You *will not* come into my courtroom and make accusations against me."

"Your Honor. My apologies to you, sir. Ladies and gentlemen of the jury, I must be mistaken. We must not make false allegations against others at any time."

"I accept your apology, Dr. Colton," Judge King said smugly. "Do you wish to recall your witness to the stand?"

"No, sir, I'll call Federal Judge Samuel Holt to the stand. Following him will be Federal Judge Nikki Myers, and then Wesley Dill."

Judge Holt walked to the witness stand. "Do I take the stand, or are you going to publicly admit Dr. Colton was not making false accusations?" Judge Holt spoke softly enough for only Judge King to hear clearly. "Nikki, will you please come forward?"

Only moments before, Judge King had enjoyed humiliating Dr. Colton when the man was forced to apologize. He'd watched Mr. Pizzo smile at the doctor's discomfort while apologizing to the jury. Now, it was his turn to squirm. Swallowing hard, he cleared his throat. "New evidence has come into light, therefore, in the interest of justice I'm retracting all petitions I've filed regarding Dr. Colton."

"That, sir, is not an apology. Please swear me in so I may tell this court Dr. Colton didn't lie to you," Judge Holt said, loud enough for all to hear.

Federal Judge Nikki Myers addressed the jurors: "It's highly unusual to have a federal judge address you in this manner. Your task is assessing the truth of this case, and only the truth relating to Dr. Colton's charge of murder. You may not take into account Judge King's behavior, nor the behavior of Prosecutor Anthony Pizzo." She paused. "Your sole purpose is to decide whether or not Dr. Colton is guilty of murdering Marco Rizzoli."

Walking over to Judge King's sidebar, Federal Judge Holt once again spoke softly: "If I'm called upon again, the consequences *will not* be pleasant. I have an envelope for you. Take ten minutes, and perhaps you can act adequately surprised when the evidence is presented."

Both federal judges returned to their seats and were silent. Thinking quickly, Judge King addressed the court. "I've just received evidence that Nurse Gina

Kelso also perjured herself in a sworn statement she gave to this court. I apologize to all parties affected by Nurse Gina's statement. Mr. Dill, do you have any additional witnesses to call?"

"Defense calls Dr. Colton to the stand." Dr. Colton took the witness seat, spelled his name, and waited for Mr. Dill.

"Dr. Colton, you have always contended that Mario Rizzoli was, or is, responsible for the death of your wife, Nancy, and son Richard Jr. Do you have any proof of Mr. Rizzoli's guilt?"

"Objection–irrelevant to this case," Mr. Pizzo protested.

"You're the one saying Dr. Colton had a motive to kill Marco Rizzoli behind his false belief–I repeat, behind his false belief–that Mario Rizzoli killed Nancy and Richard Jr.," Mr. Dill countered.

"Overruled–I'm interested," Judge King said.

"New evidence has been obtained which proves that my wife, Nancy, told me the truth when she said with her dying breath that Mario Rizzoli was the hit-and-run driver who killed her and our son."

"What kind of evidence?" Mr. Dill asked.

Dr. Colton used his computer to bring up pictures on the court monitor. "Before you is an antique Aston Martin, silver, and belonging to Mario Rizzoli. Next picture shows damage to the windshield and front of the Aston Martin. Notice the dark stain across the front. This is consistent with dried blood."

"How did you discover this evidence?" Mr. Dill inquired.

"The car was found in a storage rental room at Travis Storage. The FBI was immediately contacted and they've taken charge of the area to preserve the evidence from being tainted. I was advised the car was removed and taken to FBI headquarters."

"No further questions at this time," Mr. Dill said.

"Mr. Pizzo, your witness," Judge King directed, gesturing with his hand as he spoke.

"Thank you. Dr. Colton, don't you think it's convenient that you found the Aston Martin instead of someone else? Were you the renter where the Aston Martin was found?"

"First of all, I *didn't* find it. This evidence was brought to me yesterday afternoon while I was still in bed. Second, Travis Storage provided the renter's name."

"Just exactly who *did* find this car?" Mr. Pizzo asked.

"That, Mr. Pizzo, is classified information. Dr. Colton disclosed all the information he can legally divulge at this time," Agent Xander Ward stated as he walked forward. "I'll inform you that the Aston Martin belonging to Mr. Rizzoli wasn't reported stolen, and Mario Rizzoli was arrested in his prison cell forty minutes ago. Mr. Rizzoli has been charged with vehicular manslaughter with special circumstances, two counts–the special circumstances being his prior convictions for murder. If convicted on the new charges, he will face the death penalty." Agent Ward looked at Mr. Pizzo. "My apologies; Mr. Dill was restricted to asking only the questions you heard. No further information will be released until Mario Rizzoli is on trial."

"Are you aware that the vehicle shown on the monitor is a Special Edition?" Mr. Pizzo volunteered. "That particular vehicle has unique features that can't be disabled. They're automatically reset every 5000 miles after being downloaded to the car's VIN file at the manufacturer's headquarters."

In his own mind, Dr. Colton, thanked the prosecutor for knowing his Aston Martins.

"Agent Ward, is there anything else you or Dr. Colton are allowed to share regarding this vehicle?" Judge King queried.

"Sorry, Your Honor, everything is considered classified at this time. However, when I receive authorization to disseminate further information, you'll be notified right away."

"Thank you, Agent Ward. Dr. Colton, you may step down."

"Your Honor, we now call Gina Kelso to the stand." Dr. Colton smiled as he walked from the stand.

"Dr. Colton, are you playing some kind of twisted game?" Judge King asked.

"No game, sir. Gina Kelso filed a false report. I want to know why. She doesn't work on the oncology floor and has absolutely no access to my medical records."

"That may have been my fault," Mr. Pizzo responded contritely. "I went by the hospital and asked how Mr. Colton was feeling. Nurse Kelso assured me there was no Mr. Colton in the hospital. I arranged for her to give a sworn statement in writing. Ms. Kelso was hired less than a year ago and is still on probation. Your Honor, I don't believe Ms. Kelso meant to give a fraudulent statement to the court."

"Gina Kelso is not on your witness list, Dr. Colton. Unless you can provide me with a legitimate reason to call Ms. Kelso, I'm going to accept Mr. Pizzo's explanation and deny your witness request."

"Very well, sir," Dr. Colton replied. "I wish to press charges against Nurse Gina Kelso for fraud."

"Your Honor," Mr. Pizzo chimed in, "again, I'm certain that Ms. Kelso did not commit fraud with malicious intent."

"Get over it, Doctor. I won't order Gina Kelso's arrest just to satisfy you."

"Your Honor, we respectfully request that court be dismissed for the day in order to give you and Mr. Pizzo time to prepare for questioning by the FBI in regard to Gina Kelso's trial for charges of perjury, fraud, and conspiracy to deceive the federal government. Gina Kelso has been dismissed from her job and is in custody," Mr. Dill said without looking up from the file in front of him.

Judge King found Federal Judge Sam Holt in the audience. Their eyes met, a silent message passing between them.

"Ladies and gentlemen of the jury, and all in the court," Judge King began, "Dr. Colton addressed a matter earlier for which he apologized." Seething within he continued; "Dr. Colton spoke the truth, owing no apologies. We will not dismiss for the day."

164

Next he turned to Mr. Pizzo. "Ms. Kelso may have inadvertently given false information in her sworn statement. We'll gladly answer any questions asked of us at a later time. Mr. Dill, call your next witness." Judge King swore to himself that Dr. Colton would pay for his games.

"Please recall Mr. Canyon," Mr. Dill responded.

As the witness entered the courtroom, Judge King reminded him that he was still under oath.

"At least the witness is dressed more appropriately," Mr. Pizzo said disparagingly.

Wesha Canyon, standing in front of the witness seat, responded, "Objection; is he really going to be allowed to make snide remarks again?"

"I happen to agree that you are dressed a lot more appropriately today than the last time you were in court," Judge King said.

"So, because I'm not a fancy-pants dresser like you all, it's okay for you to be rude, or are you rude because you believe me to be beneath you?" Mr. Canyon looked toward the audience. A slight nod brought a well-dressed man to his feet. "Let me introduce Mr. Van Webster."

Mr. Webster signaled Marshal Marshall to get his attention. He handed him three envelopes which were then handed to the court bailiff. The bailiff distributed them to Judge King, Mr. Dill, and Mr. Pizzo. When the bailiff returned to his position, Mr. Webster loudly announced, "*Gentlemen, you have been served!*" and then exited the courtroom.

Judge King initially had handed his envelope to the court clerk. Upon hearing that he had been served, he quickly ordered the envelope returned and opened it.

Mr. Pizzo had his envelope partially opened when he heard Mr. Webster proclaim they had been served.

"Mr. Canyon, how old were you when Dr. Colton saved your life, and how did he save you?" Mr. Dill inquired, his envelope remaining unopened on his briefcase.

"I was six."

"Wait a minute!" Judge King shouted. "What's the meaning of this garbage?"

"I'm asking my witness questions," Mr. Dill replied.

"Not that! This!" Judge King stood and leaned forward toward the witness, angrily waving his envelope.

"I don't deal in garbage, Judge. I'm suing you and Mr. Pizzo for defamation of character, malicious statements about me, and the misuse of your power of authority. It's all outlined in the papers you received from Mr. Webster."

"You called me 'Princess'," Mr. Pizzo asserted.

"Regrettably, I can't press this issue any further," Mr. Canyon calmly asserted.

"Watch yourself, young man," Judge King angrily interjected. "I'm not a person with whom you can trifle. Watch what you say and how you address people in my court. Mr. Dill, ask your question again."

"What's your occupation?" Mr. Dill calmly inquired.

"You won't win, Mr. Canyon. Your frivolous lawsuit won't make it to court for years," Judge King exclaimed, still filled with barely controlled rage. "People, we're adjourned for the morning. Return at one o'clock this afternoon." Judge King banged his gavel and left.

"You went too far, Mr. Wesha Canyon," Mr. Pizzo snapped as he angrily slammed his briefcase closed. "You've filed your last lawsuit. I'm going to bury you!"

"A suggestion, Mr. Pizzo," Wesha offered. "Look me up on the internet, sir. I'm not the young punk kid you seem to believe."

"Wesha, lunch at the house. Mr. Dill has a few questions he wants to ask you," Dr. Colton invited.

"Can I put on some real clothes and get out of this monkey suit? It's totally uncomfortable. And I need a ride."

Mr. Dill waited until they were in the car to ask his first question: "Are you really a sniper?"

"No, I'm just an excellent shot using the rifle I invented, and I like Swiss made telescopes."

"Why'd you tell Mr. Pizzo to find you on the internet?"

"He'll learn that I sold my rifle design, my body armor patents and smart bullet designs to the military."

"Are you another genius?" Mr. Dill asked.

"No, sir, I just like solving problems and all things electronic."

"How'd Dr. Colton save your life?"

"When I was six years old, we were in my aunt's car. I liked looking out the window pretending I was running instead of riding in the car. I heard a loud thump and my aunt screaming. My aunt lost control of the car. When I woke up, Dr. Colton was holding me."

"Yes," Dr. Colton began, "I didn't know anything about Wesha, whose name was originally Franklin Bush, until I reached his aunt's car, which had gone off the road and tumbled two hundred feet to a section of the same road lower down. The Bush family was headed south; Barbara and I were going north. Mrs. Bush was the only person who remained in the car. She automatically knew Franklin was alive and everyone else was dead. Millicent Bush lived for thirty-nine minutes after we arrived. Barbara found Franklin and told me where he was lying. I examined him and then carried him to our car where he woke up in my arms.

"Mrs. Bush told me she gave her boy the nickname 'Kila Wesha', which she said means 'sun red savage' because he liked running around in his Indian clothes her sister made for him. Millicent died from internal bleeding before reaching the hospital. I promised Millicent I'd keep Franklin safe. He had no living relatives according to the authorities. August and Lisa Canyon adopted Franklin and changed his name to Kila Wesha at his request."

"Dr. Colton found the right parents for me," Wesha declared. "My parents encouraged me to stretch myself. They had me tested when I was eight after I fixed some clocks and an electric radio in my dad's junk pile. It turns out that I'm really smart."

166

"Excuse me, but how smart is 'really' smart? You told me earlier you just like all things electronic. Explain," Mr. Dill said.

"Oh, Wesha is boiling smart," Dr. Colton teased. "Mr. Canyon graduated high school when he was twelve."

"Whoa!" Mr. Dill exclaimed. "I know Dr. Colton is considered a freaky smart genius, but oh my God, you're freaky smart, too."

"I don't have his memory," Wesha admitted. "I've made millions from my government contracts. Now I earn money by inventing video and computer software. If I were evil-minded, I could destroy Mr. Pizzo's computer by easily hacking into it and inserting a virus nobody would ever find. Our government has been using my inventions for the last three years."

"I think we can let you go home," Dr. Colton said, changing the subject. "You rattled Mr. Pizzo and Judge King with your lawsuit. Do you think much will come of it?"

"They'll settle out of court. I expect a small amount, but I'm just going to insist on a public apology."

"Judge King is going to seethe when we don't recall Mr. Canyon," Wesley told his companions.

"I expect his anger will skyrocket when I ask him why Mr. Pizzo was allowed to defame Mr. Canyon with his Daniel Boone remark. I'll probably get another court fine, but hey, it can only help your lawsuit," Dr. Colton smiled as he talked.

"Who are we going to call next?" Mr. Dill asked.

"No idea," Dr. Colton responded. "I want to irritate Mr. Pizzo a little more. He hasn't had many questions for our witnesses and that frustrates him to no end. We need another witness who doesn't crack under a little pressure."

"I can still go back to testify," Wesha offered.

Chapter 33

"We are back in court. This morning was definitely strange. I look forward to a more productive afternoon. Mr. Dill, you may call your witness," Judge King said, trying to project a calm demeanor.

"Your Honor, Defense calls Dr. Ian Kendall."

"Counselor Dill!" Judge King snapped in exasperation. "You can't seat a witness, ask them questions and then arbitrarily dismiss the witness. Mr. Pizzo has the right to question your witnesses."

"Your Honor, Mr. Canyon was prepared to testify. However, Mr. Pizzo's demeaning comment about Daniel Boone, simply because of Mr. Canyon's clothing, followed by his succeeding comments without court intervention, caused us to deem it unwise to bring Mr. Canyon back as a witness." Dr. Colton spoke with deliberate intent to bolster Wesha Canyon's lawsuit.

"Dr. Colton, you *will* call Mr. Canyon and instruct him to return in order for Mr. Pizzo to cross-examine him."

"No offense intended, sir, but which question would Mr. Pizzo inquire upon? As I remember: 'Do you know Dr. Colton?' Reply: 'Yes.' Next was: 'How old were you when Dr. Colton rescued you?' Reply: 'I was six.' At which point you banged your gavel and dismissed court for the morning." Dr. Colton sat down before adding, "If we recall Mr. Canyon, I fear he'll face further character assassinations by Mr. Pizzo."

"Your Honor, I have no further questions for Mr. Canyon at this time," Mr. Dill said.

"I'd ask how Dr. Colton rescued the witness," Mr. Pizzo asserted.

"I believe that I asked about Mr. Canyon's occupation. There was no answer, and his age is nineteen," Mr. Dill offered.

"Listen up people, you'll either call Mr. Canyon back to court or I'll issue a warrant for his arrest. Tell me which it's going to be," Judge King said, his face reddening in anger.

"Okay, I'll call him and see if he is willing to return," Dr. Colton consented, "but it is his decision."

"It is not his choice—" Judge King began.

"May I be heard?" a man in the audience requested.

"And who are you?" Judge King barked impatiently.

"My name, Your Honor, is Ronald Worth, attorney for Mr. Canyon.

"Speak your piece, sir." Judge King was becoming even more agitated.

"If you wish to speak to Mr. Canyon, you'll write out your questions and submit them to me. My client won't be returning. And, gentlemen, you're not to contact Mr. Canyon for any reason."

"Who are you to tell this court what it will or won't do?" Judge King said, fighting to maintain his composure.

"These, Judge King, are restraining orders. Judge Noah King and Prosecutor Anthony Pizzo shall not contact, or come within one hundred yards of Mr. Kila Wesha Canyon. Both orders are signed by Federal Judge Samuel Holt." Ronald

Worth handed two envelopes to the bailiff. "My contact information is inside each envelope."

"Are you serious?" Mr. Pizzo interjected. "Mr. Canyon needs to grow up. His lawsuit is ridiculous."

"I really don't care about your opinion at this time, sir. You'll abide by the signed restraining orders or face the consequences. My job here is complete. Good day to you."

"Mr. Worth, tell your client his lawsuit is a waste of time and money," Judge King announced loudly.

"If you want to end this, make a public apology and restrain your prosecutor's behavior. Reprimand him as should've been done at the beginning." Ronald Worth turned and left the courtroom.

"Your Honor," Mr. Dill interrupted. "Is that a federal seal on your envelope?"

Judge King looked more closely. "Ronald Worth, Office of the Attorney General." Judge King stared at the envelope. "Mr. Dill, who is that kid?"

"He's on the internet," Dr. Colton replied. "Here, let me show you an article." Judge King read for about fifteen seconds before reacting.

"You may close the article. Mr. Pizzo, I want to see you in my office immediately. Court is dismissed until tomorrow morning."

"Your Honor," Dr. Colton interrupted. "Our witness is a busy man. We promised he'd be finished by tomorrow afternoon."

"Then I suggest you don't call him on Monday," Judge King snapped.

"Excuse me, Judge King," Mr. Dill interjected. "Today has been a nightmare so far. Can we take a deep breath, step back, and make this afternoon productive, please?"

Judge King leaned back in his chair. "Actually, that makes a lot of sense. I'll talk to Mr. Pizzo after court today. Jury will remain seated. Court is back in session. Mr. Dill, you may call another witness."

"Defense calls Dr. Ian Kendall."

After promising to tell the truth and spelling his name. Dr. Kendall took a mere ten minutes to briefly detail his expertise and experience in forensic investigation. He then submitted to the court a copy of his licenses in the medical field.

"Dr. Kendall, what specifically did Mr. Dill ask of you?" Dr. Colton inquired, waiting for Mr. Pizzo's objection.

"I specialize in DNA testing and the results. Mr. Dill submitted two samples of DNA to be tested. The two samples of DNA turned out to be from two different individuals."

"Were you able to identify whose DNA you tested?"

"Yes, sir, since DNA is collected from all convicted persons, I was able to determine that one of the samples belongs to Mr. Mario Rizzoli."

"Do you know the origin or where the sample came from?" Dr. Colton queried.

"Yes, sir, Mr. Dill provided proof that the sample had been obtained near a pile of ashes thought to be the remains of Marco Rizzoli."

"And the second DNA sample, Dr. Kendall?"

"That sample came from you, Dr. Colton, sir. It is your DNA. Mr. Dill submitted an affidavit explaining that he collected hair while you were in the hospital being treated for cancer."

"Objection, Your Honor. Mr. Kendall is a biased witness, skewed to favor Dr. Colton. Not to mention that he only spoke briefly regarding his qualifications as an expert witness."

"Your Honor," Dr. Kendall interrupted, "I'm not biased. I am, however, offended, so I offer Mr. Pizzo an opportunity to prove otherwise. I'll send a lab assistant to Mr. Pizzo's office. He can submit his own DNA samples labeled so only he and the lab assistant know whose DNA is submitted."

"Can you take DNA samples here in this courtroom, and if so, how long will it take to perform the test, and get the results?" Judge King asked skeptically.

"This is Friday. I can have the results on Monday if I get the sample, or samples immediately."

"Mr. Dill, do you have another witness available at this time?" Judge King asked.

"No sir, we don't," Mr. Dill admitted.

"Mr. Pizzo, do you accept Dr. Kendall's offer? Your own DNA expert witness was killed in an auto accident, so you might want to consider the witness's offer."

"On one condition: I alone will know the origin of each sample until your results are given. I'll seal the information into separate envelopes, then turn the envelopes over, one at a time, to the court clerk."

"I have an additional condition," Dr. Colton said. "I want two unbiased witnesses to observe everything."

"Granted," Judge King responded. "My bailiff and Marshal Marshall, is that unbiased enough for you, Dr. Colton?"

"Agreed, let's do it."

"Dr. Kendall, if Mr. Dill does not object, you may step down. Contact your lab assistant; let's get this started right away. Mr. Pizzo, your objection is tabled until Monday morning."

Once Dr. Kendall's assistants arrived, he was escorted to an anteroom. He was unable to observe DNA samples taken from three people, and labeled as "A", "B", and "C" with only Mr. Pizzo, the bailiff, and Marshal Marshall knowing which belonged to whom. Blood was not needed, as a swab of the inside of their mouths was quite sufficient.

"We'll adjourn once Dr. Kendall has returned," Judge King announced.

"Your Honor, if it please the court, we can take time after Dr. Kendall's assistants are finished with their task, to qualify him as an expert in the field of DNA analysis. He can testify regarding his qualifications in DNA technology." Dr. Colton offered.

"Very well, we'll remain in session until after Dr. Kendall is examined on his qualifications," Judge King smiled smugly.

Mr. Pizzo used sleight of hand to exchange a swab with his own DNA for that of Dr. Colton. To misdirect attention from his underhanded switch, Mr. Pizzo

170

addressed the court, "I'd like to submit the dried blood sample from the Gibson Road scene for further analysis." Three jurors, who were intent on every aspect of the DNA gathering, still saw Mr. Pizzo's actions. Each juror remained silent.

With the two assistants finished, Dr. Kendall returned to the courtroom "I'd like to request an escort for my assistants once Mr. Pizzo is finished with his part of this qualifying test," he said addressing the judge.

Marshal Marshall volunteered and was ordered to escort the assistants. He was instructed to remain with the assistants by his superior, Agent Xander Ward, until such time as they returned on Monday morning.

Judge King addressed Dr. Kendall: "You may take the witness stand and remember you're still under oath to tell the truth."

Dr. Kendall resumed the witness stand and took a deep breath. "I'm ready, sir."

Mr. Dill stepped forward. "Dr. Kendall, could you please tell the court; what is your profession?

"I'm a Forensic Science Technician-slash-Expert."

"Please tell us your educational background, and what degrees, certificates or licenses you hold."

Because of his extensive background, it took the remainder of the day for Dr. Kendal to testify to his qualifications. He testified to academic and professional achievements; including three papers published by major academic organizations over the last five years. It took over an hour just to document his training in the field of DNA forensics, biochemistry, microbiology, and infectious diseases. It took equally as long to enumerate individual cases and studies he had handled in his lengthy career as a senior forensic technician for the FBI. Lending more weight and credibility to his expertise was his testimony about a high profile case in which he had gathered the necessary evidence to gain a conviction of the person the media had odiously deemed "The Hollywood Bomber".

Even the questions Judge King had hoped would show he was less than qualified, were answered with the ease and skill that only an experienced professional could offer. It became clear to everyone present that Dr. Kendal was going to be acknowledged as an expert witness when he testified he was responsible for much of the training of the prosecution's now deceased expert witness.

When he concluded, Dr. Colton addressed the court: "Your Honor, the defense wishes to submit Dr. Kendall's credentials as evidence of his qualifications as an expert witness in DNA technology,"

"For argument's sake, the prosecution will agree that Dr. Kendall appears to be an expert. However, I do wish to table this stipulation until Monday, when we receive Dr. Kendall's analysis of our DNA samples."

"So agreed," Judge King acquiesced. "Dr. Kendall, you may step down. I remind you not to discuss this case with anyone outside this courtroom. Dismissed until Monday at nine o'clock in the morning."

"Your Honor," an observer in the audience spoke out, "my name is Ethan Rau. Is Dr. Colton free to leave?"

"Dr. Colton has given his DNA, so he's no longer needed. Agent Ward, your party is free to leave until Monday."

Outside the courtroom, Dr. Colton offered to give Ethan Rau a ride to the house. Inside the car, Ethan received a file from Dr. Colton.

"That's my recollection of the events as they happened," Dr. Colton said.

"This says 'Journal Entry'. Is this in your journals?" Ethan asked with concern.

"That's the only copy," Dr. Colton answered. Ethan Rau began reading.

Chapter 34

"Dr. Colton, Doctor!" Nurse Barbara Manners called out to me.

"Yes Nurse Manners what is it?"

"Doctor, there's a boy in the emergency room who cut his foot on some glass."

"Okay, how bad is it?"

"Dr. White Eagle, our on-call intern, believes there is more glass in the child's foot, but he's fresh out of med school and this is his first emergency room duty."

"Very well, I'll check it out."

"Dr. Richard Colton, my name is Dr. White Eagle. The boy's foot–"

"We'll do everything we can to help him," I said, walking over to the four-year-old boy's side. "I see you started an IV. I trust your judgment so far. Let's see if there's any more glass in his foot."

"I removed three pieces so far," Dr. White Eagle said, "but his foot won't stop bleeding."

"Where're his parents?"

"Doing paperwork out front," Nurse Manners spoke up. "The boy's name is Charles Piper. His mother said her son broke a vase in their dining room. He cut his foot walking through the glass."

I was so angry all I could do was shake my head. The whole time I examined the boy's foot not a single whimper was heard. Two more shards of glass were found in his foot. I personally admitted the boy, Charles Piper into the hospital and spoke to his mother.

"I must inquire, is Charles adopted? The reason I ask is because there was a tag in his underwear with the name 'Benjamin Beam' on it."

The woman was a fast thinker. "Benjamin is our older son. And yes, Charlie is adopted. When can I take him home?"

"Hopefully tomorrow, after I change his bandages."

I silently prayed I would not see Benjamin, a.k.a. Charles again. I couldn't have imagined how soon it would be. Benjamin Beam arrived at the hospital unconscious. His mother, Skye Beam, a professional model, stated that her son was injured when he fell down the stairs at home. Benjamin remained in the hospital for three days before he was released to return home. His father, Cody Beam, hadn't stopped by the hospital to visit his son even once. Mrs. Beam explained that her husband was a long-haul truck driver who was gone for up to a week at times. Six days following his return home, Benjamin was back in the hospital.

"Dang kid jumped towards me from the cab of my truck," Mr. Beam told the woman at the admissions. "I tried to catch him, but I injured my right shoulder in Baton Rouge."

I read all the reports on Benjamin. I studied the x-rays and wondered why this boy was always being returned to his abusive parents. His shoulder had been dislocated, and his right side was scraped and bruised. Two fingernails of his left hand were gone and he had three bruised ribs as well. This time, Benjamin stayed in the hospital for six days before being released. There were no explanations offered for Benjamin's suspicious injuries. However, the authorities were notified and nothing happened to address the boy's condition.

Nearly a month had passed, and I was walking to my first morning patient. I heard a child screaming. I stepped into the emergency room, immediately recognizing Benjamin Beam. The boy now had a broken arm. His left knee was dislocated and he had three broken toes. Benjamin smelled of urine, and while the nurse cleaned him, she discovered he had head lice.

"Admit him until tomorrow and then send him to Lutheran Hospital for Children. Which parent brought him this time?" I asked.

"Both–and they're telling different stories," Dr. White Eagle replied. "Why send him to Lutheran?"

"Ask Lutheran to look into his past injuries. They can justify a court order to keep the boy and seek legal aid."

"Smart. I'll do it right after I finish treating his injuries," Dr. White Eagle said as he went back to work.

I walked away knowing I could do nothing that wasn't already being done. Benjamin was transferred to Lutheran the next morning and placed in foster care, which lasted three months. The boy was court ordered to be returned to his parents. Benjamin next appeared at the clinic with a broken right wrist. His mother's excuse: "He fell off the model's runway."

"How did he manage to get burned on his back?" I asked, once Benjamin was clad only in his underpants. "It looks like your son must have cut the back side of his leg, too." With his pants removed, I could see the cut on Benjamin's calf muscle.

"One of the models accidentally spilled her tea. Will this take long? I have a meeting to attend before we do a showing at two o'clock this afternoon."

"I need to take x-rays of Benjamin's injured wrist, and I'll have to sedate him to reset his bones. If you leave him with me, I'll stay until you return after your showing.

"Are you sure the little...er-uh...Benjamin won't be a bother? He can find trouble without trying," his mother said, accidentally revealing her son's true name.

"I promise he'll be fine," I told the woman. "While he takes a nap I can set his wrist, and a nurse can launder his clothes."

Mrs. Beam quickly jumped at the offer, and leaving her son behind, she went to her meeting.

"I'll be back before you close at six o'clock this evening."

Mrs. Beam accepted me calling her son 'Benjamin' and not 'Charles'. Benjamin's x-ray showed an odd breakage. He was taken to the hospital, where a CAT scan revealed a wrenching break. His hand had been twisted and wrenched backward, breaking his wrist. The burns on his back would heal. He received an antibiotic which his young body could tolerate, and a mild dose of pain reliever.

His wrist was set, a cast put on it, and he ate chicken nuggets while telling me how he was injured by his mother.

He did fall off the runway, after she twisted his arm behind his back and made him wear a small girls' dress. Benjamin didn't like dressing in girl clothing, he's a boy. When he started crying, his mother poured her hot tea on his back, which was exposed by the fancy dress. He complained of his wrist hurting as his mother's friend removed the dress and put Benjamin's own clothes back on him. Then he asked a strange question, convincing me that his story was true.

"Mister, why do Mommy and Daddy say, 'I hate you? You a mistake'."

I held Benjamin in my arms until he stopped sobbing. I gave him a lollipop and took him to my next appointment. "This is Benjamin," I said to another boy and his mother. "Do you mind if he comes in with me?"

"Doctor, this is my nephew, Lewis Lowe."

"What happened, Mr. Lowe?" I asked Lewis.

"I cut myself."

"If Lewis doesn't object, then neither do I. He'll probably need stitches. I put gauze over the cut. My name is Glenda Rau, retired Army Lieutenant and now active housewife. Colonel Peter Rau, my husband, and I are on vacation. Peter is based on the west coast. We brought Lewis with us from Arizona to give his parents a break. He has Asperger's."

I turned my attention to Lewis. "I helped Benjamin; will you let me help you? Can you take your shorts off for me? I want to see the cut on your leg."

Lewis didn't say a word; he merely pulled his summer shorts down, revealing a gauze-covered cut on his upper thigh. Benjamin watched, never saying a word.

"Is he your son?" Mrs. Rau asked.

"No, off the record, it's my belief, that his mother and father P-H-Y-S-I-C-A-L-L-Y   A-B-U-S-E him. That's probably how his arm got broken and his back burned with hot liquid."

"Parents like that don't deserve children," Mrs. Rau voiced. "You're definitely more tolerant than I am, doctor."

"Who's more tolerant?" a voice said from behind.

"Peter, this is Dr. Colton. He's examining Lewis. I'm surprised Lewis is being so accepting of Dr. Colton."

"Glad to meet you, sir," I said. "Thank you for serving our country. Your wife is correct; his cut needs to be cleaned. I think six stitches and a tetanus shot."

"Just ask Lewis if you can do it first. If you don't ask, he'll get angry–and that's always ugly."

I talked to Lewis, explaining what had to be done and how I would do it. I didn't lie to Lewis or say putting in the stitches wouldn't hurt. I used a topical numbing agent before using a lasting local anesthesia. Lewis smiled throughout his treatment.

Glenda Rau noticed Lewis holding Benjamin's hand. She heard Benjamin ask, 'Did that hurt? Did that hurt?' each time I put a stitch in Lewis's injury. When I finished the last stitch, I helped Lewis lie on his stomach. I pulled his underwear down, exposing his upper buttock for tetanus and antibiotic shots. He barely flinched as I gave him the injections, his aunt and uncle speaking German off to one side.

I smiled, eavesdropping on their conversation. I speak fluent German, Swedish, French, Japanese, and Spanish–a fact few people know. I heard Colonel Rau tell his wife, "That boy's parents need an old-fashioned ass-kicking. We can't have children, due to my injuries, and we want kids. It's unfair; he's a little kid. I could never hurt any child, but I sure wouldn't have a problem beating the living crap out of that boy's parents."

"I'd like to take that boy home with us," Glenda continued in German, "but that would be kidnapping."

"My superiors know we don't have children. How'd I explain being a new father?" Colonel Rau countered.

"Adoption from Germany–Berlin, to be exact," I said while helping Lewis with his shorts. "You finish your vacation in Michigan, New York, and then Germany." I spoke to them in German, knowing Colonel Rau and his wife would understand that I knew what they had said. "Return Lewis to his parents earlier. In Berlin, take custody of an adopted son. I have a friend in Hamburg who'd help you adopt. All the paperwork will be legal."

"We're only in Berlin for two weeks," countered Peter.

"Can it be done that quickly?" Glenda inquired.

"Not if you don't try," I told her. "I'll contact my friend and he can meet you at the Brandenburg Gate."

"Sweetheart, we'll be in Berlin," Glenda said. "We've nothing to lose."

"We'll be in Germany in two weeks. We're spending ten days in Berlin. Then we have plans to visit the Isle of Sylt for two days and return to Stuttgart. I'm slated to fly General Brooks' aircraft back to the United States. My wife will be returning with me. If I bring back a son, they'll ask why we didn't mention the adoption."

"Go now and cut out Michigan. Call your superiors and tell them you might be adopting a child. Offer no further explanations, saying you don't want to jinx things. That way any child will be expected. On your way home, make a call, asking for no celebrations. You want a quiet, uneventful transition."

"I'll call Lewis's parents," Peter offered.

The Raus left with smiles on their faces. I took Benjamin with me to my office. I made two phone calls and left the clinic. I returned an hour later with food for myself and Benjamin. When Benjamin's mother arrived, I gave her medicine for her son. I explained that I wished to keep him overnight, but being home in his own bed would undoubtedly be best for him.

On the drive home, Skye Beam wasted no time in taking the medicine meant for her son. Cody Beam returned home the following day and found his wife out cold. He saw the cast on his son's wrist and immediately began yelling. He snatched up the remaining medicine. He read the label: *Take one every twelve hours as needed for pain.* Mr. Beam removed two capsules, walked to the refrigerator and swallowed them with a cold beer.

"I'll beat her within an inch of her life when she wakes up," Cody Beam yelled in anger. "Get away from me, you worthless snot-nosed turd–or I'll beat your stupid head right now! God, how I hate you!" Mr. Beam yelled at Benjamin who was gently touching his father's leg.

Cody Beam awoke hours later when his wife poured ice-cold water on his face. "Benjamin's missing. The front door was wide open and he's gone."

Cody and Skye sobered up fast. They went through their neighborhood looking for the son they despised. It took a mere thirty minutes for them to stop looking for Benjamin.

"Where's them pills you had?" Mr. Beam asked his wife.

"You must've taken all of 'em," Mrs. Beam replied. "Help me clean up the house. I'm going to report Benjamin missing."

"Clean it up yourself. I just got home to find my son missing and my worthless wife sound asleep in our filthy house."

The couple began arguing, playing the blame game, entirely forgetting their son was missing. Benjamin was safely asleep, away from his abusive parents. Everything they'd done and said was being recorded by cameras, hidden in the open–'nanny cams' which I'd placed in their house during the hour I was gone from the clinic.

Benjamin cried himself to sleep. I lifted him from his bed, with his abusive parents passed out in the living room. I removed anything that could be considered evidence, except one video recorder which revealed everything the authorities needed to see. When Benjamin awoke, he hadn't eaten for nearly thirty-six hours. He was strapped down to his bed with an IV in his arm, lying at an incline, so he could watch popular children's television cartoon shows. He didn't recognize the man who entered his room. I wore a mask and a gown.

"Are you hungry? Do you want something to eat?" I asked Benjamin.

"Yes, please," the boy responded.

The short cast on his wrist had been removed and replaced with a cast up over his elbow.

"I pooped," Benjamin said, in shame. "Sorry."

"Not your fault. It's okay to get up after I unstrap you. Hold still while I take the needle out of your arm, then you can take a bath. I'll put clean sheets on the bed.

"Mommy won't let me take my bath alone. Mommy helps me."

I looked at Benjamin. "Can you use the toilet by yourself? I'll put water in the bathtub for you."

Benjamin replied by saying, "Yes, sir–and thank you."

The food Benjamin and I ate was the same. Fruit juice, milk and water were given to Benjamin whenever he was thirsty. The majority of his day was spent alone, watching various cartoons or sleeping. He was no longer strapped to his bed, but being alone made him sad.

Three days after rescuing Benjamin from his abusive home, I'd still heard nothing regarding his disappearance. When I drove by the Beams' rented house there were no lights on and Mrs. Beam's forest green car was missing. On day four, two short paragraphs appeared on page eight of the newspaper. It read:

> *Parents of four-year-old Benjamin Beam are suspected in their son's disappearance. The clothing his mother described when he went missing was found in the parents' bedroom. Police detectives discovered the boy's blood stained clothes under his parents' bed. Additional blood was found in Mr. Beam's truck bed along with blood-stained towels and strands of hair believed to be that of the missing child.*
>
> *Both parents were discovered to have drugs and alcohol in their systems when officers interviewed them. They accused a local physician, Dr. White Eagle; however, the Beams remain as primary suspects. The physician implicated by the couple has provided authorities with evidence which clearly shows Benjamin Beam had been physically abused by his parents for some time. This has been supported by other evidence discovered at the residence. The physician implicated has been cleared by police.*

The morning I was leaving for Germany with Benjamin, I read, on page two, in the newspaper:

> *Following an anonymous call to police, a search warrant has been served at the country club of Mario Rizzoli. Police found an unknown set of fingerprints, believed to be those of Benjamin Beam, on Rizzoli's golf cart. Police found the boy's bloodied pajamas in a trash receptacle. Blood and urine were discovered on Rizzoli's golf cart. Mario Rizzoli is a person of interest. The Beams' relationship with Rizzoli is being investigated. Marco Rizzoli, son of Mario, disappeared nearly ten months ago. Authorities found Marco's charred remains after the boy's father failed to pay a ransom for his son. Rizzoli insists that all but $300,000 of the ransom was paid. When police retrieved the briefcases, they were empty."*

It was risky, putting the evidence on Rizzoli's golf cart. Thank heaven for drainage ditches and culverts! Hopefully the police will find the $3,000 I hid in Skye Beam's car. That should tie them together fairly solidly. I put Benjamin in footie pajamas for our flight to Germany. My flight plan for Odense, Denmark, was changed in flight. I changed Benjamin's name to Ethan Rau the day we left for Germany. I left him in the aircraft while I cleared customs. There were no complications with his passport. He was admitted without incident. A taxi took us to a home in Berlin. I paid the taxi driver and walked with Ethan to the house.

"Johan, I thank you for offering your home during my stay. I promise we'll show respect in your absence, leaving this, your beautiful house, in pristine–ah hell, who am I kidding? Johan, you need new furniture. Well, the least I can do is go shopping for supper." I spoke to an empty house; Johan wasn't home. One hour later, Johan Mann arrived.

"Is this the boy you called me about? Food smells good."

"Yes, his papers name him as Ethan Rau. His parents are in Germany now, somewhere in Berlin. You can call them this evening at the number they gave me. Set up a meeting for tomorrow morning and turn the boy over to them."

Examining the adoption forms, Johan asked, "Where'd you get these forms? They're perfect."

"For the right price, you can obtain anything you want in America–including German adoption forms. Even his passport is authentic."

Before Ethan was taken to meet his new parents, I got him used to saying his new name. "Who are you?"

"Benj–"

"No! Let's try again, what is your name? Do you remember?"

"Ethan!"

"Yes."

This was repeated over and over until the boy automatically called himself Ethan.

Johan was cool when handing Ethan over to Peter and Glenda Rau. "This boy is Ethan; on his adoption it says Ethan Rau. He speaks English. Be good to this boy. His parents were bad people. They don't deserve a child, now or ever."

Johan handed Peter Rau five thousand dollars, all in hundred-dollar bills. "If you're mean to this child I'll know. This boy is a good boy, you give him lots of hugs and love."

Full of joy at their answered prayers for a son or daughter, Glenda Rau beamed as she held Ethan close to her.

"Mister, anybody ever hurts this boy again, I'll personally hunt them down and make them wish they were dead," Peter Rau promised.

"Mommy, I have to go number one," Ethan interrupted.

Johan handed Mr. Rau all of Ethan's papers, including a birth certificate. Johan followed Peter and Glenda for two days, watching how they treated Ethan. Had he seen anything that might cause him to doubt their sincerity, he would have taken Ethan and told the Raus to leave. Benjamin was taken out of love; Ethan was given into love."

End of Journal Entry – Now Ethan Rau

Following a pause after reading the journal Ethan told Dr. Colton, "This is awesome. It answers questions that Mom and Dad couldn't."

"Richard, we have visitors," Barbara said as I entered the kitchen through the garage door.

"It's me and Dad, Pa-pi," a smiling, reddish-blond haired teenager announced, walking into the kitchen.

"Who the hell are you?" Wesley Dill asked.

"I'm Connor; Pa-pi is my godfather."

Dr. Colton embraced the boy. "This young man is Connor Bolger. Let's go into the living room so I can sit down. Xander, call Judge Holt. When he gets here, I'll tell everyone about Connor and his dad."

Chapter 35

"Okay, Doc, what's the story with you being Connor's godfather?" Mr. Dill inquired, once Judge Holt was seated with a beer in hand.

"Let me tell you," Dr. Colton replied. "I enjoy fishing, both freshwater and ocean. After talking with Barbara, I decided to lease a forty-two-foot Nordic tug and take the family from Bremerton, Washington, down through the Panama Canal and end up in Portland, Maine. Barbara and I decided to take the boys on their first commercial airline flight to California. They hated it!

"We rented a thirty-six foot motorcoach for the drive to Bremerton. We stopped along the way at Dirty Socks, where the boys came to us. Royce took me to where he remembered them huddling together after Ted and Myra abandoned them. I wasn't surprised when Royce asked to walk back alone. What did surprise me was when Royce and Kent asked me to cut their hair. Once I finished cutting their hair, using just a pair of scissors, both boys laughed and had fun cavorting in the sulfur spring water.

"Our voyage from California to Washington took seven days, as we were in no hurry. We stopped in Tacoma, Washington, to buy supplies. Barbara bought new diving equipment, intending to teach the boys how to scuba dive. I invested money in fishing equipment and beer–lots of beer. Beer and nuts...all right– chips, too. Our Nordic tug was fueled and waiting. I raised a small ruckus upon finding the tug had no potable water in its freshwater tank. We were given instructions on various aspects of the tug, then left alone to fill its water tank. Kent stepped up to fill the tank without being asked. He helped his brother load their gear onto the tug, keeping track of the boat's water level as well.

"We left Bremerton at eight-thirty the next morning. Our tug performed extremely well and by the time we reached Port Angeles, Washington, Barbara and I could guide the tug with ease. At Port Angeles I took Kent with me to purchase fuel for our carry-aboard skiff. Barbara remained behind with Royce to prepare dinner. When Kent and I returned to the boat, Royce was wrapped in a large towel. Barbara informed me that Royce had jumped into the cold water to rescue a small child's puppy that fell off the dock. Royce was a cold, cold, cold hero to that child. After Royce saved the puppy, we decided to travel towards Vancouver, Canada. Before we pulled anchor, Barbara helped the boys into cold-water gear. We traveled at a steady ten knots for two hours, sighting the lights of Victoria, Canada, to our left which Kent informed me was our port side. It was so dark that I couldn't see anything in front of or around us. I wanted more lights on our boat.

"We stopped for three days in Victoria, outfitting the boat with extra temporary lights. The boys added to their collection of video games, music, and junk food. Me, I just bought more beer and a couple of bottles of good wine. The wine I'd share with Barbara.

"We headed north once again. The twins were allowed to wear regular clothing, keeping their cold water-gear close. We didn't push the tug for speed. I rested during the day, leaving Barbara to navigate. Our second night out of

Victoria was warm. Water temperature was 48°. I saw a fire blazing high off our starboard side and began steering in its direction. I dropped anchor in the bay of an island a short distance away and turned off all unnecessary lights. Our map showed us to be north of Waldron.

"Around six in the morning, I heard shouts and yelling coming from the island where the night before there had been a bonfire. Looking through my binoculars I could see a group forming around a person lying prone. I called Barbara and the boys. Royce helped me launch our skiff. Kent did everything his mother asked and within minutes of me leaving in the skiff at full throttle they were moving. Three minutes after I landed the skiff I began treating a teenage girl for deep cuts on her back, legs, and knees. The girl had slipped while walking to the beach. She stumbled, tumbling head over heels. The last thing I did was set her leg. My family was thanked by being invited to one of the biggest island parties anyone ever imagined. We stayed with newfound friends for three days. The girl and her family returned to Vancouver.

"We headed south after spending just two days in Vancouver, Canada. Our next stop was Coos Bay, Oregon. Three weeks later we anchored along the central coast of California, exploring some caverns Kent spied from our tug. We were in no hurry to go anywhere. Over the next month, we leisurely motored as far south as the beautiful town of Avila. Barbara managed to rent a car and spent two days replenishing our supplies. Giving in to twin pressure, I went exploring with Kent and Royce. We found two more caves, one of which was easily accessible from the beach. Cave number two, while visible from land, was accessible only by water.

"I told the boys, cave number two would have to be an adventure for the next day. I also explained it would give us the opportunity to use the skiff and snorkeling gear. We started with cave number one. Now, where those two boys pulled their flashlights from, bewildered me, considering they wore only board shorts and sneakers. Our exploration ended about one hundred and fifty feet into the cave. A lot of sand, rock all around and plenty of evidence indicating that people had built fires inside.

"While waiting for Barbara's return, I allowed the twins to go swimming. We were visited by a local resident who told me many facts of Avila's past. Although our guest, Stephen Bolger, never mentioned the twins, he kept an eye on them the entire time he was aboard our boat. When Mr. Bolger left, I took the boys and followed the man at a distance. He went into an older house. A short time later he left, carrying a camera and a tripod. I quietly observed Mr. Bolger for fifteen minutes, eventually realizing he was taking pictures. I also realized he needed to move a mere fifty feet for a clear view of our boat.

"Barbara arrived around four-thirty with food, new clothes, and gifts for the family. And, just as I thought, Mr. Bolger moved so he could begin taking pictures of our boat and family. I didn't like what I saw, so I decided Barbara should know I didn't trust the man.

"Later, while shopping in Avila, it occurred to me that I could spy on Mr. Bolger in return. My plan was simple. A fast trip to the city of San Luis Obispo would provide me with the items needed. Barbara liked my plan and agreed that she and the twins could help the most by keeping Mr. Bolger distracted while I visited his home. By using our binoculars to scan the picture-taking location, we knew when Mr. Bolger was watching us. Once he was in position, I made it obvious that I was leaving. Kent and Royce lay on the tug's roof to sunbathe. Barbara joined the boys and read one of her novels. The end of my plan seemed more difficult, but was in fact quite easy. I wore dark clothing, a ski mask, black latex gloves, and socks covering my shoes. I left three video and three audio recorders at various places in Stephen Bolger's home.

"Upon my return to the tug, Barbara suggested we take the skiff southward around the jutting hillside to see what might possibly attract Mr. Bolger's attention. What we found was a beach, roughly two hundred yards long by forty yards wide. We easily saw that this was a beach where people sought seclusion from the public eye for clothing-optional activities. We traveled south for another fifteen minutes before we returned to our boat. Our black water tank needed to be emptied, so we headed to San Luis Obispo to refuel, refill her freshwater, and empty our sewage. Barbara insisted on fresh fruits and vegetables, while I journeyed to the hospital for medical supplies. Although I wasn't from California, nor did I practice medicine there, the medical staff provided me with everything I requested. I paid for the items, asking what I might need that I had not thought to obtain. The hospital staff was helpful with their suggestions and I thanked them profusely as they added to my medical stores.

"We dropped anchor close to our previous location offshore at Avila. I scanned Mr. Bolger's observation spot to find him absent. For the next half-hour we bathed, cooked supper, and put our supplies away properly. It was two days after I secreted the video and audio recorders in the man's home that I was able to retrieve them. I watched the videos on our computer. Mr. Bolger had definitely taken pictures of Royce, Kent, and Barbara. A second video showed a strawberry-blond-haired boy on Mr. Bolger's computer being abused. There were numerous photos of the child and none of them in Stephen Bolger's house. I decided to visit the man.

"'If you move, I'll shoot your twisted ass,' I told Mr. Bolger, after walking silently to within twenty feet behind him.

"'Dr. Colton, what pray tell makes you think I'm the twisted one?' Mr. Bolger asked me.

"'Why are you taking pictures of my family? I've seen you through my binoculars.'

"'I assure you. sir, my intentions are not evil. You have a wonderful family. I intended to visit you this evening. I'm a professional photographer. I intentionally came here to get pictures of the town. What I eventually discovered makes me sick.' Mr. Bolger slowly turned to face me. 'You can either shoot me or let me gather more information for the police.'

"I spent the next three hours talking with Mr. Bolger at his house. He kept all of his information, videos, and photographs of the boy I'd seen on an external hard drive. Mr. Bolger then called the county sheriff and requested a deputy stop by his house.

"When the sheriff's deputy arrived, Mr. Bolger introduced himself. 'Stephen Bolger; I called to have you come and see me.' The two men shook hands. I noticed two dots in the web between the thumb and forefinger on the deputy's right hand.

"'I'm Richard, Stephen called you for me. I want to file a complaint against the people of Paradise Cove. They need to cover up so my sons aren't forced to see them.'

"'Mister, you're wasting my time. Keep your kids away from the beach so your tenderness isn't offended. Good day to you.' The deputy turned to leave.

"'But, I–' Mr. Bolger started to stop the man.

"I put my hand on his arm, softly saying, 'Let it go.'

"When the deputy departed, I asked to see Mr. Bolger's evidence again. 'You have to leave the area,' I told Stephen. I pointed out the bird tattoo on the strawberry-blond boy's arm. 'You have been observing them. They've probably been watching you as well. This is a dangerous organization. If you stay, expect a sheriff to come back with a search warrant of some kind.'

"Two days later, Stephen Bolger was arrested on drug charges. His cameras and other equipment were confiscated. Barbara and I read of his arrest in the local newspaper. The following evening, around 11 o'clock, I paid a visit to the house Mr. Bolger had been watching. I found a boy zip-tied to a bed. He was freed and we disappeared into the night.

"From a payphone I called the San Luis Obispo police. 'There's an envelope containing evidence of a dirty sheriff deputy at light post 'C' in the Cal Poly parking lot.' I hung up and removed some cotton from my mouth.

"Barbara and the twins were ready to leave once I returned with an anxious young male in tow. Royce navigated as Barbara assisted me in removing an RFID from the boy's arm, and a second one from his right ankle. While the boy was still out, I took six vials of his blood. I dropped both chips into the ocean, well away from shore, in over two hundred feet of water. They were smashed into pieces using a hammer before disposal.

"During the rest of the night, in calm water, I removed a small seagull tattoo. We stopped our speedy ten-knot escape from Avila Beach three days after leaving when we arrived at Catalina Island. The new boy volunteered his name when he awoke.

"'I'm Davey North. Is my daddy here? He was mad at me again. Are you friends with my daddy? What happened to my arm?'

"'Hello Davey. Why were you tied to your bed?'

"'Daddy said Deputy Barry told him I was a bad boy. I was being punished. Mister, I don't want to die. I did everything people told me to do and I didn't say 'no' to anyone.'

"'Were you a Dragon boy? Is your daddy a Dragon?'

"'Yes sir, I'm a Dragon boy. I don't like the Dragons, they're mean. My daddy is a Grand Dragon. He gave me a star around my seagull. Daddy said I won't be a Dragon boy after next week.'

"'I'm not a Dragon, Davey. You won't be a Dragon boy anymore, and we'll help you. Do you want me to call your daddy?'

"'No! Please, don't make me go back. Daddy let the Dragons kill Mommy because she didn't like the Dragons. Mommy told the police my daddy hurt me and then Deputy Barry arrested Mommy. Deputy Barry killed Mommy with a knife.'

"We stayed in Catalina for a month with author Blake West. I rented a small plane from an island resident and flew to San Luis Obispo. It took three hours to find out that Deputy Barry and Davey's father had been arrested for crimes against children, thanks to the evidence I left for the police at Cal Poly.

"A quick search for people living in Avila resulted in me obtaining Stephen Bolger's phone number. I thought about calling him, but decided not to. Mr. Bolger was home when I knocked on his door.

"'I should've listened to you,' he told me. 'If I hadn't given you my external hard drive I'd be facing prison. I bailed out yesterday.'

"'Stay near your phone. I'll call to see how you're doing,' I told Stephen.

"'The cops think the boy is dead. I was too late. I told the city cops about my videos. They want me to give them my external hard drive.'

"'Bad idea,' I replied. 'The Dragons want that boy. He isn't safe around the cops.' Then I explained how to detect an adult Dragon member by their dots. I gave the police enough evidence to convict the two men they arrested.

"'You said *they* want the boy. Is he alive? Where is he?'

"'Too many questions. He's alive, his name's been changed and he's safe for now. You're being investigated. Move away from Avila. Let this whole thing be taken care of by the police. Tell them your external hard drive was stolen, and get the hell out of here.' I left Stephen's home within ten minutes after I arrived.

"I left San Luis Obispo, flew to an airfield in Mojave, California, and then returned to Catalina. Blake West was playing a game of 'Simon Says' with Davey the next day, when the boy said, 'Simon Says bark like a dog.'

"I turned to him and asked, 'What'd you tell Mr. West to do, Connor?'

"'I'm sorry, sir, I thought we were playing.' Davey started to cry. 'Please, I'm sorry.'

"I stepped over to the trembling boy. 'It's okay, you did nothing wrong.' I held him close and spoke softly. 'From now on, your name is Connor. You get to live with a good family. No more mean people to hurt you and no more Dragon punishment.'

"'Do you have any ideas or prospects as parents for the boy?' Barbara asked me.

"'I called Sam and he is checking out Stephen Bolger for any sketchy background problems. I think Mr. Bolger might well be a decent father for Connor. He plans on going to Germany for a few months. Then he'll live in South

America for two years and take pictures of and in the rainforest. If Stephen is clean, then Connor will be safe.'

"'What're we going to do with Connor until Sam does his investigation?' Barbara inquired with genuine concern.

"'He stays with us. I sent Mr. Bolger's external hard drive to Sam,' I replied. 'We need a bigger boat or else the boys won't have room to be comfortable.'

"After a family meeting, we decided to continue our voyage on the tug. Blake offered to give Connor a brown tan in a matter of a few hours and darken his hair. I explained to Connor what we planned to do and he never complained once, a smile on his face. Blake mixed baby oil with another oil, then rubbed the mixture all over Connor's body. Within minutes, he went from a pasty white to a deep, rich tan-skinned boy with dirty blond hair. When Blake finished, he took Connor outside to let the boy get some sun on his body. I accompanied Blake and Connor down to the bay, where Blake rubbed any excess oil off of Connor. It seemed as though nobody noticed us as we walked to the beach. I realized why nobody paid attention to us when I saw my own sons cavorting in the bay.

"'Hey, Robin!,' Blake called to his adopted daughter. 'Come say hello to Dr. Colton.'

"'Bring those two black-haired dippers with you,' I added. 'Their names are Royce and Kent.'

"Robin introduced me to her children: seven-year-old James, five-year-old Eric, and two-year-old Cynthia. Robin sent her children with their grandfather and Connor back to the house. She guided the twins and me to her husband's office at the airport.

"'Hank, this is my godfather, Dr. Colton. He's my hero and I wanted you to meet him. Hank is my husband.'

"'I'm no hero,' I protested.

"'Robin and Blake told me everything you've done for us,' Hank confessed. 'Not too many people are willing to risk their lives to help others the way you do. Thank you.'

"We left Hank's office a few minutes later. Our evening was spent watching the kids playing on the street without fear they could be run down. Blake West invited me to accompany him on a trip to the mainland of Santa Barbara aboard the *Lucky Lady*, his trawler. It took us over nine hours to make our round trip, and upon return, we spent another thirty minutes unloading the trawler. I tied our tug against the trawler to transfer our own supplies.

"The day after we left Catalina, Connor no longer had any tattoos. A once-withdrawn boy was becoming an outgoing person who offered to help whenever he could. All three boys wore lifejackets when out on deck and all three sported sun-darkened bodies. Our next stop was San Diego. Royce and Kent helped with water and fuel while Connor remained below deck, studying his schoolwork. At nine years of age, he lacked any education above first grade level. He was learning, and we did our best to make him want to learn more.

"Sam Holt called me one afternoon. Stephen Bolger was no longer a person of interest for law enforcement. The boy named Davey was now considered deceased. Sam gave me Stephen Bolger's phone number in Germany. I used a pay phone to call him.

"'Stephen Bolger Photography.'

"'You have a package for pick up at La Paz in Baja California.' I disconnected after delivering my message.

"Back on the tug I called a family meeting. 'I found a good dad for Connor. We may be saying goodbye to him in La Paz.'

"'Did Sam clear him?' Barbara asked.

"'Yes, he did,' I answered.

"'How much longer before we reach La Paz?' Connor asked.

"'We're here for a few more days and I expect one or two weeks to reach La Paz.'

"'Will my name change again? I like the name "Connor".'

"'I'm flying out of here to get your adoption papers signed. Your name from now on is Connor Jude Bolger. Your dad's name is Stephen Bolger. When I return I'll have your birth certificate, passport, a visa, and a social security number in your name.'

"Our trip to La Paz was uneventful. I enjoyed sitting at the helm, watching the boys and Barbara soak up the vitamin D-filled sun. We ate fish caught by the three fish-happy boys. Stephen Bolger had been in La Paz two days prior to our arrival. He brought a skiff out to the tug once we anchored. He looked surprised to see a healthy, evenly tanned boy smiling at him as he came aboard.

"'Are you my dad? My name is Connor.'

"'Hello Connor. Yes, I'm going to be your dad. My name is Stephen Bolger, but you may call me Dad.'

"Connor smiled. 'My last name is Bolger, too. It says so on my birth certificate,' he boasted.

"'Connor's passport and other papers all have Bolger as his last name. Even his fingerprints say he is Connor Bolger.'

"'So, Connor is my son now?' Stephen Bolger asked.

"'Yes, he is, and you're free to take him to live with you,' Barbara replied.

"'I can't take Connor with me.' Stephen sighed heavily.

"'He doesn't want me,' Connor started to go inside the cabin.

"'Stop!' Stephen commanded. 'Connor, come over here, please.' Stephen Bolger wrapped his arms around the boy. 'Don't run away. I want you to be my son. I can't take you to the Arctic research station with me. I'll be gone for just one month. Then you and I will live in Peru with some Indians.'

"'I want to go with you, please,' Connor began to plead.

"'Connor, your father can't take you,' I explained. 'The Arctic research station is really cold. It's colder than the freezer you were locked in–do you remember telling me about that time?' I spoke looking directly at him.

"'Yes, sir, I remember the freezer. I don't like being cold.'

"'Could Connor stay with you for another month?'

"We agreed to keep Connor and take him with us to Puntarenas Costa Rica where Stephen would accept custody of his son. He signed papers giving Barbara

186

and me permission to take Connor into Costa Rica. He'd arrive in Costa Rica on a specific date to reunite with his son. The document explained the obvious scars and that Mrs. Bolger was deceased.

"Barbara bought Connor a camera and asked him to take pictures as we traveled. Kent and Royce received cameras when they were younger. The weather was warm and we stopped often, allowing everyone to swim as they wanted. Our family cruise was a time of relaxing fun. Having the boys full of energy, helping each other do chores, and posing for each other's pictures made our journey the experience of a lifetime.

"After leaving La Paz, Barbara and I enjoyed the tug's air conditioning while the boys lazed about outside on pads in their usual state of undress, often checking their fishing lines. Their favorite activity while at anchor was jumping from the tug roof into the water."

Chapter 36

"That's all?" Conner asked after listening intently to what Dr. Colton had said.

Dr, Colton continued, "When the time came, I was sad to see you leave. You'd been with our family for five months. You received all of your childhood immunizations at the age of nine, never complaining. Your dad joined us for ten days before the two of you departed for Peru. He praised your photographs and helped you understand why the pictures had to stay with us."

"We kept Connor's pictures and albums for him," Barbara said. "Now it's time to return his property."

Connor sat beside Dr. Colton as his story was told to everyone in the house.

"Pa-pi, Dad said I can't testify in court for you, why?"

Dr. Colton chuckled. "If Mr. Pizzo knew your story, he'd insist I be arrested for child abduction. Everyone in this house knows I'll keep no secrets from them. I trust the people who are here. The Dragon Society is still very dangerous."

Xander Ward turned to Connor. "You were a Dragon boy. The Dragons think you're dead. If you were to testify, they'd try to hurt you because they have kill orders on all Dragon Kids who have escaped. Don't let them know you're alive, youngster."

"My next assignment is in Australia," Stephen volunteered. "We leave on Monday. I promised Connor he could see Dr. Colton to say 'thank you'."

"Happy birthday, Connor," Dr. Colton said, handing the teenager an envelope with his name on it. "For you when you go to college. Study hard and become the doctor you're meant to be."

"I start med school next month in Australia. My girlfriend lives in Sydney. Thank you, sir." Connor was truly grateful.

"Dr. Colton and my dad kept people from killing me," Connor told those gathered. "I lived with my dad in an Indian village. I went hunting with the other boys. The women and men taught me about plants. I'm only eighteen but I have a degree in herbology. Pa-pi has been drinking a tea I made using plants from the rainforest. These plants are rich in antioxidants and have other healing nutrients. Dad and I drink the same tea at least twice a week."

"Connor taught the twins and me how to make his tea. He's going to be a doctor, so I want him to have this." Dr. Colton reached down beside the couch and produced a new doctor's bag. "Or, you can have this one," Dr. Colton said, setting his personal bag in front of Connor. "You may take your pick."

"Doctor, are you sure about this?" Stephen asked.

"Yes, I am. Connor will be a good doctor. I consider it an honor to give him his first bag."

"I want this one," Connor held up Dr. Colton's personal bag.

"Good choice," Barbara Colton said with motherly approval.

Connor leaned over and hugged Dr. Colton. "When we lived in South America with the Indians, I lived like them. My hair was short with grease in it. They treated me like all the other boys. Dad took a lot of pictures down there, but he didn't take pictures of me with his camera. The only pictures of me were taken with the camera you gave me on the boat. Dad kept all my pictures separate and we finally put them on an SD card. We even sold some of the pictures I took. We lived with the Indians for over three years, and even though I didn't wear clothes all the time, nobody ever treated me like the Dragons did.

"I swam in a river with piranhas in it. I hunted monkeys, which we ate. The Indians killed pigs plus all kinds of birds. The only bad part, I had to do schoolwork at least four times a week. I did get credit for learning their language. An Indian girl, a lot older than me, drew a design on my body from head to foot. I asked Dad to use my camera to take pictures of what she did from beginning to end. I didn't realize it when she drew the design because I didn't understand their language, but what she drew was a blessing. Another time, two older men painted me and another boy with their history in a sacred ritual. We weren't allowed to touch the ground for one whole week. Any time we went somewhere, an adult carried us."

"It was a great honor for them to be chosen for that ritual," Stephen added. "If either boy violated the ritual, they both would've been sacrificed. The Indians chose Connor and the other boy as a way of honoring them. Whenever those two boys went hunting, they always returned with food. After the ceremony and celebration other boys, even a lot of men, looked at Connor in a different way. I've been nothing but proud of this boy since day one."

"Dad and I went to Iquitos, Peru, every year to renew his work visa. Dad let me buy a saw, some nails, rope, and other stuff. When we got back to our village, I built a platform twelve feet off the ground. It took me two weeks to build it and all of the villagers laughed at me. I just laughed with them, but in all honesty I was afraid of one man in the village. He kept threatening to burn my platform at night.

"We had a little girl who was attacked by a jaguar one day. The women scared it away by throwing sticks and rocks at it. Dad let me use his crossbow and every night I slept on my platform. Six days after the little girl was attacked, I saw the jaguar drinking water about forty feet away from me. It was barely light outside, but I could see the jaguar, so I used Dad's crossbow. I hit the jaguar and it ran off. I went to the village and told everyone what happened. Some of the men grabbed their spears and after I showed them where it had been drinking they found blood. They found it dead about a hundred yards away and I was taken back to the village. An old man, called a 'shaman', painted me with white grease, followed by black rings all over my body and every day called me 'Jaguar'. Then they began calling me 'Little Jaguar'."

"The South American Indians we lived with believe only a jaguar can kill another jaguar. The Indians adopted Connor," Mr. Bolger told those gathered.

"I admit, I was scared," Connor confessed. "Dad knew I was afraid of the jungle. He told me jaguars couldn't get me if I was up high, and he helped me build my platform. Then Dad let me use his crossbow. What I learned about the Indians we lived with is that they're more scared of jaguars than me. Two men offered to help me throw the dead jaguar into a river to get rid of it. They didn't keep the skin for anything. It took piranhas less than five minutes to devour the

189

carcass. I had to stay in a separate hut with two men for seven days, because they believe a jaguar's spirit will seek revenge for up to that length of time."

"Connor told me his two companions always made sure he ate before they would eat. When their isolation ended we learned Connor could take a wife. He had proved himself to be a man at age eleven by providing food for the village and killing the jaguar by himself. Those people considered my eleven-year-old son to be a man," Stephen related with obvious pride.

"I was almost twelve, Dad!" Connor protested. "But I didn't want a wife." They both laughed. "My platform got a lot of use by other villagers."

"When we left South America, Connor was known in Iquitos as 'Jaguar Boy'. He brought back two blow guns and twelve darts," Stephen boasted.

"The Indians taught me a lot about plants. I gave my best friend a machete when we left. My other stuff was given to the two families of the men who helped me get rid of the jaguar," Connor explained.

His dad continued: "Connor went with me to all of my assignments. We spent four months in Alaska at a gold mine. Then we got to stay in Arizona with Native Americans. Two weeks before Connor turned thirteen, we were in Japan. I was doing a piece on sumo wrestling and Connor celebrated the big one-three dressed in a sumo wrestling garb with dirt all over his backside."

"At least I won two matches," Connor defended.

"You won your first match because you lifted your opponent and put him down outside the ring. Your second win was after your wrap fell down, exposing you for all to see. What nobody expected was you running up to your opponent and pushing him out of the ring."

"Everyone was yelling and clapping," Connor reminisced. "Some man came up to me and put that sumo belt back around my waist."

"He was the tournament's lead judge and our host. His name was Minanoto Tenno. He later died eating *Fugu,* which is puffer fish. It's poisonous if not prepared correctly."

"Mr. Tenno also taught me karate," Connor added. "He didn't do that 'wax on, wax off' nonsense, either. Dad did seven jobs in Japan. We got to see the old armor for samurai warriors. Being in Japan was fun."

"The two of you traveled a lot," Dr. Colton observed. "Who taught you your schoolwork?"

"I taught Connor," Stephen admitted. "After Japan ended, we lived off-grid at an old dude ranch I bought for $120,000. We still live there, and it's still off grid."

"I love my dad," Connor confessed openly. "Dr. Colton gave me a new life." Moving to stand directly in front of Dr. Colton, he continued, "I told Dad that I love you. If I could take your cancer, I would do it right now. You gave me a father who loves me."

Dr. Colton looked at Connor. "This is your last gift." He then handed Connor an envelope. "It's a title deed for a house on Catalina Island. Learn how to fly airplanes."

Connor, visibly shaken, simply said, "Thank you."

Chapter 37

"We are on the record. Dr. Kendall is on the witness stand. Let me remind our witness that he's still under oath," Judge King said. "Do you have the DNA results?"

"Yes, Your Honor, I do," Dr. Kendall replied confidently.

"Mr. Pizzo gave my clerk three envelopes, plus the blood sample. She'll now read the contents."

Dr. Colton interrupted, "Your Honor, could Mr. Pizzo verify that these are the originals and nobody has tampered with the envelopes?"

"Do you not trust my clerk, Dr. Colton? I assure you, she hasn't tampered with them."

"I trust your clerk. However, someone else may have done so."

"Very well, Mr. Pizzo, are these envelopes, as they were when you handed them to my clerk?"

Mr. Pizzo examined the envelopes then handed them back. "Yes, sir, they're the same envelopes."

"Please open them to see if they're correct," Judge King instructed.

Opening the envelopes, Mr. Pizzo said, "I must have been tired. This doesn't look like my handwriting, but I'll confirm nobody has altered them, Your Honor."

Dr. Kendall, please reveal your results."

"My results are written on the back side of your blackboard. The bailiff allowed Marshal Marshall and me inside the courtroom earlier to record them," Dr. Kendall explained.

"Sample 'A' did not come from Dr. Colton," the clerk stated as she read the results. "Sample 'B' has no known match in the DNA data banks. Sample 'C' came from Marshal Marshall. And *finally*, the dried blood sample Mr. Pizzo submitted belongs to Mario Rizzoli."

"Wait just a minute!" Mr. Dill interrupted, holding up his hand. "One of the samples submitted was that of Dr. Colton. What happened to his DNA sample? Whose DNA is in its place?"

"That DNA belongs to Prosecutor Anthony Pizzo," Dr. Kendall stated emphatically.

"How can you be certain it's my DNA?" the prosecutor asked.

"I'm an observant man, Mr. Pizzo, I saw you palm one of the samples. Which one, I didn't know, but I accepted it as a challenge. Your DNA is in the national data bank which is where I found a match to the mystery sample."

"Busted," one of the jurors muttered to himself.

"What was that you said, sir?" Judge King asked.

"I said; 'BUSTED'," the juror replied. "I, too, watched the prosecutor palm a swab from his mouth in exchange for another. I meant no disrespect by my comment. I think Dr. Kendall is the real deal and not some phony trying to pass himself off as an expert."

"The prosecution will concede, and stipulate Dr. Kendall is an expert in DNA analysis. We accept his testimony in the field of DNA." Mr. Pizzo thought nobody had seen him switch the samples.

"Mr. Dill, your questions please."

Mr. Dill approached his witness. "The blood sample labeled; *CRIME* then beneath that is written *Unknown Blood Sample*. This was analyzed by your laboratory and determined to be whose blood? How did you match the DNA taken from that sample?"

"First of all, let me make it clear that the particular blood sample provided was tainted. Now, by 'tainted' I mean it was not fresh from an individual's body. Regardless of that factor, we were able to obtain viable DNA from the sample given to us. The blood sample is from Mario Rizzoli, whose DNA is in the national data bank due to his current incarceration.

"It is also common for a prosecuting attorney to receive death threats from organized crime. Like many others in his field of practice, Mr. Pizzo was asked to voluntarily submit a DNA sample. It's a means by which an individual's mutilated body can be identified, should they be killed by something like an explosive device. I would reference the prosecutor who was killed by a Mafia car bomb less than two years ago."

Scratching his head, Mr. Dill turned to Dr. Colton. What he saw was a man in deep thought. "Nothing further at this time, Your Honor."

"Your witness, Mr. Pizzo," Judge King instructed.

"Dr. Kendall, I cannot fathom why Mario Rizzoli's blood would be at a crime scene where his son's ashes were discovered. Could someone else have planted that blood where it would be discovered?"

"OBJECTION!" Mr. Dill shouted. "Mr. Pizzo is asking the witness to give an opinion which is not allowed. It's pure conjecture for the witness to respond–especially when the witness would be giving an opinion not directly related to DNA analysis."

Dr. Kendall lifted his hand. "Allow me, please." Turning to face the prosecutor, he continued: "I deal with hard-core evidence. I leave all conjecture up to individuals like you. But–and I do mean this–maybe, just maybe, Mario Rizzoli is the one who cremated the individual whose ashes were found, and in the process injured himself. Could it be that Mario Rizzoli murdered his own son and nobody thought to consider that possibility?"

Mr. Pizzo shook his head. He'd asked a stupid question, and the answer given did nothing to bolster his case against Dr. Colton.

"I'm going to overrule the objection simply because the witness answered. And, because I think Mr. Pizzo now realizes his mistake."

"Dr. Kendall," Mr. Pizzo addressed the witness, "you said the DNA sample was tainted. Would you please explain what you mean?"

"'Tainted' means *not pure*. There were traces of dirt, ash, and pollen in the blood sample we were given. That which is not DNA must first be removed before we can extract the DNA. This process can be time consuming. For

192

example, had someone poured bleach over the blood–well, then you'll not have viable DNA; it would be destroyed, not tainted."

"Would a person in the medical profession know how to destroy a DNA sample?"

Dr. Colton held up a hand, "Objection! Speculation, hearsay–and *yes*, for the record, I *would* know this information."

"Sustained," Judge King responded.

"Dr. Kendall, can you get DNA from ashes?"

"NO! You absolutely cannot."

"Your Honor, could we take a twenty-minute recess? My new medication has to be taken at this time," Dr. Colton requested.

"We'll take a twenty-minute break," Judge King said as he banged his gavel and recessed court proceedings. "The witness may step down."

As Dr. Kendall exited the courtroom, he handed Dr. Colton an envelope. Inside was a hand-written note which read: *Well done, sir. You have my respect and admiration.*

"All rise, the Honorable Judge King presiding, Dr. Kendall, to the stand," the bailiff announced twenty minutes later.

"Doctor, you're still under oath. Mr. Pizzo, your witness."

"Dr. Kendall, how long have you known Dr. Colton?" Mr. Pizzo asked.

"Objection: irrelevant, and goes beyond the scope of direct questioning," Dr. Colton said, remaining seated.

"My question goes to ascertaining the relationship between Doctors Colton and Kendall."

"Until this trial, I never met Dr. Colton. You questioned my integrity on Friday. The court played your game and yet my results are still the same. Now you question my integrity again."

"Your Honor, the defense has accommodated Mr. Pizzo at every turn. He's done his best to contaminate this trial with false evidence, dishonesty, and multiple lies. At this time we move for a dismissal of the charge of murder. If not a dismissal, then a mistrial," Mr. Dill said, controlling his anger with great difficulty.

"Or, I can talk to the press," Dr. Colton said softly. "I'm sure they will be interested."

"Dr. Colton, I take that as a threat, sir," Judge King's spat.

"Oh no, Your Honor, I'd never threaten the court. I merely stated what I *can* do–not what I *will* do, Sir."

"Objection sustained. Mr. Pizzo, ask your next question or release the witness." Judge King decided to ignore Mr. Dill's motion to dismiss the murder charge.

"Dr. Kendall, you stated the blood sample taken from beside the ashes, and thought to belong to Marco Rizzoli, actually belongs to his father, Mario Rizzoli. Is that correct?"

"Yes," Dr. Kendall replied simply.

"Could that blood belong to young Marco Rizzoli and not his father?" Although Mr. Pizzo already knew the answer, he hoped to sow the seeds of doubt regarding the DNA results into the jury's minds.

"No! Absolutely not! Each DNA is unique to the person it belongs to, and that is why *I* am the expert in this field."

"But you could've made a mistake," Mr. Pizzo asserted.

"I don't make mistakes. DNA testing has been my area of expertise for twenty-five years. I *do not* make mistakes or assumptions. It would be my mistake if I tried to practice law—just as it is your mistake in attempting to assert any knowledge regarding DNA science."

"Dr. Kendall, you previously testified you can't take DNA from ashes?"

"That's correct."

"Is there a chemical you can add to ashes in order to extract DNA?"

"No, there isn't," he said with an impatient sigh. "What you suggest is impossible."

"So, to be clear: the ashes in the photograph aren't identifiable through DNA."

"That's also correct," Dr. Kendall said, reaffirming his previous testimony.

"I have nothing further," Mr. Pizzo concluded.

"Dr. Kendall, you may step down."

Chapter 38

"Mr. Dill, call your next witness."

"Your Honor, we call ten-year-old Renée Miles to the stand," Mr. Dill responded.

A little girl with a red ponytail and green eyes entered the court. She stopped in front of the witness stand and raised her right hand.

"I'm waiting, sir," she chirped.

"Before you raise your hand and make any promises, I want to ask you some questions," Judge King said gently.

"Sure," was the polite reply.

Judge King looked at the expectant girl. "Do you know the difference between telling the truth and telling a lie?" he inquired.

"Sure, everyone knows that," Renée replied with disarming sincerity.

"Have you ever told a lie?"

"Yes, sir, and I got grounded. It's not good to tell lies."

"If I said your name is Mindy Castle, would that be the truth or a lie?"

"That's a mistake, not a lie, because you could forget my name is Renée. Now, if you said I was pretty, that'd be a lie. I'm not pretty, I'm beautiful," Renée expounded.

"If I told you I'm the president of the United States—"

"That's a lie, sir; you're the judge. I'm not a princess and I'm not a doctor, but I know the truth."

"Your Honor, prosecution accepts that the witness knows the difference between truth and lies," Mr. Pizzo said.

"Agreed," Mr. Dill echoed.

"Very well," Judge King said, addressing both prosecution and defense. Turning to Renée, "If you would like to raise your right hand now, I'm going to ask you: do you promise to tell the truth, the whole truth, and only the truth while sitting in that truth chair?"

"I promise to tell the truth," Renée answered.

Renée pronounced her name and spelled it for the record.

"You may question your witness, Mr. Dill."

"Thank you, Renée, do you know Dr. Colton?"

"Yes, sir."

"Are you afraid of Dr. Colton?"

"Nope! I mean—no, sir."

"How did you meet Dr. Colton?"

"Uncle Royce took me out of my mommy and daddy's house. He took me to Dr. Colton. That's how I met him."

"Why did Royce take you out of the house?"

"It was on fire."

"Where were your mother and father?" Mr. Dill queried.

"In the house, sir."

"Did you get hurt in the fire, Renée?"

"Yes, sir," the girl replied with a shudder.

"Your Honor, I have photographs that might make this a bit easier to understand. May I share them?" Dr. Colton stood, offering his photographs to Judge King.

"Because the witness is still very young, I must insist you wait. She's been through enough trauma."

"Renée, what happened to your parents?" Dr. Colton asked in response.

"They died. Three men in masks killed them and cut my back. Those men started the fire."

"Was anybody else in the house?"

"My big brother, Lee. He shot one of the men with Daddy's gun. Then another man stabbed me with a knife."

Dr. Colton sat down, taking a drink of water.

"Did Dr. Colton hurt you?" Mr. Dill asked.

"No, sir, he made me stop hurting. He kept me with him until I was adopted."

"Renée, have you ever told anyone about your family, or the fire and those men?"

"I talked to my new daddy. He's a doctor, too."

"Is your new daddy Dr. Milo Miles, psychiatrist?"

"Yes, sir, I talked with him."

"No further questions, Your Honor."

"Mr. Pizzo," Judge King said, "remember the witness is only ten years of age."

"Yes, Your Honor," Mr. Pizzo replied. "Renée, other than Dr. Miles and us, who did you tell about the fire and those men who hurt you?"

"I don't remember every name," Renée answered.

"Did you tell the police?"

"Yes, sir, I told the police everything."

"Did you tell them Royce and Dr. Colton kidnapped you?"

"Objection. Mr. Pizzo is testifying for the witness," Mr. Dill quickly protested. "He's attempting to convict Dr. Colton of a kidnapping for which he's not charged."

"Your Honor, the witness clearly stated Royce Colton kidnapped her," Mr. Pizzo countered.

"Objection!" Dr. Colton joined in. "Mr. Pizzo is blatantly misstating the facts. Renée Miles never used the word 'kidnap'. Her words were, and I quote: 'Uncle Royce took me out of my mommy and daddy's house. He took me to Dr. Colton. That's how I met him,' unquote. Mr. Pizzo is attempting to prejudice the jurors, hoping they'll convict on a bogus charge when he has no evidence to prove the murder allegation."

"Your Honor, she said they kidnapped her," Mr. Pizzo protested vehemently.

"Mr. Judge, you asked me if I knew what a lie is. Well, that man just told a lie!" Renée declared, pointing at Mr. Pizzo.

"Okay people, let's take a deep breath, and relax. The court recorder will read back the witness's testimony." Judge King sat silent and listened as Renée's testimony was read by the court recorder.

196

"Mr. Dill, objection sustained. Dr. Colton, objection sustained. Mr. Pizzo will apologize for his behavior. I applaud the witness, Renée Miles, for knowing when she heard Mr. Pizzo state an untruth."

"Your Honor, I believe the words 'took' and 'kidnapped' are synonymous in this case. I simply stated the truth as I both see it and understand it."

"Mr. Pizzo, you *will* apologize. Failure to do so shall result in one of the following, and quite possibly all: If you choose not to apologize, you shall be found in contempt and jailed immediately. Should you be jailed, it will force me to either dismiss with prejudice any charges against Dr. Colton or declare a mistrial. Regardless of how I rule, you will be sanctioned and face disbarment. Need I say more?"

"Very well, I don't want to see a guilty man go free. My choice of words was wrong. I apologize for my perceived attempt to testify for our witness. My memory recollection isn't photographic, like some people's. For making that mistake in memory, I apologize. I do hope the jury won't hold this against me, but make their decision based on the facts."

"Humph," Renée reacted. "That was psychobabble."

"Excuse me, little lady," Judge King interrupted. "You weren't asked a question. You do not make comments."

"Your Honor, is it possible for Amy Miles to sit off to one side of her daughter for support?" Mr. Dill asked.

"I don't think that's necessary, Mr. Dill."

Dr. Colton stood to contest the judge's decision. "Your Honor, Renée Miles is clearly crying. Now, I'll jump to conclusions and say it is due to your rebuff for telling the truth even though she wasn't asked a question. Her father, Dr. Milo Miles, will testify that his daughter has a good command of the English language and she most definitely understands the word 'psychobabble'."

As Dr. Colton spoke, Judge King glanced at Renée, who was still softly crying. He listened to Dr. Colton's words and thought of how to let Renée Miles explain her remark.

"Bailiff, bring Amy Miles into the courtroom. Dr. Colton is quite correct. I, too, believe a bit of support is in order for our witness." Judge King then looked towards Renée. "When your mother comes in, you may step down and give her a hug."

Amy Miles comforted her daughter and then sat so she could watch Renée as she testified. When Renée appeared more composed, Judge King spoke again. "Renée, you used a very big word. Can you explain it?"

"It means that man over there," she said, pointing at Mr. Pizzo, "said stuff meant to confuse us and make everyone think he was sorry. He didn't apologize for saying I said something I didn't say. It sounded like an apology, but what he said was nugatory, sir."

Judge King turned to Amy Miles and gave her a puzzled '*do I dare ask*?' look.

"Ask her," Amy Miles boldly asserted.

"Renée please tell us what *nugatory* means," Judge King politely requested.

"It means, 'of no importance, worthless or ineffective', sir." Renée again pointed at Mr. Pizzo, "You are mendacious."

"Thank you," Mr. Pizzo responded.

"Uh...Mr. Pizzo, the witness just said that you were given to deception or falsehood. You're dishonest and deceitful," Mr. Dill educated his uninformed colleague.

"You're a very smart girl," Judge King complimented. "Mr. Pizzo, do you have any more questions for the witness?"

"Yes! Renée, you said Royce *took* you. Did you *want* to go with him to Dr. Colton?"

"No, I didn't know him."

"Did Dr. Colton take you somewhere?" Mr. Pizzo was being careful how he asked the questions.

"Yes, sir."

"Did you *want* to go with Dr. Colton?"

"He didn't ask me if I wanted to go with him. He just took me."

"And you didn't want to go, did you?" Mr. Pizzo was pleased.

"No, I did not," Renée replied.

"So, you were forced to go with Royce Colton and Dr. Colton when you didn't want to go with them. Is that true?" Mr. Pizzo knew the answer, but he wanted to hear it in front of the jury.

"Yes, but–"

"Nothing further, Your Honor," Mr. Pizzo interrupted before Renée could qualify her answer.

"Mr. Dill, redirect?"

"I have a few questions," Dr. Colton answered. "Renée, when Royce took you out of your house, did you want to stay with your family?"

"Yes, sir."

"Did you know how bad the cut on your back was, or how badly your feet and legs were burned?"

"No, sir, I didn't."

"Can you tell me why Royce and I took you away when you didn't want to go with us?"

Renée visibly choked up a bit. "Uncle Royce took me away because Mommy and Daddy were dead. I was bleeding and Uncle Royce took me to a doctor. You stopped the bleeding and took me to a hospital. Uncle Royce and you took me to save my life."

"Is Royce really your uncle?"

"No, sir. I asked if I could call him 'Uncle'."

"Your Honor, I have no further questions," Dr. Colton announced.

"Nothing for me, Your Honor," Mr. Pizzo added.

"Thank you, Mrs. Miles. You may escort Renée from the courtroom."

Dr. Colton next presented the photographs showing the injuries suffered by Renée Miles. When he was finished, it was evident to everyone present that he had saved the girl's life.

"Mr. Dill, do you have any more witnesses to call?" Judge King asked in exasperation. "This is beginning to annoy me."

"Yes, Your Honor, I do have more witnesses. However, my next witness will be a bit late due to vehicular difficulties."

"Forgive me," Mr. Pizzo said querulously. "Can't you call a different witness? I mean, one would think you'd be a little better prepared in scheduling your witnesses."

"Objection, Your Honor. Mr. Pizzo is attempting to impugn Counselor Dill's ability. Could you please ask Mr. Pizzo to be a bit more tolerant with things we have no power in controlling?" Dr. Colton chose his words with care so it would not appear as though he were attacking the prosecutor.

"I'll sustain the objection and remind Mr. Pizzo that his apology lacked sincerity. Albeit I must agree with our prosecutor in regard to calling a different witness," Judge King said.

"Your Honor, I received notification of this delay through the court clerk moments before court was called to order. Had I known five minutes earlier, it might have been possible to call a different witness and request that they appear sooner," Mr. Dill asserted in his defense.

Judge King spoke briefly in a low whisper with his clerk before addressing Mr. Dill: "We will take a short break. Mr. Dill, you're to notify my clerk the minute your witness arrives."

"Yes, Your Honor," Mr. Dill answered.

"Court is in recess. Jury will go to the deliberation room."

"Your Honor, if it pleases the court, we'll provide fresh doughnuts for the court and jurors during the delay," Dr. Colton offered. "And just so there is no hint of bias, I invite Mr. Pizzo to join in the purchase."

"I agree," Mr. Pizzo stated. "Our jurors deserve some consideration. I'll gladly help with the purchase of fresh pastries."

"So be it. Give the money to our clerk. She can purchase the items and see that they get to our jurors. Dismissed," Judge King said.

Dr. Colton handed the clerk forty dollars. He watched as Mr. Dill handed over another twenty. He smiled upon seeing Mr. Pizzo hand ten dollars to the court clerk.

Looking at the court clerk, Dr. Colton spoke: "I hope you don't mind. I took the liberty of ordering from the Dough-Knots Donut Shoppe."

"Good, it's only two blocks away. I should be back really quick," the clerk replied.

"The doughnuts will be here in a few minutes," Dr. Colton said. "They offered to deliver because we're so close."

"Thank you," the woman responded.

"Mr. Dill, there's a man here who is looking for Dr. Colton," Marshal Marshall interrupted.

Dr. Colton and Mr. Dill followed Marshal Marshall out of the courtroom.

"Now, isn't this a nice surprise," Dr. Colton said, extending his right hand. "This, Mr. Dill, is the Talon family."

"We heard about your trial, so I arranged a two-week leave from the resort," Mr. Talon said in greeting. "It's good to meet you, Mr. Dill. Doc, we already met Judge Holt."

Looking at his watch, Mr. Dill said, "Let me give my witness a quick call. I need to know where she is, and how long before she arrives."

Mr. Dill's witness needed ten minutes, but the court clerk informed him that Mr. Pizzo was headed to urgent care. The prosecutor had cut his hand on a metal binding clasp. Judge King dismissed for the morning with instructions that there would be no afternoon break.

When Mr. Dill joined Dr. Colton and the Talons at the coffee shop, he suggested they go to a nearby pancake house for breakfast and juice for the doctor.

"Come on over and grab a seat, Judge," Dr. Colton called out. Sam Holt and his wife, Sandra, joined Dr. Colton, Mr. Dill, and the Talon family for breakfast.

"Wesley just asked a question, but I wasn't paying attention," Dr. Colton confessed.

Mr. Dill feigned shock saying, "I just asked Mr. Talon, how'd you folks meet?"

"Let's let Sam and Sandra order breakfast and I'll tell you everything," Dr. Colton responded.

Chapter 39

Draining his coffee cup Dr. Colton began:

"This all started on the twins' thirteenth birthday. We gave both of them their very own one-man pontoon boat, which could be set up in less than six minutes. The small storage area in the motorcoach which once held the generator was perfect for storing the inflatable boats. Even the small electric motors, swivel seats, collapsible oars, and rechargeable batteries fit.

"At age thirteen, each could carry his own boat and attachments. The boats were used regularly and we ate fresh fish just as often. Barbara and I love the noble redwood forests in California. It was on our way to visit these behemoths that Georgia Pittman crossed our path. Georgia was nine years old, with light brown hair down below her shoulder blades and brown eyes. We first encountered her and her father in the ghost town, Bodie, when Barbara informed me a little girl had cut her leg when she fell through a rotted walkway. Identifying myself as a doctor, I offered to clean the child's wound and give her a tetanus shot. Georgia's father, Todd, stayed by his daughter's side while I treated her.

"Later that afternoon Barbara and I went for a walk, leaving the boys inside our motorcoach doing homework. Bodie had been very prosperous at one time. The buildings were old and dangerous, with 'NO TRESPASSING' signs attached to them—which obviously didn't mean much to those who tried the door knobs hoping to look or go inside. It was during our walk that we saw Georgia's father accept an old coffee pot and cast iron skillet passed to him from inside one of the buildings. One or two minutes later Georgia crawled through a hole in one of the walls.

"We stayed overnight at a campsite about two miles away. Kent and Royce rode their collapsible bicycles after supper. Later, while playing a board game, Kent mentioned that he and Royce rode down to Bodie, where they saw Mr. Pittman and Georgia breaking into another building. Around seven o'clock, Mr. Pittman parked their trailer about three campsites away. By eight o'clock Mr. Pittman was completely drunk. When drunk, his voice raised to an eight, on a scale of one to ten. It became obvious that Georgia had failed to find enough items for her father to sell. They were going to return in the morning, and if Georgia didn't bring better things to her father, he promised to use his leather belt on her.

"The following morning, Mr. Pittman left the campground before seven. We departed at nine-thirty, heading for our destination; the Silver Dollar Saloon. Ten miles down the road, Barbara told me to go back. Mr. Pittman was using his daughter to steal historical artifacts from the town of Bodie. I argued with Barbara for another mile or two, but finally gave in and turned around.

"When we pulled into Bodie, there were two sheriff's cars and a park ranger truck parked beside the Pittman's trailer. They'd caught the man coming out of a house dragging an old cast iron potbelly stove. His trailer door stood open, with stolen items sitting on the ground outside. As we drove past the town jail, Barbara said, 'Stop'. She'd seen Georgia peek over the edge of a water trough. Stopping where we did blocked her from view of the sheriffs and park ranger. Quickly leaving the motorcoach, Barbara stepped over to the girl while I told Royce to open the table bench seat, which disclosed a hiding place. I instructed Kent to put a mover's pad inside. Upon entering, she followed Barbara directly to the hideaway.

"'If you don't want to go to jail with your father then I suggest you keep quiet,' I told the girl. We took a few pictures, then went to our previous campsite. Georgia was brought out of hiding. 'Do you want us to take you back?'

"'No, please, I didn't want to steal those things, but my daddy made me. I was hiding when the cops caught him. I ran away because I was scared. I'm still scared.'

"'Where's your mother?' Barbara asked.

"'Daddy said she's in heaven. She was shot by a man in a post office where she worked.'

"'We'll take you to the sheriff's office. They'll find a family for you to live with. They don't put little girls in jail. The sheriff will find your family.'

"'I don't have any family. Daddy said it was only him and me. And, *I am not a girl*. My real name is Clyde.' Tears appeared in the child's eyes. 'Daddy made me wear dresses and gave me a girl's name. I hate him! I wish they'd put him in jail for the rest of his life. He treated me like a girl since Mama died three years ago.''

"'What's your father's name?' Barbara gently asked.

"'His real name is Clyde Brown, Senior, but he changed it to Todd Pittman after he stole money from the stores in other states before we came here. When he robbed a bank in Corpus Christi, Texas, he wore a mask and shot a man inside the bank.'

"'What kind of a mask?' I pressed for more information.

"'He looked like President Washington. After we were in New Mexico, I hid his gun and mask inside our trailer. I was going to shoot him.'

"'First, we get out of here. We can stop up ahead and buy you some boys' clothes. Royce can show you how to use the motorcoach shower. When we stop for the night, I'll give you a haircut. Then we'll burn the dress and shoes.'

"'Why don't we stay at Red Rock Canyon tonight,' Barbara suggested. 'The boys can swim in Cottonwood Creek after you cut Clyde's hair.'

"We stopped in the town of Cramer Junction to buy some basic clothing for Clyde. As I drove to Red Rock Canyon, Royce showed Clyde how to use the shower. After parking and leveling the motorcoach, I gave Clyde a crew cut. His appearance changed drastically. No longer would you mistake him for a girl, even if he did wear a dress.

"'We need to change your name,' Royce announced.

"'There was a cute boy who lived next door to my family when I was a little girl living in Virginia,' Barbara recollected. 'His name was Owen.'

"'Owen sounds good,' I replied. 'What do you think, little man?'

"'I like it better than Clyde. Can I be called "Owen" instead of "Clyde"?'

"'Royce, take Owen outside and rub some of your coconut tanning cream on him. Don't forget to apply some on his head to cover the color of his hair. Remember, no white skin anywhere.' I turned to Clyde, whom we named Owen. 'Do what Royce says and when he is finished, you boys can play in the stream. Tomorrow we'll start on a new birth certificate which will say your name is Owen.'

"Barbara and I fixed dinner while the boys found enough water for swimming. I realized we'd have to register Owen's fingerprints with the FBI. The boys quit playing in the stream an hour before sundown.

"'Can we go north and get out of this state?' Barbara asked.

"'Are you giving up on the Silver Dollar Saloon? We still have to pass right by it on our way north,' I countered.

"'We can stay at Silver Lake and fish while you go to the Silver Dollar Saloon,' Kent suggested.

"'You'll stay inside the motorcoach and do your schoolwork, or watch movies on your bunk televisions,' I stated firmly.

"'Can we at least play video games?' Kent haggled.

"'Only if you keep the noise down,' I answered.

"Barbara and I enjoyed our day at the Silver Dollar Saloon. When we returned to the motorcoach, we were greeted by the smell of homemade lasagna. All three boys had taken showers, their clothes washed, dried, and put away. Sporting his deep brown tan, Owen smiled as we entered the motorcoach. He wrapped his arms around Barbara.

"'I made the salad and tea,' Owen said proudly.

"We ate supper in the Silver Dollar Saloon parking lot. Seeing Owen helping Barbara with the dishes, I went outside to a pay phone. I made an anonymous call to the sheriff's office informing them of Todd Pittman's true identity, thefts, and suggested they search his trailer for a gun and mask.

"All three boys were dressed in summer pajamas as we headed northwest once again. They were belted into their seats, playing a board game with Barbara. After sundown, Barbara joined me while the boys played their electronic football games. We spent the night in a small place named Garlock.

"Fifty miles north of the Silver Dollar Saloon, I instructed the twins to get dressed. Twenty minutes later, Kent helped me refuel the motorcoach as Royce checked the air pressure in each tire.

"Barbara took the boys shopping for over an hour. I stayed with Owen, parking where Barbara could easily see the motorcoach. While waiting, I talked with Owen about what I'd observed since he joined us. He hadn't spoken of the abuse he went through at the hands of his father.

"Owen began crying, begging me not to tell anyone. I promised to find somebody for him to live with who'd never allow him to be hurt. I suggested he tell someone whom he trusted about the abuse.

"I was getting my ass handed to me in a card game when we heard a knock on the door. Barbara, Kent, and Royce had returned. Helping Barbara put our supplies away I told her what I'd learned about Owen. I explained that I removed a splinter of oak wood from inside of his left thigh. Knowing how painful it must've been, Barbara was surprised when I told her he'd hardly made a sound. I told her I was proud of the kid.

"Later, I could hardly believe my ears when I was ordering pizza over a payphone and Owen asked for jalapeños. I motioned him to me, and handed him the phone. 'Order your own pizza–anything you want.'

"Before hanging up, I requested our pizza order be doubled, with only the first order to be cooked. King John's Pizza Palace made excellent pizzas. The following day, once the sun went down, Owen asked to sit up front as we traveled. I drove until nearly midnight before stopping to refuel, both tanks being nearly empty. At one o'clock in the morning I pulled into a rest stop, Owen sleeping soundly in the front passenger seat. I unbuckled his seatbelt and carried him to his bed.

"I hooked up the motorcoach to the public black water dump to empty our waste. Turning around to double check all hose connections, I saw Owen standing beside the motorcoach in his pajamas. He said, 'I can't sleep, sir. I'm afraid that when I wake up, I'll be back with–'

"'You're not going back,' I interrupted. 'He'll never hurt you again. Go inside and go to bed. I promise, you'll wake up in the motorcoach.'

"'Can I stay out here with you? I've been inside all day.'

"Owen helped me with the motorcoach. He refilled our freshwater tank, getting soaked in the process. I forgot to tell him not to fill the tank too fast. Owen did whatever I asked of him without complaint.

"Barbara left the rest stop before dawn. She drove north on the freeway. I awoke to the smell of freshly made coffee. As I drank my second cup, Kent and Royce staggered to their chairs. They each drank half a cup as we crossed the state border. We were parked at the top of the mountain pass, fixing breakfast, when Owen staggered forward, still sleepy. Breakfast consisted of bacon, eggs, and fried potatoes with onions, and fresh garlic.

"I drove away once everyone was dressed and seated with seat belts buckled. We exited the freeway at Exit 33. We heard nothing on the news regarding Owen, so he joined us when we stopped in Eagle Rock to buy warm clothes, fishing gear, and more beer.

"Barbara reminded me to stop at a boat-rental place. We leased a twenty-four-foot pontoon boat with a cabin and two 90-horsepower outboard motors.

"We ate lunch at a quiet little place that served the most delicious pies. We arrived at Pyramid Lake an hour-and-a-half after eating lunch. We launched our boat and I parked our motorcoach in a nearby parking lot, then returned to Barbara and the boys. I ushered everyone aboard with their fishing gear. Before I could say anything, Barbara handed each of us a life jacket. Trying to set a good example, I smiled, struggling to put on the one she handed me.

"After anchoring about twenty yards from other boats, the boys proved themselves: eleven fish in two hours was better than we expected. Owen caught a twenty-six-inch trout, followed by Kent, who landed one measuring twenty-two inches. When we pulled anchor, I motored to the north end of Pyramid Lake. There we stopped, and dropped anchor in four feet of water.

"'Owen, are you ready to meet your new family?' I asked, sitting down next to him. 'Jeremiah and Ingrid aren't rich, but they have a lot of love. Jeremiah is the Pyramid Lake Resort manager. He and Ingrid live in a two-bedroom house with a fireplace. It has running water, a bathroom, and a big family room with a screened-in porch for use in the summer. The house sits two feet off the ground in case of high water. You'll have your own bedroom, and you can dig up worms for fishing.'

"We pulled anchor; then, with Owen sitting by himself, we headed for the resort. Jeremiah and Ingrid were gone until the following day. The assistant manager allowed us to park our motorcoach in the dirt area behind the resort mini-market and boat rental. Kent and Royce unloaded their one-man pontoon boats, set them up and went fishing. Owen and I excused ourselves, leaving Barbara to relax alone. Back aboard the rental boat, I guided us past the marina docks. Once we cleared the docks, Owen tossed a line to Kent and Royce. We towed them a short distance before their fish finders, attached to their electric motors, began indicating schools of fish.

"Owen dropped anchors front and back while the twins slowly trolled in circles a short distance away. Owen and I caught six fish between us. Royce trolled close, shouting his count was two, and Kent one. After tying off to our rental boat, they caught their limits. Owen teased them that he and I had been waiting for over thirty minutes.

"Owen eagerly began learning basic watercraft skills using one of the twin's boats. He smiled more often, showing signs of becoming relaxed and less fearful. Sitting in the motorcoach eating lunch the next day, I asked Owen 'Are you ready to meet your new family? Shall we try again?'

"'I'm scared, sir. What if they don't want me?'

"'Trust, you have to trust somebody. The world is full of men and women who will give you nothing but love. Royce and Kent are adopted. They went through a lot of abuse but they trusted us,' I said, looking into Owen's eyes.

"'Our mother and father took our clothes, then left us to die in the California desert,' Kent interjected.

"'Before that, our father used to cuss, yell, and tell us we were trash, worthless, and even said they didn't love us. Mom and Dad saved our lives. They loved us even after we told them what happened,' Royce explained. 'You didn't ask to be treated like a girl and we stopped calling you Georgia once we learned that you're a boy. I saw the marks on your back. You're our friend,' Royce added.

"'You wouldn't like me if I told you what my father did, or what I...,' Owen broke down crying.

"'Owen, we all know you didn't ask for what happened. You probably didn't like it or want to do any of it,' Royce offered as comfort, kneeling in front of Owen.

"'I hated all of it,' Owen admitted.

"'None of us like being hit, yelled at, told we are trash, or hearing we're not wanted. Our father hated us, but Mom and Dad love us,' Kent said.

'Let's go over to Jeremiah's house and see if they're home yet,' I suggested. 'We can do some fishing in the bay using the little boats. Owen can find out if there's any fish close to the Talons' dock.'

"'Dad, may I talk to you alone?' Royce asked as we walked to the dock. We held back to talk.

Owen was towed on Royce's boat. As usual, the boys wore lifejackets. Sixty minutes of exploring revealed many fish. We loaded the small boats onto the big one and returned to the docks. Having thought about my conversation with Royce, I came to a decision.

"'Royce, my answer is yes. You'll tie off the bow, please? Kent, tie off the stern and one of you can show Owen how it's done.'

"'Go with Royce,' Kent said. 'When he's done, you can try doing the stern.' Kent looked askance at me–if that's okay with my dad.'

"'Do it! Doing is a good way to learn. Why didn't I think of that? Congratulations son, you had an original idea.' It was the truth, and I focused on showing Owen that mistakes aren't always met with anger and or violence.

"Slowly walking to the resort restaurant, I stepped over next to Kent. 'I'm proud of you, son. Letting Owen tie off the boat was a good idea.' I hugged Kent. 'Bring your mother to the restaurant, please.'

"'Thanks, Dad. I checked Owen's tie-down. He did really good.'

"Inside the restaurant, I had Owen sit down beside me. The waitress seated us in a booth. Before she returned, I leaned over to Owen. 'Kent said you did an excellent job when you tied down the boat. You can order anything you want for supper.'

"'Make sure you order vegetables,' Royce remarked. 'Just remember ice cream and cake aren't vegetables.'

"'Can I have a bacon cheeseburger?' Owen asked as Barbara and Kent set down.

"'Yes, and carrot cake will pass for a vegetable tonight,' I answered in reply, 'but only tonight.'

"The waitress took Owen's order last, and he ordered jalapeños. After double-checking each order, she left. Less than ten minutes later a tall, dark-haired man approached. I smiled and nodded towards Owen.

"'Excuse me, may I sit down?' the man politely asked. 'I'm looking for a boy who wants to be adopted. Does anybody know a boy who wants to live at a mountain lake?'

"'Owen needs someplace to live,' Kent volunteered.

"'I'm looking for a boy who wants parents that won't make him do bad things. My son has to like swimming, fishing, and will have to learn how to hunt, using guns and bows and arrows.'

"'What about going to school?' Barbara offered.

"'We have home-schooling here. My son has to do his best to get passing grades. He'll have to help cut firewood, make fires in the fireplace, take a bath

206

every night, make his bed, and help keep our house clean. There'll be times when I'm not at home, so I have to trust my son to behave. After his chores are done, he can play video games. It'll be cold when there is snow on the ground, and I expect my son to learn how to use snowshoes, skis, the quad runner–and later, a snow blower."

"'What about you Owen?' Barbara proposed. 'What would you expect from your mom and dad or want them to know?'

"'My hair is really light brown. Royce made it turn darker. I'm nine years old. I like spinach, I stole food from stores, and I drank beer and whiskey. Dr. Colton cut my leg and it still hurts.'

"'Yeah, I removed an old oak splinter that was infected. I suspect you got the splinter crawling through small holes in Bodie. I also stabbed you with the syringe. It was a tetanus shot. I put four stitches in your back after you sliced it on a rusty nail coming out of the Bodie jail.'

"'Well, my son learns from his mistakes and doesn't repeat them,' the man stated, after Owen had briefly opened up about his past and a few of the things he had experienced. It was clear to everyone he was upset, shaking from what he had just shared.

"'Owen told me that if he didn't help steal things or do other bad things he'd be whipped. I don't believe he did those things because he wanted to,' I told everyone.

"'My mom and dad have to want me, even after I did all of that. If all they want is to be mean, then I'll run away. I hate what Clyde Brown did to me. I like swimming, and I like to go exploring–but that doesn't mean stealing stuff.'

"Our food arrived, giving Owen a chance to calm down. Our guest turned to Owen as the boy took a bite of his food.

"'My son has to be willing to accept that we'll probably make many mistakes. He has to be able to forgive us and not run away when we screw up. I expect him to love me as I'll love him even after I know his past. But, the most important thing about my son is: he must know my name.'

"'What is your name, sir?' Owen asked sheepishly.

"Mr. Talon turned his chair to face Owen. Looking straight into his eyes, he replied: 'My name is Jeremiah Talon. My friends call me Jeremy. My son calls me Dad. What do you want to cal me?'

"'If you want me, I'll call you Dad, but my dad learns from his mistakes, too, and he tries not to repeat them.'

"'Jeremiah, we brought Owen here, so you and Mrs. Talon could adopt him. He's afraid that you won't want him, or he'll be abused again. He's a very intelligent boy,' Barbara said. 'Richard has all of Owen's legal papers.'

"'Including the last name, Talon. If need be, I can change it,' I added.

"'Owen, will you be my son? I promise to be a good dad. If you want to live with your mom, Ingrid, and me, be at the house after one o'clock tomorrow afternoon.'

"I watched Owen finish eating his double bacon cheeseburger with fries. He was sold on being Jeremiah and Ingrid's son. Instinctively, I knew Owen would do well with the Talons.

"'Jeremiah, take Owen home now. In the morning we'll be fishing. Owen can go with you tomorrow to bring Ingrid home from Eagle Rock. It'll give him a chance to meet his mother. We'll come by about two o'clock with the adoption papers for you to sign. If you decide not to sign them, we'll take Owen with us when we leave.'

"'Well. little man, it sounds like you're going home with me. Do you have anything warm to wear?' Jeremiah Talon smiled as he spoke.

"'Owen has a footlocker full of clothing in the motorcoach,' I responded. 'We'll take his belongings to your dock and drop them off.'

"'Why don't you walk back to the coach with us? You can check Owen's clothes and fishing equipment,' Barbara suggested as the waitress brought us our desserts and the check.

"'We have to leave early in the morning,' Mr. Talon said. "We can go to a superstore and buy anything else you need. If we're finished eating, let's get out of here. I want to check my son's belongings.'

"Jeremiah approved of Owen's clothing and fishing equipment. When we dropped it off, he and Owen were on the dock to help us unload. Barbara sat watching.

"'That small pontoon boat isn't mine,' Owen blurted out honestly.

"'Yes it is,' Royce responded. 'Mom and Dad bought you clothes, Kent bought your fishing poles and a tackle box, so I asked Dad if I could give you my one-man pontoon boat without the fish finder. Your boat is brand-new. Your dad will have to help you set it up, but it's yours.'

"When we returned the next afternoon to Jeremiah's dock, we were greeted by Owen.

"'Dad said he and Mom want to sign my adoption papers. I want to stay here. *Please!*'

"'Did you tell them everything in your past?' I inquired.

"'Not yet, sir,' Owen replied candidly. 'I want you to be there when I tell them the rest. Please!' he pleaded.

"'Should I take Royce and Kent out fishing?' Barbara asked.

"'I meant all of you,' Owen quickly asserted.

"It was hard for Owen to describe the abuse he had been through. Numerous times, his eyes filled with tears. Yet each time he stumbled, one of the adults gave him encouragement.

"Once Owen finished speaking, Mrs. Talon hugged him tightly to herself. 'There's a saying that goes: *It is what it is, now get over it.* Also: *What doesn't kill you makes you stronger.* But what I'd say to you is that your past is behind you. Now we get to help you have a better tomorrow.'

"Looking at Owen, I asked, 'How many of us did you count before you started talking?'

"'Six… seven if you include me,' Owen answered.

208

"'How many of us are still here? How many of us left or laughed at you?' Mr. Talon asked him softly.

"'Nobody laughed,' Owen replied. 'Everyone is still here.'

"I asked Jeremiah and Ingrid, 'Do you still want to sign Owen's adoption papers, or do I take him when we leave?'

"'You take your family, our son will be staying here at home with us,' Ingrid protectively asserted, holding him close.

"And *that* is how Owen came to live at Pyramid Lake." Nodding towards the door, "Wesley, your witness is here. Shall we go back to court?" I asked.

"I'm still curious about Pyramid Lake. We have time," Judge Holt indicated, looking at his watch.

"Growing up at Pyramid Lake was more than any kid could ask for," Owen expounded. "Being home-schooled, I was able to graduate at sixteen. Now, I travel a lot with my dad as an apprentice wildlife guide in three states and Canada. I also regularly do private fishing guide work at Pyramid Lake. I even help with search and rescue. If you ever decide to visit, we'll let you use the house Dr. Colton gave me when I graduated from high school.

"Whoa, wait a second," I chimed in. "Wasn't it your parents who gave you the house *they* lived in when you were adopted around age nine?"

"Oh, yeah, I forgot," Owen teased. You didn't give me a house. "Mom and Dad moved into the 1700 square-foot house you built, and gave me their old house," Owen smiled. "I have the best life anyone could ever hope for, and I owe it all to you. Mr. Holt is always welcome at my house."

"That's *Judge* Holt," I corrected.

"Owen forgot to tell you his big news," Ingrid Talon announced excitedly.

"Owen, what's your mother talking about?" I inquired.

"I turned seventeen last week. You know everything about my past that was ugly. Now I'm in love, something I never thought would happen."

"I took a family fishing at the lake. I kept looking at their oldest kid, who I thought was really cute. I hated being around the family because I thought the kid was a boy, mainly because Mr. Dixon introduced his wife and two kids: Betty, Reggie, and Chip. It turned out that 'Reggie' is short for 'Regina'. Her brother, Chip, is fourteen, but it's Regina who, as Dad says, 'flips all my switches'. They live at Pyramid Lake. Mr. Dixon is a forest ranger and I help him with search and rescue whenever my parents say it's okay."

"You're stalling, Owen," I interrupted. "Let me tell you what I know. You didn't make many friends growing up because you hated what happened to you, and there was fear it would happen again. You, young man, have always had to be in control of your relationships, but that was only possible with people outside of your family. You're an excellent guide and you have excelled at everything put before you. The long story made short is...?

"I invited the Dixons to dinner. Mr. Dixon knew I thought Reggie was fantastic. At dinner I told them my past. They haven't judged me, except to say that Reggie and I can't be alone together. There has to be a chaperone whenever we go out. Regina accepted my proposal to become my wife when we're both eighteen."

"Congratulations, you scamp,' I declared, smiling proudly.

"Thanks to you, we have two other children now. Juanita and Louis are at the hotel with Regina. We'd like you to meet them," Jeremiah said.

"Of course I want to meet your family," I replied. "I especially want to meet Regina. Boy, do I have tales to tell her."

Chapter 40

"All rise," the bailiff instructed. "The Honorable Judge King–"

"Okay, be seated. Come to order. Mr. Dill, your next witness, please," Judge King was visibly irritated.

Mr. Pizzo immediately rose to his feet. "Your Honor, we have a visitor this afternoon; his name is Arie Bendier. He is an Inspector with the French Police in Paris."

"Mr. Pizzo, what's the significance of this visitor?" Judge King demanded.

"He's going to arrest Dr. Colton on behalf of the French government and begin extradition proceedings." Mr. Pizzo announced, clearly enjoying his news.

"Mr. Prosecutor, I'm not amused," Judge King spat.

"Your Honor," Dr. Colton interrupted, "May I inquire of the prosecutor exactly how this French inspector came to be in the United States?"

"And, even more to the point, how he came to be in this courtroom," Mr. Dill added.

"My office was contacted by the inspector's office in Paris. They indicated that Dr. Colton is wanted for questioning in regard to two abductions in France."

"Surely you're not entertaining thoughts of bringing Mr. Bendier into the court? Mr. Pizzo has rested his case. This is not only illegal, but unethical as well," Mr. Dill interrupted.

"Mr. Dill, Inspector Bendier–" The Prosecutor began.

"Pardon me, the name is pronounced, 'Ah-ree Ben-dee-ay,'" Mr. Bendier interrupted. "My first name is Arie. I have the cooperation of your federal government regarding a matter of great importance. Federal Judge Holt invited me to interview Dr. Colton."

Dr. Colton remained silent. Taking notes, he typed on his computer.

"Doctor, are you interested in these proceedings? Or are you hoping I'll disallow the inspector's claim?" Judge King asked.

"I find it amusing that Arie would come to America and accuse me of kidnapping someone. I suggest, put Mr. Bendier on the stand and let him present his evidence."

"Your Honor," Mr. Pizzo chimed in, "I must object!"

"Excuse me," Mr. Dill said, getting to his feet. "I should be objecting, not Mr. Pizzo. He brought this man into court. I would object; however, Dr. Colton has already suggested we put Mr. Bendier on the stand. I, sir, am going to request a recess so we can sort out this entire mess."

"Move to recess denied. Mr. Bendier, step forward and be sworn in to testify."

"I do not wish to testify, since I'm here to interview Dr. Richard Colton." he said in good English, but with a distinct French accent.

"Take the stand," Dr. Colton urged. "I really do want to hear this."

"Inspector, please take the stand. Didn't you say that Federal Judge Holt invited you?" Mr. Pizzo was pleased with himself.

"Objection," Mr. Dill protested. "If Mr. Bendier isn't sworn in he shouldn't be answering any questions–*especially* from Mr. Pizzo."

"Mr. Bendier, if you won't take the witness stand, I must insist you leave," Judge King said.

"Very well, I shall leave."

"Unless you wish Mr. Pizzo to call Paris and complain, it would be wise to take the stand," Dr. Colton urged.

"Why did you say that?" Mr. Bendier asked in puzzlement.

"It will make Mr. Pizzo a bit happier and give him a sense of control," Dr. Colton answered in French.

"Objection; I'm not trying to control anything," Mr. Pizzo protested. "Dr. Colton is out of order. And I understand French."

"Overruled; even I can see this is a power-play," Judge King responded.

Arie Bendier ignored Mr. Pizzo. "Very well, I accept your offer to present my purpose in being here."

"Do you propose to tell the whole truth in this court?" Judge King quickly inquired.

"I will," Mr. Bendier answered.

"Please state your name, spell it, and tell the court your present occupation," Judge King instructed.

"My name is Arie Bendier. Spelled A-i-r-e B-e-n-d-i-e-r. You already know my occupation."

"Objection," it was Dr. Colton's voice. "The prosecution rested. Mr. Bendier isn't listed as a witness for either the prosecution or defense."

"How're we supposed to find out why the man is here unless we ask him?" Mr. Pizzo angrily protested, "and I have not rested my case."

Judge King remained silent as Dr. Colton once again demonstrated his memory of total recall.

"Yes, you did, Mr. Pizzo. You stated, "Ms. Fangel was my final witness. Prosecution will have to rest.""

"Dr. Colton's objection is sustained. However, I must confess that I, too, am curious as to why this man is in my courtroom."

"Simple solution," Dr. Colton replied. "Inspector, please tell this court why you're here."

"Object–"

"Shut it, Pizzo!" Judge King ordered. "You may continue, sir."

"Very well. In Paris several men and women have been arrested and charged with various crimes which I shall not discuss. One of our witnesses, a girl about fifteen years of age, claims an American doctor took her out of her home in Cannes and relocated her to Paris with her current adoptive parents. Her biological family had a history of being abusive towards the girl and her younger brother. One day, the girl, whom I'll call Angela, disappeared from her home during the night. Her brother was found dead in his bed. The boy had bled to death internally. Angela recently came across her biological mother on the island of Corsica. The woman had another young boy with her. This is Angela's new brother, let's call him Jean Paul. Jean Paul showed signs of abuse, so Angela

212

contacted the police with her story. She said the American doctor called himself Arman. He gave no last name."

"Excuse me, but did this girl, Angela, describe the doctor to you?" Dr. Colton interrupted.

"Yes, she did," the inspector responded. "I sent the complete drawing of the doctor to Mr. Pizzo at his request. I must say, the drawing does not look like you, sir."

Everyone in the courtroom looked at Mr. Pizzo.

"Inspector, my apologies. Please continue," Dr. Colton said.

"Angela requested we assist her younger brother to escape the abuse of their mother. Jean Paul and Angela now live together with their adoptive family. However, French law dictates that the man responsible for Angela's disappearance answer for his actions."

"I ask your forgiveness once again," Judge King said, interrupting. "You mentioned Mr. Pizzo, can you tell us more about your interaction with him, please?" Judge King was not making a request; he was directing Mr. Bendier to explain in more detail Mr. Pizzo's actions.

"Two weeks ago, Mr. Pizzo contacted my office with information regarding the American doctor on trial for kidnapping children. He claimed it may well be the same person we are searching for regarding Angela."

"So I hear you saying that Mr. Pizzo implicated Dr. Colton in Angela's abduction," Judge King stated, with rising anger in his voice.

"I do not understand all of your words, sir," Inspector Bendier answered.

"Allow me to translate your words," Agent Xander Ward offered.

"Thank you," Judge King replied. "I had no idea you spoke any language other than English."

"Fluent in four languages, Your Honor." Agent Ward then began speaking in French.

Mr. Bendier responded to Agent Ward's translation: "Mr. Pizzo believes the man I'm looking for is in your courtroom. He claims Dr. Colton has kidnap–"

"I'm going to stop you at this point," Dr. Colton said, speaking in French. Switching to English, he continued, "Nobody here is on trial for kidnapping. I'm being tried for the murder of a child who is not dead: however no one believes me. I, sir, believe the man you are searching for is Arman Baylock. He is a member of the organization, 'Doctors for All Nations'. He works for Carmel Enterprises as their on-call doctor. I'm surprised Mr. Pizzo didn't recognize the man's name or face. And, I believe he was arrested in conjunction with Arie's current investigation."

"So, I have wasted my time in coming here," Inspector Bendier stated.

"No, sir," Mr. Dill interjected. "Your being here has once again demonstrated Mr. Pizzo's disregard for Judge King's instructions in this court."

"Tell me, Inspector, who paid for your trip to America?" Dr. Colton spoke in French, so Agent Ward translated.

"Your Mr. Pizzo sent me an airline ticket to come here. I believe he hoped I would request the extradition of Dr. Colton to face French justice." Agent Ward again translated for the benefit of Judge King, and the jurors.

"Excuse me, I'm not ignorant," Mr. Pizzo said. "I've kept silent, hoping Dr. Colton might confess his crime to the inspector in French. I speak French, and yes, I contacted Paris when I learned about Angela's abduction. It matches certain other crimes which we cannot prosecute due to time constraints. I sent the ticket so Mr. Bendier could come here and interview Dr. Colton."

"Mr. Pizzo, you've stretched the limits of my patience," Judge King shouted. "I find anything you may say in your defense distasteful. Therefore, I order you to remain silent. Your actions are contemptible. You're ordered to serve three days in jail, beginning immediately following court today. You shall be released Monday morning at six o'clock. You'll be in this courtroom at eight-thirty with a written apology to this court–including our jurors, who've had to tolerate your insolence."

"Your Honor, are you finished with Mr. Bendier?" Agent Ward asked.

"If it pleases the court, I have a question," Mr. Dill said.

"Carry on," Judge King replied.

"Inspector, may I ask what is your–scratch that. How do you know Angela? Do you know her adoptive parents?"

"I fail to see the relevance of your inquiry," Judge King interrupted.

"Forgive us," Dr. Colton responded. "I think it is quite obvious that Inspector Bendier is Angela's adoptive father."

"*Oh, please!*" Mr. Pizzo said in exasperation. "Where did *that* come from?"

"Dr. Colton is correct," Inspector Bendier asserted. Then, in French; "Her biological parents are now deceased. Angela was attacked by her mother three weeks ago. When arrested, the woman stabbed an officer with a kitchen knife. She was killed by the officer. Angela's father died in prison. He slipped on wet steps, hitting his head. He died on the steps. Angela's brother, Jean Paul, now lives with us. However, I am here to find Arman."

"I'll put out a warrant for his arrest," Judge King said. "Thanks to the information, we now know he should be in custody shortly." He turned to his court clerk and nodded.

"Should I remind them that Arman is already in custody?" Dr. Colton whispered to Mr. Dill.

"No, let it go," he answered. "Your Honor, would it be inappropriate to ask Mr. Bendier if he is willing to answer a few more informal questions?"

"Objection; I asked the inspector to be here," Mr. Pizzo protested. "If anybody asks him questions, it should be me."

"Mr. Bendier is not a witness in this trial. If either defense or prosecution wishes to ask a question, you may submit it to him through me. Mr. Pizzo, your actions have been appalling, to say the least."

Agent Ward continued to interpret the proceedings for Inspector Bendier. "Forgive me, please," the French inspector said. "Is it common practice in America for prosecution attorneys to lie when they contact foreign agencies? The

214

only positive thing in all of this is that your prosecutor paid for my travel expenses. However, with everything that has happened, I have a few questions for your prosecutor."

"You may ask whatever you wish," Judge King responded. "Mr. Pizzo will gladly answer truthfully."

"I want to inquire how you got my name, my workplace and my home address? Why have you said that my office contacted you when in fact you contacted my office? And when we ignored your phone calls you began attempting to contact me at my home. You only stopped when I answered my home telephone."

Getting to his feet, Dr. Colton cleared his throat. "That would be my fault. You have to understand I left your contact information in my witness list which came up missing. I must apologize to you."

"Just stop!" commanded Judge King. "What the devil are you saying? Dr. Colton, do you know Inspector Bendier?"

"Yes, Your Honor. I know Aire; we're friends. Inspector Bendier is my wife's neighbor in France. Mr. Pizzo somehow acquired his name from my files."

"Why did you not inform this court of your friendship with Inspector Bendier?"

"In all honesty, Your Honor, this court didn't ask if the inspector and I knew each other. I didn't mind if he was to testify, because if he was looking for me he would have asked for me by name. And Mr. Pizzo called one of my good friends to testify against me. The only list Inspector Bendier's name appeared on, went missing from my briefcase when this trial began."

"Well, Mr. Pizzo, you put your foot in it big time," Judge King said. Turning to Mr. Bendier, he continued, "Inspector, you may leave if you wish. Please accept this court's apologies for all inconveniences."

Arie left the witness stand. Speaking in French, he looked at Agent Xander Ward. "Thank you for your help."

Xander Ward ceased translating. "I shall now depart," Inspector Bendier announced, leaving the courtroom.

"Do you have any further surprises for us, Mr. Pizzo? If not, I'm going to dismiss court until Monday morning. Bailiff, escort the prosecutor to jail. He'll stay there without phone calls or visitations except for legal counsel if he desires. Court is adjourned," Judge King declared loudly, banging his gavel.

As he exited the courtroom under sheriff escort, Mr. Pizzo glared at Dr. Colton and Mr. Dill. "I won't forget this," he told the two men. Speaking French, Dr. Colton responded, "One shouldn't steal papers from people smarter than them. When one lies, cheats, and steals, one loses." Then, in English, "Enjoy your weekend, Mr. Pizzo, *sir*"

"Don't forget to pay your fines," Mr. Dill chided.

Once they were done, Dr. Colton called his wife. "Your neighbor will be dining with us this evening. He's here with me now. I think you'll also be interested to know the jury became aware that Pizzo stole my phony witness list. Our prosecutor is *not* very happy with us."

Inspector Bendier waited until Dr. Colton had ended his phone call to be certain they were totally alone. "My wife and children thank you for your willingness to bring joy and love to our lives. I have two fantastic children who may well have died or been killed had they not had the fortune of being rescued. Every day I give thanks for having wrecked my Porsche 911. Had I not crashed, you and I would forever be strangers. And, contrary to what your prosecutor desires, all of my superiors know we adopted rescued survivors of abuse."

"Thank you for coming," Mr. Dill said. "Your testimony has hurt the people's case. Mr. Pizzo and Judge King have conspired together to present false evidence as the truth."

"Anything for my friend, Arman—or should I say 'Richard'? And you are not in custody, my friend."

"Arie, when you return home, please take this card to your beautiful wife. I'm sending her a token of our appreciation." Dr. Colton handed an envelope to Inspector Bendier. "No peeking, sir!"

"You already know my wife will become emotional when she opens this envelope."

"You realize what you're saying is considered an S.E.P., don't you?"

"Yes my friend," Inspector Bendier said with a smile on his face.

Puzzled, Mr. Dill queried, "S.E.P., what...?"

"Somebody Else's Problem," Dr. Colton responded, chuckling.

As they entered the underground parking lot, Inspector Bendier spoke, "May I ask a question?"

"No! Arie, I didn't kill anybody."

"I know that! I was going to ask, what's for dinner?"

"Barbara is cooking fresh salmon and king crab in honor of your visit," Dr. Colton answered. He then dialed the local pizza place and requested a delivery. He ordered pizzas for the jail officers. He sent a message along with the pizzas: "Tell Prosecutor Pizzo 'thank you for the pizza.'" The food was paid for by Inspector Bendier.

"How many French or non-Americans did you rescue?" Xander Ward asked.

"Let me see… six French, four German, three Italian, and six Asian. It was amazing that only the Italians weren't interested in adoptions. They placed their rescuees in foster homes."

"Does Judge Holt know this information?"

"Yes, this and more. He even knows your past, which I willingly shared with him and four other federal prosecutors. When they asked for my help, I agreed and then spent two entire months sharing everything."

"Does that include why you killed Marco Rizzoli?"

"Xander, I actually like you," Dr. Colton said. "But if you continue to insinuate I have lied to you about Marco Rizzoli, you and I will have problems. And I promise, cancer or not, I will kick your ass."

"Take it easy, Doc. I've been briefed on you being a black belt."

Dr. Colton smiled. "Maybe you ought to call your martial arts sensei. Then when you do, ask him about me, and tell him hello for me." Dr. Colton knew

Xander would call his old martial arts instructor. He also knew what he would be told.

Mr. Dill looked in his rearview mirror at Xander. "Dr. Colton used to go into Chi-town, below ground, where even the police don't go without backup. Have you ever been there?"

"Forget it, Wesley," Dr. Colton said. "Xander went to Chi-town as a little boy."

"Richard, Wesley, the two of you are incorrigible. Stop picking on Agent Xander," Inspector Bendier parried.

"It's okay, Inspector," Xander responded. "I know they only want me to get defensive. I'm not worried over little things. I've no intention of retaliating."

Xander Ward began remembering what he had been told about Dr. Colton. At dinner that night, Xander looked at Dr. Colton with a new sense of respect. The man who rescued and saved his young life was a definite enigma.

Chapter 41

"Your Honor, defense will now call Clara Gibson, daughter of the Gibson magistrate– uh–scratch magistrate and make that matriarch," Dr. Colton scratched his head. "Such is the fun of cancer," he said with a wry smile.

"Way to go, chemo-brain!" Mr. Dill quipped.

"Is that what you meant by–and I quote, 'Remember, you're supposed to have cancer, act like it'?" Mr. Pizzo bellowed venomously.

"Your Honor, objection!" Mr. Dill's voice sounded displeased.

"Let it go, Wesley," Dr. Colton interceded. "Anthony spent the weekend in jail. He's just being hateful, reciting something I wrote on a piece of paper and left in my briefcase. It's also what I told Caleb when he was in hiding."

"Bailiff, call Clara Gibson," Judge King instructed.

Clara Gibson walked to the witness stand, took an oath to tell the truth, and then sat down.

"Ms. Gibson, do you know the man to my left?" Mr. Dill queried.

"It's Clara, and yes, sir, he is the Gibson family doctor. Well, not anymore, but he used to be our doctor. Dr. Colton delivered my children and the majority of my grandchildren."

"To the best of your knowledge, has Dr. Colton ever caused any of your children to suffer pain?"

"Yes, sir, he surely did."

"How'd he do this?" Mr. Dill asked.

"Them babies wailed every time Doc stuck a needle in their little arms. You should've heard my Bobby scream bloody murder when the doctor pulled glass out of his hand and then cleaned the hole," she answered.

"Dr. Colton didn't go out of his way to hurt anyone, did he?" Mr. Dill asked.

"Mister, the onliest thing that man goes out of his way to do is *help* people."

"Your last name is Gibson. Do you know if Gibson Road has anything to do with your family?"

"My great-grandad named that road. He bought land and made that road to reach his property. Our family eventually bought more land along both sides of Gibson Road."

"Clara, who was Philip Matthews?"

"Philip James Matthews was my grandson. He died almost 25 or 26 years ago."

"Objection! Irrelevant, Your Honor. This testimony is totally pointless," Mr. Pizzo spat.

"Your Honor, Clara Gibson's testimony is extremely relevant and we shall prove it shortly," Mr. Dill continued.

"I'll allow Ms. Gibson to continue testifying."

"Clara, where is Philip buried?"

"Objection!"

"He ain't buried. We cremated him just like we do all male Gibsons," the woman answered.

218

"Overruled, Mr. Pizzo," Judge King said.

"You need to let folks speak without interrupting. You might learn something," Clara told Mr. Pizzo."

"You said 'we', who do you mean?" Mr. Dill asked, without waiting for Judge King or Mr. Pizzo to speak.

"I mean, *we*, the Gibson family."

"How old was Philip?"

"Five, his older brother, Malcolm, accidentally caused Philip's death."

"We're sorry for your loss," Mr. Dill said with genuine sorrow. "Where was Philip cremated, Clara?"

"Philip was cremated on my property beside Gibson Road."

"Clara, are you aware that Dr. Colton is accused of killing Marco Rizzoli and burning his body to unrecognizable ash out on Gibson Road?"

"Dr. Colton never kill't nobody. He saves lives, he don't take them," she declared in her homey country manner.

"I can't believe this charade!" exclaimed the prosecutor.

"You don't believe me? Take a look at these photographs and then tell me how unbelievable I am, mister."

"May I approach the witness, Your Honor?" Mr. Dill requested.

"She's your witness."

"Thank you," Mr. Dill said, as he received an envelope from Clara Gibson. "Your Honor, the defense wishes to enter these photographs into evidence as Exhibit Number Four. I also request they be enlarged for our jurors to see."

Dr. Colton nudged Attorney Dill and whispered. Moments later, Mr. Dill addressed Judge King once again: "Your Honor, Dr. Colton has informed me that Royce can scan these photographs into his tablet and present them to the jury as he did with the photographs of himself and Kent."

"Objection; Royce Colton is too close to this trial. He already testified on behalf of the defense."

Getting to his feet, Dr. Colton spoke: "Your Honor, this is ridiculous. Mr. Pizzo objects to everything. He won't be happy until you sustain his objection. May I request you agree with him? Then grant us a short recess so I'm able to see Dr. Boot briefly."

"Prosecutor's objection is overruled. Young Mr. Colton has a skill which will benefit this trial. We'll take a short fifteen-minute break. Bailiff, escort Royce Colton to my chambers. Please invite Mr. Xander Ward as well."

"Yes, sir."

"Clara, you may wait outside if you wish," Mr. Dill offered.

"No, thank you," the woman replied. "I'll stay here. I think I make your prosecutor friend nervous. I kind of like it."

"Yes, Ma'am, you stay right there and make him nervous," Mr. Dill said as Mr. Pizzo glared at him.

Clara Gibson sat in the witness chair and stared at the prosecutor. She was a woman, unintimidated by his overinflated authority. She stared at Mr. Pizzo for the entire fifteen minutes.

Sitting down, Wesley Dill waited for the recess to end. "I do believe we've hit this one out of the ballpark," he told himself softly. "You're one cagey man, Doc. Your motions get denied and yet you still get important information to the jury."

"Stop mumbling–here comes the judge," Dr. Colton teased.

"Remain seated and come to order. Mr. Dill, your witness is on the stand. She is still under oath."

Royce briefly explained how to use his tablet. He then left the courtroom without glancing at his dad. What the jury saw was a series of pictures showing Philip Matthews' body lying atop a stack of pallets surrounded by oak logs and chunks of magnesium engine blocks.

"We laid Philip on top of a one-inch-thick sheet of marble so we could keep his ashes separated from fire debris." Clara Gibson explained each picture as it appeared on the courtroom monitor screen. At no time did Dr. Colton appear in any of the photos, but Clara Gibson could be seen in nearly all of them. To everyone it became clear: the ashes proclaimed to be Marco Rizzoli, were in truth the remains of a different boy, a boy named Philip Matthews.

"Clara, how'd you come to be in possession of Philip's body?" Mr. Dill inquired.

"My family prepared Philip's body for burial. We sealed the casket and put Philip in my SUV. When people came, they paid their respects to one of our guard dogs."

"Did you know the police thought Philip's ashes were the remains of Marco Rizzoli?"

"Yes, but we broke the law by cremating him. We had honored our boy so we let Mario Rizzoli bury his ashes. Where he buried Philip's ashes, I haven't a clue."

"Clara, I have one last question. Were you paid any money for your testimony?"

"Nope, no money. All I get for my testimony is satisfaction of knowing the truth has finally been told."

"Why didn't you say something sooner?" Mr. Dill asked.

"Didn't know about the time limit. That is, not until I got a phone call from a nice lady named Gigi Green from the prosecuting attorney's office a few weeks ago. We talked for over an hour. That's the onliest reason I called your office, Mr. Dill, and agreed to testify."

"I've no further questions," Mr. Dill said, returning to his chair.

"Your witness, Mr. Prosecutor."

"Thank you, Judge. Who did you say called you from my office?" Mr. Pizzo asked in bewilderment.

"She claimed her name was Gigi Green. Her words were that she was working with you and all time limits against us expired, so I was cleared to testify at this trial."

"How old was Philip?"

"I told you, Philip was five."

220

"Didn't he die from a ruptured aorta which Dr. Colton repaired through surgery?"

"The coroner said it wern't Dr. Colton's fault. Philip's older brother was told by their daddy to practice his punches using Philip to spar against."

"And you've not been paid to testify here today?"

"No, sir, nobody gave me anything to be here."

"Explain if you can, where the deposit of $5,000 came from? You know, money deposited into your bank account five days ago. And I warn you, lying to the court is perjury."

"I bought Dr. Colton's old house. When this trial started, Sam Holt leased the house for six months at $2500 a month. The government paid for the first two months. Would you like to see a photocopy of that check, Mr. Prosecutor?"

"Isn't that a bit much?" Mr. Pizzo asked.

"Objection," Mr. Dill blurted.

"Sustained, Mr. Pizzo, do you have anything useful to ask?"

"I have no further questions, sir."

"You may step down," Judge King said.

"One moment, please," Dr. Colton requested. "Clara, if I'd been present at Philip's cremation, would you tell the court?"

"Yes, sir, without a doubt, I tell the truth."

"And even though I've been your family doctor for years, if you knew I was guilty of a crime, what would you do?"

"I'd call the po-po and tell them everything I knew. If I thought you was guilty of harming that Rizzoli boy, you'd never been the Gibson family doctor."

"I'm good with that," Dr. Colton concluded.

Mr. Pizzo didn't look up, waved his hand in dismissal, "No questions."

"You may leave, unless Dr. Colton has further questions."

"No, sir, we have nothing further," Mr. Dill answered. Then holding up his hand he corrected himself. "I'm sorry, Clara, please forgive me. I actually do have one or two more questions for you. I also wish to clarify that, in fact, Dr. Colton has been testifying every time he questioned our witness, filling in the blanks."

"And yet Mr. Colton has failed to share any information regarding Marco Rizzoli," Mr. Pizzo remarked sarcastically. "And forgive me; I meant '*Doctor*', not '*Mister*'."

"Mr. Prosecutor, per my previous agreement with this court, I *will* take the stand to testify. However, I'll allow you one question at this time, only one. And please be careful of the question you ask. Evidence already proves that what was thought to be Marco Rizzoli was a different boy, Philip Matthews."

"Are you keeping secrets about Marco Rizzoli which could possibly send you to prison?"

"I said *one* question. You asked a disguised two-part question," Dr. Colton admonished.

"Fine. Are you keeping secrets about Marco Rizzoli?"

"Yes," Dr. Colton answered candidly.

"Could you go to prison because of the secrets?" Mr. Dill quickly interjected.

"No," Dr. Colton responded immediately and without hesitation.

Mr. Dill turned to Ms. Gibson. "Clara, did Philip's body drip any blood before you burned it?" He asked the question while Dr. Colton displayed a photograph showing drops of blood next to the ashes.

"No, sir, them drops of blood got there after we finished cremating Philip."

"Do you know how they got there?"

"No, sir, I picked up the only bone of Philip's body that didn't get burnt to ash."

"Clara, what'd you do with that bone?"

"It's part of my fish aquarium. I boiled that thing clean before I put it in with my fish."

"Where's Philip's older brother, Malcolm?" Mr. Dill asked.

"Malcolm shot his father after Philip died. He always blamed his father for making him hit Philip."

"What do you mean, 'making him hit Philip'?"

"Their father used a leather strap to beat Malcolm when he refused to hit his brother. When that no longer worked, the boys' father started using his belt on Philip. Malcolm told me–"

"Objection; hearsay," Mr. Pizzo immediately protested. "This testimony has no bearing on this trial."

"Your Honor, the witness is stating what she was told, not what she heard secondhand. It's not hearsay," Dr. Colton argued.

"Overruled; continue," Judge King replied.

"Malcolm said he started punching Philip lightly because he was pulling his punches."

"Why didn't anybody notify the police regarding their father's violent behavior towards his sons?"

"Malcolm's father was a reserve deputy. It didn't do no good to report his behavior."

"Is Malcolm in prison?" Dr. Colton inquired.

"No, sir, Malcolm's in the loony bin. He'll spend most, if not all, of his life there. We pray not, but it is possible."

"Thank you, Clara; I've no more questions," Dr. Colton said.

"Mr. Pizzo, recross questions?"

"Ms. Gibson, would you allow a DNA test on the bone you claim is Philip Gibson's bone fragment?"

"It's Philip *Matthews'* bone fragment, Mr. Pizzo," Dr. Colton corrected.

"Apologies, Philip Matthews' bone fragment," Mr. Pizzo acquiesced.

"Sure, but it won't do no good. That poor boy's little bone's been in that aquarium a long time. Plus, there's a bit of algae covering it."

"You said that to burn Philip's body you used magnesium. Is that correct?"

"Yes, sir, magnesium burns super hot. When you spray it with water, it only gets hotter."

"And you swear that the ashes we saw earlier are the ashes of Philip Matthews?" Mr. Pizzo pressed.

"Yes, sir, I promise them ashes *are* Philip's."

"I've nothing further, Your Honor. I promise," Mr. Pizzo said mockingly.

"Go, quick–before they change their minds," Judge King urged.

"Your Honor, may I approach the bench?" Mr. Pizzo asked.

"Mr. Dill, please join us," Judge King responded.

"Your Honor, I realize the prosecution has rested; however, I request to be allowed one final witness. I know Mr. Dill would be within his rights if he objected, but the prosecution has been tolerant in accepting Dr. Colton's partially testifying without questioning due to his promise to testify here in open court," Mr. Pizzo stammered nervously.

"Okay, Mr. Dill, I'm going to allow our prosecutor's request. You may enter your objections, if any."

"By all means, Your Honor, the defense does object."

Judge King sent the men back to their tables.

"We'll have one final witness for the prosecution. Mr. Pizzo, call your witness," Judge King announced.

"Your Honor, prosecution calls Signa Benson to the stand." Mr. Pizzo announced with a smile.

"Objection," Mr. Dill said as Signa Benson walked to the witness stand.

"Overruled," Judge King quickly rebutted.

"Do you promise the testimony you are about to give is the truth, the whole truth and nothing but the truth?" the witness was asked.

"Nothing but," Signa Benson replied. She then pronounced and spelled her name.

"Mrs. Benson, do you know a young lady named Susan Tishwood?" Mr. Pizzo inquired.

"Susan Tishwood is my granddaughter."

"Objection," Mr. Dill interrupted. "What does this witness's testimony have to do with Dr. Colton's case? Her testimony is irrelevant."

"Your Honor, allow me a couple more questions and the relevancy of this witness will be made clear." Mr. Pizzo continued, still smiling.

Dr. Colton nudged Mr. Dill. "Withdraw your objection," he whispered as Mr. Pizzo spoke.

"Would you care to share with the rest of us what is so important that you found it necessary to disturb Mr. Pizzo as he argued your objection?" Judge King voiced testily. "And your objection is overruled."

Standing, Dr. Colton spoke. "My apologies, Your Honor. I advised Mr. Dill to withdraw his objection. I briefly told Mr. Dill that Mrs. Benson is going to be doing a fifteen-year prison sentence for child abuse."

"Objection," Mr. Pizzo shouted.

"Sustained; the jury will ignore what Dr. Colton just said," Judge King instructed. "I will not tolerate any more of your underhanded tricks."

"Forgive us, Your Honor," Mr. Dill replied. "Mr. Pizzo, please continue with your witness."

"Mrs. Benson, do you know Dr. Colton?" Mr. Pizzo asked.

"Yes, my granddaughter was seen by Dr. Colton, who accused my husband and me of abusing the girl when she lived with us."

"Why was your granddaughter living with you?" Mr. Pizzo asked, building up to his main question.

"My daughter and her husband were killed in a plane crash. Susan was court-ordered to live with us. Her brother, Hayden, quit high school at seventeen and went to work for an electronics company. The court awarded Hayden emancipated adult status. He's a computer hacker."

"How old was Susan when her parents died?"

"Six. We wanted Hayden to live with us, but he rebelliously refused."

"Where are Hayden and his sister now?" Mr. Pizzo asked.

"Nobody knows," Mrs. Benson replied. "I believe somebody is hiding them. I received a letter from Susan, which I turned over to your office. The letterhead read: *The Nancy Colton Medical Clinic*."

"Your Honor, prosecution offers this letter as evidence that Dr. Colton is an accomplice in Susan and Hayden Tishwood's disappearance," Mr. Pizzo said, walking up to the bench.

"Court clerk will accept the document and enter it into people's evidence," Judge King acknowledged.

"Objection, Your Honor," Dr. Colton stood. "This letter has not been seen by the defense as Mr. Pizzo has deliberately withheld it from us. Therefore, it's being improperly submitted."

"Overruled," Judge King smugly responded. "You may argue the point in your appeal."

"As you wish, Your Honor," Dr. Colton said as he sat down.

"Mrs. Benson, is it safe..., uh..., scratch that. Am I correct in saying your granddaughter was first seen by Dr. Colton for medical reasons? Then Dr. Colton accused you and your husband of physical abuse? He testified against you in court? Now your granddaughter has disappeared, with nobody knowing her whereabouts. However, you received this letter from her with *The Nancy Colton Medical Clinic* at the head of the letter?"

"Yes, sir, all of that is correct," Mrs. Benson stated.

Mr. Pizzo returned to his seat. "Mrs. Benson, have you been offered compensation for your testimony today?"

"No, sir."

"At this time, I have nothing further," Mr. Pizzo concluded.

"Your witness, Mr. Dill."

"Mrs. Benson, you've received nothing for your testimony?" Mr. Dill questioned.

"That's correct, sir."

"Then how, pray tell, do you explain the prosecutor's office granting bail while your appeal is being heard?"

224

"I've no knowledge regarding that subject," Mrs. Benson professed.

Dr. Colton reached down beside the table and removed a paper from inside a file box. "Your Honor, please accept this document into evidence as a defense exhibit–"

"Objection," Mr. Pizzo hastily interrupted. "Defense hasn't told the court what this document purports to be, nor have they disclosed its source."

"Your Honor," Dr. Colton quickly responded, "this document is the agreement between Mrs. Benson and Mr. Pizzo's office. It was discovered as a document in the court files as a matter of public record. It clearly shows Mr. Pizzo's signature, along with that of Mrs. Benson. It provides irrefutable evidence of perjury and fraud by the witness, who swore to tell the truth."

"Your Honor!" Mr. Pizzo exclaimed. "I don't know where or how, but what the defense proposes is impossible."

"We're in the age of information," Dr. Colton calmly explained. "Your Honor, during Mrs. Benson's testimony, I searched public records and located this agreement between the witness and Mr. Pizzo's office. I used a portable battery-powered wireless printer to print the document for the court."

"Again, I object," Mr. Pizzo protested. "Dr. Colton hasn't followed proper protocol in submitting this document."

Dr. Colton held up the document in his hand. "Mr. Pizzo set the standard for entering evidence when he submitted his letter."

"I'm overruling Mr. Pizzo's objections. The court accepts this document into evidence." Judge King realized he couldn't deny Dr. Colton's submission. "Is that all you have, or are there more questions for this witness?"

"I have further questions," Dr. Colton asserted.

"Proceed," Judge King ordered.

"Mrs. Benson, do you smoke, or did you smoke?"

"Irrelevant," Mr. Pizzo objected. "Goes beyond the scope of direct examination."

"Your Honor, Mr. Pizzo brought up the witness being accused of physical abuse."

"Dr. Colton is correct; overruled. You may answer the question," Judge King instructed.

"No, sir, I don't smoke."

"Mrs. Benson, I'm still a licensed physician. I can tell that you're a smoker, or rather, you smoked just before you came into court. Would you care to revise or correct your answer? Before you respond, allow me to remind you of an incident regarding tobacco in your jail cell just last month."

"Your Honor," Mrs. Benson protested. "I just quit smoking. Therefore, my answer that I don't smoke is true."

"Dr. Colton, please continue your questions," Judge King urged. "The record will show that Mrs. Benson did smoke, yet claims to have quit."

"Thank you, sir," Dr. Colton responded. "Mrs. Benson, will you please explain how your granddaughter, Susan Tishwood, sustained round cigarette burn marks on her neck and back. Especially since Mr. Benson doesn't smoke. He is, however, an alcoholic."

"Objection!"

"That's okay. I retract the last statement," Dr. Colton said.

"Answer the question," Judge King instructed.

"I didn't burn my granddaughter," Mrs. Benson defended.

"Cigarette butts with Susan's DNA on one end and yours on the other end were found immediately following your arrest. The only smoker in your home was you."

"Objection; argumentative," Mr. Pizzo asserted vehemently.

"And well presented," Mr. Dill added.

"I'm not arguing with the witness, Your Honor. I'm simply pointing out that Mr. Pizzo's witness continues to lie under oath, after swearing to tell the truth."

"Objection sustained. Cease the argumentative dialogue or face a contempt fine."

"Yes, sir," Dr. Colton responded. "Mrs. Benson, why didn't your grandson want to live with you and your husband?"

"Hayden dropped out of school. He's a computer hacker who went to work for a big company."

"Your Honor, we have nothing further for this witness at this time. I'll ask the court to accept into evidence the following document as a defense exhibit. It's a sworn statement by the Tishwood parents, stating that should anything ever happen to them, their children were not to be placed with Mrs. Benson and her husband because both children feared their grandparents. Hayden Tishwood accused Mr. Benson of throwing a large rock at him, resulting in Hayden's right arm being broken."

"Submit the document to our clerk," Judge King calmly replied. "Mr. Pizzo, do you have any more questions for this witness?"

"Mrs. Benson, did Susan run away from home?"

"No, she was kidnapped. The police received a ransom note two days later."

"Mrs. Benson, let's not use the 'K' word," Mr. Pizzo quickly corrected. "Susan disappeared. Do you know when she disappeared?"

"To the best of my recollection, Susan disappeared right after her last appointment with Dr. Colton at the Nancy Colton Medical Clinic."

"Nothing more, Your Honor," Mr. Pizzo said.

"Your Honor, may we take a short fifteen-minute break for Dr. Colton to eat and take his medicine?" Mr. Dill inquired before being asked if he had questions.

"You have five minutes," Judge King responded.

"I have a ten minute IV drip: therefore I'll need at least fifteen minutes," Dr. Colton continued.

Judge King was now clearly exasperated. "*Fine*, we'll recess at this time for lunch. Everyone will return at one-thirty. Dismissed!"

Dr. Colton sat with an IV in his arm, talking with Mr. Dill. "Call Detective Cassidy and ask him to come for testimony."

226

While Mr. Dill made his phone call, Dr. Colton doodled on the corner of his legal pad.

"Detective Cassidy will be here when court resumes," Mr. Dill said, once he ended his phone call. The two men conversed for another ten minutes before Dr. Boot removed the IV.

"Shall we eat a sandwich for lunch?" Dr. Colton asked. "I need a double bacon cheeseburger."

Chapter 42

"All rise; The Honorable Judge King presiding."

"Be seated," Judge King instructed. "Bring Mrs. Benson back." The judge waited until Mrs. Benson was seated. "You're still under oath," he admonished. "Mr. Dill, your witness."

"Mrs. Benson, where were you when Susan, as you claim, disappeared?"

"I was in the hospital, being treated for skin cancer. I used to be a sun-worshiper."

"Was Susan living with you?" Mr. Dill asked calmly.

"No, she was with friends," she replied.

"Is it not true that even though you were in the hospital, in all honesty, you were in jail at the time Susan allegedly disappeared?"

"Objection!" Mr. Pizzo yelped.

"That's okay," Mr. Dill quickly continued. "I'll retract my question and redirect it to Detective Cassidy, who has current information regarding Susan Tishwood."

"Do you have any further questions for this witness?" Judge King inquired.

"No, Your Honor, I don't. However, because Detective Cassidy is here, and as I have previously stated he has firsthand knowledge, we request he be allowed to answer a few questions."

"Request denied," Judge King responded. "The witness may step down."

"Excuse me, sir, I, unlike Mr. Dill, do have further questions," Dr. Colton interjected.

"Make it quick," Judge King snapped sharply.

"Mrs. Benson, do you know where Susan is living at this time?"

"No, I don't," the woman snarled.

"Did you know your granddaughter is living with Detective Cassidy and his family?"

"I didn't know that information," Mrs. Benson admitted.

"Your Honor, I made a photocopy of this document during our noon recess," Dr. Colton said. "It is a restraining order against Mrs. Benson on behalf of Hayden and Susan Tishwood."

"Objection; you haven't shown the significance of this order," Mr. Pizzo blurted out.

"The photograph accompanying this order again proves Mrs. Benson has perjured herself. She is shown standing on the Cassidy porch." Dr. Colton continued, "Because he isn't allowed to testify, would it surprise you to hear Detective Cassidy say that Hayden Tishwood was granted custody of his sister?"

"Objection," Mr. Pizzo said loudly. "Dr. Colton is now testifying for a hopeful witness who has been denied."

"Mr. Pizzo is correct, Your Honor. Detective Cassidy was denied as a witness. However, I did not testify for the detective. I could just as easily have used Judge Samantha Carr, who signed the custody order. And may I point out that Signa

Benson isn't on Mr. Pizzo's witness list and his prosecution rested. Yet he was allowed to call Mrs. Benson for testimony."

"Your Honor–" Mr. Pizzo began.

"Silence, sir. Dr. Colton is correct in regard to your witness. Granted, they could have objected, but they didn't. Objection is overruled. The witness will answer the question."

Mr. Dill wrote a note to share. It read: *But we did object. I don't think Judge King remembers it.*

"Hayden will harm his sister," Mrs. Benson insisted. "He's a criminal with no way to provide a decent home for himself, let alone his sister."

Dr. Colton turned to Judge King. "Your Honor, Hayden Tishwood is married with two stepchildren and is employed by E.H. Electronics and Gaming, earning more than $250,000 a year."

"Mr. Tishwood is not a part of this trial," Judge King retorted. "Why'd you bring him up?"

"Susan Tishwood was not kidnapped. She didn't disappear and there was no ransom note for her. Hayden Tishwood picked his sister up at school, accompanied by Detective Cassidy and her social worker. The alleged ransom note informed Mrs. Benson that she'll never see her grandchildren, no matter how much money they offered."

"Do you have any more questions for this witness?" Judge King asked angrily.

"No, sir, Detective Cassidy will be asking the witness about her perjury and how she obtained old stationery from the defunct clinic."

"Mr. Judge, may I speak?" Mrs. Benson asked.

"I think it best that you say nothing further. You're excused." Judge King banged his gavel repeatedly. This trial was definitely not going as planned.

Dr. Colton noticed a wince in Judge King's face as the gavel banged. Judge King started to rise, but sat back in his chair with a grimace. In an instant Dr. Colton was on his feet. When Judge King turned pale, Dr. Colton shouted, "Bailiff! Call an ambulance. Judge King is having a heart attack."

Bailiff Elliott didn't like Dr. Colton. He did not like taking orders from people on trial, but even he could see that Judge King was in distress. While the doctor was administering medical aid, Bailiff Elliott ushered the jurors out of court. Ten minutes later, Dr. Colton passed information to paramedics on what he'd already done for the judge. Judge King was transported to a local hospital.

Everyone was dismissed for the day by Judge Sheppard. "Judge King has suffered a heart attack. When you return tomorrow morning, I'll advise you of his condition. We'll discuss our options regarding this trial at that time. Court dismissed until tomorrow morning at nine o'clock."

As promised, Judge Sheppard was waiting the next day for the people in Judge King's current trial. "Be quiet and come to order, please. I am here to inform you that Judge King has suffered a massive heart attack. He'd have died had Dr. Colton not recognized his symptoms and acted as he did. Tomorrow morning, Judge King will have triple-bypass surgery. He'll be on medical leave for an extended period of time. Now I must conduct court business. Mr. Dill, are you and Dr. Colton willing to waive a speedy trial?"

The two men conversed for a few minutes before Mr. Dill replied. "Your Honor, we are willing to waive a speedy trial this one-time only. We desire the court's promise that there'll be no other delays, unless Dr. Colton goes into the hospital."

"I assume your request is because Dr. Colton has cancer. However, if you waive your right to a speedy trial, you open yourself up to countless delays. If you should insist on a speedy trial, which is your right, I'm authorized to dismiss the charges of murder without prejudice or declare a mistrial."

Dr. Colton leaned forward in his chair. "Your Honor, you do have another option of which you may not be aware. If you call a trial delay due to medical issues, you can order a delay in trial for up to one month." Dr. Colton handed Bailiff Elliott a file. "That contains a written contract, which, if signed by you, Mr. Pizzo, and either Mr. Dill or me, becomes legal and binding. The reason it becomes binding is because we each agree to extend the speedy trial aspect by thirty days. This contract may be used only twice before an indeterminate waiver must be agreed upon. The trial delay contract is a little-known and rarely used legal proceeding."

"Dr. Colton, I've never heard of such a contract," Judge Sheppard stated authoritatively.

"Sir, I discovered this item while studying for my bar exam. I was surprised it wasn't used by the courts," Dr. Colton replied.

"Okay, I've listened to what you said. I did a quick research scan on our legal web, and this simple one-page contract is a binding document. Bailiff, hand this contract to Mr. Pizzo. Provided the prosecutor agrees and signs the contract, I'm ready to grant a court delay of thirty days. I'm sorry—strike 'court delay' and make that a *medical* delay."

"If this is legal, the prosecution is agreeable to a thirty-day medical delay," Mr. Pizzo consented.

"Very well," Judge Sheppard said. "Our jurors are released until further notice. You shall not discuss this trial with anybody. This court is dismissed for a period of thirty days. I am invoking an agreed-upon medical delay provision in the law."

"Your Honor," Mr. Pizzo spoke once the jurors had left. "Court is in medical delay for thirty days. May I have permission to go home for two weeks? My parents live in Alaska."

"Mr. Prosecutor, the contract you signed prevents you from accepting any new cases for trial due to the nature of our delay." Judge Sheppard paused; "Maybe that's the reason medical delay contracts aren't used more often. Mr. Pizzo, you have thirty days of medical delay time. Use it to your advantage."

"He means go home, see your parents," Mr. Dill interjected.

"Listen to Mr. Dill," Judge Sheppard suggested. "Go home, gentlemen. Lock-up your files and be ready for trial in thirty days."

Chapter 43

Stepping into the court's trial area a young man addressed Mr. Pizzo. "Sir, my name is Evan Holt. My father, Judge Sam Holt, and I briefly discussed your situation."

"Just what do you mean, 'my situation'?" Mr. Pizzo bristled.

"I mean your visit to Alaska. I need to make a trip to Anchorage for business. I intended to offer you passage as far as Anchorage via my personal aircraft. Would you care to join me? From Anchorage, I'll be taking a helo to McCarthy. I promise you this case won't be an issue."

"While I appreciate your offer, I don't think it proper for me to accept. Your father is a federal judge, so–"

"Just accept the young man's offer and go see your parents," Judge Sheppard insisted. "Evan, is nearly a billionaire. You're a fool if you don't accept."

"When do we leave?" Mr. Pizzo asked.

"Midnight; you'll have a room for yourself to use during the flight. We'll fly nonstop and eat breakfast around seven-thirty in the morning before landing."

"How big of a personal aircraft do you own?" Mr. Pizzo inquired in bewilderment.

"It's only a 747, but I don't own it," Evan replied. "Games Inc. owns the plane, I just use it."

"And Evan owns Games Inc.," Dr. Colton added. "I read about him in a gaming magazine Kent has at home."

"Be at Gate 10 at eleven o'clock. Takeoff is promptly at midnight, Mr. Pizzo. I'll have two people waiting to escort you. One will have a sign with your name on it," Evan said before leaving the courtroom.

"One question," Mr. Pizzo responded. "McCarthy is rather isolated. Why're you going to McCarthy?"

"There's a computer genius who lives in McCarthy. I've hired her to work for Games Inc. She and her family are moving. I believe they want to live in a warmer climate."

"Thank you," Mr. Pizzo replied. "I'll be on time–if not a few minutes early."

Evan Holt left without looking at Dr. Colton.

"Wesley, could I impose on your office to purchase a get well card for Judge King?" Dr. Colton asked.

"Anything special you want written inside?"

"Nope, just send it from your office."

Wesley Dill knew Dr. Colton had no intention of sending Judge King a card. It was a ruse to prompt Prosecutor Pizzo into sending a get-well message.

"You need to meet Pony Boy," Dr. Colton told Mr. Dill. "His real name is Paul O'Neill Boyd. I shortened it to Pony Boy."

"Do I dare wonder who Paul O'Neill Boyd might be?" Mr. Pizzo asked as he put away his paperwork.

"He's outside waiting for us with his father. Would you like to meet them?" Dr. Colton walked to the courtroom door and motioned for the Boyds to come inside.

"So what's Mr. Boyd's story?" Wesley inquired.

"It's not *my* story," a young adult around age twenty-eight replied. "Dr. Colton helped me rescue my daughter."

"Okay, I'll bite," Mr. Dill said. "How'd he help you do this?"

"It's rather simple. Dr. Colton helped me find my daughter Mia, and rescue her. Her aunt kidnapped her when she was three years old."

"Pony Boy has a flair for being dramatic," Dr. Colton asserted. "Pony Boy's wife died giving birth. Her sister, Tina, kidnapped the baby and disappeared. I found them in Trona, California."

"There's nothing in Trona except stinky air and a business which employs a lot of people," Pony Boy added.

"What happened? Did you drive to Trona, kidnap your daughter, and then leave?" Mr. Pizzo asked curiously.

"Pony Boy posted Mia's photograph all over the Internet. He asked for information about his daughter and spent almost every penny he earned looking for Mia," Dr. Colton answered. "When Oscar Boyd called and told me they had a positive identification on his granddaughter after two years of searching, I asked if they needed help getting Mia back."

"I rented a house in a place called Red Mountain. I used an alias of Joseph Hart, and Dr. Colton went to Trona for me," Pony Boy said.

"Don't give me all the credit," Dr. Colton countered modestly. "There were four of us who rescued your daughter."

"True, but it was you who flew less than twenty feet off the ground in a helicopter to bring her home."

"I don't understand; why'd you fly so low?" Mr. Pizzo posed.

"Let me explain, Anthony," Dr. Colton replied. "Trona doesn't have an airport. We landed the jet in San Bernardino. I rented an R-66 helicopter and I flew it to Red Mountain, which is nearly in restricted airspace. We loaded the R-66 onto a semi truck trailer and took it to a place the locals call 'The Pinnacles'. Two days later I went to Trona so I could make sure Tina was still at her boyfriend's house. They were gone. He lost his job and they were forced to move. I found them a week later in a small place called 'Little Lake'. Tina and her boyfriend were caretakers of the lake itself. The semi truck was parked behind the Little Lake Motel and we unstrapped the R-66. I made Pony Boy stay inside the truck's cabin sleeper so Tina wouldn't see him if she came to town. There were three of us who went to Little Lake, where we rented a room. The lake was small, but it was excellent fishing. Barbara met Tina and endeared herself to the woman simply by commenting on her clothing.

"On day three, I offered Tina and her boyfriend a ride in the R-66. To my surprise, they accepted. The tricky part of this flight is that on both sides of Highway 395 there's restricted airspace which is reserved for military operations. There's a narrow corridor, which by following the highway, will keep you in

232

uncontrolled airspace. If you inadvertently cross one of those invisible lines in the sky without clearance, you risk becoming target practice for the F-18 Hornets out of China Lake.

"While we were flying, Pony Boy took Mia away from a woman who was holding the girl's hand. When we landed, the woman waved, motioning for us to join her. Pony Boy had a ten-minute head start going south. When Tina joined the woman, I lifted off with Barbara beside me. Pony Boy and Mia were waiting at a prearranged location before we arrived. I flew to San Bernardino in the R-66, returned it to its owner, then we flew home in the jet. Because Pony Boy alerted the FBI prior to taking his daughter, her disappearance didn't cause law enforcement alarm. Tina showed up here three weeks later trying to find Mia. The police arrested her for kidnapping and now she's in prison." Dr. Colton looked into Mr. Pizzo's eyes as he spoke.

"If I were a betting man, I would've said you were going to have Mr. Boyd testify. He'd have testified how you got his daughter back," Mr. Pizzo said. "Smart!"

"It crossed my mind. However, Judge King and his heart attack shot the idea down real fast. I think we'll have a lake party for the family. I'll even let Kent do the barbecuing."

"I thought you were going to tell him about when you saved me from my crazy father in the mountains," Pony Boy said after Mr. Pizzo left.

"That was one strange case," Dr. Colton recounted. "I had no idea the crazy man being sought would show up in Rainbow Meadows where I was camping with the boys. Royce and Kent were on their first backpacking trip. We had about 300 firecrackers to scare any bears who came around at night. The boys brought their collapsible .22 caliber survival rifles. We left Cottonwood Creek on foot at first daylight. We arrived at the upper Meadow Lake where we stopped beside a stream. I chose to soak my feet; the boys chose a natural swim. The boys cooled down, then ate a beef jerky snack before we headed for Bear Meadow. I warned the twins not to be quiet and to sing loudly. They knew bears could be anywhere, so they both requested a dozen firecrackers. We camped at Whispering Pines in a state-owned, bear-proof cabin. We lit a fire to dry out wet clothing and cook our supper, when the door opened. You walked in behind your father."

"I was scared to death," Pony Boy said.

"When I first met Fred, my initial thought was that you were one lucky boy, having a dad who'd take you camping," Dr. Colton admitted. "Then I saw that neither of you had camping gear or warm clothing."

"Dad, are you ready to go home?" Kent asked from the courtroom door. "Mom wants us to pick up chicken and wine."

"Take your brother and get the stuff your mother wants. I'll be home with Oscar and Pony Boy." Dr. Colton guided his friends to his home, where he announced the news of Judge King's heart attack.

Barbara hugged Oscar Boyd. "I should've known you wouldn't allow this scoundrel to leave my beautiful goddaughter at home.

"And you!" she said to Pony Boy. "You'd best get over here and explain why I should feed you again!" She was happy to have the guests.

Once everyone was present with food on their plates the young man asked, "Do you remember my name before you started calling me Pony Boy?"

"Paul O'Neill Boyd," Dr. Colton answered immediately. "Before that, your name was Marion Orvis Denks. Fred called you 'Marion' when we met. He thought his word was law for everyone. 'You sleep there, with that boy. I'll sleep here,' your father told you. I almost laughed when Kent told your father if you didn't bring a sleeping bag you can sleep next to the fire, but nobody was going to use his sleeping bag except him. Then he and Royce showed your father their rifles."

"I remember that. It was funny, but I didn't dare laugh. Fred didn't know what to say."

"We ate our suppers, not offering a single bite to either of you. I kept two hot dogs warm until Fred fell asleep and then gave them to you. I somehow knew Fred was mean to you but I didn't want to believe he could be such a jerk. Kent, Royce and I left when it was beginning to get light, leaving you and Fred asleep. By noon we were nearing Pineridge. I knew of a hidden cave in an outcropping of boulders. We left our packs in the cave to spend the day swimming and fishing. We later relaxed, lying on the rocks and letting the sun warm us, when we heard your screams.

"I told Royce and Kent to stay in the cave while I went to investigate. Fred was angry because we had managed to disappear and you were paying for it with a beating. I returned to the twins once you and Fred continued hiking. We spent the day fishing, swimming and relaxing. The next day, we left our secret cave. We found your campfire while looking for a place to camp. I suggested we keep walking to avoid Fred. Kent grabbed my arm and pointed. He saw Fred relieving himself, so we stayed out of sight behind some bushes.

"You were lying on your stomach; welts covered your back, legs, and neck. You smelled horrible and you were bleeding. When I lifted you up, Royce quickly covered your mouth. I decided you weren't going to be there when Fred returned. I spent the evening hiking back to our cave, stopping frequently to cover our tracks. Once you were safely inside, I sent Royce to watch out for your father from a distance. It took three days for you to heal enough so walking wasn't too painful. As we passed the last place we'd seen your campfire, I constantly looked for signs of Fred, then I found his body."

"I thought he took off because we didn't see him," Pony Boy confessed. "I hated him, wishing I had one of the twins' rifles. I would've killed him."

"I pushed you boys down the trail, not to escape Fred, but to get us further from his body. He lay on his back about a mile from your campsite. When we stopped at Elk Meadow, I used a satellite phone. I told the sheriff that I was hiking with my boys when I found a body which looked like it had been mauled by a bear."

"That's why we saw the helicopter. They flew to where his body was and carried him out. Mom caught him cheating on her. She threatened to get a divorce

234

and take me. I detested my mother because she knew Fred was abusive. She'd tolerate anything except another woman taking her place. Why didn't they look for me?" Pony Boy's expression showed he was puzzled.

"It took a month to identify Fred's body. I took his wallet, removed two hundred dollars, and then burned the wallet. I later learned that we were lucky. Fred stabbed your mother twenty-three times in the back before taking you hostage during his escape. They suspected Fred had killed you long before he died in the mountains."

"I thought he was going to kill *you* that night when we met each other," Pony Boy recalled.

"When I found Fred dead, I thought it was a blessing for you," Dr. Colton confessed.

"Dr. Colton, my blessing came the night we met. Your fire in the cabin kept me from freezing, and you even fed me. I think you, Royce, and Kent were my first blessing in life. When we were hiking I no longer wanted to die."

"Well, you sure seemed to enjoy hiking with us. Didn't even hesitate at the waterfall when Kent washed his clothes and himself. You jumped right in, enjoying yourself alongside the twins."

"It was the first time I felt safe. Even when those other people caught up to us, I didn't try to become invisible."

"As I recall, you walked up to the parents and asked if their children could play in the water with you three boys."

"It was fun and nobody got hurt. It was the first night I cried myself to sleep out of happiness. I didn't deserve to be happy. My parents were dead and I was happy. It took a long time to stop hating myself. Other than you, I have to thank my adoptive mother and father for saving me from myself. Mom taught me that what happened wasn't my fault. Dad just showed me how to be a man. He demonstrated his love for us every day."

"Do you have any brothers or sisters?" Mr. Dill asked.

"Only two," Dr. Colton responded. "Pony Boy was adopted by the family who caught up to us while hiking. They almost instantly included him in everything they did, and Mrs. Boyd adjusted the pants we gave him, so they'd fit him better. Mr. Boyd and I had a few private conversations regarding Pony's past. Three days from Rainbow Meadows, the Boyds asked if I'd recommend them as foster parents."

"You told us, 'No. The boy needs permanent parents–not foster parents he could lose.' You immediately told us to either adopt the boy or forget he existed. You said that if we were serious then we had to keep his adoption quiet. The adoption would only take a month, but we had to let you handle it."

"And you thought I was crazy. Adoptions take a lot longer. You took parental custody of the little guy three weeks later. He has been your son ever since."

"I'm blessed," Pony Boy admitted. "Now, I no longer need this." He started to hand Dr. Colton a piece of crinkled paper.

"My phone number. I gave you that paper the day you were adopted. I'm glad you never used it."

"Why? What would've happened?"

"Show the phone number to your father," Dr. Colton instructed.

Having looked at the phone number his son handed him, Mr. Boyd chuckled. "This is your mom's phone number."

"Sorry, kiddo the Boyd's were your family. I was no longer a part of your life unless they contacted me," Dr. Colton offered.

Chapter 44

Judge King awoke from heart surgery to find Federal Judge Samuel Holt sitting beside him. Judge King was handcuffed to the bed.

"Hello Judge King–or perhaps I should say 'Grand Imperial Dragon Master Albert Preston'. You will not be returning to the bench, unless it's one in federal prison, out of the public eye."

"I don't know what you're talking about. I've been a judge for over thirty years. I put people like Dr. Colton in prison for life."

"Dr. Colton has hurt the Dragon Society to its very core. He's been rescuing Dragon children for the last twenty-five years. He's used Mafia connections to arrange decent adoptions for every child he rescued. Thirty-one rescues–thirty-seven if you count non-Dragon children. Funny, don't you think? One illegal organization used to destroy another. How do you think Mario Rizzoli will feel when he learns that your people were part of his organization? And that his son could've been stolen by your people?"

"You need to leave, sir. My chest is beginning to hurt; I have to rest now."

"In fifteen minutes, you're leaving for a military base in Alaska. As of today, you're dead. The hospital has already notified the media of your death. The military prison in Alaska gets unbearably cold. There won't be any communications allowed and you don't have an attorney–you're dead, remember." Judge Holt started to leave. "I nearly forgot the best part. There's a private prison in California which is home to over 500 Dragon family members, minus the children. Now that you're dead, information is being leaked regarding your role in bringing down the Dragon Society. We thank you for your assistance in making children worldwide safer. The names you've provided will assist in ending the world blight." Judge Holt smiled. "Those are the words I said less than an hour ago, following your death."

"You'll never get away with this. You can't just make an officer of the court disappear."

"Here's the funny part, your friend Mr. Pizzo is going to his demise in Alaska. I do believe there's a train accident in his near future. Too bad you won't be able to warn him. We knew he was working on Dr. Colton's trial so he could learn what we know," Sam Holt lied.

"I've committed no crime. I legally changed my name in college. I've had open heart surgery–triple bypass, to be exact."

"I suggest you examine your chest when you get a chance. You, sir, are a healthy man, with nothing wrong physically."

"Why're you doing this to me? I'm a respected judge. I've devoted my whole life–"

"To abusing and killing children. To encouraging and even propagating the enslavement of children through intimidation."

"You tell a good tale, sir. But tell me, how can you prove any of it? I sent people like you describe to prison."

"Agreed, you've sent men and women to prison. Some of those people have been what you would call Common Dragon Scales. The Dragon Scales clean up Dragon problems in prison, especially kids who become adults and jeopardize Dragon activity through their own behavior. Douglas Ray confessed that he was ordered by you to kill Corky Spiro. When he refused to follow orders, you had him freight-trained. And yes, we know what 'freight-trained' means. According to your phone records, you've ordered no less than fifty 'freight-trains.' And suffice it to say, David Kelly, Brody Green and Dyson Compton, along with numerous others, have given sworn statements you ordered David Kelly to experience such an act the night he and his friends disappeared." Judge Holt didn't stop. "The man on trial gave me these files." he tossed the files at Albert Preston, a.k.a. Noah King. "Dr. Colton's files on every child he ever rescued. One of Dr. Colton's witnesses recognized you. Through his testimony he was able to alert federal agents. The young man also recognized your mother–whom you managed to get seated on the jury."

"How dare you accuse me, Judge Noah King, of these disgusting improprieties!"

"You *are not* a judge!" Sam Holt shouted. "You're Albert Preston, despicable and evil. You deserve nothing but contempt. Every trial you have adjudicated is subject to retrial. A small price to pay in order to cut off the Dragons' head in the United States. And one more thing you may want to think about on your trip to Alaska: this morning, federal agents served warrants on Bailiff Elliott and his wife. Mr. Elliott chose to resist. He fired three shots. One struck Marshal Marshall in the chest. Mr. Marshall is alive, thanks to his ballistic vest. Mr. Elliott is lying in the city morgue. Agent Ward fired one shot, striking Mr. Elliott in his left eye. Mrs. Elliott died when she picked up her husband's weapon. Your wife is on her way to California to await trial for two counts of murder."

"Tell me, what is so important about Dr. Colton? He's a cold-blooded killer. When Mario Rizzoli didn't pay the ransom, his son was burned alive by that so-called rescuer of children."

"If anyone killed Marco Rizzoli, I believe it was the Dragon Society. Dr. Colton is a genius. He has manipulated this trial from the beginning. He's been two steps ahead of you and you never had a clue. He's richer than you could ever imagine and he uses his money to help those in need. Dr. Colton spent nearly three decades doing his best to root out and eradicate the Dragon Society. In case you didn't know, Dr. Colton's army consists of children–no sorry, my mistake– *adults* to whom he demonstrated true, altruistic love." Judge Holt motioned four heavily armed men forward. "If Mr. Preston resists or causes any problems, pull his plug." Judge Holt waited until Mr. Preston had been placed in shackles before speaking again. "The prisoner is to be transported to Alaska. His status is upgraded to 'terrorist'. Transport him to the island after ninety days. If he escapes, you shall be held accountable."

"You can't send me to Gitmo. I'm not a terrorist," Albert Preston loudly protested.

238

"I want this man placed in dungeon cell number 12. No communication, *period*," Judge Holt told the escorts. "Bottled water only, trading bottle for bottle. Food on paper trays, sandwiches, bread–sliced meat, no condiments, absolutely no hot food for the first ninety-six hours. No bedding and no clothing; you can give him suicide-watch padding, nothing more. The prisoner requires no medication. Once a month his hair shall be shaved. Give him nothing which he can use to harm himself."

"Sir, communication? Does that include books or other reading material?" one guard queried.

"Nothing, lights on 24/7, dungeon shower twice a week, your choice of day and time."

"Who died and made you God?" Albert Preston asked venomously.

"When you die, Mr. Preston, nobody will miss you. But I promise there will be a party of celebration. You'll be informed when one of your members ceases to exist." Judge Holt had no intentions of following through with any celebration or announcing Dragon Society member's deaths. "When you admit your true name you'll be allowed one book to read every two weeks. Each time you give us information about the Dragon Society you'll be granted additional privileges. And you can forget Grandpa Calvin; the oldest Dragon is dead. Strangest thing, he somehow ingested a toxin from a South American frog."

"He was murdered," Mr. Preston yelled loudly.

"Then it'll go down in history as the world's first perfect crime, because nobody's going to investigate his death."

"How do I know what you say is true?"

"Let me tell you a secret. Ten years ago I approached Dr. Richard Colton with the question of how he kept the Dragon Society from finding the children he abducted. Only I used the word 'rescued'. He merely looked at me and smiled. Then he said, 'I changed those children through love.' Mr. Preston, why do you think Dr. Colton knew you were having a heart attack so quickly? He drugged your coffee, your croissant, and your doughnuts. You breathed in a mist in your office dispensed by an air freshener. All of which were compliments of the brilliant doctor."

"I don't understand. How can I be this all-powerful Dragon?"

"Oh, you're not all-powerful. Let me explain what you already know. You are, or were, Grand Imperial Dragon Master, Albert Preston. In Russia your equivalent is Igor Raskanovich. In Japan the man's name is Ito Takashami. They were arrested while you were in surgery, not really being operated on."

"You won't be able to hide me forever. How do you expect to cover up not having a funeral?"

"You signed a 'do not resuscitate' order last year. It appears that you also signed an order for no autopsy, and cremation with no funeral. Your good friend, Representative Michael Burton, confirmed your signature. Mr. Burton was taken into custody at seven-thirty this morning. He accepted the first offer I gave him. We have six teams of four federal agents coordinating efforts to arrest Dragon members whose names we received from Mr. Burton. Your way of life is over.

No one will miss you now that you're gone. It's your turn to experience the despair you've inflicted upon others for decades.

"Before I finish and these guards take you away, I have one last bit of news. You're going to a prison strictly for Dragon Members. It took many years and a lot of money, most of which was taken from the Dragon Society. And, unlike you, I admire the man who brought you people down. Goodbye, Albert."

Chapter 45

Anthony Pizzo carried his single bag to Gate 10. He waited five minutes before a well-dressed man approached. "Mr. Pizzo, we've been expecting you. Mr. Holt hopes you have a nice flight and apologizes for making you wait. We were moved to Gate 11. Our pilot will be arriving shortly. We'll be taking off on time so there'll be no delays. I've been instructed to make sure you're comfortable. Should you need anything, just call me. My name is Daniel."

"Thank you, Daniel." Mr. Pizzo expected only a bed inside a small room. He was more than a little surprised upon finding the room quite large, with a bathroom and shower. This room was bigger than his apartment bedroom. Anthony Pizzo was relieved to be getting away from Judge King. The man, totally spineless, had failed to impress Mr. Pizzo. And Dr. Colton, a child kidnapper and murderer wasn't behind bars…yet.

"I guess I can't blame him. Mario Rizzoli killed the man's wife and son, but that's no excuse for killing the Rizzoli boy," Anthony thought to himself.

Anthony Pizzo was fast asleep when they departed for Alaska. He couldn't believe he had not awakened when the jet took off.

"Did you sleep well, Mr. Pizzo?" Evan Holt asked while eating potatoes with ham and eggs. "We have a fully stocked galley with a chef, so order whatever you desire for breakfast."

"Ham and eggs with hash brown potatoes sounds good. How do I order my food?"

"Push the green button and somebody will come take your order."

Mr. Pizzo pushed the button and waited.

"Mr. Holt, I'd like to say my room is quite comfortable. I thank you, sir. Your offer to let me fly with you is greatly appreciated." When Mr. Pizzo received his food, he was amazed at how much was on his plate. He was also impressed with how fast it had been prepared. "It must be nice to have this available whenever you want to go someplace," he said between bites of food.

"I only fly when I must," Evan replied. "Most of the time I use the motorcoach or my Learjet. This thing drinks too much fuel, but sometimes it's necessary. When I leave Anchorage I'm going to Hawaii, Japan, and then Australia."

"If I may, how many rooms are there on this plane?"

"Six state rooms, each with a shower and toilet. There's a conference room, galley, and twenty first-class seats. In addition, there's an area for up to thirty business-class passengers. We can feed up to forty people. When we leave Japan, I expect our baggage area to be full of goods for sale in Australia. I'll be able to save five to ten thousand dollars by delivering the shipment myself."

"Is that legal?"

"We own the product, so yes, it's legal. We're merely saving on shipping this time and we're allowed a certain amount of tax deduction."

Grateful for Evan's hospitality, Anthony hesitated before speaking what was on his mind. "I know you said we wouldn't discuss Dr. Colton's trial, but I need to ask: Do you really think he's not guilty?"

241

"Mr. Pizzo, I don't believe it's a good idea to discuss the trial. Our opinions of Dr. Colton are completely opposite. I have not and will not testify. I'll only say that Dr. Colton has been our family doctor for sixteen or so years. He removed my tonsils when I was seven. Dr. Colton is a good man. Who knows? If you got to know him, you might actually like him."

"Dr. Colton saved my best friend's life after I accidentally shot him," Mr. Pizzo confessed. "Your good doctor has never let me forget how he kept me out of jail."

"Mr. Pizzo, what you don't know is that Dr. Colton saved my life at least three times. And whenever he talks about what he did for me, it just reminds me of how much he cares. But how many people testified for Dr. Colton? If he was a child killer, don't you think people would turn him in? Personally, I believe if he was guilty my father would vigorously prosecute him."

"You make a good point. However, I still think he's guilty."

"And you're entitled to your belief. Would you like another cup of coffee?"

"Yes, thank you, Mr. Holt. I appreciate your hospitality. Do you mind if I use the shower I saw earlier?"

"It's there to be used. There's plenty of water, and I plan to clean up before we land as well."

Forty-five minutes later, Anthony Pizzo called his father while in flight. "I'll be landing in Anchorage. A man I met in court allowed me to fly in his corporate jet. He's even offered to fly me in a helicopter to the house."

"Mother is gone for two days. Come to the railyard and we'll go home by train this afternoon."

"I'll get a ride to the yard," Anthony told his father.

Chapter 46

"Dad, there's a man at the clinic looking for you," Kent said. "Miss Sally called to let you know. She asked if you want her to tell the man where we live."

Dr. Colton didn't respond. He knew Sally would stall until he called and spoke to her. Sally had gone to college with a full scholarship in order for her to pick either becoming a nurse or a doctor. Sally's mother had continued her medical career becoming one of the top plastic surgeons in the state. After Sally qualified as a nurse, she continued to work hard striving to become a nurse practitioner.

Dr. Colton dialed the clinic. His call was answered on the second ring. "Dr. Colton here," he said. "Is Nurse Sally available?"

"She is speaking with a Mr. Booth. Is there anything I can do to help you, sir?"

"Tell her to give Mr. Booth my address. Thank you, Betsy."

"Just one moment, Dr. Colton. Sally's walking towards me right now."

"Hello Pop-Pop," Sally said cheerfully. "Mr. Zane Booth was just here looking for you. He informed me that Mr. Hill from the Prosecutor's office contacted him, and they're supposed to meet at the Methodist Children's Park."

Dr. Colton didn't reply. He walked to Xander and spoke crisply. "I need you to call agents to intercept Mr. Hill at Methodist Children's Park. Mr. Hill is a Dragon Enforcer, and I believe his target is Zane Booth."

Xander called for agents to find and arrest Mr. Hill and to make certain no harm came to Zane Booth.

As he stood in the park waiting, a voice came from the shadows, "Mr. Booth, I presume?"

Zane turned to his right. "That's me. How can I help you?"

"You don't recognize me, do you?"

"Why should I want to recognize you? I don't think you know who I've become, or who I really am, Mr. Hill. Maybe you should leave and forget you ever talked to me," Zane suggested with a dangerous edge in his voice.

"Sorry, I can't leave. I've been searching a *long* time for you. I was sent to find you and either take you home, for Dragon justice, or eliminate you. Dr. Gunn was in charge of preparing you for Dragon initiation. But now that doesn't matter. Taking you home isn't possible. I'm going to eliminate you." Mr. Hill removed a small snub-nosed .38-caliber revolver from his pocket.

Zane remained calm, hooking his thumbs behind his belt. "How will you explain shooting an unarmed man?"

"You pulled a knife on me; I shot you. Don't worry, I have a knife for you to use."

Zane looked directly into Mr. Hill's eyes. "If I can't talk you into walking away, then you leave me no choice." Zane moved his right hand slightly over his buckle.

Mr. Hill raised the hand holding the snub-nosed pistol. As fast as he was, he didn't expect Zane Booth to react so quickly. Zane's right hand shot out, his index finger blocking the pistol's hammer from striking the firing pin. As Zane grasped

Mr. Hill's hand and pistol, he continued to move. Zane ducked, pushing his own hand upward as he positioned himself to strike Mr. Hill's face using an elbow. Zane's left elbow struck Mr. Hill's nose, breaking it. Grasping the pistol hand with both of his own, Zane lifted; then, standing, he brought Mr. Hill's elbow down hard on his shoulder. Mr. Hill's elbow gave a loud pop. His hand went numb as he released the pistol. Zane wrenched the gun free, tossing it into a large nearby sandbox. Two punches to the solar plexus, followed by a knee to the groin, and then a roundhouse kick to Mr. Hill's head brought the incident to an end.

Mr. Hill was arrested and taken into custody by federal agents a short time later. Dr. Colton arrived to give Mr. Hill medical attention.

"You should've walked away," Dr. Colton said. "He's not a little boy anymore."

Zane looked at Dr. Colton. "My parents insisted I learn how to protect myself. Once I learned a few basic moves, my brother, Jory, decided to take lessons too."

"It's good to see you," Dr. Colton said, shaking Zane's hand. "When did you grow up and get so handsome?"

"I did it while you were getting old, sir."

"You broke the man's nose, finger, and elbow," Dr. Colton responded. "He sure isn't going to be the same. His nose bent, his finger snapped, and his elbow shattered. All of which will never heal correctly."

Agent Ward walked over to Dr. Colton. "Mr. Hill is claiming your friend here attacked him with a gun. He said that he was merely defending himself."

Zane reached into a pocket. "This is the result of my parents constantly telling me to be prepared for anything. And because of what happened to me as a boy, I'm paranoid, which translates into being hyper-vigilant." Zane then handed Agent Ward an SD card. "My belt buckle has a microphone for audio recording. My glasses have a video camera in the center."

"Where did you get these things?" Dr. Colton asked.

"A store called 'I-Spy'. They cost almost $2,000, and now I'm glad I bought them."

"Bring the idiot over here," Agent Ward ordered.

"I haven't done anything wrong," Mr. Hill moaned. "That man attacked me."

"I'd keep my mouth shut if I were you," Agent Ward advised. "Mr. Booth recorded your encounter. He gave me an SD card and I'm sure it will prove you're lying."

"Mr. Hill," Dr. Colton interrupted, "I remember seeing you in court the day I called Caleb to testify."

"I don't know anybody named Caleb," Mr. Hill responded.

"He knew you," Dr. Colton stated. "He said a code word which meant he recognized a Dragon Enforcer. When he was out of the courtroom we spirited him away in an ambulance. Caleb whispered a message to Agent Ward and me. You, Mr. Hill, were a part of that message.

"You're a murderer, Mr. Colton. I help the court put people like you in prison"

"And I help people like Caleb and Zane, who as children needed to be rescued from people like you, who abuse them. My only regret is that I couldn't save them all."

"I'm not like that!" Mr. Hill shouted.

"Mr. Hill," Dr. Colton interrupted once again, "before I rescued Caleb, I watched the abuse he suffered, waiting for the opportunity to help him. I also took a lot of photographs. Caleb identified you from four of those many photographs. Your plastic surgeon forgot to remove your ear tattoo. It's the little thing which betrayed you."

Agent Xander Ward touched Dr. Colton's arm. In a near whisper, he said, "I remember him now. Our friend Mr. Hill is the man whose back we saw in the video Mr. Pizzo didn't believe was real." Then addressing his fellow federal agents, he instructed, "Solitary, transport hooded, and notify Judge Holt immediately. Sure wish I'd remembered him a whole lot sooner."

Zane rode with Dr. Colton and Agent Ward to the doctor's house. After greeting Barbara and Wesley, he pondered, "Maybe it's weird, but I remember my life from age four up to the present."

"I met you at Lumberjack Days in Townsville," Dr. Colton said. "You were ten years old. You wore a mountain man outfit with a matching cap and boots."

"Yeah, I remember," Zane replied. "I was also crying, had blood on my shirt, and a broken arm. My father's friend, George Bane, threw a baseball at me when I ran away from him."

"What the heck did you do?" Wesley Dill asked.

"It was cold outside. George wanted me to take my clothes off and wear a different costume he made. I didn't want to be an Indian who wore only a loincloth and moccasins. I said no, not in cold weather."

"You had a friend who had to see the same doctor in Townsville. He broke his arm one day after you did," Dr. Colton recalled. "His name was Greg."

"What's with this place?" Agent Ward asked.

"It's a small mountain town. It was a good place to live before Dr. Gunn came and it's even better now that certain people have died," Zane told him. "I'll never go back, because I'd have to explain what happened to me and why I didn't return to live with my father."

"What happened?" Xander asked. "I mean, if Dr. Colton helped you, it had to be bad."

Zane looked around at the group of men gathered. "What happened to me? Well it's embarrassing," he said.

"Embarrassing?" Royce asked. "You mean like not being loved? What about being beaten or stripped naked and left to die in the desert because you aren't wanted?"

"Zane, there are three or four of us here who've been through a lot of abuse," Mr. Dill assured him.

Xander Ward told a portion of what he'd experienced. Kent Colton explained what he and Royce had suffered before Dr. Colton adopted them. Finally, Mr.

Dill gave a brief account of his life before Dr. Colton stepped in. "We were all *taken out of love*," Mr. Dill said– "Dr. Colton's *love*."

Chapter 47

Zane began to relate his story: "It all started with a boy called Whitey. I was about four. I used to play in a concrete ditch in front of our house. Whitey saw me one day and offered to help me dry me off when it was time to quit playing. He'd do this every time I played in the ditch. That was the beginning of Whitey who was about five years older than me, being around all the time. Before I turned five Whitey brought another boy, who was three years older than me, to the house. They made me bark like a dog. There were three boys, all older, who did this to me. If I didn't do what they wanted, I got beat up and forced to do it anyway.

"I hope you don't mind if I write down some of their names," Xander said. "These individuals are going to get a visit real soon."

"I met Dr. Gunn when my mother got sick. He came to the house to see my mom and said she had heart problems. He talked to my parents, telling them it was hereditary. I was taken into my bedroom and examined from head to toe. He didn't pass over a single inch of my body. At first I thought he was cool. I got to listen to my heart. Every kid wants to hear their heartbeat; I was no exception. Heck, I still like hearing my own heart. I listened to my heart when he told me to cough. When he finished examining me, I hated him.

"Later that night, I told my parents what Dr. Gunn had done. They said it was okay, he's a doctor. Dr. Gunn came to our house every week. When I had tonsillitis he took me to the hospital, removed my tonsils and then took me to his office which had a room with two beds. I begged my father to take me home. I was afraid of the man. That's when my father told me; 'You do whatever he tells you. He doesn't charge us for house calls—including his health checks for you. He only charged us for your operation and hospital time. Dr. Gunn is our friend and he loves you.'

"I stayed at Dr. Gunn's office for a week. Yeah, okay, he gave me ice cream and a lot of Jell-O, but nothing is worth the pain I experienced. One day my father came to see me. 'Your mother needs heart surgery. You'll do everything Dr. Gunn wants.' Then my father leaned close to my face. 'I'm not stupid, son. I know what Dr. Gunn is doing. You'll be good to him and you will not complain or tell anyone else, *ever*.' My father leaned back. 'Dr. Gunn is taking care of your mom. If he stops, I can't afford your mother's medical care.' Then he slapped me. 'If you love your mother, you'll wait until I leave, then you'll get out of your bed and go tell Dr. Gunn that you love him. Do you understand?' That's the day I hated being alive. I wished I'd never been born. I did what my father told me to do.

"I met Greg on my eighth birthday. Dr. Gunn paid for my party and he brought Greg to our house. The other kids lived on our street. Two of them were Whitey and Devon. Greg was the same age as me. His birthday is March 15; mine is April 1. I'm an April Fool's boy."

"I sense anger over your birth date," Dr. Colton interjected. "I changed it to the day you wanted."

"I like Valentine's Day, but it's still a lie. On my birthday, Greg and I stayed overnight at Dr. Gunn's. We had to prove we loved him; saying it wasn't enough. Greg's sister had leukemia and Dr. Gunn treated Greg the way he did me. Greg and I became best friends, so if his sister or my mother needed rest, we'd stay with the doctor. He'd found two boys who had sick relatives. He traded on our love for our families, and our parents traded us for expensive medical help.

"One day at school, Whitey, Devon, and Carl showed up at the swimming pool. I went to the deep end to get away from them, but I couldn't swim. I almost drowned trying to avoid them. That summer Greg and I took swimming lessons. For three weeks nobody bothered me."

"Did you have any brothers or sisters?" Royce asked.

"No, I was an only child. I'm actually glad I didn't have a brother or sister. They'd have had Dr. Gunn to deal with, too. Mom died two weeks before my tenth birthday. Dad came to my bedroom and wanted to know everything Dr. Gunn had done to me. I thought he finally cared, but all he did was the same thing, only worse. I cried myself to sleep at night. I started wetting my bed because I was afraid of waking my father if I went to the bathroom. My punishment for wetting the bed was taking my sheets outside to the ditch and rinsing them out. I also had to take my bath in the ditch, where anybody could see me, as part of my punishment.

"When Greg's sister died, he and I decided to run away. I was leaving to meet Greg when George threw the baseball at me. Dr. Colton saw my father push me toward Dr. Gunn's office."

Dr. Colton picked up the narrative, saying: "I watched in anger as Pat hit and pushed Zane. When I saw Dr. Gunn's sign, I decided to stop by and say hello, just as a professional courtesy. I heard Dr. Gunn screaming obscenities at you, telling you exactly what he expected you to do before he would set your arm or put it in a cast. I quietly went back outside. When I came inside again, I called out to announce my presence. Dr. Gunn entered the outer office, adjusting his scrubs. I decided not to reveal that I was a doctor, instead, I asked if he could help me with a migraine headache. The good doctor wrote the fastest prescription in history. I left, walked to my rental car, and drove to where I could watch his office. I watched your father whip you as the two of you walked home. I heard your screams and begging for him to stop. I waited two days before you appeared again. Your friend, Greg, looked happy to see you. That day I spoke to both of you."

"Yeah, I thought you were the worst. Just another adult who only wanted to have fun at my expense. You said if we wanted to escape what Dr. Gunn and others were doing to us, be at the airport together early the next morning," Zane recalled.

"I drove to a place called Mojave and rented an airplane," Dr. Colton continued. "I flew back to Townsville and waited. I stayed in my motel room until the following morning. Before I could check out of my room, two sheriff's deputies knocked on my door and searched the place. When they left, I walked a

248

short mile to the airport where you and Greg were waiting. I know you both thought I was just like Dr. Gunn after I told you to give me your clothes."

"You're right, we did, but you explained it was to put our clothes down by the river to make it look like we had been playing there. Dr. Gunn must've been madder than all hell when he found we'd disappeared."

"I knew about Greg because of what I had heard in Dr. Gunn's office. The sheriff's visited my room, because, while they found nothing, I had broken into Dr. Gunn's office and stolen his files containing the names and pictures of all his 'special' patients.

"By the way, did you know that Dr. Gunn died in an automobile accident? He rolled his Pinto doing eighty miles an hour. He died while Tom Dice was cutting him out of his car. Tom was also a special patient when he was little. Mr. Dice is about twelve years older than you, and because he knew what the doc did to kids, I personally think he let him die,"

"I'm not sorry we left," Zane said.

"How'd you get away with it, Doc?" Wesley Dill asked.

"I flew the boys to the desert. We landed on a dirt road and I hid Zane and his friend in a rundown desert cabin with food and water. Next, I flew to Mojave, returned the plane, and then drove my rental car back to pick up the boys. We went to a motel room where I left the two of you, explaining that you must stay inside. I drove back to Townsville, stopping for gas in a small place called Onyx. If I hadn't thought to buy two rainbow trout while paying for my gas, the Townsville sheriff would've had reason to ask me more than three or four questions. I had fishing gear, so when I said I'd spent the day fishing they believed me. The deputy sheriff stopped by my room and informed me that the authorities were convinced both boys ended up in one of the quicksand pits along the river. Searchers found the boys' clothing and I was free to leave. I drove to Garlock, where I bought clothing for both, then returned to the motel where they were located."

"Dr. Colton drove us to an airport and told us to lie on the floor of the car. Then he drove his car into a big hangar and parked it next to another plane he called a Learjet. Greg and I waited in the car until it was safe to get on the plane. We hid inside while he drove the car away."

"It took me about ninety minutes to return the rental car, preflight the plane, and get a tug to pull me out of the hangar," Dr. Colton remarked.

"Greg and I laughed all the way to Dr. Colton's house. We were smiling and giggling. We were free from our fathers, Dr. Gunn, and Townsville. I didn't know what happened to Greg. Dr. Colton put us in separate rooms and said we couldn't see each other any longer. Two months later, Dr. Colton took me to live with Riley and Jan Booth. They lived on a ranch which was over 80,000 acres. Their house had four bedrooms, three and a half bathrooms, and a recreation room with two pinball machines and a pool table. They also had a ping pong table. There was a large screen television, plus a huge fireplace. There was a stream on our land which fed a 200 acre lake. My dad, Riley Booth, gave me a quad runner which I rode all over the place.

One day I heard voices down at the stream. Playing Indian, I sneaked through the bushes to see who was making so much noise. I smiled because my new parents were skinny-dipping. I moved back and listened to them talk.

"'How can we expect Zane to join us when we come out here to go swimming? Dr. Colton told us he has been through a lot of abuse,' my mom said.

"'Just be a good mother,' is what Riley urged. 'Zane will learn that he can trust us in time. Not all adults are evil.'

"I went home to do my chores. I was lucky; not all kids had what I did at eleven. My life went from total abuse to unconditional love. That afternoon I cried myself to sleep, not wanting to lose my new parents. I woke from my nap smelling Mom's cooking. Riley Booth gave me the one thing I wanted more than anything else; a real father.

"Riley and Jan had already accepted me as their son, even with all the bad stuff. Now it was my turn; I needed to accept them as my parents. Knowing Mom would call me for supper soon, I took a shower. Fifteen minutes later, I walked from my bedroom to the living room. I was shaking, wondering, 'Am I doing the right thing, or is this a stupid idea?'

"'Mom! Dad! Will you come into the living room, please?' When they entered the room, both of them stopped in their tracks. 'I saw you swimming in the stream and I heard what Dad said. That's why I'm standing here like this. I love you.' I ran to them and hugged them both. 'When I was younger, around four, I played in the water like this,' I told them. I was shaking as my dad hugged me. Then I knew this was my home forever. That's when my dad dropped a bomb.

"'We have guests. They're in the kitchen.' Riley turned and called, 'Would you please join us in the living room?'

"My heart beat faster and faster; my palms sweated profusely. I refused to move; or my feet refused. Mom wrapped her arms around me when Dad let go. As I saw our first guest enter, I froze like a deer in a car's headlights.

"'Zane, meet your new brother, Jory,' Dad said, as my old friend started to walk towards me.

"Quickly padding over to Dr. Colton, I hugged him, sobbing. 'Thank you for caring enough to help us.'

"'Now I know you're both safe.' Dr. Colton said before leaving.

"My best friend, Greg, who ran away with me, was now my brother Jory. We grew up in Oregon and love the place. We lived close to a town, so Jory and I rode four-wheelers to pick up stuff for our parents at the post office and store.

"We never told anyone, but we had a plan if Dr. Colton hadn't come back to take us away from Dr. Gunn and Townsville. We were going to go to Dr. Gunn's office and kill him. I planned to shoot my best friend, and then kill myself. We'd written suicide notes to leave in our bedrooms for the cops to find."

"Dad," Royce interrupted, "security just called. Kent's bringing in a visitor. They said it's Mr. Booth."

"Show him where we are; he's expected. Zane, you're welcome. I must also thank you," Dr. Colton responded.

"Why're you thanking me? What'd I do?"

"You just provided the FBI with information that corroborates Dr. Colton's part in your disappearance," Agent Ward explained.

"But I'm still alive because he took me away from that place, and from a father who sold me to others," Zane protested.

"Zane, it's okay, your statement confirms what Dr. Colton told the FBI regarding your situation. Now I wish he'd tell *us* what he's done with the good booze," Xander smirked.

"I sent it to Mr. Pizzo," Dr. Colton jested.

Kent arrived with the visitor as those already gathered ate and quenched their thirst with beer.

"I'm looking for a guy who calls himself Zane."

"Right here, little brother," Zane replied.

"Well, big brother, did you tell them the news?" Jory asked.

"What news?" Zane inquired.

Doctor Colton held up a hand, then informed the party; "Whitey, Devon and Carl were drunk when Whitey missed a turn in the road. They went over a cliff doing fifty-five miles an hour, barely missing a guardrail. The car plummeted over 100 feet nearly straight down, landing on its roof. All three were trapped inside Whitey's car in about four feet of water. I'm sorry—did I ruin your surprise?"

"That happened two days ago," Jory said. "How'd you find out so fast?"

"A man with a conscience who despised Dr. Gunn," Dr. Colton replied. "He not only told me about the accident but thanked me for saving two boys when he couldn't."

"Well, I guess those three boys got paid back for what they did to you and the other kids. Karma is such a bitch," Marshal Marshall said.

"Three sheriff's deputies went to George's shop to arrest him, but he was already dead. George hung himself. He left a note saying his stepson broke two of George's ribs fighting over a boy Whitey and Devon kidnapped. George sabotaged the brakes on Whitey's car. His note told the police where Whitey hid the boy and he confessed to all of the abuse he committed while living in Townsville. George's note gave the names and addresses of over ten Dragon Society people where he lived before moving to Townsville." Zane sat down next to Wesley as he spoke.

"Zane and I own property in Townsville. His property has two houses on it. My property just has the house my parents owned. If we want our property, City Hall said we can file for it in Townsville," Jory informed those assembled.

"I'm not going to file. They can keep the damn property," Zane retorted angrily.

"Let me make a few inquiries," Judge Holt proposed. "Maybe you can sell the property. That way there won't be any property taxes building up."

"I'll sell everything for $1,000," Jory offered. "I'm done with Townsville."

If someone gave me $500, they can have the houses. I want nothing to do with Townsville either," Zane added.

Dr. Colton waited for people to offer their advice before speaking. "Child Adoption Resources, which I'm now changing to Child Advocacy and Rescue (CAR), will purchase both properties for a fair value. CAR will sue Townsville for employing George and Dr. Gunn."

"What are you going to do with those places?" Jory asked.

"What if we tear down Zane's houses and turn that property into a community garden. Jory's property, if big enough, can be used as a hatchery for quail, pheasants and other birds," Dr. Colton answered.

"I think the 'Adam Worth Community Garden' and the 'Greg Whitt Bird Hatchery' are what you should call them," Jory proposed.

"Yeah, let Townsville live with seeing our names when they go to those places," Zane agreed.

"Maybe you can give a brief history of why our boys feel betrayed by the community they once lived amongst," Judge Holt suggested.

"All of that sounds good," Jory asserted, "but you'll never win a lawsuit."

"We don't want to win," Mr. Dill replied. "Townsville won't want to be exposed in newspapers or on television for the reasons we'll be citing. They'll settle out of court, which is what we want."

Zane looked at Dr. Colton. "May I ask you to do me a super-big favor?" Zane hesitated before continuing. "I think Jory will agree that you're a hero; our hero."

"Cut to the chase, please," Dr. Colton teased; "I'm not getting any younger."

"Give the boy a chance, Doc," Judge Holt chimed in. "He's trying to ask you a life-changing question."

"Excuse me, Mr. Holt. I'm a big boy now," Zane responded. "Dr. Colton, Lindsay wants to name our baby 'Richard Daniel'. Is it okay with you if we name him Richard?"

"Oh hell no! The poor kid will go through life being called everything *but* Richard. Spare the child. And shouldn't you get married before you have a baby?"

"We can't afford a wedding that satisfies her parents, and they can't pay for a big wedding," Zane admitted.

Dr. Colton looked from person to person, settling last on Jory. "Did you put your brother up to this stunt?" Dr. Colton smiled and made a quick phone call. After a brief but quiet conversation with the other party, Dr. Colton announced: "Call Lindsay and her parents. You get married in one week. Your honeymoon will be in the south of France for seven whole days and nights."

"This is Evan," the voice on speakerphone said. "Zane, I'll help with flying friends and family to your wedding and back home. I have a father who's a federal judge."

"It would be my pleasure to perform the ceremony," Judge Holt told Zane.

Offers for Zane's wedding came from each person gathered around him. Jory waited for everybody to speak before adding his own offer: "I'll do your bachelor party. When you get plastered and pass out, I'll put you on a bus to California. Understandably you won't be able to make your wedding, so I'll stand in for you, then escort Lindsay as her stand-in husband. I mean, let's face it–she's beautiful." Jory ribbed his brother.

"No, thank you, little brother. I want you to do the most important thing for our wedding; we need a flower girl; but we want you to be the ring bearer," Zane smiled smugly. "Seriously, be my best man. Evan said he'll help us bring everyone here for the wedding."

Evan Holt broke in over the speakerphone. "I'm traveling, but will return in a few days." Then, addressing his father, Evan added, "I'm picking up passengers in Japan and Australia, per your instructions."

"Thank you, Evan. Take them to California and call me when you get home. The wedding is one week from today at nine o'clock in the morning."

Chapter 48

"Richard," Barbara interrupted her husband, "I just thought I might let you know Chad and Melanie Hyde will be here shortly with their daughter and grandson."

"Do we have enough food for everyone?" Dr. Colton inquired.

"Vince is sending Peyton over with food I ordered a few minutes ago. I promised we'd take Peyton back to the store," she answered.

"Ask Royce to send an invitation for dinner to the Hydes before they arrive."

"Mr. Hyde and family were just admitted through the gate," Marshal Marshall said.

A few minutes later, Chad Hyde entered the Colton home with his wife, daughter, and grandson. "Where's the Beauty of this place?" Mr. Hyde voiced loudly for all to hear. "I can see the beast; he's standing right in front of me."

"Thank you for coming," Dr. Colton replied. "How are Dawn and her son? The boy's name is Wyatt, right?"

"Under the circumstances, Wyatt and his mother are doing well. Dawn graduated high school last year, and Wyatt's sixth birthday was two weeks ago," Mr. Hyde said. "Dawn wants to ask you a question."

"Is she still denying Wyatt is her son?"

"No sir, I accept that Wyatt is my boy," Dawn Hyde responded as she walked into the living room. "I want to know if you can help me find out who his father is. Wyatt is sick, and he'll die if I can't find a bone-marrow donor. We've been searching for a donor, but in six months we haven't found even a close match."

"I'll want to talk with Wyatt's doctor. Bring Wyatt into my office in five minutes. I have to make a phone call."

"Thank you," Dawn said. "Mom claimed that if anyone could help us, it'd be you."

Dr. Colton made two phone calls before Dawn knocked on his home office door. "Come," he called out.

"Sir, this is my son, Wyatt. He's grown since you last saw him," Dawn said as she guided the boy inside.

"Hmm... the last time I saw you was when you were one. Dawn, remove Wyatt's clothing except his underwear. I need to examine him, and get a basic feel for his needs. I contacted a friend who is going to perform a DNA test."

"We already had a DNA test done, *twice*," Dawn protested.

"And I will do it again, and again, and again, if it helps me find what we're looking for. Dawn, you should know I won't hurt Wyatt."

A knock at the door interrupted Dawn's reply. "Richard, when you're finished with Wyatt and his mother, there's a fudge bar waiting for Wyatt," Barbara called through the closed door.

"Thank you," he acknowledged. Taking Wyatt by the hand, he led the boy to a bar stool. "Let's see how smart you are," he told Wyatt. "How old are you?"

"Six, and I had a big party."

"Do you know your birth date?"

254

"July 12, sir."

"Do you know who I am?"

"Mommy said you'll help me get better."

"I'm Dr. Colton. My friend, Dr. Kendall is going to help too. May I look in your ear?"

Wyatt turned his head. He hummed as Dr. Colton examined both ears and eyes.

"What is this?" Dr. Colton asked.

"My belly button," Wyatt replied proudly.

"Say 'Ahh' for me," Dr. Colton instructed.

"Ahh, for me," Wyatt mimicked with a smile.

Dr. Colton continued his examination, asking Wyatt questions.

"What is your mother's name?"

"Mommy," the boy answered confidently.

"Do you have a puppy or a dog?"

"No, Mommy gave me a goldfish."

"Do you know how to swim?" Dr. Colton distracted Wyatt as he put a tourniquet on Wyatt's arm.

"No sir."

"Okay. Wyatt, turn your head towards Mommy and count for me. You're going to feel a little pinch, but don't move." Dr. Colton quickly inserted a needle into Wyatt's arm vein. In less than thirty seconds, he had two vials of blood and removed the tourniquet.

Wyatt made it to a count of twenty-three before stopping. He winced just once, when he felt the needle pierce his arm. He then filled a small plastic jar with urine and smiled when complimented on being a big boy.

When Barbara entered the office with Dr. Kendall behind her, they found Wyatt sitting on the doctor's desk with a towel beneath him as Dr. Colton examined his feet.

"I came right over," Dr. Kendall said. "We'll get this done fast, and there's no charge for my services."

"Dr. Kendall, this is Wyatt and his mother. I am requesting a DNA database search for all Dragons in custody. I believe one of them is Wyatt's F-A-T-H-E-R."

"Excuse me," Dr. Kendall said, looking at the young woman. "May I ask how old you are?"

"Dawn is seventeen," Dr. Colton responded. "She was initiated into womanhood at age eleven. She became pregnant, and now we have Wyatt, who now needs our help. I intend to do everything possible to get him healthy."

"I'll put a rush on the boy's results. We'll have an answer within two days if I get started right away."

Dr. Colton handed the two vials of blood to Dr. Kendall, then helped Wyatt get dressed. "Call me, regardless of the time, when you get the results. I'll arrange to have a private jet ready, so we can get Wyatt his needed bone-marrow transplant as fast as humanly possible."

"We'll need a court order to take bone-marrow from any of the detainees," Dr. Kendall pointed out.

"I'll take care of the court order. Let's get this dance going."

Dr. Colton tied Wyatt's shoes, then exited behind Dr. Kendall. Minutes later, Wyatt was eating his fudge bar. Dawn watched her son as she talked with Kent. After finishing his treat Wyatt walked up to his mother, fudge covering his face and shirt. Dawn began to get upset, until Kent started laughing. Getting to his feet, he lifted Wyatt's shirt over his head. "You rest," he told Dawn. "I can clean up Wyatt's face. We'll be right back."

Wyatt returned to his mother without a T-shirt. He was barefoot, hair combed, his face was clean and smiling, holding Kent's hand.

"I put his shirt in the washer. It's nice weather outside so I thought he would be okay without a shirt."

"Thank you, Kent," Dawn said upon seeing Wyatt. "He likes you. He's usually standoffish, even when he knows the person."

Dr. Colton entered the room. "Kent, call in the pilots. I want the jet ready to fly by nine o'clock tonight. Keep it that way until further notice. We'll have twelve people flying and I want enough food for five days."

"Will you be needing a chef?" Kent asked.

"No, you're coming as one of the twelve. Pack a small bag. Take Dawn and Wyatt to the store for travel bags. Buy each of them some new clothing. Let Dawn buy some shoes as well. Charge everything to the CAR fund."

Kent wasted no time in doing as his father instructed. Shoes and coats were purchased for both mother and son. Kent handed Dawn a two-piece swimsuit.

"Try it, you might actually like it. You can only make it look good. Even Wyatt has two new swim shorts."

Upon returning home, Kent escorted Wyatt into his bedroom to change for swimming. Dawn joined them then; the trio spent an hour in the swimming pool. Wyatt slept in Kent's arms when they left the pool. Dawn watched as Kent laid Wyatt on his bed and put new pajamas on the boy as he slept.

"He's really tired," Dawn commented.

Together, Dawn and Kent walked into the kitchen. Wasting no motion, Kent prepared dinner for over fifteen people. At six-thirty, Kent sent Dawn to announce dinner was ready in the dining room. When she returned to the kitchen, Wyatt stood next to Kent, who seemed to have magically changed clothes.

"You're amazing," Dawn said. "I could never change my clothes that fast."

"I'm Royce. Kent asked me to bring Wyatt in for dinner. My brother will be here in a couple of minutes.

"Oh, I'm sorry! The two of you look identical."

Kent laughed. "You're not the first to say that."

The night passed uneventfully. Wyatt fell asleep in Kent's lap and Melanie Hyde remained pleasant, not trying to psychoanalyze anyone's words or actions. She even went so far as to halfway apologize to Dr. Colton.

"Richard, I used to think you helped people out of a deep-seated need to feel important. I was certain you'd come by the house to see if we were treating Dawn with kindness. You surprised me. Richard, I was wrong."

"Thank you, Melanie. I decided to help you and Chad adopt Dawn because you're good people. To your credit, you're also great parents. Now my only request of everyone is to not get in the way while we work at keeping Wyatt alive. He's now my number one priority. I want him in the hospital at least one day before we obtain donor bone marrow. You'll all need to know that he'll be sick before he gets better. Dr. Boot will take care of Wyatt if I'm not able."

Kent excused himself after getting to his feet with Wyatt in his arms. "Dawn and Wyatt are using my room tonight. I'll be sleeping in the basement. Pilots are on standby, ready when needed. I'm going to bed after putting this little guy to bed himself. Good night."

"Young man, you seem overly interested in my daughter and grandson," Melanie blurted. "Just *exactly*, what're your intentions?"

"My intentions are to be a friend. Wyatt seems to like me and I seem to like his mother. She is intelligent and I find myself intrigued by such a lady."

Getting to her feet, Melanie Hyde stepped over to Kent. "I can take my grandson to bed," she said harshly.

"*No!*" A small voice blurted. Wyatt's arms wrapped around Kent's neck. "I want him to take me." Wyatt hadn't been asleep after all.

Kent looked down at Wyatt. "Why don't you ask your grandma to read you the book we bought you? I'll bet she can do it better than me."

"No! Kent, you take that boy to bed and read him the book you bought," Mr. Hyde said emphatically. "Melanie, these are honorable people and we owe them our happiness. Maybe Kent isn't offended but Dawn sure looks as though you insulted her."

Turning to Dawn, Mrs. Hyde responded, "I'm such an overprotective fool. Please forgive me."

"Mother, I know you love us, but the Coltons have done nothing except give us unconditional love." Dawn began crying softly. "Kent knows I can't have any more babies, and yet he still likes me. We've been friends for the past three years. We talk on the phone at least twice a week."

"Sorry, Dad: I should've told you," Kent said to his father.

"If I didn't approve, you would know. Chad and I both know about your friendship. Dawn is a good gal." Dr. Colton smiled, "Trust your heart, son. I did, and I've been blessed beyond belief. You, Royce, and your mother are my three biggest blessings."

Barbara stood. "Enough!" she asserted. "Richard needs to rest. Kent, take Wyatt to bed. Chad, Melanie, you are welcome to stay in the great room. This conversation is over for tonight."

Dr. Colton got to his feet and walked with his wife to their bedroom. From the mini-fridge he took two beers and joined Barbara on their bedroom couch.

"Your turn to pick our movie," Barbara said.

They watched a movie and went to bed.

Chapter 49

Two days later, Dr. Kendall called at two o'clock in the afternoon. "We have a match. Wyatt's father is in custody; it's Mr. Hill.

"Thank you. I'll handle the necessary preparations." Dr. Colton hung up, and went to find Kent. "I need you to take Wyatt, his mother, and grandparents to the hospital in New York. I'll be there as soon as possible.

Less than an hour later, Kent was aboard the jet with his four other passengers. "Once Wyatt is admitted to the hospital, you can stay in the motorcoach in the staff parking lot. It was delivered yesterday and is fully stocked, ready, and waiting for you."

Dr. Colton, Agent Ward, Marshal Marshall, and Mr. Dill headed to the nearby detention center where Mr. Hill was being held. The four men easily obtained his release into their custody for as long as needed.

"Realized you're wrong about me, eh?" Mr. Hill asked sarcastically.

"No, we actually have *more* evidence to prove you're part of the Dragon Society, but today is your lucky day," Dr. Colton told him. "Today, you get to donate bone marrow for a sick child. You can do it willingly, or I can just shoot your ass and take what I want."

"You can't do that," Mr. Hill protested. "I've got rights. I'll report you to the feds when you take me back."

"Doc, let me shoot him," Agent Ward pleaded.

"Not yet; let Mr. Hill consider his options. You can shoot him or break his neck once we get him to the clinic. That way, I can keep his heart pumping." Dr. Colton had no plans to harm Mr. Hill; at least, not until after they had acquired the needed bone marrow.

"What are his options?" Mr. Dill asked.

"Simple: Give the bone marrow willingly or by force. If willingly, he may well live. If forced, he *will* die."

The next day, Mr. Hill awoke in a hospital bed. His back hurt and he remained handcuffed to the bed. Nobody came to check on him. His only company was an angry marshal. Finally, Dr. Colton entered the room. "We no longer need your worthless hide. I actually took enough bone marrow for more than one donation. I figure the only thing you're good for now is information. Nobody knows where you are, because I reported that you escaped. In order to live, you'll tell us everything you know regarding the Dragon Society."

"You don't scare me," Mr. Hill spat. "You only kill little boys."

Dr. Colton put a needle into Mr. Hill's arm, injecting him with a substance which would cause pain but not death. Mr. Hill gritted his teeth. The fire in his arm was intense. The next needle-prick injected pain into his foot.

"You hurting? Your pain will only get worse as I choose. Tell us what we want to know and the pain will go away." Dr. Colton next injected a tiny amount of liquid fire into Mr. Hill's abdomen. Then, to prove he could remove the pain, he injected another substance into Mr. Hill's arm and the pain subsided. "You have one last chance. If you refuse to answer our questions I'll make the next

258

injection into an artery. Your entire body will burn and I *will not* stop it." To further prove his point, Dr. Colton hung an IV bag in plain sight, then inserted a needle in Mr. Hill's arm.

"I want the names of all Dragon members in Germany whom you know," Agent Ward said. "I was one of the boys you abused when I was young, so I really hope you lie. That way, I get to watch you scream and beg the way I used to beg you. Please, lie to us, Mr. Hill."

Questions were asked for an entire day before Mr. Hill was returned unconscious to the detention center. Dr. Colton handed Xander the information they'd obtained from interrogating Mr. Hill. He also gave him a second envelope.

"*That* is Marco Rizzoli's file. You'll know when the time is right to open it. It will lead you to him."

"Do I want to find him?" Agent Ward inquired.

"Of course you do–and once you do find him, let Barbara know. Like you, my wife doesn't know this one secret."

"You have my promise. Without your help, I'd be dead. You fought the Dragon Society for over twenty years, and now it's our turn."

Upon returning home two days later, Dr. Colton was greeted by his wife. "Dawn called. Wyatt will get his first transfusion tomorrow. His doctors believe he has an excellent chance of full recovery. Kent is coming home today. Chad said they'll be back once Wyatt is released from the hospital."

"I have a question," Marshal Marshall interrupted. "Of all of the kids you rescued, which one would you say was the most rewarding? And you can't say Kent and Royce."

"That's an unfair question. Royce and Kent have been the greatest blessing of my life–after Barbara, of course. Each time I rescued a child, they spent time with me. I love every single one of them. I'm truly proud of each one. The parents who adopted our rescued kids have done a wonderful job raising their children. I'm tired; please excuse me, I need to rest."

Chapter 50

Dr. Colton spent two days in bed. All he asked for was rest. When he joined friends and family, it was for Zane's wedding. After the ceremony, Dr. Colton called the groom over to join him. "Your reception is in our community center. Be sure to thank the Holt's for everything they've done for you. They're good people."

"Thank you for everything," Zane said, leaning over to give Dr. Colton a hug. "I'll never forget you. I asked my mom and dad if I could tell you something."

"What?" Dr. Colton replied.

"I love you! God put you in Townsville to rescue us. I guess it sounds weird, but it's the truth."

"I agree, it does sound weird, because I love you, too, kid. All the kids I rescued were taken out of love. I'm proud of you, you're a survivor. You've risen above adversity. Be proud of yourself."

Barbara Colton entered the room, carrying a file box. "I found this box labeled; vacation to Puerto Rico. Do you remember it?"

"Of course. Royce and Kent were fifteen and we bought that power catamaran we considered luxurious. It was our last sailing vacation, and you spent most of your time entirely–"

"Okay! Stop!" Barbara yelped. "I remember the catamaran, too. Are there pictures of me in this box?"

"Yep, you, me, the boys, and other people we met along the way."

"*Do not* share those photographs with anyone outside this house or you won't live long enough to die of cancer," Barbara teased, smiling as she spoke.

"I'm hungry. May I have a cup of coffee?"

"Doc," Zane interrupted, "thank you for everything. It's time to leave for the reception."

"Goodbye," Dr. Colton replied. "Go spend time with your family before going to France with your beautiful wife."

Zane left, followed by Royce who returned with his father's favorite coffee mug and a pot of coffee. "Kent is fixing something for you," Royce said. "The newlyweds have left."

"Wedding is over, so tell us about this vacation," Wesley Dill encouraged.

"Oh, my goodness, Wesley!" Barbara exclaimed. "It took nearly eighteen months to plan and take this vacation, not to mention the $930,000 Richard spent on that boat of his."

"I thought it was a sailing catamaran until we went to check it out," Dr. Colton defended.

"*Puh-leasee,*" Royce taunted. "You just told that lie with a straight face. You kept telling Mom you'd lose money when you went to sell the catamaran. You wanted to fly the jet."

"Don't you have a daughter who needs her diaper changed?" Dr. Colton shot back.

"You leave that boy alone," Judge Holt told him, joining the conversation. "Sounds like he just pulled your covers."

"Richard loved our catamaran, once he saw how big it was inside and out. When he heard it had a 3000-mile range, I could see in his eyes he was losing the battle not to buy it," Barbara explained.

"I still remember how big it was," Royce recalled. "Huge, seventy-two feet long, two master suites, and two VIP suites. Kent and I each had a head–that's nautical for a toilet, but the shower was shared by everyone. The galley/dining room was huge. There was tons of room inside, especially in the shower."

"Food is served, m'lord," Kent jested as he walked into the room. "Crispy hash-brown potatoes, two venison, elk, and pork sausage patties, three eggs–each inside a bacon ring, with two slices of rye bread toast smothered in gooseberry jam."

"Excuse me," Xander interrupted, "can I get something to eat like that, maybe?"

"Nope, only Dad gets this food. He saved my life in the hot California desert, and Mom adopted me, so no, you can't get food like this…not even 'maybe'."

"Kent!" Dr. Colton exclaimed between bites.

"Okay, fine; how many eggs do you want?"

"What? You selling out on me?" Dr. Colton queried. "I wanted to tell you this is excellent."

"I'll take two eggs," Xander said quickly.

"Okay, tomorrow." Kent looked at his father. "And we all know tomorrow never comes."

"Thank you Kent; my food is delicious."

"You're welcome. There're platters of food in the kitchen if anybody else is hungry." Kent smiled when his father winked at him. "What're these pictures?" Kent picked up one of himself jumping into the water off of Florida's coast. "Isn't this the catamaran we sold for $1.5 million to an oil guy in Corpus Christi, Texas?"

"Thanks, Kent," Dr. Colton chided. "You really didn't have to bring that part up."

"Hey, the guy liked having the captain's chair in the main cabin with the galley and living area. He also loved those enormous master suites. What I liked was lying on the front deck tanning my whole body, then jumping overboard whenever you killed the power."

"Not me," Royce countered. "My favorite thing was sitting at the helm when it was blistering hot outside. Inside, it was nice and cool. I liked steering the catamaran."

"I think my favorite place was on the fly bridge," Barbara offered. "You can see for miles up there."

"As much as you liked the sun, it was the best place to make sure another boat didn't sneak up on us," Dr. Colton teased.

"Excuse me," Barbara snickered. "I recall being joined by three others from time to time. And all of you seemed to enjoy the same kind of bathing suit."

"Hey, I admit it," Royce ventured. "I'm still a naturist. If you don't believe me just as my wife." He smiled looking around at everyone gathered. "My parents never made Kent or me feel self-conscious. Blame them!"

"Regardless, we each agreed the catamaran was a lot more stable than the tug we previously leased. We all enjoyed it more, as well." Dr. Colton spoke between bites of food.

Barbara sat down with a plate. "We had to leave our vacation supplies in Portland, Maine, because Richard decided to take possession of the catamaran in Nova Scotia. We saved three thousand dollars by not having it delivered to Portland."

"The two crab pots we bought were cheaper in Nova Scotia, and our wetsuits cost less there, too," Royce added.

"When we stopped in Portland, the catamaran took very little fuel. We used sea water in three sun showers, which held five gallons each. This allowed us to conserve fresh water. One nice benefit of our boat was the consistent all-day sun for making tea," Dr. Colton reminisced. "And before anyone asks–yes, we had a water maker on board as well."

"Dad rented a truck so we could take our supplies to the cat, which Mom named *Nine Lives*. There was a residential refrigerator and when we finished stocking it, there was no room left. Kent and I kept our favorite snacks in our rooms. I bought sodas, powdered drink mixes, and twenty pounds of beef jerky. Mom insisted we buy sunscreen, so before we left Portland, I called Mr. West in California. He explained how to make his tanning oil. I bought everything Mr. West described. I made the oil and took thirty-two ounces with me to the inn where we had stored our provisions. When I picked up more supplies, I had a deep tan. Miss Martha, the store owner, saw my nearly instant suntan and she asked me how I did it. I showed her the oil, and she offered me ten dollars for sixteen ounces. I turned her down, and gave her an eight-ounce bottle. I showed Miss Martha how to apply the oil to her daughter's back. Miss Martha loved the oil so much she insisted I accept twenty dollars.

"We left port at nine the following morning. Mom's brother, Uncle Gene, who lives in Providence, Rhode Island, gave us fishing poles, lures, some homemade wine, jam, and dad's favorite; beer. We stayed in Providence for two days before heading for New York. Dad let me navigate past the Statue of Liberty. That was the most awesome thing I've ever done. Mom and Kent took tons of photographs while Dad and I sat on the fly bridge enjoying the scenery." Royce paused for a bite of food.

"We ambled slowly down the eastern coastline about a mile offshore," Dr. Colton joined in, having finished eating. "Each of us took turns at the helm. When we first started, everyone's turn was six hours. After leaving New York, we changed our helm duty to every four hours unless we got into bad weather or waves; then it was either Barbara or me navigating.

"I decided to restock in Virginia Beach. I was surprised when the boys bought six bottles of water. The bottles were two gallons each, with a spigot. We turned those bottles into tea, juice, or plain drinking water. I bought another six bottles and those became our emergency supply of water.

"*Nine Lives* cruised easily at twenty knots and handled superbly. We restocked again in Fort Lauderdale. While Kent and Royce took care of *Nine Lives'* needs, Barbara and I drove a short distance to visit with the adoptive parents of a rescued boy. They followed us back to the boat, where they met Royce, who was installing an LED security light. He rigged it to work off a battery for the entire day if needed. He also attached solar panels to the fly bridge top, so we could use electric lights when anchored. They met Kent when he came out of the shower. He had checked *Nine Lives'* hull and propellers after refueling. He filled our water tanks and helped Royce purge the wastewater tanks. Then he made sure dinner was nearly ready before showering."

"That boat was freaky awesome." Everyone turned toward Wesley Dill. "What? I'm not allowed to admit I was there? I got to grow up healthy, raised by two people who love me."

"We weren't going to tell anybody you were on the *Nine Lives*," Barbara said.

"Hey, I'm proud to be one of the Coltons' rescued kids. When we were on the catamaran I was jealous. I envied Kent and Royce. When Kent came out of the shower that night wrapped in a towel with wet hair, it was easy to tell him apart from his brother; otherwise it was nearly impossible. My mom gave Kent the ear stud he wears all the time."

"Helpful hint for telling us apart," Kent offered. "My ear is pierced higher than Royce's."

"We enjoyed being in Florida, but the fun came when we departed. I programmed our navigation system for Puerto Rico. Two miles out of Fort Lauderdale, I turned the helm over to Kent. We all wore life vests and safety lines whenever we went out on deck while cruising," Dr. Colton said.

"The boys had schooling, even in the summer," Barbara interjected. "They graduated high school during our brief stay in Fort Lauderdale and began college correspondence courses."

"We didn't rush the catamaran, keeping its speed down to between fifteen and twenty knots. We left Florida, heading for the Bimini Islands; roughly fifty miles east of Florida. The natives greeted us openly, paddling canoes out to *Nine Lives* once we dropped anchor. We enjoyed swimming in the warm water. Barbara bought a few fruits. The following day we puttered down to Nassau, taking ten hours to travel about a hundred miles before dropping anchor. Royce and Kent used Royce's skin-darkening oil as we cruised south. When they went swimming, we were surprised to see youngsters swim out and join our boys. We stayed in Nassau for two nights."

"I was thankful for Royce putting up the solar panels with batteries," Barbara said. "When not cruising, we were able to stay cool. We didn't have to leave *Nine Lives*, so each of us relaxed in our own way."

"Puerto Rico was casual, from island to island. Eventually we eased into San Juan, the capital. It felt strange to wear board shorts, a T-shirt, and sandals when we docked to restock. Numerous times we thanked Royce for calling Blake to learn his secret of making the tanning oil. Thirty minutes after we docked, six armed men approached us. They'd seen our American flag and were coming to greet us. Sergeant Pedro Romero advised us that staying close to land while cruising around Puerto Rico would dissuade any predatory boaters from attacking us. He asked us if we had any weapons on board for defense."

"I remember Sergeant Romero," Royce said. "I told him that I didn't like guns, they scared me."

"Well, Sergeant. Romero's guys didn't find any weapons on *Nine Lives*, so I'm sure he believed you," Dr. Colton replied. "They searched three yachts that day. They used deception to search for drugs. I laughed when their dog went crazy on some of the prescription meds we had with us. I thought Sergeant Romero was going to have a heart attack when he found out I was a doctor married to a nurse practitioner." He paused for a drink of coffee. "Sergeant Romero checked us out to see if we really were on vacation. That's why I decided we needed to move. However, before we could cast off, the sergeant was shot less than thirty yards away on a large yacht when one of his men found contraband. The yacht was owned by a drug runner."

"And he was lucky we were still there," Barbara added. "Richard ran towards where we heard the shots being fired."

"The good sergeant was barely alive when I got to him. He didn't even have a chance to defend himself. I used his radio to call for help. Royce and Barbara arrived about three minutes before the police. Barbara went to a second officer suffering a minor wound and Royce pulled a third man out of the water once Kent arrived to help him. Before an ambulance could arrive I started an IV and applied a compression bandage to Sergeant Romero's abdominal wound. One of his men told the other officers I was a doctor, so they requested that I accompany him to the hospital."

"I was left behind with the twins, and we were all covered in blood. Cleaning up was quick. We jumped into the water, splashed for a short time and then, one by one, we went inside to shower. Richard returned about six hours later," Barbara recollected.

"It turned out they had excellent medical facilities and I was asked to assist in surgery. Their chief medical surgeon went to school with me in California. That's where I met Blake West. We graduated together, and then he went to Puerto Rico to practice.

"Later that evening, Barbara and I decided it would be in our best interest to find a better place to anchor. Around two in the morning, we quietly left the dock and headed east. I kept *Nine Lives* to a crawl making very little noise. I took us a half-mile off the coast before heading for a town called Luquillo. At daylight we headed for the San Juan passage. *Nine Lives* gracefully cut through the water with Kent pulling helm duty. By three in the afternoon, we were anchored at Culebra Island in a sheltered cove. The boys and I went swimming, leaving Barbara to rest on the fly bridge."

"I wasn't resting," Barbara protested. "I was watching out for pirates."

"And even though we know different, it's Mom's story and she is sticking to it," Kent teased.

"For the next month, we slowly cruised along with another family boat, visiting all of southern Puerto Rico's coastline. The weather was bright, sunny and relaxing. Both families spent hours soaking up vitamin D with our kids snorkeling or scuba diving." Dr. Colton enjoyed reminiscing with their friends gathered around. "My suntan deepened and my supply of beer diminished. We finally ended up in Mayagüez.

"When we left San Juan I accidentally left my medical bag at the hospital. I was able to rent an airplane in Mayagüez and fly to San Juan. Royce flew with me, which was a blessing. He noticed my picture at the airport. The statement beneath my picture read: *AUTHORITIES SEEK INFORMATION REGARDING THE WHEREABOUTS OF THIS MAN*. I found an attorney who promised to contact the authorities on my behalf. An hour later, I was informed that the government wanted to thank my family for our actions in helping Sergeant Romero and his team. Royce and I stayed overnight, then returned to Mayagüez."

"While Richard and Royce were gone, I took Kent into town to resupply a few items," Barbara remarked. "There was a six-year-old boy walking in front of us, crying. He carried a banged up metal cup with nothing in it. Two older kids had taken his money and run off. Kent learned the boy's name was Pablo; he didn't know his last name. Pablo lived in the slum area. His family was dead and he was bullied by other boys every day. At first I thought, 'Well, I don't believe him.' Kent asked some of the adults about Pablo. He was told that Pablo's parents had died. First, his mother cut her foot and it became infected. She died within a month. Pablo's father worked at the docks. He was crushed by a large vessel when he slipped and fell into the water. One of the women, who spoke with us, led Kent and me to Pablo's three-year-old sister. Both of the little ones were dirty. Neither of them had eaten in days."

Dr. Colton waited until his wife had finished speaking before he continued: "Royce and I were able to retrieve my medical bag, plus pick up more supplies. Additionally, we took time to visit Sergeant Romero, who was still in the hospital. He insisted we meet his family. Then Mrs. Romero offered to bring food to the hospital for us. We politely declined their generosity, but promised to visit San Juan again on our way home. I let Royce take over our flight, assisting him only a small bit on takeoff, and I landed the plane. I had the opportunity to talk with Barbara over the radio on a prearranged frequency while Royce and I flew back to Mayagüez, so we weren't surprised to meet Pablo and his sister when we returned.

We were greeted by Kent when we arrived back at the catamaran. Barbara was in town buying food, clothes, and a couple of toys for our new crewmembers. Together, Barbara and I decided we'd return to San Juan, where we could have the jet pick me up. City officials granted us custody of Pablo and Maria, provided we agreed to keep them in our family until they were adopted. I immediately began calling the girl Juanita, and her brother became Rico.

"Being in no rush, we slowly meandered toward San Juan. Royce and Kent began teaching Rico how to swim. The boy was fearless; therefore he had to wear a life vest whenever he went out of *Nine Lives*' cabin. Whenever we anchored at a major port we were neither the largest nor the only yacht, but we always anchored for maximum privacy. Numerous times the twins joined other kids from neighboring yachts who swam 'textile free'. Barbara and I took every opportunity to meet yachting couples or families around us. We spent nearly three weeks with two families, one from Germany and the other from Brazil. The German family had four children. Their oldest, a fourteen-year-old girl, kept Royce and Kent busy improving their German. Their twelve-year-old son took over teaching Rico how to swim. The Brazilian couple had a two-year-old girl. The two families stayed with us all the way back to San Juan. I flew home and took a week getting all of the papers for Rico and Juanita completed, then returned to San Juan.

"What happened to Rico and Juanita was known all across Puerto Rico. It surprised me when people didn't care to help their own. They left it to total strangers; yet what we were doing was approved of by the Puerto Rican people.

We resupplied *Nine Lives*, including extra beer which I brought from home. Royce bought two dozen coconuts, six pineapples, and enough bananas to last us a week, providing we each ate two per day. Royce really liked coconut milk, or coconut water and he accidentally discovered that by putting hot water in the coconut you can get coconut butter. He added his darkening oil to some butter he extracted and got a nice coconut smelling cream. Royce's newly discovered cream gave each of us a bit more sun protection thanks to darker skin.

"Once we left San Juan, our destination was the tip of Florida. On deck in the open water everyone wore both a safety harness and a life vest. Our journey came to its final end at Corpus Christi, Texas. Rico and Juanita were adopted by Carlos and Raynata Moya, who met us in Corpus Christi. We hosted the Moyas on *Nine Lives* to meet their new adoptive children. Raynata watched both youngsters swim confidently alongside Royce and Kent, whom they called 'Uncle' or 'Tio'. The Moyas departed for home, Rico and Juanita would no longer go without food. Corpus Christi is where I sold *Nine Lives* for a profit and we flew via jet to Portland, Maine, where we left our motorcoach.

"Due to a broken bathroom faucet in our motorcoach half-bath, I decided to upgrade all of the faucets. I took the twins with me to the hardware store, allowing each of the boys to ask questions and make a single purchase. As we walked around I took the opportunity to teach Royce and Kent different lessons.

"Kent said he needed to replace the light switch in his bunk area, so we headed for the electronics aisle. Turning into the plumbing aisle by mistake, we saw a man who was yelling at his younger daughter. *I TOLD YOU NOT TO TOUCH ANYTHING. WHAT ARE YOU, STUPID?* the man screamed while holding onto a movable staircase for restocking shelves.

"Thinking quickly I went up three steps. *WHAT ARE YOU, SOME KIND OF MORON? DO YOU LIKE BEING YELLED AT, YOU BIG DUMB BULLY? HOW DOES IT FEEL? DO YOU LIKE IT?* All of my words were directed at the man who had been yelling at his daughter. The man had been snagged on the stairway

266

by his belt loop. As he finally started walking away, other men and women around him began clapping. One woman went further and warned the man, 'Don't you dare blame that little girl because you got yelled at, Mr. Brinkman.' Then, turning to me, she continued, 'Thank you! It's about time somebody showed Mr. Brinkman what it feels like to be yelled at by someone who is bigger.'

"'I don't think Mr. Brinkman enjoyed me embarrassing him,' I said, 'especially in front of his daughter.'

"'You're right,' Mr. Brinkman said, turning the corner, 'but more importantly, I didn't think about what I was doing to my daughter. I can't thank you for making me feel like a fool, but I can thank you for showing me how scary it must have been for my daughter. Right now I feel really small, because while I detest all abuse, you made me realize I just verbally abused my daughter. I have to apologize to Angela because I don't like what I've done to her. You may not believe it, but I love my daughter.'

"'I'm not a psychologist, Mr. Brinkman, however, you may want to think about why you yell. And in all honesty, I'm glad to hear you don't like what you did to your daughter. That sort of thing causes untold harm.'

"'Dad, I found the light switch,' Kent interrupted.

Still irritated, I turned to face my son. My irritation wasn't with Kent, so naturally my expression changed. 'That's excellent. Is it the right switch?'

"'Everything matches, but I would like you to check my work for me,' Kent held out the old and new switches.

"There are two differences,' I told Kent. 'One is broken and the other has to be paid for.' Kent stood just under six feet, thereby making it easy for me to look him in the eye. 'Good job, young man. Do you have enough money?'

"'Why do I have to pay for it?' Kent half whined.

"'Because you broke the toggle when you got angry at your handheld video game and threw it.'

"'Oh, yeah, I forgot.' Kent hung his head slightly. 'Dad, I don't have enough money. I'll have to put it back.'

"'Maybe we can find a less expensive light switch,' I suggested. 'Why the sad face, big guy?'

"'I didn't think the light switch would cost so much,' Kent admitted.

"'You bought your mother a new chair for use around our campfire. Kent, you put your mother's comfort before your own. Let's go find a different light switch,' I said, acknowledging Kent's thoughtfulness for his mother. However, I let him know that, while what he had done was commendable, he still had to live with his choice. I liked the new light switch we found, so I picked up new switches for both bunk areas. As we were checking out with our purchases, the cashier said 'thank you' and refused payment. 'Mr. Brinkman left his credit card information. He insisted on paying for your purchases,' the clerk informed us.

"'Please tell Mr. Brinkman thank you,' Kent responded.

"'Oh, excuse me,' the clerk said. 'Mr. Brinkman asked me to give you this envelope. He purchased a light switch similar to yours. He returned it and requested I give you the refund.' The woman was smiling. 'You did all of us a major service. Mr. Brinkman owns a construction business and almost everyone is afraid to offend him.'

"'I only hope he stops yelling at people; especially his daughter,' I replied. Back at the coach, we installed the light switches, but I forgot the faucet. Royce and Kent laughed *at*–not *with*–but *at* me the entire time we were back at the store. They took great pleasure in telling everyone who remembered us about my big foul-up. I tried bribery to silence my two blabbermouth sons, only to be reminded by Kent that I had to live with my forgetfulness.

"We changed all the faucets and I bought new LED lights to replace the ones that needed it.

"On our trip to see the Dill family in Florida, the twins asked if they could learn how to fly. We lived in Florida at Austin and Helen Dill's vacation resort while Royce and Kent took flying lessons.

"A month before we left Florida, we took possession of a new, upgraded motorcoach which gave the twins their own area. Royce shared his tanning coconut butter cream with Helen Dill, who wisely contacted a patent attorney. Together they licensed the cream. Barbara advised Royce to contact Blake West regarding the patent.

"The tanning coconut cream became a staple of families worldwide. Blake and Royce shared the profits of their joint invention. The first commercial was filmed at the resort. The second commercial Royce insisted be filmed on Catalina Island to honor Blake.

"By the time Kent and Royce were seventeen, they'd become millionaires. Kent earned his money through teenage endorsements and commercials. I retired full-time, taking the family across the United States. Barbara encouraged the boys to write about their lives. They titled it *From Hate to Love; A Real Life Story*. Our RV lifestyle continued even after the twins were living on their own. I love my sons, and I'm proud of them."

"I remember the three days it took to film one commercial," Wesley Dill interjected. "When they were filming, Mom was worried that people would cancel their vacations. Instead, the resort was packed with no extra room. I worked myself ragged after the commercial aired."

"Helen asked us to do another commercial. We made a total of three, using guests as extras. It was all great for business," Royce concluded.

Chapter 51

Having called his father before landing, Anthony Pizzo went to rent a car. He arrived at the railyard office expecting to find his father, Jonathan, in the office.

"Anthony, your father had an emergency repair job on one of our engines," the receptionist said.

"Thank you, Rebecca," he replied. "Any idea how long it'll take?"

"Your dad said he'd call in on his radio when he knows what the problem is."

"I'll come back. Dad probably won't call for at least an hour. When he calls, tell him I went to Donovan's."

"I'll let you know what he says when I hear from him."

Jonathan Pizzo called via radio to his office. "Tell my son to get a room. This looks like it'll take several hours."

Rebecca relayed the message to Anthony and hung up. After eating a hearty meal, Anthony remembered that the sun shone bright until late this time of year. All around Anchorage, flyers were posted for the Alaska State Fair in Palmer. He walked around the area after he rented a room. He just needed time to acclimate himself. He was about a mile from his room when he heard yelling coming from a rundown shanty type of house.

"We'll freeze to death this winter if you can't bring wood in for the fireplace," the man shouted. "Get outside and cut that firewood or you'll go without supper."

A boy of around eight appeared wearing jeans, boots, T-shirt, and gloves. The boy limped as he walked. "Alaska has no place for weak people," Anthony told himself.

He drove to Anchorage, to what was, in his opinion, the best clothing store, where he purchased new clothes. From there he went to Guns and Ammo for all Alaska, which was owned by friends of his parents.

"I need a shotgun or a handgun," he told the unfamiliar sales clerk. "I'm going to Ferry tomorrow and I heard they have bears around that area."

"I'm sorry, sir, but it'll take a week just to get clearance for you to purchase the gun of your choice," the clerk said politely.

"Oh, well. I hope no bear thinks I'm his next meal. Thank you for your help." He was starting to leave when he heard a loudspeaker blare.

"Tony Pizzo, do not leave. We want your money, but you may not buy any guns. Tony, this is not your imagination; it's Jacob Miller."

Moments later, Anthony was greeted by Mr. Miller. "Why didn't you tell the clerk we're friends?"

"I thought pulling the friendship card was wrong. I have a .45 semi-auto at my parents. I just thought maybe a 12 gauge shotgun could help until I got home."

"Bring me a colt .45 with shells. I want a 12 gauge shotgun, eight rubber slugs and a box of steel slugs," Mr. Miller instructed the clerk.

"Jacob, who lives in that shanty house on Spring Street?" Anthony asked.

"That's Dave Clark and his boy, Bailey. Dave's wife died in a house fire. Little Bailey gets more than his share of beatings. We keep expecting to find

Dave dead from alcohol poisoning, or the boy from all the beatings he gets," Mr. Miller replied.

"How long has this been happening?" Anthony queried.

"It began about a month following Mrs. Clark's death. Some folks swear they hear the boy screaming in pain after nine o'clock at night. Bailey's a good kid who doesn't deserve the abuse his father metes out every day. The sick part is, nobody's willing to help the boy."

"Why hasn't anyone called the state troopers?" Anthony found himself becoming angry over Bailey's mistreatment.

"Dave Clark is an ex-state trooper. He's a decorated veteran. Who do you think people will believe? Nobody's willing to cross the man."

"It's a shame," Anthony replied. "I never thought any Alaskan would allow that sort of thing to happen."

When Anthony returned to the railyard office he learned his father had encountered further necessary repairs and would return the following day.

"Please tell my dad I went to Palmer. I need to unwind." Anthony then went to the room he had rented, changed his clothes, and went for another walk. He purposely stayed away from Mr. Clark's home. Thirty minutes of walking failed to improve his mood. "I hate you, Richard Colton," he yelled. Walking back to his motel, Anthony realized a few things: 1) He loved his parents, 2) growing up in Alaska had been fun, and he missed his friends; 3) he didn't want to live in Alaska ever again; 4) learning to fly airplanes was a must; and 5) he hated Dr. Richard Colton, but for reasons he was just now beginning to realize had nothing to do with why the man was on trial.

Anthony used his rental car and drove to Palmer. There he made purchases for his parents, along with minor items for himself. After three hours in Palmer, his anger having increased and fully frustrated with himself, he returned to his room.

Sleeping was full of Bailey Clark's face. Nightmares of the boy being found dead, abused beyond anything he could imagine, haunted him. Tossing and turning, he awoke without any perceptible evidence of having been asleep. At six-thirty in the morning, Anthony left and drove to the railyard. Jonathan Pizzo walked outside to greet his son.

"Shall we go home?" Jonathan asked his son. "I'm off for the next two days."

"Can we get a bite to eat first? I'm a little hungry and I've got some things for the house."

"Let's go eat, and then we can go shopping. How long are you able to stay?"

"A week, maybe two. Judge King is out for at least a month, due to having a heart attack in court."

"You might want to call the court. I received a call from Mr. Xander Ward. He asked me to inform you that Judge King took a turn for the worse this morning. Just remember we're three hours later than them."

"Maybe I should go back right away. I want to advise my boss that we need to prepare to retry Dr. Colton. He's flaunted his kidnapping of children in the face of justice."

270

"Mr. Ward said Dr. Colton's trial is on hold until the court decides whether they'll dismiss all charges or seek other action. It'll take at least another week depending on Judge King's status tomorrow morning."

"I'll call Agent Ward after I eat," Anthony proposed.

"Son, I know you think Dr. Colton has done a lot of evil. My opinion is that he's saved many children's lives by what he did. However, regardless of how either of us feels, a Learjet will arrive tomorrow for whenever you choose to leave. The aircraft has been made available by Evan Holt."

The two Pizzo men enjoyed a delicious breakfast. They went shopping for food and Jonathan ordered four propane tanks filled while Anthony called Chicago. Agent Ward advised him to take a week and relax.

They used Jonathan's high-rail truck, which enabled them to head home on the rail line, not worrying about traffic. Father and son talked about different topics, including Dave Clark and his son. What shocked Anthony was his father's statement regarding the Clarks.

"If Dr. Colton wasn't dying of cancer I'd call him and ask if he could get away from that trial to come rescue Bailey. Let's face it, you folks have been in the news and I know many people consider him to be a savior of children."

"The man is a child killer, not a savior. Personally, I detest him. I mean, how'd he like it if somebody took one of his children?"

"Mario Rizzoli took the lives of Nancy Colton and Richard Jr. Their DNA was positively identified on the front of the silver Aston Martin registered to Mario Rizzoli. I know this because of the news, and I asked Agent Ward when he called."

"Dad, you don't know the whole story," Anthony protested.

"Son, I know more than you give me credit for. I've followed your career and I'm proud of you. But now, think on this: Dr. Colton is brilliant. He's been in charge of the trial, even though it may not seem that way. My advice to you is, call him and ask point blank: 'Where is Marco Rizzoli?'"

"Good idea provided the man would answer such a direct question." Anthony paused briefly. "If he takes the witness stand; *I will ask him.*"

Jonathan stopped his truck on the tracks so he could raise the rail wheels. Slowly, he drove off the rails onto the road crossing which was installed for four-wheelers to use. He drove up the dirt road to the house where Anthony was raised.

Father and son worked together once they arrived home. Anthony took their purchases inside, while his father started a fire in the wood stove. For the next two days, Anthony split wood and did minor repair jobs around the house. Jennifer Pizzo arrived from Fairbanks the day following Anthony's arrival at home.

Each night Anthony's dreams were invaded by the face of Bailey as he gasped, dying from being choked. The boy's fate plagued Anthony all night, resulting in little rest. On day five, he caught a ride with his father to Anchorage. Once in Anchorage, he drove to the airport and found a Learjet standing by to take him back to Chicago. Locating the pilot was easy; he was asleep in the Learjet bedroom.

"My name is Bob Bravo," the pilot said. "When you're ready to leave, just let me know. We can be airborne in forty-five minutes."

"I paid for two weeks' rent at a motel down the road. Why don't you stay there until I call you?" Anthony suggested, holding out the key. "I'm staying with my parents in Ferry. I'm going to hire a helicopter to fly me back there later."

Mr. Bravo accepted the offer, thanking Anthony repeatedly.

A Robertson R-66 helicopter was hired to take Anthony home. Before returning, however, he bought items from a hardware and lumber store. He also purchased more warm clothing and a new snowmobile for his parents. He spent nearly $15,000 before buying the snowmobile. His father arranged to have the purchases delivered by tundra truck that afternoon.

Before returning to the airport to meet the helicopter, Anthony drove past Dave Clark's shanty. Eight-year-old Bailey was outside, doing his best to chop firewood. Twice Mr. Clark threatened to whip his son if the boy didn't cut enough wood for the night. Having seen Bailey's welted back, Anthony made an anonymous call reporting child abuse. He saw the state troopers take Bailey away. Then they took Mr. Clark as well. One hour later he was flying towards his parents' property. The tundra truck carrying supplies was already underway.

For two days Anthony removed and replaced his parents' tin roofing and cleaned the wood stove flue, then changed four filters for drinking water. Jennifer watched as her son labored to build a 16'x20' frame for a hothouse so they could grow vegetables in cold weather. Upon seeing her son install a wood-burning stove for heat, she had an idea. Walking out to where he was working, she asked, "Can you put a wood floor in this building?"

"Why? It's supposed to be your hothouse. What's up, Mom?"

"You've saved the old tin from the house. Can we use it to cover the roof of this building?"

"Yeah, there's enough tin for a roof. Why?"

"Your father will be home late tonight. He needs a work shed with heat for winter use. He does a lot of work outside, even when it's thirty to forty below zero."

"If I'm going to build a floor, I better get busy. I know there's enough lumber but I'll need more plywood."

"What size and how much?" she asked.

"Ten sheets of half-inch and ten sheets of one-inch. The one-inch plywood will support anything Dad puts in his shed."

"I'll call and have it delivered today."

Anthony gave his mother permission to use his credit card to buy numerous other new items for his father, including a new chainsaw.

"There's enough insulation for two layers in the walls. I'll use one layer in the ceiling to keep it warmer inside. It'll be warm when we give it to Dad."

Anthony worked hard preparing his father's new work shed. Flooring went in first, followed by framed walls and a roof. He built a workbench along one wall, then installed a forty-eight-inch-wide door. He finished construction minutes before his father arrived home at midnight.

Mother and son were patiently waiting when Jonathan entered the house. "We have a surprise for you," Jennifer proudly proclaimed. "Come outside with me please."

Jonathan was delighted with his work shed, but once inside with his wife, he gave her some bad news. "Tony has to leave. Somebody's died and they've ordered him home." Back in the house he spoke to his son. "Agent Ward called today. You've been ordered back to court. You leave as soon as possible."

"I'll eat supper with you, then call for the helicopter to take me back to Anchorage." Anthony had enjoyed a short vacation but was glad to be getting out of Alaska. On arriving in Anchorage he drove his rental car to his rented room. The pilot had moved out. Minutes later Anthony was headed for the airport. He went to the Learjet, only to find Mr. Bravo absent. A note had been left inside: *Will return at 0830 hrs.* When Mr. Bravo returned, Anthony requested they leave immediately. He'd been waiting impatiently inside the aircraft.

Three days after leaving Alaska, Mr. Pizzo walked into the courtroom. Only Mr. Dill was present for the defense. "If your client thinks he doesn't have to be here, he's wrong," he told Mr. Dill.

"Charges are being formally dropped. The jury is being dismissed, and I can go back to being a federal defense attorney." Mr. Dill reached inside his briefcase, "This is for you. Dr. Colton sent it to you."

Looking inside the envelope, Prosecutor Pizzo stared in disbelief. How the–."

"All rise; the Honorable Judge Sheppard presiding," a deputy sheriff announced loudly.

"Be seated and come to order. Bailiff, bring in the jurors." Silence filled the courtroom as the jurors entered. When they were all seated Judge Sheppard continued: "Ladies and gentlemen of the jury, today we'll meet for our last session. All charges against Doctor Richard Daniel Colton have been dismissed with prejudice. You're free to go home. Please accept our sincere thanks for your time."

"Judge Sheppard," a juror interrupted, "would it be acceptable to allow us to say, in court, how we would've voted; guilty or not guilty?"

"It's not required," Judge Sheppard replied. "However, if any of you wish to do so, you may indicate your disposition. Simply stand and state 'guilty' or 'not guilty'."

"Excuse me, Your Honor," Juror Three interjected. "I was elected as jury foreman and none of us believe it's that simple. We posed the following to ourselves: Is Dr. Colton responsible for removing children from abusive situations? Yes. Did Dr. Colton assist the children in being adopted by loving people? Absolutely, yes! Did Dr. Colton kidnap Marco Rizzoli? This is irrelevant! And finally, did Dr. Colton kill Marco Rizzoli? We'll tell you our individual opinions. Mine: Not guilty."

"To save us time, let me assist," Judge Sheppard interrupted. "All who say Dr. Colton is not guilty raise your right hand." All jurors raised their hands.

"Your Honor, from the beginning we believe there's been no evidence against Dr. Colton. Mr. Pizzo's behavior offended each of us," the jury foreman stated.

273

Standing up to face the jury, Mr. Pizzo said, "I apologize for my behavior. I was focused solely on convicting Dr. Colton of the death of Marco Rizzoli. I admittedly agree with dismissing all charges, because there's insufficient evidence. I ask you to please accept my sincere apology."

"Judge Sheppard," Mr. Dill said, interrupting Mr. Pizzo. "I've been asked to read something to the court regarding Marco Rizzoli."

"Speaking of Dr. Colton, where is he?" Mr. Pizzo inquired.

"Dr. Colton is in the hospital," Mr. Dill explained, "which is why he's absent from court today."

The courtroom door silently opened and closed. Special Agent Xander Ward walked in and motioned to the bailiff. He was summoned to the bench moments later.

"Agent Ward has an announcement to make," Judge Sheppard told the court.

Looking at Mr. Pizzo, Xander smiled. "Dr. Colton said you're welcome, but that's not why I'm here." He paused before speaking again. "Dr. Colton sent another envelope to Mr. Pizzo. I'll read its contents. However, Mr. Dill needs to read a message from Dr. Colton."

"I don't mean to be arrogant but can't this wait? I mean shouldn't Dr. Colton be here?" Mr. Pizzo protested.

"Dr. Richard Daniel Colton died this morning at 4:13a.m.," Agent Ward announced solemnly. "He wants everyone here to know about Marco Rizzoli. I have a written statement from him."

Judge Sheppard turned to face Agent Ward. "Please read what you have for us."

Xander picked up a folder and removed its contents. He cleared his throat and began reading: *I, Dr. Richard Colton, apologize for what I've done. However, I'd do it all over again. I'm gladdened to know the Dragon Society will no longer be able to hurt innocent people. I ask only one person to forgive me for not giving him closure until now. Marco Rizzoli, please, I beg your forgiveness.*

Mr. Pizzo, you have lied, used deception, and false witnesses to convict people in the past. You're a good attorney. I hope you accept the position you'll soon be receiving. Had you simply asked me, man-to-man, where Marco Rizzoli could be found, I would've told you.

When Xander finished reading, he looked to Mr. Dill, and said, "It's all yours, Wesley."

Chapter 52

"These are the words of my friend and hero, Dr Richard Colton." Wesley Dill began reading:

"Marco Rizzoli first visited the clinic for a puncture wound in his left foot. An older boy playing a prank put a piece of wood with a nail sticking out in a paper bag. The older boy set the bag on fire on the Rizzoli's front porch. After ringing the doorbell, he ran away. Marco stomped on that bag. Marco's next visit was for a bruised tailbone. Mario Rizzoli kicked his son for getting cookie crumbs on the family room carpet.

"Marco was brought to see me after being hit on the head by one of his father's bodyguards, using a lead filled leather sap. I kept him at the clinic with me for twenty hours before letting him go home. Marco had suffered a concussion.

"Mrs. Rizzoli brought Marco to the clinic following a whipping for theft of an apple from the family kitchen. His back needed stitches in two places, and his legs were heavily welted. Less than a month later, I was looking into two brown eyes that had been blackened. I treated three cracked and bruised ribs at that time as well.

"Before his fourth birthday, he was again brought to the clinic, his right arm bandaged. A nurse took his vital signs. The problem this time was a severely infected tattoo. The tattoo was actually two-in-one. It was the Rizzoli family crest with a seagull beneath it. It hurt Marco to move his right arm. Even when I touched him lightly he cried out in pain. Part of me wished Mario Rizzoli would suffer one-fourth the amount of pain his son had endured. Marco had also sustained a broken jaw; the result of his father striking him with a closed fist for telling him, 'no'.

"I next treated the boy in an operating room to repair a ruptured spleen, which had occurred from multiple beatings. At this time I removed five studs from piercings. Mrs. Rizzoli was unhappy, but my patient came first regardless of whom I was treating. Two weeks after his stitches were removed, he and his mother flew to Italy.

"While in Italy, Maria Rizzoli and three bodyguards were shot and killed from an ambush. Maria and her bodyguards were reported to have been killed by terrorists. In reality, Mario Rizzoli ordered that his wife be killed after he discovered she was going to seek a divorce with full custody of their son. Mario regretted having to order the deaths of three good men, but in his eyes, it had to be done.

"One week after his mother was buried in Italy, Marco entered the clinic under supervision of a nanny. Two bodyguards accompanied them. Marco coughed up blood twice during the consultation. Throughout my examination only his nanny was allowed to be in the room with us. I sent the boy for x-rays. He was accompanied by his nanny and the bodyguards. While they were gone I began making plans to remove Marco from the abusive environment. I'd thought of taking him for quite a while, but hadn't done so because his mother had spoken of leaving her husband. Two months later he returned, complaining that his tummy hurt. I knew why he complained of abdominal pain; the dumb idiot who pierced his navel did a lousy job, causing it to become infected. I informed the two bodyguards and the nanny, I was sending the boy to the hospital. I told his entourage it would be thirty to forty minutes before the ambulance arrived.

"When one of the bodyguards asked about a coffee machine, I decided to take advantage of his request. It took less than the blink of an eye to slip a slow-acting muscle relaxer and sleep aid into a pot of coffee. I gave each of them a mug with plenty of sugar. I laughed at their jokes, refilling everyone's cup before making a fresh pot. Marco Rizzoli slept soundly. Dark red bandages covered his abdomen. I made a big deal of leaving the clinic twenty minutes before the ambulance arrived.

"The private ambulance company I called for came from a competitor of Mario Rizzoli's brother-in-law's legitimate medical transport service. The clinic loaded Marco into the ambulance. I used a blind four-way-stop intersection as a place to take over the vehicle. I used traffic lights and alleyways to lose Marco's heavily drugged nanny and bodyguards. The driver was told to remove his shirt and jump out the door in one of the alleyways. The bodyguards and nanny were trapped in traffic as I made my escape. I made certain my disguise: a Richard Nixon mask with a company driver's shirt was seen by a witness, plus two traffic cameras. I abandoned the ambulance one block away from the entrance to Chitown. I removed the bloodied bandages and left them inside. Marco Rizzoli never stirred during the entire process of taking him from his father.

"I was diligent in leaving no trace of ever having been in the ambulance. To thwart any scent dogs, I splashed a gallon of bleach all over the interior followed by an equal amount of ammonia. Everything I did pointed towards Mario Rizzoli's competition, including leaving a bit of Marco's clothing in the ambulance, soaked in bleach. Forty-five minutes after I left the clinic, I carried a very sleepy boy into the basement of my house. I knew that maintaining my daily routine was of utmost importance. I further decided there must be a call to Mario Rizzoli demanding a ransom of one million dollars.

"On Marco's second day with me, he was moved to a secret location inside my garage. At that time I began calling him by a different name. I gave him toys to play with when he was alone. I treated him with antibiotics for his infection, and I knew he wouldn't cough up any more blood because nobody would ever strike him again. I retained every item used in his piercings. On day three I placed a small inflatable surgical balloon beneath his skin to one side of his ugly tattoo. I fed Marco chicken nuggets for dinner and watched a movie with him. One week later I gave Marco a sedative to make him sleep. As he slept, I removed a small wart and a brown birthmark. I allowed him two days of rest before removing his most insulting hideous piercing. A short time later, I gave Marco new clothing, and a toy truck. I read him the name which was printed on the birth certificate, telling him it was his new name.

He was smart enough to know I was trying to help. I wasn't going to return him to the person he feared. I knew he feared his father because while sleeping he often mumbled, "Please Daddy...don't hurt me." It took two months for me to perform all of the minor surgeries needed to change the defining characteristics of Marco's appearance.

"I was interviewed by police, FBI agents, and the one man I detested above all others: Mario Rizzoli himself. Everyone wanted to know where I was, what I had been doing, and who saw me. Every statement I gave was verified by one source or another. When I stood in front of Mario Rizzoli, I never flinched or faltered in my responses. We then had a short conversation which I remember as follows:

"'My wife worked for you when she was killed taking our son to school. She loved working for Rizzoli Enterprises even though she vocalized some shortcomings. Now, you ask me of my involvement in your son's disappearance. I sent him to the hospital with your guards and his nanny. My only question for you is this: How can any father trust his child's safety to someone who drinks alcohol while supposedly protecting that child? My wife and child were killed by a hit-and-run driver. Richard Jr. was thrown over forty feet by that car. He died on impact. My wife bled out and died in the street. No one was ever arrested, so I understand your pain.'

"'I'll be watching you Doctor,' Mr. Rizzoli threatened.

"'Then you'll be watching me fly to Germany on vacation. I'm going to Berlin, Stuttgart, and the Isle of Sylt or more properly, the Sylt Peninsula. I'm going to buy a cuckoo clock made of wood from the Black Forest. Would you like me to bring one back for you, too?'

"'Only if you want, sir. Only if you want. However, know this; if you bring me a cuckoo clock it will be displayed here in my office for all to see.'

"'On my way home, I'll be stopping in France for a few days. I'll bring you a bottle of the finest French Merlot.'

"'You know, Doctor, if I didn't know you'd made a small fortune winning the lottery, I'd wonder where your money came from.'

"'I still earn an easy $100,000 a year from just one of my surgical inventions. And, I might add, I have six medical patents.'

"'A man like you could retire and take a vacation all year long. Why continue being a doctor?'

"'I like helping people. I wish I could invent a way to end all suffering.'

"'Very commendable, Doctor. Enjoy your vacation.'

"I'm no fool; I knew Rizzoli ordered men to follow me. What he didn't know was that I visited the Chi-town transients daily by way of the hospital's old drainage system. I used the tunnels to purchase items for Marco without being seen by Rizzoli's henchmen.

"Marco was asleep when I took him from my secret underground bunker. His jet-black hair was bleached and dyed red. I dressed him in ragged clothing and carried him to the motorcoach I'd rented. Once he was carefully concealed, I left my house and headed for a prearranged meeting. Marco's new parents flew from their home to Chicago. Dressed as a taxi driver, I picked the couple up at the airport in a taxicab look-alike. I dropped them off at a large shopping mall, pointing out the motorcoach as we passed it. 'I was instructed to tell you that the boy was abused before his parents were killed by the mob. Treat him kindly and enjoy your son.'

"'Our son will love it at home,' the woman replied with tears in her eyes."

Using the motorcoach I had rented under the couple's own name, they drove from Chicago to Florida. Once there, they planned to fly home with their newly adopted son following a two-week vacation in Orlando.

Chapter 53

"The day after Marco Rizzoli disappeared, a ransom note appeared under the windshield wiper blade of a police cruiser:

IF YOU EVER WANT TO SEE THE BOY AGAIN, ALIVE, IT WILL COST YOU ONE MILLION DOLLARS. YOU WILL RECEIVE ANOTHER NOTE LATER.

"The FBI immediately began scrutinizing the note. It held hundreds of fingerprints; none could be identified. The only thing discernible was that the fingerprints were those of a child. For nearly a week Chicago police officers canvassed the neighborhood seeking information on who placed the note where it had been found. Other cruisers were parked in the area with hopes that another note would be left. An undercover police van was parked nearby with cameras inside focused on each of the bait cars.

"A foot-patrol officer found the second note. Ironically, it was stuck to a completely different cruiser's driver's side front tire. When the patrol officer called dispatch he stated, 'The note is stuck to a tire with an ice pick.' This time the note read:

I listen to WWDS. I will kill the boy if you do not broadcast these words: 'PALADIN HAVE SON WILL TRAVEL.' To prove I have the boy, there is a tattoo on his shoulder. He has a birthmark on his buttock and two moles on his back. You have twenty-four hours to broadcast this message. It is now three in the afternoon, Monday. I'm listening.

"The note had been found around six p.m. the same day. By eight p.m. the message had been read three times. WWDS radio was owned by Rizzoli Enterprises, so it didn't surprise me when Mario Rizzoli made the announcement himself. He added words of his own: 'Return my son. Forget the money and run. If I ever catch you I'll kill you myself. You're a dead man.'

"I'd heard the message and decided to further misdirect both the police and Mario Rizzoli. I also decided to up the ante. My next note arrived from a garbage truck worker, who after discovering the note called the police. This note read:

You have one last chance. Ransom is now two million. I don't like name-calling, but now you go by the name, 'Cupcake'. I'll explain the delivery location within twenty-four hours, tell me Cupcake understands. I'm listening, and I'm losing patience.

"FBI Agent Francis Toth advised Mr. Rizzoli not to pay the ransom. 'I hate to say this, but I fear your son is no longer alive. It's apparent the man is playing with us.'

"The police chief agreed: 'I must say that Agent Toth is correct. I suggest we keep an eye on the Banducci outfit. After all, their ambulance was used in the abduction.'

"When Mario Rizzoli announced; *Cupcake Understands*, he added, 'the FBI and other officers say you've already killed my boy. I'll pay the extra if you prove Marco is alive.'

"The next day, a photo of Marco holding the day's newspaper appeared stapled to a small convenience store bulletin board. Along with the photo was another note:

I'm always watching. Mr. Rizzoli is to place the money into two briefcases. Only non-sequential $100 bills in one briefcase. In the second briefcase I want old non-sequential twenty and fifty dollar bills. The first briefcase is to be placed in the trash can at Third and Central. The second at Tenth and Main. If I see any cops near either drop site I'll walk away and the boy dies. Final instructions will be delivered after you make the second drop. You have one hour to get the money. Your first drop is at twelve noon. Your second drop, ten minutes later. Remember, I see any cops and you never see the boy alive."

Chapter 54

"I watched my wall clock tick off the minutes. My last patient of the day had left at three o'clock that afternoon. The sound of my phone startled me as I was working on the wording of ransom note number one.

"'Dr. Colton, may I help you?"

"'Your young patient died at 2:56 p.m. this afternoon. His body is scheduled for autopsy tomorrow afternoon.'

"'I'll be by to sign the papers. Please advise the medical examiner that I'd like to speak with him.'

"'Consider it done,' Dr. Jamison replied.

"'Dr. Jamison, the child's name is Philip Matthews. I diagnosed him with a hole in his heart five months ago. He had surgery two months ago. I'd appreciate it if you could let me know the cause of death.'

"'Well, being as I'm pulling double duty until Dr. Edmonds returns from vacation, I'd welcome you to join me and see for yourself.'

"'Is there any chance we can do it today?'

"'Be at the hospital in half an hour, and yes, I can release the body right away. For the life of me, I can't figure out why you are going out of your way for this kid's parents. They're trailer trash.'

"'Kids can't pick their parents. They aren't his fault.'

"Three hours later the cause of death was evident. The boy's heart had never healed. Philip had literally died from a broken heart. Someone beat the boy, using him as a punching bag.

"'Have you got your answers?' Dr. Jamison asked.

"'Yes, I do," I replied. 'What the paramedics told me makes perfect sense now.'

"'What'd they say?'

"'They gave me an audio of the run, trailer-to-clinic. Philip kept saying, 'I didn't break the window Daddy–Amy did it.' Then he said, 'My scar hurts.'

"'Was his father in the ambulance?' Dr. Jamison queried.

"'Yes, you can hear the man screaming to stop lying or else God would punish him."

"'This wasn't accidental or natural,' Dr. Jamison continued. 'I'm legally obligated to notify the authorities.'

"'Won't do much good. The mother has pancreatic cancer. She doesn't have the strength to do this kind of thing. Mr. Matthews uses a belt, not his hands. When you contact the authorities, tell them to talk with Philip's older brother and twin sister. I'm certain the older brother used Philip for punching practice.'

"'How do you figure that?'

"'Mr. Matthews is a washed-up MMA fighter. He knows better than to ever hit his kids. During his last interview, he said he's training a fighter to be champion at age eighteen. A lot of people believe he meant his oldest son.'

"Dr. Jamison filed his report allowing me to remove Philip's body from the morgue. I took him to Clayton Mortuary, which was hired to do a closed-casket funeral."

Chapter 55

Attorney Wesley Dill opened an envelope addressed to him from his friend Dr. Richard Colton. Mr. Dill removed several sheets of paper and began reading aloud:

"Mario Rizzoli refused to listen to FBI Agent Toth. Mr. Rizzoli dumped the FBI's money, replacing it with his own. It was a chance he knew might not work, but it was his decision, not Agent Toth's. Rizzoli openly admitted that he was $300,000 short of the money demanded. His first drop went smoothly. The second drop was equally uneventful. Once the money was placed it was time to get his son back, then find the trash who took his boy. In his mind he was convinced his son's kidnapping was ordered by Don Banducci, his sworn enemy.

"What Mario Rizzoli didn't know was that his money had been taken nearly immediately following the drops. Having spent countless months in the sewers near Chi-town, beneath the city, I knew where certain manhole covers were located. All trash cans had been placed over open manholes, with small pieces of wood holding the interior container up inside the exterior trash can cover. When the money was placed inside I easily removed the wood, lowered the trash can, and extracted all of the money. I replaced the empty briefcase and put things back in proper order. The second money retrieval went smoothly. I knew that to use this money meant being caught. I had to be careful when handling the $1.7 million. To help place suspicion on Mario Rizzoli, I tacked a preprinted note against the police cruiser door parked at a donut shop. The note read:

YOU WERE WARNED ABOUT PLAYING TRICKS. NO MONEY MEANS NO BOY. YOU MADE YOUR CHOICE, NOW LIVE WITH IT.

"Prior to being in position to retrieve the money, I quietly visited Mario Rizzoli's building. I dressed as a janitor, made my way to the main office, and placed more evidence to implicate Rizzoli in his son's disappearance. What I left was a 24-karat gold earring with a diamond, a finger ring with Rizzoli's crest, and a 24-karat gold three-quarter ring which had been in Marco's small navel. All of these had been inflicted upon him by his parents.

"I placed two mini-cameras capable of transmitting a maximum of a block when the receiver was within range. I didn't do this for myself, as I hid an audio transmitter inside his cuckoo clock. This was only partial payback for Mario Rizzoli killing my family years ago. I planned to contact the FBI, alerting them to the location of my receiver. On my way out of the building, I dropped one last item on the floor of his office.

"Mario Rizzoli found his final instructions: *TAKE GIBSON ROAD TWO MILES OUT OF THE CITY WHERE YOU WILL FIND YOUR REWARD.* Mario Rizzoli quickly phoned Agent Toth. He immediately informed him of his latest discovery, stating his son was two miles out on Gibson Road.

"The plainclothes officers watching both money drops reported no activity. At drop one, they had three people stop at the trash can and put something inside. Finally a young Hispanic man reached into the trash can and removed the briefcase. He managed to take half a dozen steps before being swarmed. When police opened the briefcase it was empty.

"'Drop two, this is drop one. We just arrested a suspect. There is no money inside the briefcase. Abort drop two, abort immediately,' was the radio transmission.

"'Drop two, I'm checking now,' came the reply. 'No money. I repeat, there's no money inside the briefcase."

"'Abort, Abort,' announced the lead detective. 'Proceed to Gibson Road and arrest Mr. Rizzoli.'

"'Sir, Detective Decker here. Detective Sullivan and I are on site at Gibson Road. Mr. Rizzoli isn't here. We have a body, or more precisely ashes believed to be human remains.'

"The final note found on the office floor, concluded: *I SAID NO COPS OR FBI. YOUR SON PAID THE PRICE FOR YOUR STUPIDITY.*

"Mario Rizzoli threw his autographed Cubs baseball across the room. 'Whoever you are, there's no place to hide. I'll find you, you son of a bitch, and then you'll suffer like no one else has ever suffered at my hands.'

"Picking up his office phone, Mr. Rizzoli called his attorney. 'Victor, my son is dead. His body is on Gibson Road. Make sure the incompetent cops and FBI can't keep his remains. Whoever took my boy and burned his body is dead. I know for a fact it's Marco. I'm holding proof in my hand."

"'I'll get right on it, sir. My condolences on your loss. Do you want Franco on this?'

"'Yes, tell Franco I said it's an-eye-for-an-eye payback.'

"Twenty minutes after hanging up his phone, Mario Rizzoli found himself in handcuffs. A picture of Marco, naked and appearing dead, lay on Mario Rizzoli's desk. FBI Agent Toth read Mario Rizzoli his rights, stating he would be interviewed later.

"Agent Toth searched the office. He found the evidence I had left behind, including one of Mario Rizzoli's legitimate business cards. A card I had taken when I delivered Mario Rizzoli's cuckoo clock and wine. I hadn't actually left the United States. I already had the clock and wine at home. The card had Marco Rizzoli's smeared bloody fingerprint. I knew they could identify Marco's blood on the card because his blood would also be found on the items used to pierce his body.

"Mario Rizzoli wasn't tried for his son's disappearance or alleged death. He did remain in jail for six months after being charged with other crimes, yet no convictions occurred. Marco had been with his new family for over three months when Mario was finally released from jail.

"Anthony, thanks to you, Rizzoli has spent these last years of his life in prison, but only on charges for racketeering. Now, thanks to accidentally discovering his silver Aston Martin I can rest knowing the man will not escape the death penalty. My soul is at peace. I can finally forgive him for killing my wife, Nancy, and son, Richard Jr."

After finishing reading Dr. Colton's statement, Mr. Dill turned to Mr. Pizzo. "Would you like to read the letter Agent Ward handed you?"

Agent Xander Ward interrupted. "Judge Holt and I have read your letter. I suggest that you read it to yourself first. Then you can share your letter if you choose." Mr. Pizzo began reading to himself:

Anthony, as you well know, you were adopted at age four. Now let me tell you, Marco Rizzoli is alive and healthy. I ask your forgiveness for waiting to disclose this information. Let me tell you what I have kept a secret for so long. I met the Rizzolis through my wife, Nancy Marie. You heard that name during my trial. Excuse me, but if you can tell fibs, then so can I. My first treatment of Marco was for a dog bite on his right hand. Thank God Marco is left-handed.

You believe that I kidnapped Marco for the two million in ransom. To you, it was evident that I killed Marco. Hold your excitement. I did not kidnap Marco for money, nor did I kill the boy. I rescued him from a life of abuse and pain. You scream, 'What abuse, what pain?' Let me explain:

Marco was given a family crest tattoo on his right shoulder at the age of four by his father's tattoo business. I treated Marco for a major infection. When I gave him a tetanus shot, I saw strap marks along his back, left from being beaten.

This is what I did for Marco after taking him away from his abusive father: I surgically removed the tattoo, a birthmark, his moles, and I repaired a hernia. Marco's ears were pierced in three places, plus he suffered an infected navel piercing. I cleaned his navel so it would heal with minimal scarring. But what angered, disgusted, and totally sickened me was the mutilation of Marco's dignity through all the abuse he suffered at such a young age.

I hid Marco for quite some time as he healed. It took a while to find just the right parents who would love an adopted son. Marco's name was changed and he was taken to another state to live. His adoptive parents were never told of his true identity. What I did was never about money. It has always been about love for the child.

You have been angry over my special treatment during my trial. My entire trial has been based on being able to disclose how many children were helped because they were taken out of love; taken away from abusive parents–mostly the Dragon Society. I've disclosed to the federal authorities every child taken out of love over the last twenty-five years except one. I have said Marco Rizzoli was taken out of love, but I purposely did not disclose Marco's new name or whereabouts in order to protect him and his new family.

Ironically, I used Rizzoli Enterprises for adoption papers, birth certificates, and court endorsements. Marco never once tried to leave during his stay with me. I thought it funny Marco didn't like chocolate and wouldn't drink hot cocoa. He asked for coffee and tea. When his adoptive parents picked him up, I gave them fifty pounds of coffee and $10,000 of my own money. Later, those adoptive parents received $10,000 from my child adoption resource fund. (That is what CAR stood for. It now stands for Child Advocacy and Rescue.)

I know in my heart I did the right thing for Marco. It may not have been legal, but sometimes we have to bend or break laws in order to protect the innocent. I hope you will accept the fact I have only taken children from situations which would result in painful death if left where they were at the time I intervened. Remember your best friend, Kenny, and how I gave time and resources to make certain two boys knew their parents loved them?

At this point Anthony Pizzo stopped reading. "Now the bastard is rubbing it in my face that I nearly killed my best friend," he said aloud, before he resumed reading to himself:

Anthony, look into the mirror placed on your table. Yes, I arranged for it to be there. As you look at yourself in the mirror, repeat these words: YOU HAVE LIVED IN LOVE SINCE YOU WERE FOUR YEARS OLD. YOUR NAME WAS MARCO RIZZOLI. YOU WERE TAKEN OUT OF LOVE. NOW YOU CHOOSE WHO YOU ARE: MARCO OR ANTHONY.

Amazement struck Anthony Pizzo. Looking up, he stammered, "Thank you, Dr. Colton." Turning to the courtroom audience he announced: "Marco Rizzoli is alive! However, I do believe he wishes not to be found." Anthony Pizzo repeated his last sentence and finished reading.

Please accept my sincerest apology for ruining your career. My sole intent and purpose is to destroy the Dragon Society. The only people who know your true identity are you, Barbara, Agent Ward, and Sam Holt. Judge Holt, along with others, have assisted me in securing a judicial appointment for you in San Juan, Puerto Rico, where you can raise your son.

Forgive me, and congratulations on adopting Bailey Clark, or should I say Sander Pizzo.

A postscript was added at the end:

Inside your envelope is a safe-deposit key. In the safe-deposit box is $1.7 million. Money paid for you. Included with that money is interest accrued over the past twenty-five years.

Written in a totally different hand were the words: *Dave Clark was found dead, mauled by a brown bear. It is believed Bailey Clark was also killed by the bear that mauled his father. Be kind to your son. You will now submit your resignation. Go to San Juan.* This was signed by Judge Samuel Holt.

Getting to his feet, Anthony realized how unsteady he was; his hands and legs were shaking, his stomach was in nervous turmoil. In a trembling voice he tried to speak, "Ladies and gentlemen," he paused, cleared his throat loudly, and then continued with effort, "I've discovered the location of Marco Rizzoli. I can assure you that he is alive. Judge Sheppard, I hereby tender my resignation. It's my sincere hope Mario Rizzoli is held fully accountable for the deaths of Nancy Marie Colton and her son, Richard, Jr."

~ The End ~

Made in United States
Troutdale, OR
04/23/2025

30850166R00166